THE
SKEWED
THRONE

THE SKEWED THRONE

JOSHUA PALMATIER

DAW BOOKS, INC.

DONALD A. WOLLHEIM, FOUNDER

375 Hudson Street, New York, NY 10014

ELIZABETH R. WOLLHEIM
SHEILA E. GILBERT
PUBLISHERS

http://www.dawbooks.com

First Printing, January 2006
1   2   3   4   5   6   7   8   9

This novel is dedicated to the memory of my father,
Cdr. Philip F. Palmatier, Jr.,
lost at sea in a midair collision of two A-4 Skyhawks
December 10, 1990

Acknowledgments

First and foremost, I want to thank my editor Sheila Gilbert and my agent Amy Stout, for taking a chance on a new author and for not only believing in the story, but for helping to make it that much better. Baked goods will be had by all! Thanks as well to Steve Stone, the artist who captured the essence of the entire book in the cover art. I'm still stunned. Getting a first novel published is exciting enough; working with Amy, Sheila, Steve, and everyone else at DAW to get the story into book form and on the shelf is truly exhilarating.

Thanks also to everyone who read this novel in any or all of its various forms: two great friends and fellow writers, Patricia Bray and Jennifer Dunne; the best cycling partner in the world, Cheryl Losinger; the person who kept me sane while writing *and* teaching, Jean Brewster; the Vicious Circle—Carol Bartholomew, J. Michael Blumer, Kishma Danielle, Laurie Davis, Bonnie Freeman, Dorian Gray, Penelope Hardy, Heidi Kneale, Robert Sinclair, Larry West— an experimental critiquing group at the Online Writing Workshop that experienced greater success than I expected; and everyone else at the OWW who at some point critiqued one of my many novels and short stories posted there. All of them offered invaluable insight into this book.

I must acknowledge one first reader in particular: Ariel Guzman, a true best friend and critique partner, who was there from the very beginning, when I first set words down on paper in the eighth grade and announced I wanted to be a writer. He's suffered through everything I've ever written, and that first novel attempt was truly horrid. I still shudder. Without his encouragement along the way, I would never have made it to this point.

I must also thank Alis Rasmussen, for offering to read my first real (and as yet unpublished) novel and for offering two particularly relevant pieces of advice: "patience and persistence" and "cut at least half of the words out." She guided me through the rough terrain between the plateau of simply writing, and the heights of actually being published. She also introduced me to my first con . . . and everyone has regretted it ever since.

And last, but certainly never least, my family: my mother, who showed me that strength comes from the inside; my brothers, Jason and Jacob, who are the only other people more excited about this book than I am; and George, who has taught me more about myself than I thought anyone possibly could.

Nothing is more important than the people that support you and encourage you throughout life, especially those that encourage your dreams. These people not only made this a better book, they made me a better person.

·⟨ *The Palace* ⟩·

OVER one thousand years ago, a great fire swept through the city of Amenkor. Not a fire like those burning in the bowls of standing oil that lined the promenade to the palace, all red and orange and flapping in the wind that came from the sea. No. This fire was white, pure, and cold. And from the legends, this fire burned from horizon to horizon, reaching from the ground to the clouds. It came from the west, like the wind, and when it fell upon the city it passed through walls and left them untouched, passed through people and left them unburned. It covered the entire city—there was no escape, it touched everyone—and then it swept onward, inland, until it vanished, nothing more than a white glow, and then nothing at all.

It is said the White Fire cast the city into madness. It is said the Fire was an omen, a harbinger of the eleven-year drought and the famine and disease that followed.

It is said the Fire murdered the ruling Mistress of the time, even though her body was found unburned on the wide stone steps that led up to the palace at the end of the promenade. There were bruises around her throat in the shape of hands, and bruises in the shape of boots on her naked back and bared breasts. There were bruises elsewhere, beneath the white robes that lay about her waist in torn rags, the robe held in place only by the angle of her body and the gold sash of her office. There was blood as well. Not gushing blood, but spotted blood.

But the legends say the Fire killed her.

Fire, my ass.

Tucked into the niche set high in a narrow corridor of the palace, I snorted in contempt, then shifted with a grimace to ease a cramped muscle. No part of my body moved out into the light. The niche sat at the end of a long shaft that provided airflow into the depths of the palace.

Any blind-ass bastard could tell what had really happened to the Mistress. And the blind-ass bastard who killed her should have rotted in the deepest hellhole in Amenkor. There were quicker ways to kill someone than strangulation. I knew.

I drew in a slow breath and listened. Nothing but the guttering flames of the standing bowls of burning oil which lit the empty corridor below. The airflow in the palace was strong, gusting through the opening at my back. A storm was coming. But the wind took care of the smoke from the burning oil. And other smells.

After a long, considering moment, I slid forward to the edge of the niche and glanced down the corridor in both directions. Nothing.

With one smooth shift, I slipped over the lip of the opening, dangled by white-knuckled fingers for a moment until steady, then dropped to the floor.

"You, boy! Help me with this."

I spun, hand falling to the knife hidden inside the palace clothing that had been provided the night before: page's clothing that was a little too big for me, a little loose. But apparently it had worked. I was small for my age, and had no breasts to speak of, but I definitely wasn't a boy.

The woman who'd spoken was dressed in the white robe of a personal servant of the Mistress and carried two woven baskets, one in each arm. One of the baskets was threatening to tip out of her grasp. She'd managed to catch it with the other basket before it fell, but both baskets were now balanced awkwardly against her chest, ready to tip at the slightest movement.

"Well, what are you waiting for?" Her face creased in irritation and anger, but her eyes remained focused on the baskets.

I straightened from the instinctual crouch and moved forward to catch the basket before it fell. It was heavier than it looked.

My hand brushed the woman's skin as I took the basket and a long thin slash of pain raced up my arm, as if someone had drawn a dagger's blade across my skin from wrist to elbow. I glanced at the woman sharply, tensed.

The woman heaved a sigh of relief and wiped a trembling hand across her forehead. "Thank you." After a moment to catch her breath, she motioned to the basket again. "Now give it back. Carefully!"

Relief swept through me. She hadn't felt the contact, hadn't felt the slash of pain or anything else out of the ordinary at all.

I set the basket back into the woman's arms, careful not to touch her skin again, the woman grunting at its weight. Then I stepped aside and let her pass. She huffed out of the corridor, vanishing around a corner.

I watched her receding back, then my eyes narrowed. I wasn't supposed to run into anyone, especially not one of the true Servants. No one was supposed to know I was here.

I'd have to be more careful.

I fingered the knife again, considering, then turned away, moving in the other direction, shrugging thoughts of the woman aside. She'd barely glanced up from her baskets, too intent on not dropping them. She wouldn't remember meeting a page boy. Not inside the palace. And there wasn't any time to spare, not if I was to get to the Mistress' chambers before dawn. I was in the outermost portion of the palace, still needed to get to the linen closet with the archer's nook, get past the guards at the inner sanctum. . . .

I shook my head and moved a little faster down the narrow corridor, running through the mental image of the map of the palace in my head, reviewing the timing. The incoming storm prickled through my skin, urging me on. I reached into an inner pocket and fingered the key hidden there.

I had to get to the Mistress' chambers tonight. We'd waited too long already . . . had waited six years hoping that things would get better, looking for alternate solutions. Six long years since the Second Coming of the White Fire, and since that day things had only gotten worse. Legend said that the first Fire had cast the city into madness. The second Fire had done the same. A slow, subtle madness. And now winter bore down on us, the seas already getting rough, unsuitable for trade. With the mountain passes closed, resources low . . .

As I turned into a second corridor, I frowned, with a hard and determined expression. We'd tried everything to end it. Everything but what legend said had worked the first time the Fire came. Now there was no choice.

It was time for the Mistress to die.

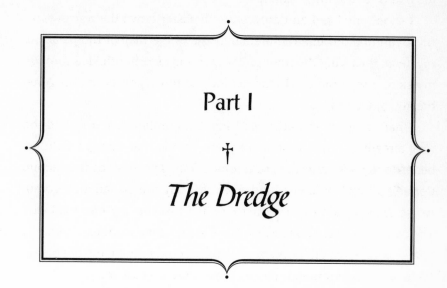

Part I

†

The Dredge

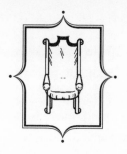

Chapter 1

I FOCUSED on the woman with dark eyes and a wide face, on the basket she carried on her hip, a cloth covering its contents. The woman wore a drab dress, had long, flat, black hair. A triangle of cloth covered most of her head, two corners tied beneath her chin, easy to pick out in the crowd of people on the street. She moved without rushing, head lowered as she walked.

An easy mark.

My gaze shifted to the basket and my hand slid down to the dagger hidden inside my tattered shirt. My stomach growled.

I bit my upper lip, turned back to the woman's downturned face, tried to catch her eyes from across the street. The eyes were the most revealing. But she'd moved farther away, paused now at the edge of an alley.

A moment later, she ducked into the narrow.

I hesitated on the edge of the street they called the Dredge, fingers kneading the handle of my dagger. People flowed past, not quite jostling me. I scanned the street, the people, noticed a guardsman, a cartman with brawny shoulders, a gutterscum thug. No one openly dangerous. No one overtly threatening to a fourteen-year-old girl pressed flat against a wall, mud-streaked, clothes more tattered than whole, hair so dirty its color was indistinguishable. A small girl—far, far too small for fourteen; far, far too thin to be alive.

Eyes hardening, I turned back to the mouth of the narrow where the woman had disappeared, watched its darkness.

Then I cut across the Dredge, cut through the crowd so smoothly I touched no one. I slid against the wall of the narrow, crouched low, until my eyes adjusted to the darkness. I listened. The noise of the street faded to a background wind, the world grayed. . . .

And in the new silence I heard the sound of footfalls on damp stone, steady and quick. I heard clothes rustling, heard the creak of wicker as a basket was shifted. The footsteps were receding.

In the cloaked darkness of the alley, I glanced back out toward the street, toward the movement, the sunlight. No one had seen me follow the woman. Not even the guardsman.

I turned back, slid deeper into the darkness, into the stench of refuse and piss and mildew. I moved without sound, with a cold, hungry intent, my stomach clenched and empty, thinking only of the basket, of the food it might represent. The woman's footsteps continued, shuffling ahead on the dirty stone, splashing in unseen puddles. I drew in the stench of the alley, could almost smell the woman's sweat. My hand closed on the handle of my dagger—

And the footsteps ahead slowed, grew wary.

I halted, drew close to the wall, hand pressed against its damp mud-brick.

Ahead, feet shuffled in place. The cold of the alley grew deeper, a coldness I felt echoed in my chest like the harsh burn of hoarfrost.

Then I heard another footstep, a heavier tread, a gasp as the woman cried out, the sound suddenly choked off.

Something heavy hit the cobbles, followed by rolling thuds, by the sound of a struggle: clothes rustling, harsh breaths, a horrifying gasping sound, choked and desperate. Like the gasping sounds of the man I'd killed three years before. Except these gasps were not wet and slick, choking on blood. These were dry and empty.

A sick, feverish shudder of horror rushed through my skin and I pressed against the mud-brick at my back, trying not to breathe. The coldness of hoarfrost prickling in my chest tightened, began to burn white, like the touch of the Fire that had passed through the city three years before. Fresh sweat prickled in my armpits, the center of my chest, making me shudder. My hand clenched on the handle of my dagger.

The gasping quieted, slowed. A strained grunting filtered from the darkness. It escalated, tight and short, then released in a trembling sigh. Almost like sobbing. This faded into soft breathing. Then there was a weighted thud, heavier than the first, and even the breathing faded.

I fidgeted, breath held close, hand gripping the sweaty hilt of the dagger. I'd let the dagger slip completely free without thinking. Had brought it to bear.

But no one emerged from the darkness. Not after twenty shortened breaths. Not after fifty.

And the icy Fire in my chest had died.

I relaxed, drew a steadying breath, then edged forward. A trickle of black water appeared, running through the alley's center. I kept to the left wall, the bricks wet, left hand against the dampness, right hand holding the dagger.

Eleven paces farther on I found the basket turned on its side, potatoes littering the cobbles. The cloth that had covered them was already stained with filth.

Three steps farther, I found the woman's body.

She lay crumpled to the ground, on her back, her feet bent beneath her thighs. One arm lay thrust out, the other close to her side. The kerchief covering her hair had been pushed askew and tangles of her hair lay matted to the stone. Her head lay in the trickle of scummy water, tilted slightly away.

I hunkered against the wall, scanned the darkness ahead, listening. But there was nothing but the sound of dripping water, the taste of damp growth.

I turned back to the woman, edged past her outflung arm, and knelt.

A dark band of blood encircled her neck, cut into her flesh. Her eyes were open, staring up past me into the darkness of the alley. Her lips were parted.

She looked like she was asleep, except she wasn't breathing and her eyes were open.

I looked at the line of blood across her neck again, leaned forward—

And saw a thin cord loop down in front of my face.

I brought the dagger up instantly, but not before the cord snapped tight across my neck, not before I heard a guttural, masculine grunt as a man crossed the cord behind my neck and jerked it tight. The cord caught the dagger on its flat side and yanked it flat against my neck.

Then the man leaned upward and back, pressed his knee hard into my spine and pushed.

My body arched outward, the cord drawing tighter across my neck. My head fell back against the man's shoulder so that his bearded cheek rested against mine, his breath hot against my chest. It stank of ale and fish and oil.

"A little young and thin for my tastes," he gasped, drawing the cord tighter with a jerk, "but I'll takes what gifts the Mistress gives me, eh?"

The icy pressure flared again in my chest, at the base of my throat, spreading like frost. I tasted the air from the night of the

Fire three years before, felt the Fire itself burning cold deep inside me. I sucked in a hard, painful breath of air in shock.

And then my breath was cut off.

I threw myself forward, felt the cord dig deeper, felt a trickle of blood flow as the cord sawed into my skin. The man's gasps ground in my ear and I jerked to the side, felt the cord cut deeper still. And then the grayness of the world focused even more, focused down and down until the only thing I could feel was the cord, the hot fire of not being able to breathe beginning to burn in my chest—

The cold metal of the dagger pressed tight against my neck. I still held its handle in my right hand, held it in a death grip.

As the fire in my chest seethed outward, sending tingling sensations of warmth into my arms, down deep into my gut, I twisted the dagger. Its edge bit into my skin, drew a vertical slice from the back of my jaw downward to my collarbone that stung like a sharp needle prick. I twisted, pushing the dagger outward as the man grunted in my ear, his breath a hissing stench, spit flying from his clamped teeth onto my neck. My focus on the world began to slip, the grayness seeping forward, narrowing to a hollow circle, to a point. Tingling hot fire filled my gut, seeped downward into my legs, into my thighs. A thousand needle pricks coursed toward my knees, through my shoulders and into my arms. The cord cinched tighter. My chest heaved, spasmed—

And then the dagger sliced through the cord.

The man grunted with surprise as his hands jerked wide. The knee pressed into my spine thrust me forward, sent me sprawling onto the dead woman. The man fell backward into the rank alley wall.

My gasp for air was like a warm, shuddering scream.

I lurched over the woman, stepped on her arm, felt it roll beneath me, but the motions felt soft and drawn out. As I fell to my side, I twisted, turned so that I landed facing the man.

He'd already thrust himself away from the wall, was already looming over me, descending, his face a grimace of hatred. His hands reached for me, the cord still twined around his fingers, its cut ends dangling as he reached for my neck.

I brought the dagger up from my side without thinking. The world was still too gray, too narrow for thought.

The dagger caught him in the chest. I felt it punch through skin, felt it grind against bone as it sank deeper, deeper, until it was brought up short by the handle. Then the man's weight drove the handle into my chest.

I had a moment to see a startled look flash through the man's eyes, a moment to feel his hands encircling my throat loosely, and then the pain of the dagger's handle drove the breath from my lungs. I lurched forward, threw the man to the side, and rolled to my hands and knees, coughing like a diseased cat. Pain radiated from the center of my chest. Not the fiery pain of no air, nor the cold pain of the warning Fire, but the dull pain of being punched too hard, too fast.

I coughed a moment more, then vomited.

I was still hunched over, on hands and knees, bile like a sickness in my torn throat, when someone said, "Impressive."

I jerked away from the voice, a tendril of spit and bile that dangled from my mouth plastering itself to my chin as I moved. I came up short against the alley wall with a thud, body tucked in so I was as small a target as possible. A bright flare of pain radiated from my bruised ribs. My hand went reflexively for my dagger, but it was still embedded in the man's chest.

My heart lurched and I cowered lower, head bowed, arms wrapped around my knees. I was trembling too much to do anything more, too weak from the struggle with the man to run. So I cowered, eyes closed, hoping the voice would go away.

After a moment I realized I hadn't heard retreating footsteps. I hadn't heard anything at all.

I opened my eyes, aware of the wetness of tears on my face, and tilted my head, staring out into the alley through the matted tangles of my hair.

A guardsman leaned against the alley wall twenty paces away, the bodies of the man and the woman between us. It was the same guardsman I'd seen on the street before. His arms were crossed over his chest, his posture casual. He wore the standard uniform— breeches, leather boots, brown shirt, leather armor underneath— but no sword belted at his waist. A dagger lay tucked in his belt instead. The Skewed Throne symbol was stitched in red thread on the left side of the shirt.

Red. A Seeker. A guardsman sent to mete out the Mistress' punishments, to pass judgment. Not one of the regular guardsmen; the stitching would have been gold instead.

A new fear crawled into my stomach.

He'd seen me kill a man, had witnessed it.

He watched me with a strange look in his eyes. A confused look that pinched the skin between his brows and tightened the corners of his mouth.

After a moment, his gaze shifted from me to the body of the man.

"Very impressive," he said again, then pushed himself away from the wall.

I flinched back, my shoulders scraping against the moldy dampness of the alley's mud-brick, my breath hitching in my throat. I tasted bile again, felt fresh tears squeeze through pain-clenched eyes.

I heard the guardsman halt.

"I didn't come for you," he said, his voice brusque but soothing. Reassuring.

I opened my eyes to narrow slits, just enough to see him, to watch.

He moved toward the dead man, knelt on his heels near the man's head.

For a long moment, he simply stared at the man's face, at the small trickle of blood that had leaked from the corner of the mouth. Then he spat to one side, his face twisted with contempt. "Vicious bastard. You deserved worse than this."

He jerked my dagger free from the man's chest and in a strangely fluid motion made three quick slashes across the man's forehead. He stared at his handiwork a moment more, then turned on the balls of his feet until he was facing me, elbows on his knees, my dagger dangling loosely from one hand.

I watched the dagger carefully, aware of his intent look. I hadn't realized how important the dagger had become to me over the last three years. I felt exposed without it, helpless.

I wanted my dagger back. Needed it.

The guardsman began swinging the blade back and forth, taunting me, and my gaze shifted back to his eyes. This close, I could see they were a muddy brown, like mine, like most of the people who lived in Amenkor, on the Dredge. There were scars on his face, lots of scars. Scars that ran up into his thinning, gray-brown hair. They made him seem hard, like worn mud-brick bleached by the sun.

"And you," he murmured, the confused look returning. "You don't seem dangerous at all. You're what? Ten?" He leaned slightly forward, eyes narrowing, then shook his head. "Older than that, although you could fool almost anyone. Thirteen at least, maybe more. And you don't talk much."

He paused, waiting. The dagger stilled.

"Maybe you don't talk at all," he said finally, dagger back in motion, the action careless, as if he didn't care.

I narrowed my eyes. "I talk."

The words came out harsh and gravelly, like brick grating against brick, and they hurt—in my chest, in my throat. I wiped the thread of spit and bile from my chin and coughed against the burning sensation. Even the coughs hurt. Hurt worse than anything I'd ever felt before.

The guardsman hesitated, then nodded, the barest hint of a smile playing at the edges of his mouth.

"So I see. You just don't talk much, do you?"

I didn't answer, and his smile grew.

He turned his attention to my dagger, still swinging between the fingers of one hand. With a smooth gesture, he swung it upright in his grip, then stared at me over its tip. All traces of the smile were gone, his eyes flatly serious, expression hard.

"This is your dagger, isn't it?" All hints of the reassuring, casual voice had disappeared. This voice was hurtful, threatening.

I cringed back. "Yes."

He didn't react, eyes still hard, intent. "It's a guardsman's dagger."

My eyes flicked to the dagger tucked in his belt, then back. I felt my stomach clench and tensed, even though it hurt. In my head, I saw the first man I'd killed leaning against the second story of the rooftop, hand outstretched, grasping for me, saw the blood coating his neck, heard the wet rasp of his last short breaths. And I saw the ripped-out gold stitching of the Skewed Throne on the left breast of his shirt.

For the first time since the night of the Fire, the thought of the first man I'd killed didn't frighten me. Instead, defiant anger seethed just beneath the pain.

I glared at the Seeker. "Yes. But now it's mine."

He frowned. He wanted to ask how I'd gotten it, where it came from. I could see it in his eyes.

But he simply shrugged. "What's yours is yours."

He tossed the dagger low across the ground, metal clanging on stone as it struck the wet cobbles and slid to a halt just in front of me.

I reached out slowly and picked it up, unbelieving, the blood on the handle still tacky, my eyes on the guardsman the entire time. He didn't move, just watched. But something had changed. There was a new, considering look in his eyes, as if he were judging me, coming to a decision.

I pulled the dagger in close to my body, kept it ready.

After a long, drawn-out moment, he stood. "I bet you know the warren beyond the Dredge like I know the scars on my own skin," he murmured to himself. And then he tilted his head.

I shifted under his gaze, suddenly aware of the darkness of the alley, of the seclusion and the smooth fluidity of his movements.

"Go away," I said, pulling in tight, ready to flee.

He smiled, a slow, careful smile, as if my wary stance had convinced him of something.

Instead of turning to leave, he crossed his arms again and said, "I could use your help."

"Go away," I repeated with more force, even though the suggestion piqued interest deep inside me.

"You can leave if you want," he said, but he didn't move himself, simply stood, waiting. It was like the dagger again. He was dangling escape in front of me, letting it swing back and forth, taunting me.

I glanced toward the potatoes scattered across the cobbles, barely visible in the light. Hunger twisted in my gut.

The guardsman shifted and I tore my gaze back to where he stood. He hadn't moved forward, only shifted his weight, his eyes on me. "Everyone runs to the slums of the Dredge, you know. Almost everyone. Murderers, thieves, brawlers. Merchants who've lost their businesses, gamblers who've gambled away their lives. A few run to the sea, to the ships in the harbor and the cities they can take them to elsewhere on the coast, but not many. They come here. They think they can hide here. That among all this crowded filth, these warrens of alleys and houses and narrow courtyards, they can somehow disappear."

He paused, still staring at me. Then he frowned, and his voice darkened. "And they're right. Five years ago, before the Fire, they wouldn't have had a chance. The Seekers would have found them, if we were sent after them by the Mistress. The Skewed Throne would have found them. But now. . . ."

His gaze dropped to the dead man in the middle of the alley, his eyes flickering with a black hatred, and I shrank back until my shoulders pressed against the collapsing wall.

"Now the Dredge is more crowded. All the merchants hit hard by the panic after the Fire are drifting here. All of their families. They're desperate. And they have nowhere else to go. You must have noticed how crowded the Dredge has become, little *varis*." He paused, glanced up, then nodded his head. "Yes. You've noticed. You live off of it, don't you?"

The question struck like a physical blow, harsh enough to make me wince. I narrowed my eyes at him, jaw set, and said, "Yes."

It came out bitter and hopeless.

He nodded again. "You know the Dredge and its underbelly. You live here. You can help me find these men that run."

He paused, still watching me, letting the offer sink in. After a moment he pushed away from the wall and walked toward me, knelt a few steps away, so close I could see his scars clearly, could see his eyes.

I cringed back from him, from the heated danger that bled from him, that set all the warning senses I'd honed on the Dredge on edge except for one, the one I trusted the most: the cold Fire in my chest. That Fire remained dormant, and because of that I stayed instead of fleeing to the street, or in the other direction, deeper into the warren of dark paths beyond the Dredge.

"Do you know where Cobbler's Fountain is?" he asked.

I nodded. I hadn't been to Cobbler's Fountain in years. It was too far up the Dredge, too close to the River and the city, to the real Amenkor. I'd be noticed there, my rags and dirty hair. It wasn't good hunting ground.

"Good," he said, sitting back slightly. "I can help you, and you can help me. Think about it. If you want to help find these men for the Mistress, come to Cobbler's Fountain tomorrow, at dusk. I'll be there."

Then he stood, turned, and strode from the alley, pausing at its edge to adjust to the sunlight before entering the crowd. He didn't look back.

I waited for ten heartbeats, wary, then rose from my crouch, wincing as I drew in a deep breath. I approached the two bodies slowly, every movement sending dull pain across my chest and into my arms, still watching the far entrance to the alley, still uncertain the guardsman had left. A stinging fire burned in a circle around my neck where the dead man's cord had cut into flesh, and a thinner line of fire ran from the back of my jaw down my throat from where I'd pressed my own dagger into my neck to cut the cord, but the pain in my chest . . .

I coughed again, hissed through clenched teeth as I knelt beside the man.

His face was strangely slack, his eyes open. Blood had filled his mouth, had leaked from one corner and matted in his beard. The guardsman had carved the Skewed Throne into his forehead, the cuts raw, with only a trace of blood. A single horizontal slash across the top, two slanted vertical slashes beneath, one shorter than the other. The man had been dead too long for them to bleed much.

I leaned over his face, breathed in his sour smell—piss and blood and sweat and something deeper, something rancid, like rotten butter. I stared into his vacant eyes, frowned as I brought one hand up to the scored line encircling my neck. There was no frigid flare of Fire in my chest now. No reaction at all. The danger had passed.

But as I stared into his eyes I felt again the coarseness of his beard on my cheek, heard his ragged, desperate gasps. I smelled his breath.

Anger grew, deep in my chest, a hard lump beneath the dull pain. An anger I recognized. I'd felt it many times during my life on the Dredge—for the wagon master who'd kicked me, for the nameless gutterscum who'd slid into my niche and stolen my bread. A hatred that was there and then gone. Fleeting.

But this time the anger, the hatred, wasn't fleeting. It was solid. And the longer I looked at the dead man's face, the harder it became. It began to take form, shifting and slithering.

I leaned closer, breathed in the rancid musk of the dead man even deeper.

And then I spat into his face.

I leaned back, startled, my spittle running down the man's skin beneath one dead eye. I was strangely . . . thrilled, arms tingling as if with numbness, with cold. But I wasn't cold. A hot flush covered me instead, lay against my skin like sweat.

I turned to the woman, a pang of regret coursing beneath the heated, sickening exhilaration. Then I crawled to the spilled potatoes, the dropped basket, and collected it all together, as quickly as possible.

I fled toward the back of the alley, away from the Dredge, trying not to think about the dead man, the woman, or the guard.

I focused on the pain in my chest instead. And beneath that, the still lingering anger, coiled now, like a snake.

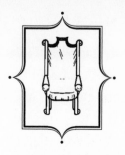

Chapter 2

I WOKE in my niche deep in the slums beyond the Dredge to vivid sunlight outside, my chest bruised a livid purple-black. I moaned as I rolled into a sitting position, lifted up my ragged shirt, and examined the bruising. Every breath drew a wince, every motion a twinge, yet I prodded the edges of the bruise anyway.

I sat and stared at the basket of potatoes and thought about the round face of the woman the man had killed. The pang of regret returned, but I shoved it aside in annoyance and focused on the guardsman, on the offer to help him.

I frowned and pulled out my dagger, stared at the band of sunlight caught on the flat of its blade.

I didn't need the guardsman. I'd survived without him since I was nine. I'd survived without anyone since Dove and his gutter-scum thugs went after that woman and I refused to follow.

I frowned. I hadn't thought of Dove since that night, tried not to feel the ghost of the throbbing bruise on my cheek where he'd punched me after I'd told him I wouldn't help him catch the woman. I'd known he wasn't going to simply rob her. He meant to kill her. I'd seen it in his eyes.

I scowled. I'd decided then that Dove had served his purpose. He'd taught me enough so that I could survive on my own.

I hadn't needed anyone else then and I didn't need anyone else now.

I hesitated. Except, of course, the white-dusty man. I needed him, relied on him occasionally. But that was different.

So I rose with a grimace of pain and crawled out into the sunlight through my niche's narrow opening, the guardsman and his offer pushed aside. The potatoes wouldn't last forever. I needed to hunt.

The Dredge is the only real street in the slums of Amenkor, running straight from its depths, across the River, and into the real city on the other side of the harbor. The Dredge is where those from the city proper mingled with those that lived beyond the Dredge, those that lived deeper, like me—the gutterscum. At fourteen, the Dredge was the edge of my world. I'd never stepped beyond it, never walked down its broken cobbles, past its taverns and shops, across the bridge over the River and into the city of Amenkor itself. The Dredge on this side of the River *was* Amenkor for me. I preyed upon its people, on the crowds of men and women who had somehow fallen on hard times and had been forced to abandon the real city and retreat across the harbor.

And the Seeker had been right. Since the passage of the Fire three years before, the number of people in the slums had increased. Not just people from the city proper either, but others as well, people not from Amenkor at all. People who wore strange clothing, who had different colored hair or eyes, who carried strange weapons and spoke in accents . . . or didn't speak the common language at all.

But those people were rare.

I peered out from the darkness of the slums now, huddled low, mud-brick pressed into my back. On the street, men and women moved back and forth. I watched each of them as they arrived, caught their faces, scanned their clothing. That man wore tattered rags but carried a dagger at his belt. Yet there was no danger in his eyes. Hard, but not cruel. He carried nothing else, and so he faded from my mind, nothing but a darker blur against the dull gray of the world. Unconsciously, I kept track of him—of all the people—but he'd ceased to be interesting. Not a target; not a threat. Gray.

A flash of fine clothing and my eyes shifted. Not truly fine clothing—frayed edging, a tear down one side of the gray shirt, breeches stained, oily—but better than most. He wore boots, one sole loose at the heel, the nails visible when he walked. He also carried a dagger, hidden, his hand resting over the bulge of its sheath at his side. He walked quickly, tense, and his eyes . . .

But he turned before I could catch his eyes, his torn shirt and loose sole vanishing through a doorway.

He faded.

Gray.

I settled into position next to the wall, wincing once over the bruise on my chest, and let the flow of the street wash around me. When the pain had receded, I focused on the street, squinted in concentration, and felt a familiar sensation deep inside.

With a subtle, internal movement, like relaxing a muscle, the sensation rushed forward.

The world collapsed, slowed, blurred. Buildings and people faded, grayed. Those men and women I'd determined to be possible threats slid into washes of red against the background gray, like smears of blood, moving through the flow of the street. Occasionally, I'd concentrate on one person and they'd emerge from the gray, sharp and clear, so I could watch them, consider them. Casual glances would draw others out of the gray, their actions entering the field momentarily, and then I'd lose interest, determine they carried nothing I could eat, nothing I wanted, and the people would return to gray.

The sound of the street blurred as well, voices and footfalls and rustling clothes all merging into a single sound like a gentle wind rustling in my ears. Threatening noises slid out of the sound, catching my attention, until I'd made certain there was no danger. Then they faded back into the wind.

I submerged myself in the world of gray and red and wind with a sigh, a world that had helped me survive all these years alone, and searched for my next mark.

An hour before dusk, I leaned back against the alley wall, an apple in one hand. The woman hadn't even noticed the apple was missing. She'd set it down on the edge of the cart to pick up the sack she'd dropped. All I had to do was reach out and take it. It wasn't much, not after an entire day's work. But the pain in my chest had kept me from trying for anything more difficult, and I still had the potatoes back at my niche.

I'd just turned away, ready to return to my niche, when I thought I saw the guardsman.

It was a subtle movement, thirty paces farther down the Dredge. As if he had pushed himself away from where he was leaning against the corner of a building, turned, and rounded the corner. All I saw for certain was the vague shape of a man's back vanishing behind the mud-brick, into the darkness of the narrow.

A casual movement, but one that sent a prickle down the backs of my arms.

I hesitated, watched the narrow farther down the Dredge. When no one reappeared around the corner, I finally turned and moved back into the warren beyond the street, letting the world of gray and red and wind slip away, shrugging thoughts of the guardsman aside.

But something had changed.

As I made my way back toward my niche, I stared down at the apple and frowned. It was a good apple. Hardly any scabs, mostly ripe, a small gouge in one side that had browned and begun to spoil, but still a good apple. I should be running back to my niche in triumph, should be huddled against its back wall, body crouched protectively around the apple as I devoured it.

But I didn't feel any triumph. I didn't feel anything at all. My stomach was strangely hollow. Not with hunger either. With just . . . nothing.

I slowed to a halt in the middle of a dark narrow. It was still light out—sun glowed bright ahead—but here there was only a dense darkness, like a smothering cloth. I halted in the darkness and simply stared at the apple. An entire day's work.

The hollowness had started after I'd killed the man, after I'd spoken to the guardsman.

No. The hollowness had always been there. I'd always just ignored it.

But now . . .

I was still staring at the apple when someone said, "Give it to me."

The voice was harsh with violence, a dry, rumbling croak, but I didn't jump. I squinted into the darkness and picked out a figure sagging against one wall. It took me a moment to realize it was a woman, sitting back on her haunches, body piled high with rags. Her hair hung in matted chunks about her face, her skin so wrinkled and ground with dirt it appeared as cracked and dry as mud. Her eyes were tainted a sickly yellow, but were alive and fixed on me.

On the apple.

"Give me the apple, bitch."

I'd seen her before, always huddled in a niche, an alcove, always in darkness. A heaving mound of rags that shuffled from one location to the next. I knew her.

But now, as I looked into the yellowish taint of her eyes, into the blackness at their center, I actually *saw* her. And the hollowness in my stomach took sudden and vivid form.

I recognized those eyes.

They were mine.

I ran, bolted from the narrow into the sunlight with the woman I would become screeching, "Give it to me! Give it to me, you bitch!" behind me. I ran back to my niche and huddled against its back wall and cried. Harsh, bitter tears that only made the hollowness inside me swell larger. I cried until my arms and legs ached and grew numb, until the sobs faded into hitching coughs. I watched the sunlight through the niche's narrow opening and tried to think of nothing at all, ended up thinking of Dove, of the five years since I'd been on my own, of the woman with the potatoes lying dead in the alley, strangled by the man I'd killed. Tremors ran through my arms, shuddered through my shoulders. Every now and then tears burned in my eyes for no reason and I'd squeeze them tight, the dark, hollow, twisted sensation burning in my chest. I'd pull in on myself, hold myself hard, until the burning receded, until my chest loosened.

Until finally the light outside began to fade and I realized what I needed to do.

I avoided the dark alley where the rag woman had been, skirted it by four narrows. The depths beyond the Dredge seemed somehow darker, dirtier. A boy no more than seven pawed his way through a heap of refuse outside a recessed doorway, buried so deep I wouldn't have noticed him if the heap hadn't suddenly heaved upward. He stumbled from it, sludge streaking his face, his legs, his arms. He held a twisted spoon in one hand like a knife, sank to one knee with a snarl like a dog when he saw me, then bolted for the shadows.

The carcass of a rat dangled from one of the boy's hands. It swung wildly as he ran.

That was me, digging through the garbage, snarling.

My chest tightened again, but I shoved the sensation back, began moving faster. The light was beginning to gray into dusk. There wasn't much time.

I slid up the Dredge, keeping to the walls, to the alleys. I watched the people as I moved, suddenly conscious of my clothes . . . no, not clothes. The farther I moved, the more it became obvious I wore nothing but dirt and slime, the Dredge draped over my bones like lichen. I felt myself shrinking and I drew in upon myself, twice halted to turn back—once when a woman stared at me with blatant shock and disgust, and once when a boy spat at my feet, laughing loudly when I jerked back in a cower.

He might not have laughed so loudly if he'd known my hand was on the dagger beneath my rags.

I pushed on, until I crouched in the darkness of a narrow that looked out on the fountain, at the crumbling stone of a woman, one arm raised to hold an urn on her shoulder. Her other arm had once been poised on her hip, but it had been broken off years before so that only a jagged piece jutted out from her shoulder, and only the tips of her fingers remained at her waist. Water had spilled from the urn into the surrounding pool, but now the pool was empty except for dark patches of mold, the mouth of the urn stained with water residue.

I settled back against the narrow's wall. I'd been here before, when I was younger, many times. But the memories were vague, blurred with sunlight. The light glinted off the water in the basin, sparkled with childish laughter. Closing my eyes, I could feel the water from the urn spilling down into my hair, could taste its coolness as it washed down into my mouth. But everything was too bright, too blurred.

I felt a woman's hands touch my shoulders, reach beneath my arms to bring me up out of the water—

"I never expected to see you here."

I opened my eyes and stared up into the Seeker's face, half seen in the dusk. He'd spoken gently, and now frowned as he looked down at me.

"Is anything wrong?"

I wiped at the tears. "No."

His frown deepened, as if he didn't believe me. His stance shifted and the cold, hard danger that edged his eyes softened.

For a moment, I thought he'd reach out and touch me, touch my face. I felt myself cringe back, hand on my dagger, even as something deep inside tried to lean forward. And he did reach out. . . .

A small sack dangled from his outstretched hand.

"Take it," he said when I hesitated.

My dagger clutched hidden against my side, I reached out and took the sack, stifling a surge of disappointment. The sack was heavy, bulged with strange shapes.

I opened it. There were oranges inside. Good oranges—skins firm, unblemished. And a chunk of bread. And cheese.

My eyes teared up, burned so fiercely I had to squeeze them tight. And my stomach seized.

I thought of the rag woman, of the boy with the sharpened spoon and dead rat, and asked hoarsely, "What do you want me to do?"

The guardsman sank down into a crouch before me, the sky dark behind him. "I'm looking for a man, black hair cut down to here, about this tall. His face is thin and sharp, like . . . like a hawk. And his eyes are dark and sharp, too. He carries a knife with a hilt shaped like a bow, sort of bent backward so it curves slightly around the wielder's hand. Just watch for him. If you see him, follow him. See where he goes, where he hides out. Then come find me. I'll be here at dusk every day."

"Every day?" I reached into the sack, grabbed a chunk of bread and crammed it into my mouth.

The guardsman hesitated, as if still uncertain about what he proposed. His eyes were squinted, even in the moonlight. Then he shook himself. "If I'm not here, one of the other Seekers will be here . . . another guardsman like me. Tell him to give a message to Erick. They'll know who I am."

I nodded, mostly focused on the food. The bread was gone, and not much remained of the cheese. I was saving the oranges. They were rare. I'd only seen them once or twice on the Dredge, and even then they'd been half spoiled.

"What's your name?"

I froze, eyes wide, mouth clamped shut. I breathed in raggedly through my nose, and my heart thudded in my chest. The taste of cheese burned against my tongue.

After a moment, I swallowed, the cheese going down like a large stone. I coughed against the pain, then coughed harder against the pain the coughing awoke in my chest.

Erick watched me carefully. "Do you even have a name?"

I had a name, but no one had used it in over eight years, not since my mother had died. No one had cared. Not the woman who'd taken me in at age six; not the street gang led by Dove that I'd eventually fled to after that. No one.

I dropped my head, stared down into the open mouth of the sack, into the darkness where the oranges rested. A stinging sense of shame and something else coursed through me, burned against my skin. The same something that had leaned forward when Erick reached out with the sack of oranges, that had withdrawn in disappointment. Erick couldn't see it. Not in the darkness. Not behind the fall of my hair.

He sat back on his heels. "It doesn't matter, little *varis*." He paused, and when he spoke again I could hear humor in his voice. "*Varis*. Do you know what that means?"

I shook my head, still not looking up.

"It means hunter." He chuckled softly to himself. "I think that's fitting, don't you, Varis?"

I lifted my head, just enough so that I could see him, then nodded.

He smiled. "Good."

Then he rose and walked down the narrow. Not fast, but steady.

I watched until he slipped into the shadows, then gripped the mouth of the sack of oranges tight.

Varis. Hunter.

I began to sob.

I had a name. Again.

†

The flow of the street had changed the following day. Not because it was different, but because I was different. I wasn't looking for a loose bundle, a momentarily forgotten basket, a stray piece of bread. Now I watched the people's faces.

Leaning against a narrow's wall, half in shade, moving as the sun rose so that I stayed in the shadows, I scanned everyone, looking at the eyes, at the hair, at the nose. Scars and blemishes, jowls and scabs—they all took on new meanings.

By midday—the sun so high there were no longer shadows—my stomach growled and I realized I'd spent the entire morning looking for the man Erick had asked me to find, the hawk-faced man. The initial excitement had ebbed, and with a strange sense of disappointment, I began to focus on bundles.

I slid into old patterns as smoothly as the sunlight slid into dusk.

The next day was the same. And the next.

By the end of the fourth day, I no longer searched for the hawk-faced man. The oranges were gone, and the potatoes. I hadn't seen the guardsman on the Dredge at all, didn't dare return to the fountain to ask for more food.

I saw the hawk-faced man ten days later.

Clouds drifted across the sky, casting the Dredge into gray shade every now and then as they passed over the sun. I stood at the mouth of an alley, eyes narrowed at the woman across the street. She was haggling with a man pulling a handcart. The cart was loaded with cabbages.

The woman had set her bag on the ground.

I glanced around the Dredge. It was crowded, the weather mild for midsummer. People were moving swiftly. Most were smiling.

I had just pushed away from the wall toward the woman and the cart handler when a strange movement made me pause. It was subtle, like the change in light when a cloud passed, but it didn't fit the rhythm of the street.

I frowned and let the world slip into gray and wind. A moment later, I caught the movement again, closer, and then I saw the wash of red among the gray.

It slid into focus almost immediately. A boy-not-yet-man.

I scowled, growled like a dog sensing another dog on his own territory as I shifted into a better position. My hand touched my dagger briefly. I'd seen this boy-not-yet-man for the first time right after the Fire, had seen him many times since; too many times. Lanky brown hair, wicked eyes, thin mouth. A birthmark shaped like a smear of blood at the corner of one eye marred his smooth, sun-darkened face. Clothes like mine—matted, torn, and stained with the Dredge.

Gutterscum, just like me. Competition.

And he'd targeted the woman yelling at the cart handler. *My* mark.

I felt a surge of resentment, bitter, like ash, felt the hairs at the nape of my neck stiffen.

Without thought, I pushed forward through the crowd, focused on the woman and the cart handler. As I moved, I felt the anger tighten in my chest, tingling in my arms, and I narrowed the focus even further. The woman raised one arm, pointing toward the sky as she yelled. Her other arm clutched the ends of the shawl draped around her head. The cart handler shook his head, both hands still firmly gripping the handles of his cart.

He'd just drawn in a deep breath when my focus suddenly . . . altered.

It was like standing neck-deep in the River that ran through Amenkor to the south, near the palace—sunlight harsh on the water, noise from the shops and streets along the banks strangely heightened as they hit the waves, somehow sharper, clearer. It was like standing there, neck-deep—

And then ducking beneath the surface, into darkness.

I felt myself slide from the world of gray and red and wind I was used to into something else, something deeper. The gray darkened. Eddies of movement I'd barely noticed before smoothed out into nothing but shadowed blackness. The background wind died out completely, only the sounds of the woman and the cart handler and the boy intruding. And these sounds were crisper. Movements grew taut, and slowed subtly.

I glanced toward the boy, toward the woman, toward the bag at her feet, and with the new sense of awareness *knew* what would happen.

I didn't hesitate. I swam through the crush of people on the street, brushing an unseen arm, a shoulder—both sensations transitory, like brushing against unseen weeds beneath the river's surface—and then I was at the back of the wagon full of cabbages.

The cart handler glanced toward me as I mimicked a lurch forward, as if I'd been jostled from behind. My hand slapped onto the edge of his cart to steady myself. He glanced toward it with a suspicious frown. The woman never looked in my direction at all.

Then I was past the cart, the woman's sack clutched loosely in my other hand.

I slid into the nearest narrow, crouched down near its opening, sack resting at my feet, and turned to watch with a half suppressed grin. The anger had passed.

The boy was only ten steps from the woman and the cart when he finally noticed the sack was missing. He froze in the middle of the Dredge, so sharply someone stumbled into him from behind. His gaze jerked from side to side. His eyes narrowed viciously. His mouth tightened to a frown.

Then his eyes latched onto mine.

I grinned. I couldn't help it.

Somehow, his eyes narrowed more, became blacker, and I felt the elation inside me curdle and sour, the strange new focus shuddering away at the same moment, making the sourness worse. The real world rushed forward, the sounds of the street loud. My grin faltered.

I gripped the sack and stood, turning to head deeper into the alley. I didn't know what was in the sack, but I no longer wanted to wait on the Dredge to find out either.

I'd reached the deepness of the alley, the sourness twisting into nausea, when someone grabbed my arm and spun me around.

I reacted on instinct, my dagger out and ready before I realized it was the boy-not-yet-man. Except this close, with his own dagger drawn, he seemed much less boy and more man. We'd never been this close, never spoken except through scowls and heated looks.

He reminded me of Dove.

He stepped back, his breathing hard, anger harsh in his eyes. The red birthmark at his eye appeared black in the light from the mouth of the alley. He said nothing, only glared. After a long moment I drew in a deep breath to steady my shuddering heart and said shortly, "What do you want?"

"I want my sack."

I snorted, felt the strange nausea deepen. I tasted bile at the back of my throat, felt a cramp shudder through my stomach. I grimaced. "It isn't yours," I said through the pain.

"But it will be," he said harshly. He didn't get to continue. I gasped at another cramp, dropped the sack as I hunched over my stomach and sagged convulsively to my knees. The boy jerked back, wary and confused, then lurched forward to retrieve the sack as I collapsed to my side, my knees pulled in tight. The bile was like fire, scorching my throat, and the pain in my stomach radiated through my chest, alternately hot and cold. I sensed the boy leaning over me, felt his breath against my face as he spat in a whisper, "Don't mess with me, bitch," and then he was gone.

I saw a retreating shadow and forced myself to concentrate. "My name is Varis," I murmured to myself as the sunlight at the end of the alley came into view, a white blur interrupted briefly by the boy's form.

I was still focusing hard on the light, the strange pain just beginning to fade, when I saw the hawk-faced man. He walked across the mouth of the alley without glancing inside, there and then gone. I might never have noticed, except I was concentrating so hard on remaining conscious. In case the boy decided to come back. Or in case something worse came along.

I lay stunned for a moment. Long enough for the sunlight at the mouth of the alley to fade as a cloud began to pass.

Then I rolled onto my knees. A wave of reawakened nausea poured through me and I dry-vomited, nothing but a sour taste flooding my mouth. When it passed, I staggered to my feet, using the wall for support, and made my way to the mouth of the alley.

I didn't expect to see him. I'd taken too long getting to the street. But he'd halted about twenty paces away, back toward me. I watched as he scanned the Dredge, as if searching for someone. Then he turned and I saw his face clearly.

He fit the guardsman's description of the hawk-faced man. Black hair, dark eyes, thin face, sharp nose. I couldn't see a knife, but I knew it was him.

He scanned the Dredge one more time, eyes narrowed, then moved into the alley farther up.

I shoved away from the wall to follow, but another spasm of pain hunched me over on the edge of the Dredge, heaving again. The people on the street flowed around me, leaving a wide space, as if I were diseased. I leaned against the near wall until the spasm passed, then stood.

I felt sweaty and chill at the same time. I wiped my mouth with the back of my hand and began a cautious stagger toward my niche. I didn't feel well enough for any more activity on the Dredge. The hawk-faced man would have to wait.

†

I spent the rest of the day and most of the night passing in and out of consciousness at the back of my niche. Shudders coursed through me, so violent at times my head cracked against the worn mud-brick, my arms flopping uselessly at my sides, spittle drooling from my mouth. Once, I bit my tongue hard enough to draw blood.

When the spasms passed, I lay back against the stone and cried, so weak I could barely raise my arms. The sobs racked my body as painfully as the spasms, but I couldn't seem to stop. I didn't understand what was happening, didn't know how to stop it.

Eventually, I realized that the spasms were taking longer to come, lasted a shorter time, and weren't so harsh. They decreased, until finally I rolled onto my side, tears running down my face, and stared out at the moonlit darkness beyond my niche, the last tremors tingling down my arms.

There, in the moonlit darkness, I saw the world of gray and red and wind. Whatever had happened on the Dredge that afternoon, whatever had pushed me deeper into the grayness, had caused this. I'd gone too deep. I'd pushed myself so far beneath the gray surface of the river I'd almost drowned.

I closed my eyes and drew myself in tight, even though every muscle hurt. I'd never felt so . . . drained.

I breathed in with slow, careful breaths, slipping toward true sleep. My last, cold thought was that I'd have to be more careful when using the river, the world of gray and red and wind.

I didn't want to drown.

†

The next day I placed myself near the alley where I'd seen the hawk-faced man. Before settling in, I checked for the cart handler and for the boy-not-yet-man.

I frowned. He wasn't a boy-not-yet-man. Not now. I'd seen that yesterday, seen it in his eyes.

I shook myself, feeling a backwash of weakness slip through me, and refocused on the crowd. Neither the cart handler nor the boy-not- . . . nor Birthmark were in sight.

I frowned again, thinking of how his eyes had narrowed when he'd seen me with the sack, how *black* they'd become.

Not Birthmark. Bloodmark.

"Varis and Bloodmark," I said out loud, then grimaced.

Bloodmark wasn't in sight. And neither was the hawk-faced man.

I sighed and sat back against the wall of the alley to wait.

The hawk-faced man didn't show until almost dusk. I'd snagged two scabrous apples, a potato as hard as a rock, an entire loaf of bread, and was almost ready to give up when I saw his sharp features heading toward me.

I faded back into the narrow, moving casually, watched him as he passed. His gaze followed the people on the Dredge, eyes flickering swiftly from face to face, mouth flat. He clenched his jaw as he moved, the muscle just beneath his ear pulsing. His clothes were well made, but fading now, stained by his stay in the depths. Mud coated his boots.

Tucked into his belt was a dagger, the hilt curved like a bow.

I glanced sharply again toward his face the moment before he stepped beyond the narrow, memorized it—the faint pockmarks on his cheeks, the lines at the corners of the mouth and eyes—then shifted forward to the corner to follow him.

He paused at the mouth of the alley, just as he had the night before, and searched the crowd. After a moment I realized he was waiting—for someone, for dusk, for the right moment, perhaps.

Then he scowled at the crowd, glanced toward the cloudless sky just beginning to darken toward night, and entered the alley.

I waited five breaths, then took a deeper breath to steady myself, and followed.

Daylight fled as the hawk-faced man moved deeper and deeper into the depths beyond the Dredge. I kept close enough I could see his dagger at first, but far enough back I didn't think he'd notice me. The texture of the Dredge changed the farther we moved, worn mud-brick darkening to decayed stone. The faint scent of dampness and mildew and piss that coated each narrow deepened into reeking slime and shit. The water that slicked through the gutters thickened into sludge, and corners and niches rounded with packed, collected refuse.

Twice the man halted, looking back as I slid against a slime-coated wall and grew still. Both times he stood silently, face hidden by the darkness of night, lit only vaguely by the moonlight. I held my breath, aware that now I followed only a silhouette of the man I'd seen on the Dredge, and hoped that he saw nothing behind him but rotting debris from a thousand discarded lives.

Eventually, he'd turn and continue, and after a moment I'd push away from the wall and follow.

Finally, he halted before a bent, iron gate leading into a narrow courtyard black as pitch. The stone wall of the courtyard lay half crumbled in the alley, the curved arch above the gate completely collapsed. He slid through a gap in the twisted bars and vanished in the darkness beyond.

I huddled against a wall twenty paces away and watched the gate, breath barely a whisper. Somewhere, a dog barked, the sound vicious, and a rat scratched its way through the crevices and stone of the wall behind me. I glanced down the alleyway in both directions, saw no one, and frowned at the gate again, at the utter blackness beyond the gaping mouth of the doorway.

I wanted to follow, but when I stood to slip across the alley the hairs on the nape of my neck tingled, shivering across my shoulders. Deep down in my gut I felt the cold, shuddering stirrings of the Fire. Barely a tendril of flame, just a hint of warning.

I hesitated, drew in a deep breath—

And then headed away from the courtyard, back toward the Dredge, back toward my niche.

I knew where he'd gone. The guardsman . . . Erick . . . would have to be satisfied with that.

I ignored the fact that my arms were trembling. And that the tendril of Fire did not die.

†

At dusk the following day I found my way back to Cobbler's Fountain. Erick was waiting.

"Have you found Jobriah?"

"The hawk-faced man."

Erick laughed. A laugh that sent shivers through my arms. "The hawk-faced man. I like that." Then he seemed to harden, eyes intent, mouth tight. The scars that marked his face stood out in sudden relief. "And can you take me to him?"

I nodded, wary. He didn't seem like the man who'd brought me oranges. This man stirred the tendril of flame that still curled in my gut.

"Good. Take me there."

He made no move to touch me, but when I rose, I veered away from him.

We slid off the Dredge, into the back streets, and headed deep. Worn mud-brick shifted to decayed stone again, piss and filth to sludge and shit. Erick said nothing, just stalked behind me as I shifted from shadow to shadow. He made no attempt to hide, seemed annoyed at my scurrying crouch, but he did nothing to stop me.

By the time we reached the street outside the broken iron gate night had fallen completely and the tendril of flame in my gut had grown to a white Fire. I huddled at the corner of the narrow I'd used the night before. Erick stood at its entrance.

"The gate," I said in a hushed voice and turned to look up at the guardsman's face.

A footfall echoed down the street and without a sound Erick slid back into the narrow. He'd lowered a hand to draw me back as well, but the gesture was unnecessary. I'd already moved.

He cast me a brief, considering look, but then the man on the street caught his attention.

It was the hawk-faced man. Jobriah.

As he had the night before, he paused at the entrance to the gate, then ducked through its bars into the darkness beyond.

Erick shifted forward, body rigid with tension. He surveyed the street, listened to the sounds of the night—a gust of wind, distant clatters of movement, nothing close.

Then, without a word, he walked across the street and ducked into the courtyard, as silent as the night.

The white Fire in my gut flared briefly at the suddenness of his movements, then settled back down. But it didn't die.

I fidgeted at the mouth of the narrow in indecision. Erick hadn't said anything about staying, hadn't said to wait. I'd found the hawk-faced man. My job was done.

I turned to go, and heard another footfall on the street.

Stomach clenching, the Fire twisting its coldness deeper into my chest, I crouched down at the base of the wall and held my breath, waiting.

Another man appeared. In the darkness all I saw was a fat face, large body, sunken eyes. The white Fire surged as he stalked into view, so intense I shivered.

He stepped into the courtyard, pausing only to squeeze his body through the narrow opening.

I straightened from my crouch, placed my hands against the decaying stone of the wall, and bit my lip.

Erick knew about the hawk-faced man, not this other.

But he was a guardsman, a Seeker. He could take care of himself.

I turned to leave, the tingling Fire surging through me, and thought suddenly of the woman the man had killed. I'd stood at the entrance to the alley and listened to her struggling as he strangled her. I'd heard her gasps, his grunts, heard her body slide to the ground. I'd done nothing.

In the darkness of the narrow, I saw her body staring blankly up into the night, leg bent beneath her, hair lying in the trickle of filth running down the alley.

She reminded me of the woman Dove had gone after.

And she reminded me of my mother.

I turned, fought down the taste of sourness at the back of my throat, and sprinted across the street for the courtyard. My knife glared dully in the faint light before I slid through the iron bars into the blackness.

My eyes adjusted, but I still couldn't see anything. I crouched down in the dirt just inside the gate, drew in a trembling breath, and let the world slip into gray and wind.

I caught a wash of red sliding through a doorway at the far end of the courtyard—a fat wash of red—and then it vanished behind the walls of the building.

I held my breath, concentrated on the eddies in the gray that I'd barely noticed before—eddies that now showed me the vague forms of rocks, the dead husk of a tree in one corner—and ran across the courtyard to the edge of the door. I glanced inside. Nothing. But a strange lightening of the gray outlined another door. The lightened gray flickered.

I frowned, then let the gray and wind slip.

Candlelight flickered through the doorway from a room deeper in the building.

I picked my way across the small room, careful of the debris of crumbled stone that littered the floor. Boot prints stood out in the dust, many overlapping each other. They all led to the inner doorway. I tucked myself low at the doorway's edge, took in the inner room at a glance.

It was much wider than the outer room. Deeper. The candlelight came from a table set against the wall at its farthest reaches, where the hawk-faced man stood, looking at something on the table, one hand clutching a wineskin that sloshed as he moved. His shadow reached back into the blackness of the rest of the room, long and thin. Blankets lay in a heap next to the table.

I saw no one else in the room.

Before I could frown in concern, Erick stepped out of the shadows. In two long, silent strides he came up behind the hawk-faced man and reached around, knife in hand, ready to slit his throat.

It would have been a quick, decisive stroke, except the hawk-faced man shifted, raised the skin to take a drink.

The cut intended to slit his throat drew a deep gash across the base of the man's chin, so deep it exposed the bone along the man's jaw as he gasped in shock and jerked backward, stumbling into Erick.

The two fell, blood sheeting down the hawk-faced man's chest, a flap of flesh dangling beneath the exposed jaw. Erick cursed, heaved the man off his chest with enough force to crack Jobriah's head into the table. The candlelight jerked. The man screamed again—a low, horrible scream, like a strangling dog—and dropped to his knees before the table. The wineskin thudded to the floor as he clutched at his chin, blood coating his hand, spattering his arm.

He moaned, rocking forward and back, eyes dazed, as Erick rose from the floor and circled around behind him. Erick's eyes were flat with purpose, the spatters of the hawk-faced man's blood on his face black in the shuddering light.

Erick had just knelt on one knee behind the man, had shifted and leaned forward as if to embrace him, knife bared and black with blood, when I caught movement at the edge of the candlelight.

It was the fat man.

He never saw me.

I sprinted across the length of the room, watched as the fat man raised his dagger above Erick's back, ready to drive it down into the base of the guardsman's neck. I saw Erick reach around the hawk-faced man's chest and slide his dagger between the man's ribs. The man stiffened, gagged as blood began to pour from his mouth, his hand falling away from his chin and the dangling flesh there.

Then Erick heard me, turned just as I slammed into the fat man.

We plowed into the stone wall, the fat man grunting in surprise, stumbling over his own feet. Then the grunts turned from surprise to pain and I realized I was stabbing him with my dagger, over and over. I could feel blood against my hand, could hear it pattering against the stone, against the floor as we fell in a wild heap. I opened my mouth and screamed into his startled face, saw the startlement turn to rage, to hatred, saw the shock slide to determination as he shifted to get the arm with his own dagger into a position to gut me.

Before he had a chance, one of my wild thrusts plunged into his neck. I felt it slide in, deep, felt the blade nick the bone of his neck, scrape and slide deeper, felt the thick folds of his skin against my hand for a brief sickening moment before I jerked the blade away.

His eyes widened, and like a suddenly broken spiderweb, his arms and body slumped to the ground. Blood seeped from the wound, but not like the hawk-faced man's blood. This blood came slower.

I was still screaming, still stabbing. Then Erick's arms enfolded me and pulled me away from the dead fat man, pulled me away and carried me across the room to the shadows, where he sat and held me, murmuring in my ear until slowly, slowly, my screaming faded down into sobs.

"Shh," he breathed in my ear. "Hush, Varis. Hush."

He held me until even the sobs faded, until I lay in a heap against his body, drained.

Eventually, he set me aside, carefully, and moved back toward the bodies. He rolled the hawk-faced man over, marked the man's forehead with the Skewed Throne, then did the same to the fat man. He collected the blanket by the table, the wineskin, and the candle.

He wrapped me in the blanket, which smelled of old sweat and grease and fire, blew out the candle, and carried me out through the courtyard, through the bent iron gate, and into the night.

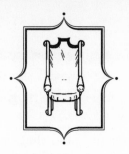

Chapter 3

WOKE in my niche, the blanket wrapped tight around me, late day sunlight angling through the entrance. The first thing I thought of was the fat man, the grate of blade against bone.

I closed my eyes tight against the sensation, pulled the blanket close. But it wasn't enough. With a shudder, I felt tears streaking down my face. I fought them. Because they were useless. Because he'd been about to stab Erick and so wasn't worth crying over.

I eventually cried myself back to sleep, my chest aching.

†

When I woke again, I was instantly hungry and thought of the white-dusty man. But someone had placed a sack just inside the entrance to my niche.

I froze, then fumbled beneath the greasy blanket for my dagger. Fear sliced through my chest that somehow I'd lost the blade, left it behind near the fat man, or that Erick had taken it. But then my fingers closed over its hilt.

I pushed the blanket aside and crawled to the sack. It contained bread and cheese. And oranges.

I only thought of the fat man twice as I crammed the bread in my mouth, then the cheese. I saved the oranges. By then it was dusk, and I thought of the white-dusty man again. I was still hungry. I was always hungry.

I slid from my niche and found the guardsman waiting. He sat on his heels on the far side of the narrow, back against the mud-brick wall. His scars stood out in the half-light. He squinted through the grayness, jaw clenched, thinking.

I sat back against the edge of the entrance to my niche and suddenly wondered how he'd gotten me inside. The opening was too narrow for him to fit. Looking into his eyes, I realized he'd been waiting all day, that he'd heard me wake, heard me sobbing.

New fear lashed through me, close to panic.

He was trying to decide whether I was useful.

He stood. "I think," he said with a careful frown, then paused and seemed to change his mind. "I think, if I'm going to have you hunting for me, I'll need to show you how to use that dagger."

He turned and began to walk away. But he halted just before turning into the nearest alley.

Without looking back, he said, "I'll meet you here at dawn for the first lesson." There was an edge to his voice—regret mixed with something deeper. As if he were about to do something he'd never be proud of, something he'd never forget.

Then he was gone.

I waited, feeling strangely hollow inside, holding my dagger in one hand. It felt . . . heavier. And for a moment—with something close to the panic I'd felt a moment before, icy and trembling—I no longer wanted to touch it.

✝

Erick took me to a courtyard the following dawn. A different one than the one near where I'd killed the fat man, this one wider, more open. He'd brought me clothes, still matted with dirt, still used, but better than the rags I'd been wearing. They still felt scratchy when we stepped through the open space where a gate had once stood into the enclosed courtyard. It was only twenty paces across at most, but I still pulled back, drew tight against the wall.

Erick set down a sack just inside the gateway, walked to the center of the courtyard, then turned. He straightened, instantly wary, eyes searching. It took him a moment to pick me out of the shadows beneath the courtyard's crumbling stone wall.

He grunted and relaxed. "You're never going to learn anything hiding beside that wall. Come here."

I bit my lower lip, forced myself to step out of the darkness into the strengthening sunlight, until I stood two paces away from him. I glared up into his eyes.

He held the gaze, then smiled tightly. "I don't normally train. That's for others in the guard. I'm not exactly certain how to do this," he said. Then he shrugged.

There was no warning. One moment, Erick stood, relaxed, face crimped in perplexed thought, the next his dagger flashed in the sunlight and he lunged.

I reacted instantly, all the years of survival on the Dredge surging forth. I ducked, twisted, and ran. I'd reached the open gateway before Erick's outcry registered.

"Varis! Stop! It was just a feint!"

I slid to a halt in a low crouch, hand against the crumbling stone of the gate's wall, and glanced back. Erick stood where I'd left him, dagger in hand but at his side. He was grinning.

"Gods, you're fast," he said. "Now come back here again. We'll try something simple . . . like holding the dagger."

"I don't want to," I said. My heart was thudding hard in my chest and my arms tingled with fear.

Erick's grin vanished and the hard, dangerous look I'd seen at the fountain rushed forward. Face expressionless, he said, "Do you see that sack?"

I glanced toward the sack he'd placed inside the entrance to the courtyard.

"You get nothing from that sack if you quit now. And you'll get nothing from me again after today unless you stay."

I shot him a defiant glare from where I crouched. The sack was only a few paces away. I could snag it and be gone before he'd barely moved.

But then I'd be back to relying on the Dredge, on the white-dusty man.

My glare hardened, but I stood and moved again to stand before Erick in the center of the courtyard. The dangerous look in his eyes receded.

"Now," he said, calm and relaxed, "let's see how you wield that guardsman's dagger of yours."

He showed me how to hold the dagger—different grips for different thrusts and slashes and jabs—and where to strike. Not just to kill. Sometimes just to maim. Sometimes just to leave a mark, a scar . . . a reminder. And he showed me stances, for balance, for distraction, so the target wouldn't know you held a dagger until it was too late.

Just after midday, Erick called a halt and pulled bread, cheese, and thick chunks of roasted pork out of the sack. My stomach growled at the scent of the meat, my eyes going wide. Meat was rare on the Dredge. Unless you included rat. This was a feast, the meat juicy and tender.

An hour later Erick packed away the remains of the food, glancing toward the sunlight before turning back to me.

"Now let's see if you've learned anything."

We faced each other again, as we had that morning, only this time Erick set his dagger aside. I kept my dagger out, held as he'd told me to hold it, even though it felt strange.

"Attack me," Erick said, his eyes glinting in challenge.

I watched him, saw the muscles already tensed, ready to react. I frowned, gripped the handle of the dagger tightly, then let myself slip beneath the river.

The world grayed, sounds receded, until the only thing in focus was Erick, the only sound his breathing. I felt my own muscles relax, saw Erick register the change with a start of surprise, and then I struck.

Erick blocked the first stab, shunted it aside, and tried to grab my wrist. I slid free, tried to step in close, to use one of the moves we'd practiced that morning. But Erick expected it. I saw his counter on the river a moment too late to react.

His hand latched onto my shoulder as he stepped back. With a quick jerk, he spun me around. I barked a snarl as his other arm snaked around my stomach and drew me in against his body, pinning my dagger arm to my side. I struggled, pushed off with my feet, snarled again as his grip tightened—

Everything he'd taught me fled my mind and instinct came rushing back. I stomped down hard on his foot, and at the same time snapped my head around and bit the hand holding onto my shoulder.

"You little shit!" he spat. He shoved me away as he collapsed to the ground.

I darted to the side, bringing the dagger back up, but halted when I realized he was laughing.

He lay on his back on the ground, hand cradled near his chest, tears streaming down his face, the laughter sharp and loud.

"Oh, gods," he gasped after a long moment, chuckling. "That's enough for today." He rolled to his side, then heaved himself to his feet, favoring one foot. He moved to retrieve his dagger and the sack, shaking his head when he glanced at me.

I followed him slowly. He paused, as if catching his breath, his back to me, then knelt by the sack.

"What about my mark?"

His shoulders stilled for a moment. Then he gathered up the sack and turned. All of the humor had faded from his eyes.

"No marks for now. Not after the last one."

He handed over the sack. I stared down at it, twisted it back and forth, then asked softly, "Who are they?"

Erick hesitated. "They're people the Mistress wants dead."

"Why?"

Erick's brow crinkled, as if he'd never been asked, had never thought about the answer before. "I don't know. Because they've done something wrong, killed someone, hurt someone. Like the man who strangled that woman, the man you killed when I first found you."

"What about the hawk-faced man? What did he do?"

Erick shifted uncomfortably. "I don't know."

Then he pushed the confusion aside, buried it. I saw it in his eyes, in the way he straightened his shoulders. "I'm a Seeker in the guard, Varis. An assassin. I hunt for those that have run to the Dredge. I don't need a reason to hunt them other than that the Mistress wants them dead. I don't need another reason. That's all that matters to me."

"But how do you know they deserve it?"

"Because the Mistress tells me they deserve it. If the Mistress says they deserve it, if the Throne says they deserve it, then they deserve it."

"But what if the Mistress is wrong?"

He stood, reaching down to ruffle my hair. That something deep inside leaped at the touch, yearned for more, but his hand dropped away.

"The Mistress is never wrong," he said, but his voice was flat, as if he were reciting something he'd been taught.

"We'll continue with the training tomorrow," he said, and then he walked away.

†

And we did. Every morning I'd leave my niche hoping Erick would be there. Sometimes he was, sometimes not. If not, I'd return to the Dredge. Not always for momentarily forgotten bundles, or the stray potato. No. Erick kept me fed and clothed now, although I still scavenged the Dredge when Erick's food ran low and I hadn't seen him, still went to the white-dusty man if I was desperate. No. After a few weeks of training, Erick started giving me new marks and so I went to the Dredge for the people, to search for the men and women who'd run, who were trying to hide from the Skewed Throne, from the Mistress . . . from Erick.

I trained, but for a long time I didn't have to kill anyone. Erick took care of that. All I did was find them, then lead Erick to wherever they'd hidden in the slums beyond the Dredge.

It worked well.

Until Erick had me find Garrell Cart.

†

Garrell Cart: about my height, a little older, dirt-blond hair, muddy eyes, and a wide, light-brown birthmark near the base of his jaw that looked as if someone had spilled ale and it had pooled on his neck.

Garrell.

Squatting on the Dredge, back against a sun-baked wall, its warmth seeping through the worn shirt Erick had given me, I searched the passing crowd. I didn't expect to see him. I'd been watching for over twenty days now. I was waiting for Erick to give up and give me someone else to find.

I glanced down the Dredge, not really seeing the people, only the movements of the crowd, and caught sight of Bloodmark.

I frowned, heard again his whispering voice, *Don't mess with me, bitch.*

A brief stab of anger shot through my chest and I stood as I lost sight of him. I found him again, thirty paces down. He'd stopped, was looking at something I couldn't see across the street.

His eyes narrowed, darkened like they'd darkened the day he'd taken the sack from me, then flicked up and down the Dredge. Then they returned to whatever had caught his attention.

His head dipped slightly forward and he bit his upper lip. One hand reached for something beneath his shirt.

I stepped away from the wall and into the crowd, moving across the street. Halfway across I saw his target.

Without thought, I let the world slip into gray and wind, keeping Bloodmark and his target in focus. The crowd became shifting eddies in the gray, eddies I could move through as I continued to cross the street. I settled against the flatter gray of another wall and leaned back to watch.

The man Bloodmark had targeted stood near another man's wagon, hand resting on the back of the seat as he talked to the wagon's owner. Both men were laughing, shaking their heads. Bloodmark's target shifted his weight. As he did so, the small pouch tied to his belt swung into view.

I frowned and glanced toward Bloodmark. He'd moved closer, but not close enough for the strike. He seemed to be waiting.

My frown deepened. I couldn't see what would happen, couldn't *feel* what would happen. Not like before. I thought about the woman with the shawl, about that sensation of slipping deeper into the gray. Everything had been clearer then, crisper, easier to see.

Straightening, I drew in a short breath . . . then hesitated. Because of the nausea, the weakness and convulsions that had followed. I hesitated . . . but only a moment.

I tried to push myself deeper into the river.

Nothing happened except a faint tremor in my chest. I strained against the sensation, jaw tightening.

Then something slipped. With a fluid smoothness, the eddies in the grayness washed away, the wind of the crowd died down to the faintest murmur. Bloodmark and the two men near the wagon grew focused, the sunlight around them brighter. Their movements slowed subtly.

And farther down the Dredge, a new eddy emerged from the blackness. A group of five men, heading toward me and the wagon, at least three of the men drunk. They were slapping each other on the back, laughter sharp and biting, like spikes in the heightened sounds of the river.

I relaxed, the tension in my jaw loosening, and settled back against the wall again. The focus remained unchanged. I'd been trying too hard, trying to force it.

When the group of drunken men were almost to the wagon, Bloodmark moved.

He timed it perfectly, motions so subtle, so casual, I almost missed them. As the drunken men drew alongside the wagon, Bloodmark fell into place behind them, close, a look of annoyance set on his face, as if he wanted to get around them but there wasn't enough room. When one of the drunks slewed toward the man with the pouch, Bloodmark's hand reached out to push him that extra distance, to make the drunk stagger into the target.

Bloodmark needn't have bothered. One of the other drunks slapped the man on the back instead.

The drunk staggered, a curse spat into the grayness and wind as he reached out and grabbed the man with the pouch to catch his balance.

In the subtle, slow world of the river, I saw Bloodmark shift, saw the blade flash in the sunlight as he neatly sliced the cords of the pouch, the blade and pouch gone in the space of a heartbeat.

Then, the look of annoyance deepening, Bloodmark side-stepped the two stumbling men, the target holding the drunk up automatically.

The others in the group burst out laughing, then rescued their companion from the target. Waving toward the man and the wagon owner, they continued on their way.

Bloodmark skirted across the street, pausing at the entrance to an alley. As the group of drunks passed me, he seemed to sense that he was being watched.

He glanced up and our eyes met.

I nodded, with a slightly turned grin of grudging respect.

He scowled.

I was about to respond with a rude gesture when the cold white warning Fire that had nestled in the pit of my stomach suddenly flared, so strongly a tingle of icy prickles raced down my arms. Simultaneously, a tremor rippled across the dark gray and muted wind and I was struck by the putrid scent of blood and sweat and rotten butter.

I staggered back from the stench, eyes widening, and felt the world of gray and wind begin to slip away under the force of the Fire. Before the grayness completely fled, I reached out and held it. The gray steadied. The rush of wind that had slipped briefly into the roar of a hundred people, a hundred voices, pulled down again to a muted murmur. I'd risen in the river slightly, not as deep as when Bloodmark had lifted the pouch, but I was still deeper than usual.

And I was beginning to feel nauseous.

I glanced quickly toward Bloodmark, still in focus on the far side of the Dredge. His scowl had turned into wary confusion, the pouch in his hand forgotten, probably wondering why I had staggered back. But Bloodmark didn't matter anymore. Only the cold Fire still seething in my gut mattered. And the stench.

I turned toward it, breathing in deeply. The gray shifted sickeningly as I moved, blurring at its edges, but it held.

When I'd spun almost completely around, the stench so thick I thought I'd gag, I saw the tremor rippling in the grayness again. It'd taken on a reddish tint.

I focused with effort and Garrell Cart slid out of the rippling red.

I straightened in mute surprise, hand immediately falling to my dagger. Then the gray and wind trembled and with a gasp I was forced to let it go.

The world rushed back with a roiling twist, the noise of the Dredge almost overwhelming. I drew short, sharp breaths, trying to calm the nausea that came with it, trying to keep Garrell in sight. For a moment I thought I'd lose the battle, felt the bile burning upward in my throat, but I swallowed hard, forced it back with a painful gasp—

And then I was moving. It had taken me this long to spot him, I wasn't going to lose him now.

Instantly, the same trembling weakness that had struck me before coursed through my legs. *I didn't go as deep!* I thought to myself in anger and annoyance, and fought the weakness, pushed it back ferociously as I dodged through the crowd. Without the focus of the river I couldn't move as easily through the people, couldn't see the eddies, the currents. I swore as I stumbled over someone's foot, heard them curse in return, and then I realized that Garrell had stopped.

I halted in the middle of the Dredge, felt someone pull up short behind me, skirt around with a mutter.

Ahead, Garrell had paused near the entrance to an alley, stood leaning against the corner. A woman had spread a stained blanket out on the stone of the Dredge, broken pottery that she had repaired set out on the blanket. Her daughter sat on the corner of the blanket just before Garrell, staring down at a thin, faded green cloth in one hand. She was twisting it in boredom, her blonde hair half-fallen over her rounded face. Unusual blonde hair, the color of straw. She wore a dirty shirt that was too big for her, tied with twine at her waist like a dress. Her mother wore the same. Both were barefoot, feet dirty.

The woman stood in front of the blanket, her own long, straw-blonde hair tied back with a length of rawhide. Her features were more foreign than the girl's, her eyes desperate. A dab of blue had been painted onto her skin near the corner of her left eye, like a teardrop. She cupped a glazed bowl in both hands and held it out to the passing crowd in mute supplication.

I frowned. The two were obviously not from Amenkor. I'd heard of the blue paint mark. The Tear of Taniece, some religious sect from one of the northern cities along the coast.

I snorted. Amenkor didn't need a god; we had the Mistress.

Garrell was staring down at the girl. A slow smile crept across his face.

Something touched against the back of my neck, like a drop of water, then trickled down between my shoulders like sweat. I reached up to brush it away, but there was no sweat, only the sensation, the prickle of water against skin.

My frown deepened and I scanned the crowd behind me. Instinctively, I reached for the river and felt the nausea return, felt my legs weaken, and stopped with a grimace. I scanned the crowd again and saw nothing.

But there *was* something back there. I could feel it.

Then the Fire leaped upward again and I spun back toward Garrell.

He was gone.

So was the girl.

The green cloth lay at the edge of the blanket, twisted in on itself.

For a moment, I felt nothing but the Fire, heard nothing but the grunts of the first man I'd killed as he struggled with his clothing, his hand pressed down hard, so hard, into my chest. I smelled his musty shirt with the Skewed Throne stitching torn out as he crushed my face into his shoulder. I couldn't catch my breath, tasted the mold in the cloth as it pressed into my mouth.

Then the Fire blazed over me and I darted toward the alley where Garrell had been leaning, where the mother of the girl had just noticed that her daughter was missing. I halted at the entrance, leaned against one wall for support as a wave of weakness washed through me. But I didn't have time for the weakness.

I gasped in a few deep breaths, then plunged into the depths of the alley, into the depths beyond the Dredge.

I ran. Into the shadows. Into the familiar stench. The alley angled away after a short stretch and I slowed as my eyes adjusted. Too slow, too slow. There was no one ahead, only mud-brick slicked with mold, a trickle of sludge down the center cobbles, an alcove, a door farther down. I slipped down the alley, keeping close to one wall, my heart thudding in my chest. The Fire had died down, but still sent licks of white flame down my arms. I felt them in my pulse, in my blood, burning.

I reached out to the wall for support as I moved, fighting off another wave of nausea. I wanted to move faster, but didn't dare. Garrell could be anywhere.

The alcove was empty. The doorway had been bricked shut, the brick now beginning to crumble.

I moved on, hesitantly, toward the empty blackness of a window, another alcove.

When I reached the window, the darkness inside so complete I could see nothing, the Fire roiling inside my gut abruptly died down to a single coiled flame.

My stomach clenched and I swallowed against the sudden certainty that I was too late. I lurched toward the alcove, hesitated at its recessed wooden doorway.

Twisting the hilt of the dagger I didn't remember drawing, I pushed the door open with one hand and stepped inside with barely a sound, crouching low and to one side just inside the darkness. I breathed in deep, scented the mildew of the rotting door and something deeper, something metallic. Something I recognized.

I waited, letting the darkness recede into vague forms. Crumbled walls, another window, a second door. A broken table and shattered chair. A body.

I shifted forward.

The girl lay on her back, her too-long shirt rucked up to her armpits, her arms pulled above her head, angled and loose in death, her legs splayed. Her skin was hauntingly pale, except for the black of the blood trailing down from the knife wound in her chest.

I stood over her, stared down at her eyes—mere shimmers against the paleness of her face. The wetness of tears still stained her cheeks.

I thought again of the first man I'd killed, of his hand pressing hard against my chest, and drew in a long, deep, shuddering breath. Tears threatened to blind me.

I'd taken too long, moved too slowly.

The Fire had died, and in its place I felt hot anger. Like the anger I'd felt when I'd knelt over the man's body and spat into his face, flushed and feverish.

I turned to the second door, moved toward it without thought. No thought was needed. I could feel the anger in my jaw, hard and locked and intent. Could feel it in the hand that gripped the dagger.

The door opened onto a wall, a narrow running to the left and right. I couldn't tell which direction Garrell had taken.

I *pushed* myself beneath the river, violently.

Bile instantly rose to my throat, burning, and I collapsed to my hands and knees, hunched over as I vomited. The world of gray and red and wind vanished almost instantly.

But not before I caught the stench of rotten butter and piss and blood. It came from the left narrow.

Spitting out the last of the vomit, I forced myself to my feet, wiped the sourness from my mouth as I stumbled to the left. My legs trembled. One calf cramped.

Twenty steps along the narrow, past a sharp turn, I saw Garrell. He was walking away, his back to me, but moving slowly.

I came up behind him without a sound, touched his shoulder.

He turned with a slight start, that slow grin still on his face. Only now it was deeper, more satisfied. Sated. And now I was close enough, I could see it touching his eyes.

He was still back with the girl. I could see it there, in his eyes. Dark brown eyes.

I slid my dagger up beneath his ribs. The motion felt slow, practiced, but it happened in a heartbeat. I slid it in deep, then pulled it free and stepped back out of range.

I'd missed his heart on purpose.

He staggered back, his eyes widening. He wasn't with the girl anymore. His hands grabbed for both sides of the narrow, but only one made contact. As he stumbled, he tried to gasp. Blood poured out of his mouth with a rough, choked cough. Hand still against the wall, he swung backward, back slamming against the mud-brick. His other hand made contact with a meaty slap.

Then his legs gave out and he crumpled to one side, back skidding down the brick.

I moved forward and knelt over him. He was still breathing,

through blood and spit and snot. Blood now stained his shirt where I'd stabbed him. The stain was spreading.

He tried to raise one arm, tried to reach for me. There was anger in his eyes now, and his mouth twisted. His breath was coming in shortened gasps.

"Die, bastard," I muttered.

And he did, his last breath coming in a bubble of blood.

It held for a moment, then burst.

I stared into Garrell's muddy, death-glazed eyes and shivered in belated reaction. Not a shudder of weariness from using the river, nor of nausea. This shiver tickled along my skin and brought hot, sharp tears to my eyes.

I turned away from Garrell's body and looked up into the blue of the sky, into the sunlight that somehow never made it down into the depths of the narrows, into the rooms with the bodies of the dead, or the niches of the living. I looked up at the sky with tears stinging my eyes and thought of the first man I'd killed, the one who'd been a guardsman, the one whose dagger I carried.

After a moment, I let the tears come. Not sobbing, racking tears. Not tears for the ex-guardsman who'd tried to rape me. And not for Garrell. These tears were for the girl whose body rested inside the shattered room, her arms loose above her head. And for the girl I'd been.

I was still staring up at the sky when I heard a rustle behind me, in the narrow.

I turned where I knelt, dagger held before me. At first I saw nothing but the darkness, still blinded by the sky. But then a figure emerged, huddled close to a wall.

The figure was too far away for me to see a face, nothing more than a shape. Before I could move closer, whoever it was turned and faded into the darkness, the sounds of their fleeing footsteps receding into the silence of the narrow.

I thought suddenly of the girl and rose. Leaving Garrell behind, I fled back to the room. I didn't want to think about what I'd done, how easily I'd done it. I didn't want to think about Garrell at all.

So I concentrated on the girl.

I hid the dagger beneath my clothes, then knelt and gently pulled down the girl's makeshift dress, hiding the blood and spatter at the junction of her legs. The length of twine she'd used as a belt was gone, discarded. I scooped her body up in my arms, holding her beneath the neck and knees. Her head rolled back, unnaturally relaxed, and I subdued an urge to sob. I shifted her arms so that they lay against her body, then stood.

She felt weightless, like a bundle with nothing inside, all loose and empty and broken.

It was the most horrible sensation I'd ever felt.

I found the girl's mother where I'd left her. She'd collapsed to her knees in the center of the blanket, her face empty. But her eyes continued to dart toward the faces in the crowd, continued to search. She hadn't seen me. Her shoulders hunched as I approached from behind, hitched with awkwardly silent sobs, her hands covering her face. The green cloth was twisted through the fingers of one hand.

I knelt beside her.

Her hands dropped instantly and she jerked away, face terrified, arms raised defensively. She cried out something in a language I didn't understand. I didn't move.

Then she noticed what I held in my arms.

It only took a heartbeat. And then she screamed. A rough scream of pure anguish that pierced the noise of the Dredge, that caused those passing by to halt in shock, to draw back. But she didn't notice. Her hands returned to her face, trembling inches before her, as if she didn't dare touch herself. Then she reached forward, tentatively, and pulled her daughter to her. She clutched her daughter to her chest, one hand holding the back of the girl's head to her shoulder, the other at the base of her back, crushing the girl to her. She hunched over her as she sobbed, the blue mark of paint near her eye vivid in the sunlight, her face contorted with a pain I didn't understand.

And so I fled. Back into the depths beyond the Dredge, into the narrows and alleys and hidden rooms. I didn't care where I went. I simply moved—away from the dead girl, away from the torn, pleading expression on her mother's face, away from the sensation of weightlessness. I moved, blinded by tears occasionally, but the tears came harder now, hurt more in my chest. I was too exhausted for tears.

Eventually, I realized I was heading toward Cobbler's Fountain.

It was approaching dusk, and I'd found Garrell.

†

I waited in a recessed doorway in sight of the fountain. I didn't like to come here. Not because of my tattered clothing anymore; Erick had taken care of that. Because of the memories.

I glanced up at the broken fountain, a mere outline in the darkness, and felt sunlight and water against my face, heard laughter. My mother's laughter, soft and deep and throaty as she splashed me. I giggled, splashed back. I could taste the water in my mouth, cool as it ran into my eyes, down the curve of my neck.

Hands lifted me from the fountain. I heard my mother murmur, *Come on. You've had enough fun for today. Time to head home.*

I turned away, shoved the memory aside in anger. It didn't matter. It meant nothing. It was too vague, too bright with sunlight and reflected water, the voice too soft and fluid. I'd been too young.

"Have you found Garrell?"

Erick stood on the edge of the open, cobbled circle around the fountain. When I glanced up, his expectant face darkened and his stance shifted, became subtly more dangerous.

"What's wrong?"

His eyes shifted behind me, scanned the alley, the recesses, the doors, then back to me. He frowned.

The nausea returned when his gaze fell on me, and I turned away.

"I found him," I said.

I led him back to the narrow, through the night. I didn't look back, but I could feel him following, wary, his hand close to his dagger.

I halted ten paces away from the body and sank down into an uncomfortable crouch against the wall. Erick paused just behind me in the darkness, then edged past, his hand resting briefly on my head. The touch was gentle, reassuring, and I felt my chest clench and harden, my eyes burn again.

I hunched over my knees, pulled them to my chest.

Erick knelt at Garrell's side a long moment, then stood.

"Did you do this?" he asked. His voice was emotionless and he did not turn.

Before I could answer, someone else spat, "She killed him. I saw her."

I jerked upright, hand groping for my dagger.

Erick barely reacted, merely turned toward the voice. "Come here," he said, hard and unforgiving.

Farther down the narrow, a shadow detached itself from the wall and hesitantly moved forward. The figure kept to the deeper darknesses, kept itself hidden, but as it moved closer, it seemed to gain confidence.

When he came close enough to be recognized, he stood straight, face wary but head high.

Erick shifted toward him. "Who are you?"

"Bloodmark," I said sharply, my voice laced with hate.

Both Erick and Bloodmark turned toward me, Erick with a frown, Bloodmark with a contemptuous sneer.

"Is that your name?" Erick asked.

Bloodmark's sneer faded. "It's as good a name as any."

Erick nodded, as if he'd expected the response.

Then he seemed to dismiss Bloodmark entirely and turned toward me.

"Come here," he said.

I hesitated, uncertain what Erick intended. But all of the brittleness had left his voice, and I was used to following his orders now because of the training. I trusted him.

I stepped forward until I stood beside Erick, over Garrell's body. Bloodmark sank into a crouch less than ten paces away, but I barely noticed him.

I looked into Garrell's face, as I'd done earlier. But now all the hatred and anger had faded. I felt nothing but a trembling, weak shame.

Erick leaned forward, close enough I could feel his breath tickling the back of my neck.

"Go ahead and mark him," he murmured.

I flinched, stepped back in horror, but Erick stopped me, his hand against my back. He pressed me forward.

"No," I breathed, shaking my head.

"Why not? You killed him, didn't you?" Still a murmur, but hardened now, insistent.

"I saw her kill him," Bloodmark interjected. "She touched his shoulder and when he turned she stabbed him!"

Erick jerked his head toward Bloodmark, cutting him off. "If you say one more word, I'll cut out your tongue, gutterscum."

The threat sent a shiver down my back, to where Erick's hand still held me in place. My skin prickled.

Then Erick's breath touched my neck again.

"You killed him, didn't you?"

I nodded, felt the dagger slice up through Garrell's shirt, snagging slightly, then slipping into flesh. With a torn voice, I breathed, "Yes."

"Then you deserve the mark."

His hand left my back and he stepped away. Not far, but enough so that the world seemed to narrow down to just me and Garrell, to his shadowed face and muddy eyes, the ale-stain of the birthmark on his neck a pool of black against his skin.

I knelt, my dagger already in my hand. The stench of death, of blood and piss and shit, filtered through the stench of rot from the narrow.

I hesitated.

"But I killed the man who tried to strangle me. I killed the fat man. You marked them both. Not me."

From what felt like a great distance, Erick said, "You killed the man who tried to strangle you to save yourself. And you killed the fat man to save me. This one is different, Varis. You killed him because it was necessary. Because you wanted to."

I brought the dagger up to Garrell's forehead, placed the blade against his skin, then hesitated again.

I closed my eyes and thought about the man with the garrote, felt the cord as it bit into my neck. I still carried a faint scar, a circle of white, with a vertical line where I'd cut myself with my own dagger to get free. I thought about leaning over him, staring into his face, then spitting on him.

The hot anger of that moment returned with a flush and I opened my eyes, looked down into Garrell's face again. Only this time I didn't see the shadows against his skin, the muddiness of his eyes, the dark blood of the birthmark.

I saw him staring down at the girl with the straw-blonde hair as she toyed with the green cloth. I saw the slow smile as it spread across his face. That slow, casual grin.

The hot anger spread through my chest, down into my arms,

and I straightened where I knelt. My jaw clenched, and with firm strokes I sliced the Skewed Throne into Garrell's forehead, then sat back.

There was no blood. And the mark didn't have the smooth lines of the mark Erick had made on the man who'd tried to strangle me. But it was clear it was the Skewed Throne.

Erick moved forward, rested his hand on my shoulder. "Good."

But I barely heard him. Instead I shuddered.

Erick squeezed my shoulder.

Bloodmark snorted. "That's it? She kills him, she marks him, and that's it? You're the fucking Guard!"

Erick moved so fast I barely saw him. In three short steps he was at Bloodmark's side. His hand clamped onto the back of Bloodmark's neck where he crouched and with a sharp shove he crushed Bloodmark to the ground, face turned, Bloodmark's ear and cheek pressed into the sludge of the narrow.

"I told you," Erick said, "not another word." He drew his dagger, brought it down to Bloodmark's face.

Bloodmark cried out, began to flail, his eyes wide. But Erick pressed his knee into Bloodmark's back, pinned him hard, hand still on his neck. He leaned close to Bloodmark's ear and the struggles ceased. Bloodmark closed his eyes and whimpered, mouth drawn back in a clenched grin of pain.

"The Mistress wanted him dead," Erick said. "It doesn't matter who killed him. I asked Varis to find him, and she did. It was her mark, her choice. The only question is—" Erick shifted slightly closer, his dagger touching Bloodmark's exposed cheek. Bloodmark gasped. "—what am I going to do with you?"

The narrow grew silent except for Bloodmark's ragged breath, rushing through clenched teeth. I didn't move.

Then Bloodmark grunted, "Use me."

I straightened, panic slicing through me. And something else.

Something like what I'd felt when the rag woman had demanded my apple.

The apple was mine. I didn't want to share it. I didn't want to lose it.

Erick paused, drew back, his knee releasing some of its pressure from Bloodmark's back. Bloodmark sucked in a deep breath, coughed hoarsely into the muck. But he didn't move. Erick still knelt over him, hand clutching his neck.

"Use you?"

I shifted forward, started to shake my head in disbelief, in panic, but halted.

Erick was considering it. I could hear it in his voice.

Bloodmark coughed again, then said in a choked voice, "Use me. Like you use her." He shot a glare of hatred toward me, one that Erick couldn't see. "Have me hunt for these marks. I can find them as easily as she can."

I drew breath to tell Erick, "No," to tell him about Bloodmark leaning close and breathing, *Don't mess with me, bitch*, to tell him that Bloodmark couldn't be trusted.

But Erick looked at me. He'd already decided. I could see it in his eyes.

"Two pairs of eyes would be better than one," he said.

I let the drawn breath out in a ragged sigh.

It was already too late.

·⟨ *The Palace* ⟩·

DRESSED as a page boy, I walked down the center of the hall-way, face intent with concentration, as if I were on a cru-cial errand for someone important and could not be disturbed. I'd worked my way from the outskirts of the main palace to within a few rooms of the edge of the inner sanctum, delineated by the original castle's wall. Those stone ramparts, rather than being torn down, had been subsumed as the original castle grew in size, so that what had once been the castle's main defense now formed the walls of numerous rooms inside the palace itself. What had once been a gate was now the main door into the inner sanctum, where the throne room and the Mistress' chambers lay.

That doorway would be heavily guarded.

I referred to my mental map of the palace, then slowed as the hallway came to an end. The room beyond was lit with oil sconces set into the ceiling's support pillars, but only down its center. To either side, the room was dark and empty of people, but lined with plants—small trees in wide pots; scattered smaller bushes with scented flow-ers in urns. A complex tracery of vines clung to the wall.

I moved through the room without pausing, intent on the hallway beyond. The main entrance to the inner sanctum should be just ahead.

A moment later, the light in the corridor increased. Then the hallway opened up into a high-ceilinged concourse to the left and right.

I slowed, footsteps echoing as I moved farther out into the open space. Potted trees lined either side of the concourse, separated by huge tapestries taking up entire sections of wall between one arching support and the next. The ceiling rose at least twenty feet overhead, the stone supports curving together and meeting at a sharp peak. Windows appeared black with night high above, darker than the shadows.

Someone coughed, the sound loud in the silence of the concourse. I started and turned to the right, where according to the map, the main entrance lay.

The door was huge, banded with iron and polished to a sheen that almost glowed with its own light. It was recessed almost ten feet, and the original arch of what had been the outer gate of the wall could be seen clearly, the stone gray and stained with the exposure to the elements. Banners of all colors were arrayed around the door to either side, each on its own pole. Standing at attention in filed rank before the door were six palace guardsmen, heavily armored. If it hadn't been for the cough, I would have thought they were statues.

Suddenly aware that I stood in the middle of the concourse staring down its length at six trained men with sharp swords, I turned and hurried to where the hallway I'd used to enter the concourse continued on the far side. I tried to act like a page boy who'd been awed by the spectacle but had suddenly remembered his duty.

Once out of sight of the guardsmen, the look of awe on my face fell into a scowl.

Fool! Gawking before men who'd only want to kill me if they knew who I really was, why I was really here.

I shook my head but kept moving. A few empty rooms, a few more empty, half-lit corridors. After a moment, when there was no sound of pursuit, I allowed myself to breathe again.

There was no way to get through the main doorway, not with all of those guardsmen watching. There were a few other entrances—for cooks, maids, dignitaries that shouldn't be seen entering through the front—but all of those would be guarded as well. The page boy's outfit wouldn't work there either. The guards checked too carefully.

But there was another way.

I entered a waiting room. Pillows were scattered throughout the room amid low tables. A half empty pitcher of water and a tray of picked-over fruit rested on one of the tables. I lifted a clutch of grapes as I passed, but kept moving.

Then I froze, a grape half raised to my mouth, ears pricked. Someone was approaching. Two men, arguing.

As they drew closer, I realized I recognized one of the voices.

I scanned the waiting room, saw a latticework of carved wood screening off a small portion of the room for privacy, and dove for it. Crouched down low in the corner, I plopped the last grape into my mouth as the men entered the room, still out of sight.

"—don't think I can take another one," a man said. His voice shook. "The last one . . . I can still hear her screams. And the way she thrashed in the throne, as if . . . as if it were a bed of hot coals! As if we'd tossed her into a gods-damned bed of hot coals!" He drew in a trembling breath. "I really don't think I can stand to watch another one die. Not if it's like that."

"I agree."

I shifted forward, eyes narrowed. The second man to speak was Avrell, the First of the Mistress . . . the man who had sent me into the palace to kill the Mistress, had provided the map and the clothes and the key. Unlike the other man, his voice was steady and smooth, and soft like warm sunlight.

They were getting closer. But I still couldn't see them, not from this vantage. I pulled myself back against the wall and grew still.

Avrell continued, "You agree that there is no question now, Nathem? That the Mistress is truly insane?"

Silence for a moment, and then, reluctantly, "Yes." A pause. Then with more force. "Yes. Yes, there is no question now. Not after the fire in the merchants' quarter."

I flinched with guilt and shifted uneasily.

"It took the fire to convince you?" Avrell said. "I was convinced when she closed the harbor."

Nathem sighed. "Yes, that, too. How could she order the harbor closed? How can she keep it closed, with resources so tight, winter so close, and now the fire? It makes no sense. We must open the harbor. It's our only chance of surviving the winter."

They stepped into view.

Both wore the dark blue of the priesthood, the robes appearing black in the darkness; they walked without any light. A four-pointed gold star was stitched onto the chest of Nathem's robe, signifying his rank as Second. He was older than Avrell, with dull gray hair and an age-lined face; broader of shoulder as well, but he held his back straighter. And yet Avrell appeared the more poised, his hands hidden inside the wide sleeves of his robes. An eight-pointed star was stitched into Avrell's robe—the four-pointed star that adorned Nathem's robe but with four shorter, daggerlike triangles woven in between.

"But these attempts to replace the Mistress aren't working," Nathem continued as they walked slowly across the room. Neither looked toward the latticework. "We've tried . . . what? Seven times now? Something isn't working."

"I don't understand it either," Avrell said thoughtfully. "We're selecting the girls from the Servants as we've always selected them. We've used those with the most talent, those who've shown the most promise and the most skill at using it, but it's as if that isn't enough anymore, as if something *more* is needed." He shook his head, as if confused, but he kept his eyes on Nathem. "This has always been sufficient in the past."

"Yes, but in the past the Mistress wasn't insane!" Nathem interjected. "In the past, we were trying to find a successor because the Mistress was dead!"

Avrell halted. His back straightened, his lips pressed together. He eyed Nathem as the Second continued for another few paces before realizing Avrell had stopped.

When Nathem turned, his brow was furrowed. "What?" he asked.

Avrell said nothing, only gazed hard at Nathem. They'd halted near the table containing the pitcher of water and the remains of the fruit.

Nathem's brow furrowed further, then cleared as realization struck. His head lifted, eyes widened.

"On the Mistress'—" he began. But something seemed to catch in his throat, choked him off.

The room no longer felt open and airy and soft. Now it felt close and tense.

I drew back farther behind the screen separating me from the outer room. Nathem's face was clear through the latticework, even in the darkness.

"You said so yourself," Avrell murmured. "We've tried seven times, used the most powerful Servants, and in all cases the replacement—" Avrell halted, seemed to harden himself even further. "No. Let's be realistic. We can't afford to be anything else. Not now. Winter is too close. In all seven cases, the *women* set to replace the Mistress have died. Good women. Trusting women. Women we've found and raised and trained for this one purpose since they were children. Others have died trying to ascend the throne in the past, but none have died like this." Avrell's voice had risen slightly, but now he paused, collected himself. "Something is wrong. Something is different this time."

Nathem sighed. "The Fire."

Avrell nodded. "The Fire. And as you said yourself, in the past the

Mistress has already been dead when a successor was seated on the throne. Even when the Fire first passed through Amenkor. That time, the Mistress was murdered so that another could be placed on the throne. Murdered because the Fire drove the Mistress insane and a successor needed to be named."

"You don't know that for certain," Nathem said sharply. "We only know she was killed. Not why. It was too long ago. There are no records."

Avrell didn't answer. Avrell and Nathem held perfectly still, Avrell rigid and imposing, Nathem indignant and stern, their eyes locked. Nathem's gaze searched Avrell's face, searched hard and quick.

Then Nathem rocked back slightly, as if struck.

A subtle move, but Avrell's shoulders relaxed.

"You can't be suggesting—" Nathem began.

"I'm *suggesting* nothing," Avrell countered, and his voice fell in the room like stone.

Nathem paused. "We're sworn to serve her," he protested, but there was no force behind his words. "We're sworn to protect her."

Avrell reached forward to grasp Nathem's shoulder. "We're sworn to protect the Skewed Throne, Nathem. We're sworn to protect Amenkor. Can you honestly say the throne is safe? That the *city* is safe? Think about the fire, about the closing of the harbor. What will she do next? As it is, we may already have waited too long."

Nathem still seemed unconvinced, his brow furrowed in thought.

"And then there's Captain Baill to consider," Avrell said, stepping back, his hand falling from Nathem's shoulder.

Nathem snorted in contempt. "Baill is a fool."

Avrell shook his head. "Not a fool, Nathem. He has never been a fool. He's following the Mistress' orders to the letter. He's filled the streets with his guardsmen to protect the citizens of Amenkor as she requested, closed the harbor as she ordered—"

"But what are we protecting the people from?" Nathem spat. "It doesn't make any sense! Baill has *seen* the Mistress. He *knows* the orders make no sense!"

"And yet he carries them out without question," Avrell said, voice weighted with meaning. He caught Nathem's eye. "Not even a token protest."

After a long moment, Nathem asked, "What do you suspect?"

Avrell drew in a deep breath, held it a moment before releasing it. "I suspect everything, Nathem, but can prove nothing. In any case, Captain Baill is not an immediate concern. The Mistress is. You've seen her wandering these halls. You've heard her muttering to herself, arguing with herself, sometimes in languages neither of us have ever heard. Are any of us safe?"

Nathem dropped his gaze to the table of fruit. "No," he muttered, his voice so low I could barely hear it. Then, louder, more forceful: "No. None of us is safe. None of us has been safe since the Fire. It did something to her, changed her." He squeezed his eyes shut.

Avrell stood silently, hands again folded inside the sleeves of his robe. He waited.

Nathem finally opened his eyes.

His face clouded as he looked down at the table and paused. "I could have sworn . . ." he began, but trailed off.

Behind the latticework, my neck prickled, the tiny hairs at its base rising. I drew back, even as Avrell tensed.

"What?" Avrell said. Like stone again, all the gentleness he'd shown Nathem gone.

Nathem frowned at the table. "I could have sworn I left a clutch of grapes right there."

Shit!

Avrell turned sharply, his eyes darting around the room, hitting the shadows, the corners, the shield of the latticework.

And there they halted.

I stiffened, could barely breathe. Everything shrank down to

Avrell's eyes, to their dark blue intensity, to the narrowed, harsh lines that had formed between his eyebrows.

We held each other's gazes for eternity, for the span of three heartbeats—

Then, in a taut voice, Avrell said, "One of the servants must have eaten them."

Nathem frowned in consternation. "Then why didn't they clean up the table?"

Avrell said nothing, turned toward Nathem.

I drew in a slow breath and shuddered. I tasted fear like blood at the back of my throat.

Avrell held Nathem's gaze a long moment, until the frown faded from Nathem's eyes and he sighed, shook his head.

"Something must be done with the Mistress," he said.

Avrell hesitated a moment, not turning toward me, then said, "Something has already been done."

Nathem stood stunned, back rigid, mouth open, eyes angry. But then his shoulders slumped in resignation.

Avrell led him from the room. Against the realization that they intended to murder the Mistress, that events were already in motion, Nathem's concern over the grapes had been forgotten.

As soon as they drifted from the room, I slid from hiding and moved to the corridor. Avrell had known I'd be in the palace tonight, but he wasn't supposed to know where. And now I'd been held up, when I had to be in the linen closet at the time the guard changed. If I wasn't . . .

I shoved the thought aside, jaw set.

Then I began to run.

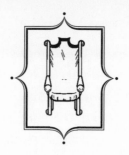

Chapter 4

"NO. Back off, Varis. Try again."

The river pulsed in my head, sweat running down my face in sheets. I barely heard Erick's order, too intent on Bloodmark's shifting movements before me, too focused on his eyes. His face was sheened with sweat as well, his hair plastered to his forehead in tendrils. Anger had locked his jaw rigid. A muscle twitched above his lip. His breath came in heaves through his teeth. We circled each other in the makeshift training yard, the light overhead beginning to fade. The Fire lay dormant inside me. Somehow it knew this was simply practice.

A surge in the currents warned me a bare instant before Bloodmark attacked. Bloodmark's dagger sliced low across my front, trying to gut me. It wasn't a smooth cut—Bloodmark's moves were never smooth—but it was lightning quick and full of violence. I slid back from the arc, moved forward after it had passed, close enough so Bloodmark couldn't maneuver easily, and made to slice across his face.

He jerked back from the stroke, anger flaring higher in his eyes as Erick barked, "Strike for Varis! Back off and reset. Bloodmark, you're not controlling your slashes! Power means nothing without control."

We began circling again. The anger had settled deeper, so deep Bloodmark was shaking. I'd tagged him five times already; he'd only managed to tag me twice. There'd been three draws. I only needed one more strike to win the bout. In all the weeks of training with him, he'd only won a single bout.

I waited, watching Bloodmark's eyes, sensing his movements. I knew if I waited long enough, he'd attempt a strike.

It didn't take long. It never took long.

He tried to control the lunge; I could see it in his eyes. I stepped to the side, attempted a counterstrike across his torso, under his reach, but he twisted, sidestepped, and cut back. His dagger whipped through empty space and I tried another lunge, but he was being careful now. We feinted and parried and lunged for what seemed an eternity, fatigue beginning to set in, but Bloodmark's anger began to override his caution. His thrusts became more erratic, sharp and loose.

When I thought his anger had built high enough, I exaggerated my fatigue, thrust forward and stumbled, presenting Bloodmark with an opening along my side.

He took it, stepping in close as I'd done before, driving the dagger home sharply. But I wasn't there. Instead, I twisted, fell down hard on my side, and cut upward, tapping his leg lightly with the flat of my dagger. I grinned.

"Strike and match! For Varis." Erick's voice held a note of controlled respect.

Bloodmark snarled, then fell on me with a roar of hatred, hand clutching at my shirt, pulling it up in a bunch as he straddled me. I gasped in surprise. I heard Erick bellow, "Fall back!" and heard his voice approaching, but it came from a distance. Bloodmark's eyes had fixed my attention, his dagger descending toward my chest.

My hand lashed out, caught his wrist and halted it, both our arms trembling. I felt a flicker of rage deep inside, hot and tingling.

"Fall back!" Erick bellowed, voice close now. It sliced through my rage, severed it. The tension in Bloodmark's arm loosened and he made as if to pull back.

I relaxed.

Then Bloodmark hissed, "Bitch," too low for Erick to hear, and the Fire inside me flared up sharply.

Bloodmark's dagger flicked outward, the motion small, and nicked my forearm. I hissed at the pain and my hand snapped out, hitting Bloodmark square in the chest, thrusting him away.

He yelped, landed with a thud, but scrambled up into a crouch in the space of a breath.

"That's enough!" Erick roared, interposing himself between us both. "What the hell happened?"

"The bitch shoved me off her, even though I was moving to get up."

I shot him a dark glare. "He sliced me with his dagger. Drew blood."

Erick's eyes instantly darkened and he turned toward Bloodmark.

"It was an accident," Bloodmark spat. "I didn't mean it."

Erick hesitated, uncertain. "Don't let it happen again," he finally said. "Either of you." Then he glanced toward the sinking sun. "That's enough for today. We'll continue with this tomorrow."

Bloodmark rose, brushed himself off with a sniff, then headed out into the warren of the slums. But not without a sly glance and a sharp grin back at me before he left.

Erick knelt as I shifted into a sitting position and pulled my arm out to inspect the cut. He frowned down at it. The blood had already dried, the pain gone.

"He did it on purpose," I said, even though I knew it was useless. "Why do you believe him?"

A look of annoyed anger crossed Erick's face and he dropped my arm. "Because he's useful."

"He hates me. And he's vicious."

"And you aren't?" Erick countered, standing. He motioned to my dagger. "What about that? A guardman's dagger. We don't part with them lightly. How did you get it?"

A surge of fear stabbed deep into my gut. For a moment, I was eleven again, felt the ex-guardsman's fingers dig into my arm like spears and wrench me into the alley, crushing me to his chest. I had no time to react, no time to scream.

Got ya, little one, he'd breathed, the words a rumble in his breast. *Got ya.*

And then he'd laughed.

I looked up into Erick's eyes, the fear hardening into anger. "He wasn't a guardsman." I pointed to where the Skewed Throne symbol was stitched into Erick's shirt in red. "The stitching had been torn out."

Erick frowned. "A deserter, then. Did he have a scar along one cheek? From the corner of one eye down to the jaw?"

I nodded, pulled my knees up to my chin, not looking at Erick. I could smell him—the man that had taken me back then—could smell the stench of ale, of dirt, of the Dredge and things deeper. I could taste the mold of his shirt as he cupped one hand on the back of my head and pressed my face into his shoulder.

Don't tremble, he'd breathed, voice as soft as rain. *Don't tremble.*

I shuddered, heard Erick kneel down in the dirt of the old courtyard beside me. I felt him hesitate. Not because he didn't want to hear, but because he wasn't certain I wanted to relive it.

"Tell me what happened."

I squeezed my eyes shut, stifling a sob as I laid my head on my knees, facing away from him. I sat that way a long moment, then felt Erick's hand on my shoulder.

He tried to pull me in closer to him. I resisted at first, then shifted back and leaned into his chest, still turned away.

When I finally spoke, my voice was muffled, distorted with the effort not to cry.

"He caught me in an alley," I said. "Crushed me to his chest so that I couldn't breathe."

And that was all it took. I was eleven again.

And the ex-guardsman had me.

✝

I could not see where he took me. I struggled at one point, but he only crushed me harder, all the time whispering, chest rumbling, breath coming in short, anticipatory wheezes. "Don't tremble, little one. Shhh. Shhh. Not far. Not far now." Then a low laugh, almost inaudible. "Not far."

Grunting, and sudden jolts, as if the man were fighting his way up stairs. Then he turned and crushed me between himself and a wall, one arm—the one holding my head—retreating. I jerked my head back from his shirt, gasped in a deep breath with a small cry of desperation, the air still filled with the stench of the Dredge, but with traces of night air as well. The man cursed, jerked hard on something unyielding that finally gave with a rotted crash, and then the hand was back, pressing even harder, and the flash of night sky vanished and I tasted rot and darkness again. He lurched back from the wall and now his wheezes were gasps, sharp and uncontrolled. His voice had deepened, grown dark and harsh. Now I could hear the death in his voice. No words, no hushes, only guttural needs.

And then the man shoved me away from him, drove me from the crushing darkness of his shoulder into a mud-brick wall. My breath rushed from my body even as I tried to gasp it in. My head cracked into stone.

The world swayed as I crumpled. I could see the stars, the moon, the narrow ledge where we had stopped. The wall I'd hit formed a second floor, smaller than the first, the ledge around its edge only five steps wide. Large enough for the gasping man to crush me where I'd fallen, hand pressed hard against my chest. He hit me, grunting as his fist connected, my head snapping to the side so that I looked along the ledge and over its edge. Dazed, the man moving atop me, scrabbling at my clothes, ripping them, I saw the city of Amenkor across the harbor. Not the Dredge and the slums, but the real city. I could see the waters of the bay, flecked with edges of moonlight. I could see the docks, the masts of ships, the strange angles of the rooftops and buildings as they rose slightly toward me. On the far side of the city, the layers of the palace glowed with firelight, faint and unearthly. I could feel a breeze from the water, clean and pure.

The motions of the man didn't register. Mind foggy, I stared at the water. I knew what was happening, what was going to happen. I'd seen it before, in the slums beyond the Dredge, in narrows and niches and empty holes. I'd heard screams, seen knives drawn, seen blood flow. I'd lived eleven years beyond the Dredge, spent one of those with Dove and his street gang of gutterscum, just long enough to learn how to survive on my own, how to steal without getting caught. I'd become numb to the death, to the disease, to the depravity. I felt nothing. Yet I was crying.

Then, through the haze of pain and numbness, through the night and the tears, I saw the horizon. The moon was high, but in the west, the horizon shimmered with white light, as if the sun were beginning to rise.

Except the sun rose in the east.

I frowned, and for the first time that day, the world began to fade to gray. The man crushing me to the rooftop slipped into a smear of red, his grunts as he struggled with his breeches slipping into the rush of wind. The world collapsed to the brightening line of white on the horizon, spreading north and south, growing in a long arc until it filled the night. It rushed out of the west, faster than the sunrise, a pure, brilliant white. And as it came closer, as the night brightened, I suddenly recognized it.

The White Fire from the legends.

It was exactly as the street-talkers had described it. A wall, filling the horizon, the flames reaching high, higher, reaching into the heavens, swallowing the stars as it came. Relentless, and so terribly swift.

The man atop me froze as the Fire entered the bay and scorched its way across the moon-flecked waters. The shadows of ships on the water and along the docks appeared against its whiteness and then were consumed by it as it swept forward. The docks were swallowed by it, and then it struck land and began sweeping through the city. As it rushed toward us, as it engulfed building after building, street after street, I heard the man atop me draw in a choked, horrified gasp.

Only then did I realize that there was no sound. The Fire was utterly silent.

In the moment before the Fire engulfed us, the instant before it descended onto the roof, I felt the clench of terror. My heart halted, my body tensed—

And then it was upon me, passing through me. I felt it scorch deep down inside me, deeper than the fear, deeper than the terror, deeper than anything I'd ever experienced before. It burned through everything, left everything exposed.

Through its whiteness, I saw the man atop me, saw his frayed clothing, his torn shirt. Something had once been stitched to the breast of his shirt, a symbol, the holes where the stitching had been torn out ragged and unraveling.

The Skewed Throne.

He'd once been a palace guard.

I glanced up into his face, frozen against the whiteness. His eyes were wide in shock, his attention turned inward. His mouth had parted, as if he'd been punched. Grit lined the corners of his eyes, his mouth, and mud streaked his hair.

I felt anger uncoil like a snake. Deep anger, resentful anger.

And then I saw the dagger.

The man's shirt was undone, the dagger exposed. Without thought, with a swiftness I'd learned long ago in the depths beyond the Dredge, a swiftness that had been honed while in the company of Dove and his gang, I snatched the dagger from its sheath.

And then the Fire passed beyond us. Night slammed down, harsh and hurtful.

There was a moment of stillness, filled with the man's tattered gasps, one hand still pressing down hard onto my chest, the other still tangled in the ties of his breeches.

Then the terror in his eyes faded as his attention shifted back to me. Shock twisted back into a snarl. His hand clenched on my chest, fingers digging deeper—

I slashed the dagger across his chest. A black ribbon of blood appeared, slick and smooth, and he lurched back. I didn't give him time to react further. I slashed again, the motion awkward and childish but purposeful. It caught his arm, a gash opening up, blood gushing outward, splattering hot across my face and neck. I slashed again, catching him in the thigh, and this time he screamed. A hideous, wet, animal scream that shattered the night.

My last slash caught him in the throat. Blood flooded down his neck and he lurched farther back, one hand jumping to the wound, the other grasping at air as his back slammed against the wall he'd thrown me against earlier. He hung there, mouth gaping wide, blood slicking his shirt, until he slipped down the mud-brick and sat. His mouth began to work, opening and closing, and still the blood flowed. Guttural, rasping sounds emerged, ragged and torn.

I rolled into a huddled crouch. He grasped at me with his free hand, fingers closing on air. Blood coated the hand at his throat, until it glistened wetly in the moonlight. His grasping hand shuddered, its motions slowing. It began to lower, fingers still clenching, until it rested on the ground. And still the fingers spasmed. The muscles in the arms relaxed and the hand slid from his throat, leaving a second trail of blood down his shirt, a mark on his breeches. Blood dripped from the fingertips.

The guttural, rasping sounds continued, then degenerated into wheezing gasps of air.

Then these ceased as well.

And I fled. Back to the depths. Back to the Dredge.

Back to my niche, the dagger still clutched in my hand.

†

In the courtyard, Erick wrapped his arms around my shuddering form and drew me in close, rocking me back and forth. The motions were awkward, as if he were unfamiliar with how to hold someone, how to comfort them. But I barely noticed, too absorbed in the memory of the Fire . . . and what had come after. I leaned into him and cried soundlessly.

I hadn't told him everything. I hadn't told him how the Fire had left part of itself behind, inside me, curled and dormant, how it flared up in warning when I was threatened. I didn't tell him that sometimes the Fire still burned.

After a long while, he gripped my shoulders and drew me away so that he could look into my eyes.

"He's dead now, Varis."

I nodded, sniffling, wiping at the tears streaking my face with both arms. "I know."

Erick stroked my hair, squeezed my shoulder once before standing. "Good." He glanced out into the night. The sun had set, the slums now dark except for the starlight. He sighed and turned back to me. "Are you going to be all right?"

I nodded again.

He hesitated, as if he didn't believe me.

I gathered myself and stood before him, looking him in the eye. "It happened almost five years ago. I'll be fine."

He held my gaze, searching, face grim, but finally nodded. "Then I'll see you tomorrow. I may have another mark by then. Someone for you and Bloodmark to search for. Together."

I grimaced but said nothing.

We never searched for the marks together.

†

"Have you found him yet, *Varis?*"

I started, Bloodmark's voice emerging from the night shadows at my back. He'd twisted my name, Varis coming out as a vicious hiss, with a tone like that of the wagon owner so many years earlier who'd called me a whore. And somehow, Bloodmark's voice had the same force as that wagon owner's kick, sharp and bruising.

Bloodmark laughed when he saw me start, then settled into a crouch behind me that was uncomfortably close.

I shifted forward. My hand rested on my dagger.

"So have you found him? The 'pug-nosed man'? Is that what you call him?" Even whispered, Bloodmark's tone was mocking.

I frowned in annoyance, then lied. "No. And I call him Tomas."

I'd seen him the day before, but not on the Dredge. In one of the narrows. I'd tried to follow but had lost him almost immediately. He'd had no scent, like Garrell, and there were too many doorways, too many paths he could have taken. If the mark was out of sight, I couldn't find him using the river unless he also had a scent.

And I did call him the pug-nosed man.

I felt Bloodmark staring at my neck, felt my skin prickle, but I did not turn. I kept my attention fixed on the Dredge before me, shifted uncomfortably again.

"Liar," Bloodmark said softly. I could hear the smile in his voice. It sent a shudder down my back, forced me to turn and look at his eyes, cold and empty in the darkness. His birthmark was black in the moonlight.

He held my gaze without flinching. His smile widened slightly.

He *knew*—knew that I'd lied, knew that I'd found the pug-nosed man . . . or at least seen him.

I felt the faint sensation of a hand pressing against my chest, the sensation limned with the frost of the Fire. It closed off the base of my throat, made it harder to breathe, to swallow.

I pulled away from Bloodmark's gaze with an effort, focused on the street ahead.

Bloodmark did the same, shifting far enough forward I could see his face out of the corner of my eye.

"What are we watching?" he asked, and this time he was genuinely curious.

My eyes flicked toward the white-dusty man's door involuntarily, toward the loose stone to the right of the doorway, and I saw Bloodmark's gaze shift, saw him frown as he settled back slightly.

The sensation of the hand against my chest grew. I suddenly didn't want Bloodmark to know about the white-dusty man, didn't want him to know about the bundles of bread the white-dusty man left beneath the stone outside the door if I left a length of linen there . . . and lately I'd needed to leave the linen more and more often. The slums were becoming even more crowded, the food more scarce. People were being less careless, had become more wary. If not for Erick and the white-dusty man . . .

I stood, startling Bloodmark enough he had to catch himself with one hand. His eyes flashed and his frown deepened. I stifled a brief surge of satisfaction at his reaction.

"Nothing," I said down to him. "Nothing at all." I suddenly didn't want Bloodmark anywhere near the white-dusty man's house.

I turned, retreated back into the alley, leaving the white-dusty man's empty doorway and Bloodmark behind. But I paused at the end and looked back.

Bloodmark still crouched near the alley's entrance, his gaze fixed on the white-dusty man's door. Though distant, I could see the frown on his face, the calculating, narrowed look around his eyes.

The hand of frost pressing against my chest flared, then died as Bloodmark shifted toward me. His frown dropped away and in a teasing voice that echoed strangely in the alley, he said, "Shall we hunt 'the pug-nosed man' tomorrow, Varis?"

Then, in a darker voice, "Yes. Yes, I think we shall."

✝

I saw Bloodmark twice the next day. Each time he stood across the Dredge, back against a wall, arms crossed over his chest. His birthmark stood out a startling red in the sunlight. Each time he grinned and nodded, then pushed away from the wall and joined the flow of the crowd, turning into the nearest alley with a backward glance.

The pressure of the cold hand against my chest returned, tightening the base of my throat. But I pushed it down and focused on a loose bundle, a forgotten sack, a wagon of produce that couldn't afford to miss a single apple or potato. Not now. And I watched for Tomas.

Toward midday, a low rumble rolled through the sky and for a moment people paused, looking up.

The leading edge of a bank of black clouds was just beginning to emerge from the west. As I watched, it began to obscure the sun.

The light shifted, grew gray. When I glanced back down at the Dredge, people were moving swiftly, bundles tucked close, shoulders hunched. Desperation fought with weary resignation on their faces.

I sighed. So much for finding more food.

I scanned the thinning crowd as the light darkened further, but didn't see Bloodmark. With a last look at the sky, I turned into an alley and moved deeper into the depths beyond the Dredge, toward the narrow where I'd seen Tomas earlier.

By the time I settled into a crouch beside a heap of crumbled stone, it was raining. Heavy at first, it tapered off as the leading edge of the storm swept past, trailing wisps of whiter clouds beneath it. I let the water wash down my face where I crouched, felt it plaster my hair to my neck, my clothes to my body. The trickle of sludge that traced down the narrow's center grew to a stream.

I scanned the alley, then shifted against the slick mud-brick at my back and relaxed. Time to wait.

A few hours later, I heard a chunk of mud-brick skitter across cobbles. I lifted my head, glanced down the narrow through tendrils of hair dripping water. But the narrow was empty.

I thought about slipping beneath the river. Not far, just beneath the surface. But exhaustion had sunk into my muscles—from lack of sleep the night before, from the wait. So I shifted position instead, dismissed the muted skitter of stone against cobble.

I had just resettled, was about to drop my head forward again, when the prickling frost of the hand returned to my chest. Lightly, like ice rimming the edge of a hand-shaped puddle.

I froze, eyes still on the narrow. When nothing appeared immediately, I let my hand drift to my dagger.

Movement. So close I stiffened in shock, hand still inches from my dagger. But the figure that stepped from a shadowed doorway only paused briefly at the edge of the narrow, then began moving away.

My hand fell onto my dagger and I shifted forward, weight now in my toes. I steadied myself as I watched the figure through the sheets of wind-gusted drizzle. Because of the icy hand against my chest, I thought at first it was Bloodmark. But no. This man was too tall, too broad of shoulder.

He halted suddenly, shoulders stiffening as if he'd heard something, then turned.

It was the pug-nosed man. Tomas. His nose had been broken, crushed and flattened against his face. He scanned the narrow, dark eyes intent, brow furrowed with suspicion.

His gaze had just settled on where I crouched when the hand against my chest flared with ice and a shadow dropped from a window onto the pug-nosed man's back.

The two men went down in a heap, Tomas grunting in surprise. I jerked forward, then forced myself to stop.

Bloodmark had crushed the man to the ground, had him pinned with one knee, as Erick had pinned Bloodmark so many weeks before. Except the pug-nosed man's right arm was trapped beneath his chest.

As I watched, Bloodmark raised one arm, dagger held in one grip, and stabbed the pug-nosed man in the back. Once. Twice. Both strikes were high, in the shoulder muscles.

It happened in a strange, rain-muted silence, the narrow glistening with dampness. The only sounds were a low gasp from Tomas when Bloodmark's dagger struck. Then Tomas seemed to relax, shoulders sagging.

Bloodmark hesitated, dagger raised for another strike. After a moment, he shifted his weight.

The pug-nosed man heaved, pushing up hard with the arm trapped beneath his body. Bloodmark hit the side wall, head thudding against stone, then collapsed.

As smooth as a rat, the pug-nosed man stood and spun. His hand closed around Bloodmark's throat, then lifted the gutter-scum's body as if it were made entirely of cloth and shoved him hard into the stone wall.

"You fucking little pissant urchin," the pug-nosed man snarled. "Did you think you could *rob* me? Huh? I have nothing you can gods-damned steal!"

Bloodmark's eyes widened as the man's hand tightened, and an instant later the gutterscum's hands flew to Tomas' arm, grasping at the muscles there.

Bloodmark had lost his dagger.

I saw the pug-nosed man's shoulders flex—even after Bloodmark had stabbed him there—and then he jerked Bloodmark away from the wall, lifted him higher, so his feet were no longer touching the ground, and shoved him back.

Bloodmark gasped again. The pug-nosed man's hand was now shoved up under his jawbone, half hidden in the folds of Bloodmark's flesh. The palm lay against Bloodmark's throat, and as I watched the pug-nosed man began crushing Bloodmark's windpipe.

Bloodmark's eyes flew even wider and his mouth opened, worked hard for breath. His fingers began to tear at the pug-nosed man's arm, gouging at the skin, drawing blood. Tomas snarled again, tightened his grip.

I hesitated. On the edge of the narrow, Tomas and Bloodmark a mere twenty paces away, I hesitated. I felt Bloodmark leaning in close as I lay helpless in the alley racked with nausea, smelled his breath, garlicky and stale, as he breathed, *Don't mess with me, bitch.* I saw him at the end of the alley the night before, his gaze on the white-dusty man's door, eyes dark and intent and unforgiving. I felt the nick of Bloodmark's blade during the bout, saw his self-satisfied grin as he retreated.

I hesitated and thought of Erick, how I'd felt when Erick had glanced up from kneeling on Bloodmark's back and I'd realized he'd meant to use Bloodmark. Erick was mine. I didn't want to share, didn't want to lose him. Erick didn't see how vicious Bloodmark was, didn't see the hatred in Bloodmark's eyes when he looked at me.

Tomas could solve that problem. All I had to do was walk away. I could pick up Tomas' trail again later.

My eyes narrowed as I watched Tomas push even harder, hand flexing as he shifted his grip.

My own hand tightened on my dagger, then relaxed. I began to turn away.

Then Bloodmark's feet began to kick, thudding into the slick stone at his back in a feeble, erratic rhythm.

I'd moved the twenty paces before I realized it, stood at Tomas' back in less than a heartbeat. He never heard me, too intent on Bloodmark's face, now beginning to turn red. My dagger slid up into his back, low, exactly as Erick had taught me. It was the only possible strike. Tomas was too tall for me to reach his throat, his body too close to Bloodmark's for me to get a clear cut in front.

I backed off instantly. In my head, I heard Erick's voice, from the training sessions in the courtyards and darkened rooms beyond the Dredge: *It won't kill instantly, but they're dead just the same. They're walking dead men and they won't even know it. But they're usually pissed.*

Tomas grunted. It shouldn't have hurt that much—if done correctly, he'd never know he'd been stabbed—but I'd purposely tugged it as I removed the dagger so that he'd feel it. His head jerked toward me. Then he snarled and dropped Bloodmark.

Bloodmark gasped, sank forward onto his hands. His arms gave out and he collapsed to his chest, face pressed into the rain-wet sludge as he hacked in deep, harsh breaths.

I shoved Bloodmark from my mind, concentrated on Tomas. He'd turned toward me, reached around with one hand to feel his back.

It came away slick with blood and rain.

"You little fucker," he muttered. He glared at me, eyes so hard with hatred I stepped back. But I didn't hide, didn't cringe. I held my dagger before me and waited, weight balanced.

Tomas grinned. "Courageous little bitch, though."

He stepped forward and his eyes widened in shock as he staggered. He reached out to steady himself with one hand, managed to stumble a few steps farther. He leaned heavily against the rain-slick wall, trembling, breath coming in deep, wet gasps. Water trickled down his face, dripped from his upper lip and chin as his gaze fell on me again.

His eyes were no longer hard. They were surprised, and strangely confused.

"What did you do to me?" he gasped, swallowing with pain.

He stood a moment more, bent slightly forward, wavering as he tried to keep his balance. Then he sagged to his knees, and like Bloodmark, fell forward onto his chest, his arms loose at his sides. He landed in the little stream of sludge near the center of the narrow and water began to fill his mouth, before pooling and escaping around his body.

I relaxed, stood straight.

Bloodmark coughed. "He was my mark," he muttered, voice broken and hoarse.

I frowned at him where he lay on the cobbles, too weak to rise. "Not anymore. Stay here. I'll get Erick."

"Wait!" he barked, but then broke out in ragged, hacking coughs. He tried to rise as I passed, but barely got his chest off the ground before collapsing again.

I ignored him, too pissed to care.

†

I found Erick at Cobbler's Fountain, standing at the edge of the circle. It was still raining. He wore a cloak—as almost everyone I'd seen outside in the rain this close to the real Amenkor did—the hood pulled over his head.

He straightened as I approached. "What's wrong?"

"Tomas is dead."

He nodded. "And did you mark him?"

"Bloodmark tried to kill him."

Erick tensed. Through the rain dripping from the front of his hood, I saw his expression harden, his jaw set. "Show me," he said.

I led him back to the narrow, the light darkening beneath the clouds even further as night fell. The drizzle slowed, then halted, and overhead the clouds began to tatter, shredding like rotten cloth. The moon appeared. The air smelled crisp and fresh and I breathed it in deeply.

Tomorrow the Dredge would reek.

I noticed Tomas' body had been moved the instant I entered the narrow. I halted, Erick pulling up sharp behind me, his hood down.

"What is it?"

I drew breath to answer, then spotted Bloodmark.

He sat on his heels, back against the wall, a few paces farther down the narrow, almost hidden in the darkness. He turned as he saw us, face hard with anger.

"He was *my mark*," he said.

I lurched forward, knelt beside Tomas' body.

Bloodmark had rolled him onto his back, had beaten Tomas' face to a bloody, fleshy pulp. One ear had been ripped free and dangled loosely against the cobbles. Bruises lightly touched his neck but had not darkened. One side of his head had been crushed in, as if kicked. Or struck with a loose mud-brick.

And carved into his forehead was the Skewed Throne. The cuts were brutal and deep, exposing bone.

I choked on anger. The hot, flushed anger I'd felt staring down into the man's face in the alley off the Dredge. The same anger I'd felt as I sliced the Skewed Throne into Garrell's forehead.

I glanced up at Bloodmark and saw him draw back, eyes widening. I stood, stepped over Tomas' body.

"He was my mark!" Bloodmark barked, jerking upright, back scraping against the mud-brick.

I'd taken a single step forward, hand already on my dagger, when Erick stepped between us, his hand latching onto my shoulder, halting me. He faced Bloodmark, his back to me.

"Did you kill him?"

Bloodmark hesitated, hand going to his throat. The bruising from Tomas' grip had already darkened—a deep, ugly purple that appeared black in the moonlight.

"He was going to kill me," Bloodmark said.

Erick let me go, took a menacing step forward, and Bloodmark skidded farther down the wall.

"But did you kill him?"

Bloodmark shot a hateful glare at me. "No."

"Then he wasn't your mark!" Erick spat, and turned. He studied me for a moment, then stepped up next to me and stared down at Tomas' body.

He frowned. Anger darkened his eyes as well, mixed with something else. A hint of doubt. As if he were beginning to reconsider using Bloodmark. He knew I would never have beaten a mark, knew I would never have slashed the Skewed Throne so deeply into a mark's forehead.

A shiver of icy hope shot through the hot flush of my anger.

"Why did you try to kill him?" Erick asked finally. There was no doubt in his voice now, only anger.

Bloodmark had relaxed slightly, but tensed again. "Because he was the mark—"

Erick turned and with a single glare cut Bloodmark off. "No. You're only supposed to find them, then find me." He began to move forward, reached as if to grab Bloodmark's throat with one hand. But at the last moment he slapped his palm against the stone to the right of Bloodmark's head.

Bloodmark flinched, his hand still raised protectively to his throat.

"You only *find them*," Erick said in a low, angry voice. "Understood?"

Bloodmark snapped a narrowed glance toward me. But then something shifted deep inside his eyes. The glare sharpened, grew sleek and edged, like a honed blade.

Eyes locked on me, he asked, "The Mistress wanted him dead, didn't she?"

Erick pulled away, frowning. "Yes."

Bloodmark turned his gaze directly onto Erick and said with a confident, mocking smile, "Then it doesn't matter who kills him. He was my mark. It was my choice."

Erick's frown deepened, his own words thrown back into his face. He said nothing for a long moment, the air between them heavy with tension.

Then Erick pushed away from the wall. "And it almost got you killed."

I felt an acid surge of disappointment.

Erick turned away, dismissed Bloodmark without a sound. He began moving toward the end of the narrow. I couldn't believe he was leaving.

Bloodmark stepped forward, away from the wall, his hand dropping from his throat. "My choice," he said to himself, under his breath, as he watched Erick retreat.

Erick halted, back stiff. His gaze found mine.

His eyes were confused, uncertain, his face taut with anger. He knew Bloodmark was dangerous—I could see it—but he did nothing.

He must have seen the betrayal in my face for his shoulders sagged. He dropped his gaze and continued on toward the Dredge without a word.

Behind him, Blookmark looked at me, eyes smug and defiant.

A cold, hard stone of hatred solidified in my chest, just beneath my breastbone.

When Bloodmark turned and left me alone with Tomas' body in the rain-soaked narrow, the stone remained.

I should have let Tomas kill him.

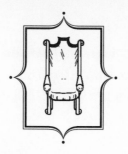

Chapter 5

I MADE my way to Cobbler's Fountain purposefully, walking down the Dredge until I was within a few alleys of the fountain, then veering off into the side streets and narrows. I was early—a full hour before dusk—but I wasn't here to meet with Erick.

I was here to stalk him.

I ducked into a narrow and crouched down, slipping from shadow to shadow, until I reached an alcove overlooking the circular fountain. Tucked into the alcove's depths, the wood planking of the door pressed into my back, I could see the statue of the woman holding the urn, her back toward me. Sunlight still touched the top of her head.

I glanced back down the alley, a nervous twinge in my stomach. It was early enough for people to be moving about, early enough someone might notice me. In the slums, no one would do anything but keep their distance. Here, closer to the real Amenkor . . .

There was no one in sight. I settled in to wait.

The sunlight shifted. Overhead, the few clouds in the sky burned a deep orange, like fire. The light began to fade.

Someone entered the area surrounding the fountain, footsteps clicking on the cobbles. I tensed, heart thudding in my chest, but it wasn't Erick. The woman cut across the open area and entered another street, a wooden box clutched to her chest.

I sank back against the door, felt sweat prickle my forehead, between my shoulder blades.

"What am I doing here?" I murmured to myself, my voice barely more than a breath, nerves making me feel sick.

But I knew. I could still taste the betrayal of the night before, like ash in my mouth. Erick should have stood up to Bloodmark, should have threatened him, abandoned him. He should have done *something*.

My brow creased with anger. Instead, he'd walked away. I needed to know why.

Something moved near the fountain, a subtle shift of shadow. I scanned the area but saw nothing.

I was just about to use the river when Erick stepped from the darkness of a narrow.

Bitterness flooded my mouth. I reached for my dagger, but halted, my hand trembling. I tried to ignore it.

Erick moved to the fountain, stared up at the woman's bowed head. In the fading light, I could see his face clearly. His eyes were troubled, the skin around his mouth pinched with worry, with doubt. He searched the woman's features for a long moment, then turned away with a sigh, still troubled. He began pacing the cobbles, circling the fountain slowly, waiting.

For me. Or Bloodmark.

I sat back. The bitterness retreated slightly, still there but not as strong. A queasy uneasiness in my stomach had taken its place beside the anger. Erick's face had been too open, too exposed. My presence suddenly felt wrong, a betrayal of Erick's trust.

But I didn't move.

Dusk fell, deepened into night.

My legs had begun to cramp when Erick's pacing halted. He glanced once up into the night sky, the stars brittle, the moon high, then headed toward the Dredge, not trying to hide, his stride steady.

I waited, felt my heartbeat skip, then cursed my hesitation—cursed the bitterness, Bloodmark, the sense of wrongness—and followed.

I kept far enough back that Erick's figure was just a shadow, seen only in the moonlight that filtered down into the alleys. He moved straight toward the Dredge, but turned before reaching it, paralleling it using the side streets and narrows, heading farther from the slums, toward the bridge where the Dredge crossed over the River into the city proper. The texture of the buildings changed. Crumbling mud-brick no longer littered the alleys, cobbles lay mostly whole underfoot. Candlelight appeared in a few windows, glowing behind chinks in the wood used to cover the openings.

My uneasiness grew. We were moving outside of the slums. The alleys and narrows—the buildings themselves—no longer felt familiar.

Erick only stopped once, half-turned as I slid into hiding behind the remains of a shattered barrel. Breath held tight, I waited—for him to turn back, to pick me out of the shadows and frown down at me in deep disappointment.

My stomach twisted in anticipation. . . .

But after a moment he continued.

A few streets later, he turned. When I edged up to the end of the narrow, glanced around the corner, I could see the arch of the bridge, could see moonlight reflected on the River, could hear the slap of water against the stone channel.

And on the far bank, Amenkor . . . the real Amenkor.

I stared at the buildings, noted with a strange disappointment that they seemed no different than the buildings surrounding me now. But different than those in the slums. These buildings were not half collapsed, stone sagging in on itself under decades of disuse. These buildings had edges and corners.

"Who goes there!"

I tensed, shrank back farther into the shadows, but the rough voice had called out to Erick.

"It's me, you bloody bastard," Erick growled, humor in his voice.

Two guards stood watch at the end of the bridge, pikes held ready. One of them shifted, pulled the pike back into a guard position with a grunt. "It's Erick," he said to the second guard, "the Seeker."

The second guard relaxed, fell back slightly as Erick approached. He appeared younger than the first. Both wore gold-stitched thrones on their shirts and were more heavily armored than any guardsmen I'd seen in the slums.

"Gave me quite a start sneaking out of the shadows like that," the first guardsman grumbled as Erick halted beside him. "You shouldn't scare us regulars."

Erick frowned. "I didn't realize there'd be guardsmen here."

The man grunted. "Captain Baill's orders, straight from the Mistress. 'All entrances to the city proper are to be guarded at all times.' The captain's set patrols throughout the city as well, and increased the night watch near the palace."

"What for?" Erick asked. "What are we guarding against?"

The guardsman shrugged. "Don't know. I don't think Baill knows either, but if the orders came from the Mistress. . . ."

Erick shifted uncomfortably, cast a glance across the river, toward the palace.

"If you ask me," the second guardsman said, "the Mistress has lost it."

"We didn't ask you, did we?" the first guardsman barked. "Now stand up! Hold that pike like you mean to use it, not like some slack-jawed lackwit!"

The second guardsman glared, but straightened, back as rigid as stone, and turned his attention toward the street. The first guardsman grunted, shot a glance toward Erick.

There was fear in his eyes. Hidden behind a thick layer of loyalty, but fear nonetheless.

It sent a shiver through my skin. The Mistress ruled the city. . . . No. The Mistress *was* the city. If something happened to her, it would affect everyone.

Even us gutterscum in the slums.

"Are you headed back to the palace to report?" the first guardsman asked.

Erick nodded, his attention still on the other guardsman, his face creased in thought. "Yes. But I'll be back tomorrow."

"Good hunting?"

All emotion left Erick's face. He turned and caught the first guardsman's eye.

The guardsman stepped back sharply, gaze falling to the stone cobbles of the road. "Forget I asked," he mumbled, voice thin, thready.

Erick didn't answer, simply stepped around him and crossed the bridge.

The guard waited a moment, then turned to the other guardsman and scowled.

Back pressed against the stone of the narrow, I hesitated. I could follow Erick farther if I wanted. The two guardsmen would be easy to distract, and they were watching the street, not the water. . . .

But I was already too far beyond the slums. If I entered the real Amenkor, I'd be stepping onto totally unfamiliar ground.

I wasn't ready to do that.

I hesitated a moment more, then slid back down the narrow, back into the darkness, wrapping it around me like a cloak.

I still didn't have any answers, but I'd seen and heard enough. For now.

✝

I was moving through the depths of the Dredge, moving toward the white-dusty man's door, when I ran across the body. The man had been thrown into a corner of the narrow, where it turned and cut left. His head rested on one shoulder, rolled slightly forward. His hands lay in his lap, his legs stretched out before him, one knee bent outward. He was barefoot, breeches coated with mud, and his muscled chest was bare and streaked with blood. He'd been stabbed four times. Twice in the chest, once in the side, low, and once in the gut.

I halted as soon as I saw him, scanned the narrow in both directions. It was littered with refuse, with broken stone. A rat skittered along the base of the wall, then vanished through a crevice in the mud-brick. But otherwise I was alone.

Stepping close, I knelt, reached forward to push the man's face into view. But I already knew what I'd find, had known the moment I'd seen the body.

It was the mercenary, Bloodmark's and my current mark. Blue eyes, brown hair, sun-weathered skin shaved smooth except for a narrow band of beard on each side of his face, stretching from his ears to the base of his jaw. He reeked of ale, his dried sweat sick with its stench. A trail of vomit touched the corner of his mouth. A pool of vomit had congealed near his side.

Carved into his forehead was the Skewed Throne. Brutal and deep.

Bloodmark.

I lowered the mercenary's head slowly and sat back on my

heels. The hot anger had flushed my skin again, but now it felt worn and used. I thought about telling Erick. But Bloodmark always killed the marks now, *our* marks. At least, if he got to them first. And Erick did nothing, said nothing.

Not after Tomas.

The thought sent a pulse of bitterness through the flush of anger, hotter and heavier, aimed at Erick.

I stood, staring down at the mercenary. He was only a shadow in the moonlight now. The sun had set.

I turned away, heading again toward the Dredge. I was hungry.

I crouched down at the entrance to the alley across from the white-dusty man's door and immediately noticed the tuft of cloth peeking out from the stone where the white-dusty man hid the bundles of food. A prickling sensation, like gooseflesh, swept through me and I smiled, my stomach growling. I'd left the linen beneath the stone a few days before, but there'd been no response. I'd thought that perhaps the desperation that haunted everyone's eyes on the Dredge now had finally forced the white-dusty man away, that he'd left, that he'd forgotten me. The thought had hurt. But the white-dusty man hadn't gone, hadn't forgotten.

I almost stepped out onto the Dredge, heading for the bundle without thought, my stomach clenching with hunger. But at the last moment, weight already shifted forward, I remembered Bloodmark, felt his breath against my neck from weeks before.

What are we watching?

I shuddered, pulled back and scanned the nearest alleys, the darknesses.

Nothing.

I hesitated at the world of gray and red and wind, then pushed deeper.

I saw nothing, felt nothing, smelled nothing, until I'd pushed myself as deep as I'd ever gone before. There, the ice-rimmed hand began to press against my chest, so faintly it barely touched my skin, as if the hand were hovering a hairbreadth above my breastbone.

I sensed that I could go deeper, but the grayness had solidified so I could see into the shadows, could see oil light flickering a lighter gray in the cracks around the white-dusty man's door and window—oil light I had not seen from the alley. And the ice of the hand seemed distant, removed.

I drew back until only moonlight lit the Dredge, the tuft of cloth.

The hand against my chest faded.

I hesitated a moment more, then scurried across the Dredge, keeping low, keeping to the shadows. I crouched in the thin recess of the white-dusty man's door, removed the loose stone, then dragged out and opened the bundle.

Inside, there was a small loaf of bread and a chunk of cheese the size of my fist.

I smiled, realized I'd been more worried than I'd thought. And hungrier.

I sniffed back the worry, and grabbed the loaf of bread. I was just about to bite into it when the door opened.

Oil light flooded out onto the Dredge. With it came a wash of dense heat—

And the heady, overpowering scent of flour, of yeast and dough.

The scent struck me like a fist and suddenly I was nine again. Nine and cowering in the shadows of an alley, watching a man and woman approach each other, both lost, their eyes vague, in their own gray worlds. The woman had straight black hair, brown eyes like the mud of the buildings after a rain, and a bundle tied too loosely and held too far from her body. The man wore a rough homespun shirt, sleeves rolled to his forearms, old breeches, no shoes. His clothes were coated with white dust . . . with flour. His hands and face were immaculately clean.

They collided, and in the brief moment they were distracted, I stole two of the rolls that fell from the woman's bundle.

I thought I'd escaped as I retreated to a narrow across the Dredge. I thought I hadn't been seen. But when I turned to watch . . .

The man was leaning over the woman in concern. After a moment of wariness, she allowed him to help her to her feet. When she reached for her bundle, the man knelt and began gathering the fallen rolls. The woman joined him.

Then the man frowned, brow creasing. He scanned the ground, searching, as the woman slid the last roll into the bundle and cinched it closed.

He turned toward my darkness and stared straight at me.

I don't know what he saw. A girl pressed flat against the wall, mud-streaked, clutching two rolls to her chest. That at least. But he must have seen something more, something else, for the frown softened, relaxed. He settled back onto the balls of his feet, hands dangling between his knees.

What is it? the woman asked.

The man held my gaze a moment more, until the woman began to look in my direction with her own frown.

Nothing, he said, and stood.

And before the woman with the straight black hair and the soft brown eyes turned completely toward me, he touched her arm, distracted her.

I fled. I ran deep, farther than I'd originally intended. Because of the man with the white-dusty clothing. Because of the way his eyes had softened. Because he'd relaxed onto the balls of his feet and dangled his hands, instead of leaping forward to snag my arm, to halt me.

I ate the bread. I cried when I did, and couldn't understand why, but I ate the bread.

I'd followed him the next day, and the next. And eventually he'd begun to leave the bread beneath the stone outside his door when I returned the linen the bread had been wrapped in.

A shadow stepped into the light spilling from the white-dusty man's door. I glanced up. Up into the white-dusty man's eyes— older now, shaded with pain, with weariness. Gray streaked his hair, and wrinkles etched the corners of his eyes and mouth, etched his brow.

But I saw none of that.

Instead, I saw his eyes as they'd been on the Dredge that day, saw them soften as he stared at a girl pressed flat against the mud-brick wall of an alley.

Tears bit at the corners of my eyes. Tears of shame, of need, of hunger. But not hunger for bread or cheese. For something more.

In the depths of the white-dusty man's house, I heard movement. Then the black-haired woman stepped into view.

She held a long wooden paddle before her, charred and streaked with soot. A heap of dough rested on the long end of the paddle, ready to be placed into an oven.

"What is it?" she asked.

I stilled, as I had on the Dredge so long ago. I stilled and caught the white-dusty man's eyes.

He held my gaze a long moment, then smiled.

"Nothing," he said.

Something—a pain, an ache—surged up from deep in my chest and forced itself out in a hitching sob. I tried to hold it in, but it was too much, too large. Tears coursed down my face, and I closed my eyes, the sobs coming hard and deep. Not loud sobs. Wet, throaty sobs that forced deep breaths through my nose, my mouth closed tight, trying to hold it all back, to keep it all in.

The white-dusty man simply waited, not moving.

The ache—the pain—released, like the tension in the bundle when the blade finally cuts through the cloth. It released and the sobs quieted. My breath came smoother, deeper.

Someone touched my face, a gentle touch, and I glanced up into the white-dusty man's eyes again. And this time I saw the gray in his hair, the lines on his face, the age.

His fingers traced down from my forehead to my chin. He tilted my head upward, stared deep into my eyes.

I felt myself trembling, still weak and fluid from the tears. The skin on my face felt tight, my eyes sore.

"You've grown," he said.

Fresh tears burned at the corners of my eyes. It was too much.

And so I pulled away, his fingers sliding down the length of my chin. I stood, back straight, no longer the nine-year-old girl cowering in an alley, no longer a child.

I glanced down at the bread, at the cheese still bundled in the cloth. Then I looked the white-dusty man—the baker—in the eye. I held up the bread a moment, and said in a tight, strained voice, "Thank you."

The baker smiled and nodded, the wrinkles around his mouth and eyes more pronounced. "You're welcome."

I hesitated, felt the wash of heat and the smell of baking bread against my face, then turned and walked away.

I headed back to my niche. I squeezed through the opening, felt the mud-brick scrape my back, my hips, as it always did now. I sat, drew my knees up tight to my chest, the baker's bundle set aside, and dropped my head.

I did not cry. Instead, after a long moment of silence, I simply sighed, raised my head, and reached for the bread.

†

Erick found me in my niche a few days later.

"Varis?"

I hesitated. I didn't want to speak to him, didn't want to see him.

But I still needed him.

"I have another mark for you and Bloodmark."

My eyes narrowed. He knew about the mercenary.

I moved to the edge of the niche, crawled out into the sunlight, then stood.

Erick stood on the far side of the narrow, back against the wall, arms crossed on his chest. He watched me carefully.

"I've searched for you on the Dredge," he said. When I didn't answer, he added, "Bloodmark hasn't seen you there either."

At Bloodmark's name, I tensed. "I haven't been to the Dredge." I couldn't keep the anger from my voice.

Erick hesitated, asked carefully, "Why not?"

I caught Erick's gaze. "Does it matter?"

Erick stiffened, and his eyes hardened. His hands dropped to his sides. "No. It doesn't matter to me at all."

I flinched inside.

"I have a new mark—two, actually," Erick said shortly, angry now, too. "A man and a woman, Rec Terrell and Mari Locke. The man is thick-shouldered, husky, bald. He had a pierced ear, but the stud he wore was torn out on the left side. All that's left is a mangled lobe. The woman, Mari, has short black hair, a rounded face, broad hips. There's a scar on her forearm, almost healed, very faint. Someone sliced her up. The Mistress wants them both."

Erick turned, began walking away.

"Wait."

Erick paused but did not look back.

I bit my lower lip, thought of the white-dusty man, thought of telling Erick about him. But then I thought of Bloodmark, of the mercenary, of Erick saying nothing, doing nothing, and the anger returned.

Instead, I asked, "Why?"

Erick turned, enough so I could see the confusion in his eyes. "What do you mean?"

I didn't know. Why are you still using Bloodmark? Why did you walk away the night I killed Tomas? Why did you let Blood-mark win?

"Why do you do this? Why are you a Seeker?"

His forehead creased as he frowned. "It's . . . what I know how to do, what I was trained to do. It's what I've always done."

He hesitated, as if uncertain he'd answered my question, or un-certain of his own answer. Then he turned and left.

I should have asked him something else.

†

I never would have spotted Mari if she hadn't reached for the cabbage.

I was standing near the wagon, the ebb and flow of the Dredge washing unnoticed around me. I'd come out of habit, having nowhere else to go. I didn't need food. I had enough in my niche for a few days. And I wasn't looking for Rec or Mari. Let Blood-mark have them. Erick didn't seem to mind.

And so, when a woman reached for the cabbage and I saw the faint scar tracing down the length of her forearm, it didn't register. Not at first.

I glanced up at her. Rounded face. Short black hair. Brown eyes. A lighter brown than I'd seen on the Dredge before, streaked with yellow.

She met my gaze, smiled tightly, nodded, then turned.

I nodded back, belatedly. I thought, vaguely, that she reminded me of someone. Of the woman the man had strangled, the one with the basket of potatoes?

I frowned.

Then it struck. Mari. My mark.

I jerked away from the wall, glanced sharply in the direction Mari had moved. The world slid to gray and wind and red, and I began searching the washes of red to find her.

She wasn't there.

I frowned, let the world return to normal. I stared down the Dredge—

And saw her. She'd halted before another wagon, this one loaded with carrots. She was talking to the wagon's owner, a bunch of carrots gripped in one hand.

My frown deepened. Keeping her in sight, I slid beneath the river again, slowly. Everything slid to gray except Mari.

I let my focus on Mari relax . . . and she slid to gray as well.

I bit my lower lip.

All of my marks had been red before, dangerous and deadly. Some had had smells, but all had been red in the end.

Mari was gray, and smelled of nothing but sweat and the Dredge.

She finished with the carrot monger and began moving away.

I hesitated, chewed on my lower lip a moment more, then followed.

The depths beyond the Dredge began to shift, as they'd done when I'd followed the hawk-faced man. Except now, five years after the Fire, the decay had crept closer to the Dredge itself, like a blight on the city and its streets. Mud-brick slipped to crumbling granite. Streets narrowed to alleys, then narrows, shortened and filled with heaps of decaying filth. Mildew thickened to slime, streams to sludge. The reek of the Dredge deepened, stank of piss and shit and rot. The light darkened, as if the depths of the Dredge were sucking it away, swallowing it as it swallowed everything that lingered too long, that hesitated. Soon, everything north of the River would be subsumed. I could see it happening, could feel the blight of the city on my skin.

Mari began to slow, and the sun began to set, the gray of dusk seeping between the stone. I fell back, crouched behind mounds of filth, behind heaps of fallen stone.

Then Mari turned into an empty doorway.

I glanced up at the sky. The light was fading swiftly, darkness descending like cloth, smothering and complete. In moments, the depths swallowed the last of the sunlight and stars pricked the sky.

I moved forward, edged up to the doorway where Mari had vanished. I stared into the blackness, focused.

An empty room, small, with three doors opening onto their own darknesses.

I stepped inside. Dust covered the floor, disturbed by tracks leading toward the central door straight ahead. Beneath the dust, a mosaic of colored clay tiles could be seen, most cracked, a few missing altogether.

I moved to the central doorway, noticed the flicker of firelight off to one side, through another doorway.

I halted at the edge of the second door.

Mari stood near the fire in the center of the room, the cabbage and carrots laid out on the floor beside her. She shifted a pot over the flames, face already sweating from the heat, then squatted down and began chopping the carrots.

Someone grunted.

Mari froze, the knife in her hand trembling. Her eyes were wide in the firelight.

In the corner, a heap of blankets moved, were thrown aside. A man propped himself onto one elbow. His ear was mangled, like a piece of gristle someone had chewed on and spat out.

His gaze wandered, bleary with sleep, then settled on Mari.

He stilled, grew suddenly focused. The bleariness faded, hardened into something terrible, something cruel.

"Where have you been?"

I drew back from the doorway, sweat prickling the back of my neck. His voice was dark—soft and fluid and dark.

Like Bloodmark's voice.

I no longer wanted to be here.

I heard a rustle of movement, then drew in a deep breath to steady myself and glanced back through the door.

Mari had turned back to the carrots. But her knife was no longer steady as she cut. "The Dredge," she said. Her voice shook.

Rec shifted, stood.

"And what were you doing on the Dredge?"

She didn't answer.

He moved behind her. His hands fell onto her shoulders and she drew in a sharp breath, her shoulders tightening, her body going rigid. She held the knife before her, pointed down, the blade halfway through a slicing of the carrot.

But the carrot was forgotten. Her eyes were locked straight ahead, strangely terrified and blank at the same time. Her lips were pressed tight together, trembling.

Rec leaned forward, one hand moving to her neck, to her shortened hair. His fingers closed into a fist in the tresses, pulled back sharply.

Mari gasped, sobbed, her chest heaving. Tears formed at the corners of her eyes.

"What were you doing on the Dredge?" Rec whispered into her ear.

Mari choked on her own words, her head pulled back, her neck exposed. "Food." Rec jerked her hair hard. "I got us food!"

Rec leaned back, but didn't release her hair. He knelt. His free hand shifted from her shoulder, reached down the length of her arm for the knife.

Her body jerked. "No," she gasped. So low I could barely hear it. "No. You said never again," she sobbed, eyes closing. "Never again." Tears coursed down her face.

"Shhh," Rec said. His hand closed about hers.

"No," she breathed, shaking her head.

"Shhh. Give me the knife."

I gripped the dagger in my hand hard, hunched forward, my free hand holding the edge of the doorway. But Rec was too far away, was faced toward me.

He'd see me the moment I moved into the light.

I clenched my jaw as the muscles in Mari's arm—muscles so tensed they seemed like cords beneath her skin—relaxed.

The knife began to slip, but Rec caught it.

Mari let out a sob—of pain, of despair, of weakness—and her arms dropped to her sides.

Rec drew the knife up to her face, let the blade touch the skin of her cheek.

Mari drew in another hitching sob, but her arms stayed lax at her sides. All of the tension had left her body. She lay slumped, head back, neck exposed, supported by Rec's body.

"Next time," Rec began, then casually stroked the knife down Mari's cheek, drawing a thin line of blood, "tell me where you're going before you leave."

Mari sucked in breath through her teeth as the knife cut.

Rec stood, let her hair free with a sudden shove forward. He dropped the knife to the ground beside her, the blade clattering on the stone floor. "What's for dinner?" he asked as he moved away.

Mari stayed hunched over, her shoulders shuddering, her face hidden.

After a long moment, her shoulders stilled. She sat back up, cheeks wet with tears but drying, and reached for the knife. She cleaned it, her eyes vacant and empty, drawn inward, the muscles of her face set. "Stew," she said.

Her voice had changed, had hardened.

Rec grunted. "Best get at it, then," he added, crawling beneath the blankets again. "Wake me when it's done."

My grip on my blade tightened, relaxed, then tightened again. But I shifted back away from the doorway.

I couldn't take them both.

And Mari was gray.

I sat back on my heels a long moment.

I needed Erick. Needed to *talk* to Erick.

I glanced into the room once more before heading toward Cobbler's Fountain. Rec was still wrapped in the blankets in the far corner. Mari knelt near the fire, staring down at the knife, blood and sweat dripping from her jaw.

†

Erick was not there.

I glanced at the night sky, at the stars. It was past dusk. I'd moved fast, but apparently not fast enough. Erick had already gone.

I sat back against the alley wall, stared out at the fountain.

The woman with the broken-off arm stared down at me, one arm still clutching the urn. I stared at her face as Erick had done weeks before, looked into its time-worn features.

I heard water, heard laughter, felt the warmth of sunlight against my face.

At the mouth of the alley, I stood, began slowly moving forward. Until I stood at the edge of the empty pool, looking down at its cracked bottom.

Except the pool was no longer empty. Not in my memory. It was full. Sunlight on water glared into my eyes and I blinked, felt warm hands catch me up under my armpits, lift me high and naked over the pool's edge. Cool water shocked through my feet, up through my legs, as I was dipped into the fountain. I screamed. A childish scream of delight. A six-year-old's scream. I kicked before my feet touched bottom, splashed water into my mother's face.

She had soft features, blurred somehow with the sunlight off the water, with the haze of memory. But I could see her eyes. Dark eyes, brown, almost black, with tiny flecks of green. They reminded me of the strangled woman's eyes, the one with the potatoes.

She jerked back from the spray, laughed with a slightly scolding tone, then set me firmly on my feet on the pool's stone bottom and released me.

I immediately knelt and began splashing with my hands, shrieking as she splashed back. I slogged away, stumbled on the uneven bottom, fell—

And submerged beneath the water. It closed over my head, enveloped me, cool and fluid, filling up my ears, my nose. The noises of the fountain's circle, of people talking, of children shrieking, of my mother's laughter, dropped away to a dull roar, like wind. The bright glare of the sunlight grayed. I'd clamped my mouth shut instinctively, but I'd kept my eyes wide.

The whole world grayed, grew muted.

Something inside me slipped. In the terror of the moment—a child's terror, riddled with exhilaration as well as fear—something deep inside . . . tore.

And something was released, surged forward. . . .

And then my mother's hands grabbed me, lifted me free of the water. I spluttered, felt water draining from my ears, from my nose. I blew out a rushed breath, water sheeting down my face, my hair plastered to my scalp, to my neck. I gasped in a breath too quickly, coughed hoarsely.

My mother pounded my back. *Are you all right? Breathe, baby, breathe. Come on. Breathe.*

Her voice sounded muted, unnaturally calm, yet edged with suppressed hysteria.

I gasped again, drew in another breath, then another. The spasms in my chest eased.

My mother lifted me from the pool, tucked me to her side so that my head rested against her shoulder, so I could see behind her.

The world was still gray, the sounds of the fountain still muted, as if I were still underwater, submerged.

Come on, my mother said. The edge of hysteria had left her voice, but now it sounded exhausted. *You've had enough fun for today. Time to head home.*

I clutched at her shoulder as she began moving away, trembling slightly, face pressed tight against her shoulder. But something in the gray of the world caught my eye, held my attention.

I lifted my head, and into her shoulder murmured, *Look, Mommy. Look at the red men.*

At the edge of the empty fountain, someone grabbed my shoulder and I spun with a snarl, the harshness of the sunlight, of the water, of the gray and wind and red men, jerking back to darkness and stars and damp, night air.

"It's me!" Erick barked, stepping back out of my dagger's range swiftly, one hand held out before him to stop me.

I halted, breathing hard, heart thudding. Then I blinked.

I'd dragged the grayness of the memory back with me. And beneath the river, Erick was a swirl of gray and red mixed together.

The sight was shocking. I'd never seen someone with mixed colors before, didn't know what it meant.

"I thought you heard me coming up behind you," he said, relaxing his stance. His hand dropped to his side.

Our eyes met, and something he saw in mine made him take another step back. "No," I said, then drew in a deep breath and pulled myself together. "No, I didn't hear you."

He hesitated at the anger in my voice, at its harshness. After a long considered moment, he said, "So you've found them."

"Yes."

He nodded. "Take me to them."

He turned, began heading toward the depths.

I straightened. "No."

Erick halted.

When he turned back, his eyes had gone blank, expressionless. "What do you mean?"

I narrowed my eyes, shifted uncertainly. "Not until we talk."

A flicker of surprise crossed his face. But then it blanked again. "Why now?"

"Because things have changed," I said without thought, and then realized what I'd said was true. Not because of the sense of betrayal that still burned inside me; and not because of the mixed gray and red of the river.

I drew in a steadying breath. "I'm not the girl you found vomiting over the dead body of that man."

Erick smiled tightly. Then the smile faded and shifted, and he seemed to really look at me, to see me standing there at the edge of Cobbler's Fountain in clothes he had given me—still worn, still tattered here and there, but not rags. I no longer crouched, no longer flinched away when someone reached toward me, no longer stayed in the alleys and narrows as much as possible when hunting. My head reached up to his shoulders, not his chest. And I walked the middle of the alleys and narrows now, walked the middle of the Dredge.

"No," he said, "you're not that little girl anymore."

We stared at each other a long moment, and somehow in the silence the heat of my anger faded away.

"So," Erick said, turning fully toward me, "what do you want to talk about?"

"The Mistress."

Erick frowned. "What about her?"

"You said that she picks the marks, that you only find them and kill them. That's what you do, what you were trained to do."

Erick's frown deepened. "Yes."

"You never ask yourself what the marks have done? Why the Mistress wants them dead?"

"No. I told you before. I don't need to know. The Mistress wants them dead, that's all that matters."

"What if she's wrong?"

Erick shook his head. The frown was gone. "She can't be wrong. She sits on the Skewed Throne."

"But—"

"No," Erick said with force. But there was strain in his eyes, doubt. "She can't be wrong. Saying she's wrong is the same as saying the Skewed Throne is wrong. They're the same. If she's wrong, then—"

But he halted, a flash of fear crossing his face—a fear that he quickly suppressed. A fear I didn't think was new, just as the doubt wasn't new. I'd seen both before, in his eyes after he'd backed down from Bloodmark, and again at the bridge leading to Amenkor.

"No," he said again. "The Mistress is never wrong. The marks deserve to die."

"Why?"

"I don't know," Erick said impatiently, not looking at me. "I don't think about it beyond that. I believe in the Mistress. I have faith in the Skewed Throne. There's a reason the marks need to die, one that only she needs to know. I don't. I'm not that important."

The doubt I'd seen in his eyes a moment before had crept into his voice. And I heard the lie. He did think about it, had been thinking about it, at least recently.

His faith in the Mistress, in the Skewed Throne, was wavering.

I hesitated, then said quietly, "Mari isn't a mark."

He looked at me sharply. "Why not? How do you know?"

I almost said, *She's gray*, but caught myself. "I've watched her." I saw Rec drawing the knife down her cheek, saw her eyes, the defeated slump of her body, her lax arms.

Erick's eyes narrowed. "The Mistress . . ." he began, but trailed off. He stared at me hard, considering, then drew himself straight. "Show me."

†

We didn't speak on the way into the depths. I led, moving fast, not hiding, not lurking, moving with purpose. Erick followed behind me, hissing once for me to slow. But after that he seemed to catch my urgency, sped up, enough that I could feel him at my back, so close he could reach out and touch me, push me.

But I felt as if I were already being pushed. I'd felt it as soon as we'd left Cobbler's Fountain. A pressure against my back, tightening my shoulders, prickling the skin.

So I moved faster. Until the night air burned in my lungs, harsh and loud and cold. As cold as it had been the night of the White Fire. Sharp and piercing. I heard Erick breathing hard behind me, heard him gasping at the pace.

But the pressure didn't relax.

Instead, it grew.

We were close—so close—when I felt the ice-rimmed hand press hard into my chest and heard the first scream. A woman's scream. High-pitched, desperate, and filled with shuddering, as if she were struggling, as if she were fighting.

I stopped cold, Erick staggering to a halt behind me, one hand on my shoulder to steady himself.

It felt eerily real against the icy pressure of the hand on my chest.

"Gods," he gasped, dragging in a deep breath. "Where is it coming from?"

I didn't answer. I knew.

I bolted forward, barely aware that Erick stayed right behind me. The scream filled the air, escalated, then dropped in pitch, fading, although still strong, still desperate. It was falling down into sobs, struggling down, trying not to give up hope.

I was at the doorway, colored tiles beneath my feet.

I was at the inner room.

I halted at the door, caught myself at its edge. Rec's body lay half off the blood-soaked bed, his torso twisted, one hand stretched out before him, reaching. The spilled contents of the stewpot created a glistening sheet of wetness in the center of the room. Two figures struggled on the far side of the fire—Bloodmark and Mari. I saw all of it in a heartbeat.

But Erick moved faster.

Bloodmark had hold of Mari's wrists, one in each hand, one grip loose and cumbersome because he still held his dagger. Mari struggled, but there was already blood on her chest, seeping from a deep gash in her side, and another higher up, near her neck, above her breast. Her arms had grown weak, and she was sobbing, her head shaking back and forth.

Bloodmark snarled, let go of the Mari's wrist with the hand that held his dagger, and plunged the blade twice more into Mari's chest. Deep strokes. Penetrating strokes. Each followed by a visceral grunt. Spittle flew from his mouth, his teeth clenched.

And then Erick hit him, body to body. Hit him so hard they flew across Mari, struck the granite floor and rolled. Bloodmark's eyes opened wide in terror. His arm flailed, scored Erick hard along his back with the dagger. Erick hissed, lurched back, away, and Bloodmark jerked into a crouch, coming around fast, like an adder.

All of us froze. Erick on the floor, on his side, ready to move, his glare focused on Bloodmark. Bloodmark in a crouch three paces away, breathing hard, dark eyes fixed on Erick. The terror in his face was gone.

Mari gasped, a sickeningly wet gasp. Her arms had fallen to her sides.

As I watched, she tried to roll over, pushing herself weakly up onto her side so that she faced me, her back to Erick and Blood-mark. Her eyes met mine and she sobbed, the sound shuddering in her chest.

She hunched forward, drew her hand up close to her face. It dragged on the floor, trailed through blood, flopped weakly beside her mouth.

She paused, gathered herself with a single breath—

And tried to lift herself up.

I watched her eyes close with the effort, watched the muscles strain, her arm tight, her chest tight, her teeth clenched. I watched sweat break out on her face, watched her eyes squeeze tighter, her neck muscles taut. Her shoulder lifted an inch. Her arm began to tremble. . . .

And then she collapsed, breath expelled in a ragged, hopeless sob. She cried into the floor, shaking, mouth flecked with spit and blood.

She drew in another breath and opened her eyes. She stared straight at me, seemed to be gathering herself for another try, her eyes intent, her palm flat against the stone before her.

And then she died.

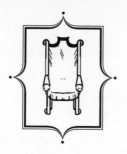

Chapter 6

THE room held silent for a moment, stilled, expectant. . . .

"She wasn't a mark."

I said it with force, looking at Erick. The fist-sized solidness of stone began to form in my chest, right beneath my breastbone. Familiar stone. Hatred and anger made real. I tasted it, thick and fluid and acidic.

I straightened at the doorway, stepped into the room.

"She *wasn't* a *mark*," I repeated, louder, and knelt down at her side, placed a hand on her shoulder. But I kept my eyes on Erick. "She didn't deserve this!"

"What do you mean she wasn't a mark?" Bloodmark spat. His breath came in ragged gasps, deep and forceful.

"I mean that she didn't deserve this! That there was a mistake!"

Bloodmark snorted, turned to Erick. "That's the woman you sent us after, isn't it?"

Erick pulled his gaze away from mine, glanced down at the woman. He stared at her a long time, then said, "Yes."

"Then she deserved it," Bloodmark said. His breath had calmed, was no longer intense, no longer . . . excited. He shifted, wiped the blood from his blade. "Besides," he added, "she's the one that killed the man. She beat me to it, the bitch."

I shot a glance at Bloodmark.

"Shut up," I said, voice hard, vicious.

He glared at me, shifted his stance again. His eyes bled hatred.

"What? Don't you believe me?" He laughed, without humor. His eyes were dark.

I shifted uncomfortably.

"Oh, yes, she killed him," he said, voice softening. "I watched her do it. She moved from the fire and stood over him while he slept. If I'd known what she was going to do, maybe I would have stopped her, saved the mark for myself." He smiled, a slow smile, like Garrell's smile as he stared down at the girl playing with the green cloth. "She stood over him for a long time. A long, long time. She had the knife in her hand, turned it as she clutched it at her side. Then she knelt down and stabbed him in the throat."

"Shut up," I said again, but this time it didn't have as much force. I saw Mari in that last moment before I'd left, saw her squatting before the fire, staring at the knife.

Her voice had changed after Rec had used the knife to cut her cheek. It had hardened. Her eyes as well.

"I saw it," Bloodmark said, and his smile deepened. "I watched her do it."

"Shut up," Erick said flatly.

Bloodmark flinched, cast a glare in his direction.

Erick had moved while we spoke, so quietly I hadn't noticed. He now squatted, facing Bloodmark, his eyes intent.

"You watched," he said quietly, his voice deadly. It wasn't a question. "Why?"

Bloodmark's brow creased. "What do you mean?"

"Why *didn't* you stop her? Why *didn't* you act?"

"Because I didn't know she was going to stab the bastard. Besides, he was a mark. He deserved it."

"How do you know?"

Bloodmark grinned. "Because you sent us after him."

A stricken expression crossed Erick's face, a grimace of regret, as if he'd tasted something sour. But it cleared, there and then gone in a breath.

"No," he said, and shook his head. "I think you watched because you enjoyed it. I think you enjoy it far too much."

I straightened where I knelt at Mari's side. Hope flared up inside me, like fire.

Erick's gaze narrowed as he watched Bloodmark. I could see him thinking, could see it in his eyes, in the muscle that twitched at the back of his jaw as he clenched his teeth.

Then he shook his head once. "No. It's over. It's gone on long enough."

I almost barked a laugh, caught myself, held it tight.

Bloodmark stilled, and when he spoke, his voice was as low and dangerous as Erick's. "What do you mean?"

"I mean," Erick said slowly and with purpose, "that I'll give you no more marks."

Bloodmark's eyes narrowed. "You can't do that."

"Go back to the Dredge," Erick growled. "I should have sent you back long ago. Should never have brought you in on this in the first place, should have listened to Varis. You're too dangerous."

"They were marks! They deserved—"

Erick took one step, but Bloodmark was expecting it. He launched himself away so fast he seemed a blur. But he halted at the door, shot Erick a dark glare, me one filled with hatred and venom. And something more, something I didn't understand.

"Bitch," he spat.

And then he was gone.

Erick remained motionless, stared at me in mute apology. The flare of hope that had suffused me a moment earlier died, the stone of hatred and anger still burning beneath my breastbone.

I knelt over Mari, trembling, hand on her shoulder, looked into his eyes.

"You shouldn't have let him go," I said. "After what you saw him do. . . ."

"They were marks—"

"No!" I spat. "Don't tell me that! Don't—"

"They were marks!" And now his voice was hard, unforgiving. "No matter what you think, the Mistress said they were marks!"

I drew in a deep breath. "Mari was gray," I said. I ignored the look of confusion that crossed Erick's face, confusion that after a moment transformed into sudden understanding, as if he'd seen something for the first time, something that had been dangling in front of his face, that should have been obvious. I thought of what Bloodmark had said instead, that Mari had killed Rec. I knew what he'd said was true. I'd seen the intent before I left, in Mari's eyes, in her stance. But I hadn't recognized it, had refused to recognize it. "She was *gray*," I repeated. "She wasn't a mark."

"She killed him," Erick said, his voice grudging. "You heard Bloodmark. That makes her a mark."

"Does it?" I spat. "If that's all it takes, then I'm a mark as well."

Erick frowned. "What do you mean?"

"She killed Rec to save herself," I said harshly. "He's the one who sliced her up. He cut her while I was here, before I came to get you. He cut her because he enjoyed it." I shook my head. "Mari killed him to save herself, just as I killed the ex-guardsman to save myself, and the man with the garrote. Just as I killed the fat man to save you."

Erick drew in a sharp breath. Fear flashed across his eyes, and doubt.

But again he pushed the doubt back, forced down the fear. He shook his head, said in a tight voice, "It was Bloodmark's decision, just as previous marks have been your decision. He killed her, just as you killed Garrell."

I flinched, felt the dagger slide into Garrell's chest, felt myself step away. "No," I said, hardening my voice. "No. It's not the same. I *killed* Garrell. Bloodmark *murdered* Mari."

Erick glanced down at Mari's body, but said nothing. The fear shimmered in the back of his eyes, pushed back but not gone.

He knew what I said was true. But if he admitted it . . .

If he admitted it, then the Mistress was wrong, the Skewed Throne was wrong. And then everything that he'd believed in and trusted would be in doubt. No matter that the city had been slowly dying since the Fire, that the Mistress seemed incapable of doing anything to save it. No matter that what the Mistress *did* do only seemed to make matters worse. I knew the Dredge was dying. I saw it every day. I lived it. I saw what it had done to people like Mari, saw what it was still doing to people like her, and to me.

"You shouldn't have let Bloodmark go," I repeated, and then I turned to Mari, shut Erick out. It didn't matter now. It was done. Mari was already dead.

Erick held still a long moment, began to shift closer, but stopped himself.

In a strained voice, he said, "We need to mark her."

I felt the stone of hatred harden further. "No. Mark him, but not her."

Erick hesitated, then shifted away, toward Rec's body. He lifted the man's head, made three clean strokes, and then set Rec's head back down in the pool of blood that was already tacky, already darkening to rust.

I sat next to Mari as he worked. I heard her screaming, saw her in my mind, her body lax against Rec's body, shuddering as he drew the blade down her cheek. I saw her eyes—a light brown, lighter than I'd ever seen on the Dredge, with streaks of yellow—saw them flinch shut as Rec began to cut her. I heard her breath hiss between clenched teeth.

She had been gray.

I should have run faster.

I never should have left to find Erick in the first place.

Erick had finished, had come to stand beside me. He reached for my shoulder, but hesitated, not quite touching me. As if he were afraid to touch me.

His hand dropped.

And then the ice-rimmed hand slammed into my chest, so frigid I gasped. Its ice burned across my shoulders, burned up into my arms. It slammed into my chest with so much force I jerked backward in shock, stumbled where I knelt—

In the next breath, I choked on the smell of yeast, of dough and flour, the scent so strong it overpowered everything, overpowered the stench of fresh blood, of sickening sweat, of oily smoke.

"OH GODS," I choked, and tasted vomit. "Oh gods, oh gods, oh gods."

I suddenly understood the look on Bloodmark's face as he'd left. Hatred and anger, but mixed with self-satisfied content.

He knew how to hurt me.

"What is it?" Erick barked, stepping forward. His eyes were wide with fear. But he was moving too slow.

I turned from him, lurched up into a crouch and launched toward the door, stumbling with the weight of the smell of yeast, with the weight of the ice-rimmed hand burning through my chest. I gasped as I hit the edge of the doorway with my shoulder, then caught myself and ran.

Ran through the outer room, through the room with the shattered clay tiles, out into the narrows, into the depths beyond the

Dredge, the depths that had swallowed me as easily as they had swallowed Mari. I ran through the niches, through the abandoned courtyards, through the alcoves and doorways and gaping windows and half collapsed walls, so fast Erick could not possibly follow. I ran through my home, catching glimpses of the other animals of the Dredge. The startled face of a man, no more than skin laid over bones, huddled over a heap of rotten garbage. The rag woman, who cackled as I veered past, her heated laughter echoing down the alley. The boy, no more than seven, who held a broken spoon like a weapon, who clutched a pitted apple in one hand, one side already rotten, already brown and writhing with maggots. I ran, gasping in the frigid night air, muscles burning in my legs. I ran for the white-dusty man's door.

The ice-rimmed hand blazed deeper, tingling now in my hands. The stone of hatred grew harder beneath my breast, grew larger, until it choked me, lodged at the base of my throat. The scent of yeast, of dough, of heat and flour, burned in my nostrils, burned on my tongue, tasting of bread, of rolls, of cheese—

And then the scent flared, so strong I gasped at the intensity, so real saliva filled my mouth, coated my tongue—

And then it died.

I staggered to a halt, cried out to the sky. A raw, unintelligible wail that drew from deep inside. A wail of pure anguish, that sucked everything from me, that sucked the strength from my legs, from my arms, from my chest.

I gasped, collapsed into the nearest wall, hit it hard with my shoulder, scraped down its mud-brick side until I lay huddled in a ball at its base, arms wrapped around my legs, face drawn tight to my knees. I cried—harsh racking sobs that tore in my chest, that filled my mouth with the taste of phlegm, that sent my blood pounding through my forehead, pulsing in my ears. I choked, not able to draw in enough breath, not *wanting* to draw in another breath. I felt a gaping hollowness fill me, a horrible emptiness that claimed everything inside me, everything in my chest, in my arms, in my legs. A hollowness that left me fragile, vulnerable, and utterly alone, that left me abandoned.

A hollowness that crushed me.

And I suddenly understood the look on the woman's face when I had handed her the dead girl. I suddenly understood that pain.

The thought brought my head up, stilled the sobs.

I'd killed Garrell. A sharp thrust to his chest, near the heart.

My eyes narrowed. The stone of hatred beneath my breastbone pulsed, its hardness seeping outward, stilling the tremors of weakness, stilling the liquid sensation in my lungs from the tears, filling the hollowness.

But it didn't touch the frigid burn of the hand pressing against my chest.

I stood, uncoiled from the tight crouch. My dagger was already drawn, already held loosely in one hand.

I had a new mark.

I slid forward, moving swiftly, but no longer at a dead run. Every muscle was tense, every sense alert. I bled from shadow to shadow, everything I'd learned of stealth and silence on the Dredge, everything I'd learned from Dove and his street gang of thugs, everything I'd learned from Erick coming forth.

Ten minutes later I slipped into a crouch opposite the white-dusty man's door. It was cracked open, oil light seeping out.

The ice-rimmed hand still burned on my chest, still tingled in my arms. But it had faded, the edge of intensity dulled.

I glanced down the Dredge in both directions, saw no one.

I moved across the street, slow and quiet, and settled next to the white-dusty man's door. Reaching out, I pushed it open farther. It creaked as it slowed to a halt.

A wash of heat pushed outward, with a scent of yeast, of dough, and of blood.

Something clawed at my throat, acidic and vicious, but I pushed it down, crushed it with the stone in my chest.

Through the door, I could see the opening of an oven, the flames licking upward inside. An oil lamp hung from the ceiling, over a long table, a few chairs. On the table I could see lumps of rising dough, a pitcher of milk, a bag of flour. Another bag of flour lay split on the floor, a white fan against the fieldstone. Tracks marred the whiteness. Farther into the room, beyond the table, the long paddle I'd seen the black-haired woman holding when I'd been here last lay on the stone as well, the loaf of freshly baked bread it had once held lying on its side nearby.

And at the edge of the door, just within sight, I could see a hand, palm up, fingers slightly curled. A woman's hand.

I swallowed, felt tears burning the edges of my eyes. I moved through the door in one quick step, crouched low. I ignored the two bodies—forced myself to ignore them—scanned the room, found it empty. I slid to the only doorway, moved into the darknesses beyond, checked the inner rooms.

Bloodmark wasn't here.

I returned to the outer room and knelt down beside the white-dusty man. I brushed at the hair on his forehead, hair lightly dusted with gray, with flour. I let my fingers trail down his cheek, stopped at his jaw. I looked into his eyes, saw them soften there on the Dredge, saw them soften here in the alcove of his door, heard him say, *You've grown.*

I cupped his face with my hands, leaned forward over him, till my forehead touched his.

Then I sat back.

Bloodmark had stabbed him in the chest, had stabbed the black-haired woman as well. But on the white-dusty man's chest he had carved a parody of the Skewed Throne—three long, deep slashes.

I stared at the bloody gashes, felt myself harden further.

I stood, moved into the back rooms, returned with two blankets. I covered the black-haired woman first, then the white-dusty man.

Then I slid back out into the night, closing the door behind me. Standing in the alcove of the white-dusty man's doorway, I looked up into the sky, gazed at the stars and moon a long moment, saw them as I'd seen them the night of the White Fire—clear and vibrant and pure. And I felt the Fire inside me, burning with its cold flame beneath the frigid imprint of the hand on my chest. I felt it seeping through me, not fiery and seething, but slow and gentle.

It filled me with a preternatural calm, as it had that night so many years before.

I glanced back down to the darkness of the Dredge. I straightened, narrowed my eyes at the depths.

And then I slid beneath the river. Deep. Deeper. Until I could feel the pull of the ice-rimmed hand, until I could scent it—like hoarfrost, burning in my nostrils, metallic against my tongue.

I drew away from the white-dusty man's door, slid into an alley—

And submerged myself in the depths.

I followed the scent, the river smooth around me. I flowed from alley to alley, from courtyard to courtyard, through twisted iron gates, past crumbling statues. I moved through abandoned buildings, their insides gutted, their walls collapsed. I saw the gray shadows of people huddled in corners, so many more people now than before the Fire. As I crossed one narrow, I heard a low growl, glanced down its short length and saw a dog, its teeth bared, lips peeled back, saliva dripping from its mouth. Its eyes were feral beneath the river, black and haunted. Snot coated its muzzle, and blood bled from its eyes. Its hindquarters had collapsed, gone numb with disease, and it lay in its own shit and piss, unable to move.

I paused, stared into the low, ominous rumble of its growl.

Then I moved on.

The scent grew, and with it the frost of the hand against my chest. And as I closed in, moving slowly, cautiously, I realized where I'd find Bloodmark. The realization came with a hard twist in my stomach. But at the same time I think I'd known. Part of me had hoped, had thought there would be a refuge, a safe place, a home—

But he'd taken everything else.

A tension fell away from me, a tightness in my shoulders. I moved forward purposefully now, without seeing the depths of the Dredge.

Until I came to my niche.

I paused outside the entrance, knelt down a few paces away to stare into the narrow darkness.

The scent of hoarfrost was strong, overpowering. It rolled from the entrance to the niche like the heat had rolled from the white-dusty man's door, but cold instead. The ice-rimmed hand against my chest burned so harshly it felt as if my skin would freeze, would peel away in chunks.

The sensations were so intense, I never felt Bloodmark approach.

I sensed the kick a moment before it struck, tensed for the blow as I'd done a thousand times on the Dredge, ready to absorb it and flee to a safer darkness.

But this time I wouldn't run.

Bloodmark's foot dug in just beneath my ribs, forced itself up into my stomach with enough strength that it lifted me, flung me to the side, twisted me onto my back. The air was thrust from my lungs, but before I could suck in another breath, Bloodmark stomped onto my chest, his heel landing squarely on the ice-rimmed hand.

I doubled over, curled up tight over the sudden, vicious pain, rolled onto my side, coughed against the burning in my lungs.

I lost my hold on the river.

The instant the darkness of true night closed around me, I felt the backlash of nausea begin in the pit of my stomach, felt the tremors of weakness begin to course down the muscles of my arms.

My eyes flew wide in fear.

"Bitch," Bloodmark said.

I struggled to rise, heard Bloodmark's footsteps as he moved around behind me. The tremors shuddered through my shoulders now, through my legs.

I focused on Bloodmark, on the sounds of his movements, on the pain in my gut, in my chest. I focused on breathing, each intake painful.

"You ruined everything!" Bloodmark spat, punctuating it with another kick, this time to my lower back.

Fresh pain sheeted up my side and I jerked out of the protective curl, rolled onto my back again, then over onto the other side with a barked cry, my arms tucked close to my chest.

But the pain pushed the tremors back.

Bloodmark moved in close, squatted down beside me.

"Did you find them?" he asked quietly, then laughed. "I left them for you. And for Erick." His voice turned bitter. "He was my ticket into the Guard."

"They would never have taken you," I gasped, the words broken, breathless.

"Why not?"

I shifted, enough so I could look up into Bloodmark's eyes, so dark and vicious, enough to free the arm tucked closest to the ground.

"Because," I muttered, so softly Bloodmark leaned down closer to hear, leaned close enough I could see the black smear of the birthmark next to his eye. I smiled—a slow, satisfied smile. "Because you're gutterscum. Just like me."

I shoved my dagger up along his neck, drawing a thin line beneath his chin before the blade punched up under his jawbone. Blood splashed my hand, hot and slick, and then Bloodmark jerked back, a strange, gurgling croak coming from his open mouth. The dagger slid free, followed by another wash of blood, and Bloodmark's hand clamped to his throat, to his jaw. He staggered backward, struck the mud-brick of the collapsing wall beside my niche, and skidded down it until he sat against the heels of his feet.

My hand, the one that held the dagger, slumped to the ground. Tremors were rippling through me now and I could no longer hold it up. I let my head rest against the dirt-smeared cobblestones of the narrow, let the tension in my shoulders release, but I didn't take my eyes off Bloodmark.

He stared at me with horrified, hate-filled eyes. His jaw worked as he tried to speak, but nothing came out except a sickening wheeze of air and a speckle of blood. Blood coated the hand clutched to his throat as well.

I thought of the first man I'd killed, of his hand clutching the cut across his own throat. I thought of the White Fire.

Bloodmark's eyes widened and his body began to slip. The hand at his throat fell away. As it did he lost his balance.

He slumped to one side, falling across the opening to my niche, his body landing with a low, rustling thud.

His blood-soaked hand flopped out toward me, as if he were reaching for me.

I stared into his dead eyes and then the tremors took me.

The world faded, and I closed my eyes. I felt the spasms shudder through my body, felt the pain from Bloodmark's kicks pierce through my chest, but it was all distant, removed. I drew myself away, too exhausted for anything to matter, too beaten down to care. I thought of nothing, simply stared into the darkness behind my eyes and waited.

It took longer than I expected. I'd stayed beneath the river far longer than I ever had before, had pushed myself harder than I ever had before.

When the worst of the spasms finally passed, I rolled onto my stomach and pushed myself up onto my hands and knees, thinking of Mari, of Erick. *You heard Bloodmark. She killed him. That makes her a mark.* Nausea rippled through me and I vomited onto the cobbles. Hanging my head, I waited for this to pass as well, then climbed weakly to my feet.

It was still night, still dark. But dawn had begun to touch the eastern sky.

I stood over Bloodmark, wavering slightly, still weak.

He'd stolen everything from me.

Erick.

The white-dusty man.

My niche.

He'd taken it all.

And I'd killed him for it. Murdered him.

I turned and stared up into the night sky, thought of the Mistress, of the Skewed Throne . . . of Erick.

A searing pain slid through me, as thin as a dagger's slice, but deeper. Tears stung the corners of my eyes and I pressed my lips together hard, felt them tremble.

I could never go back to Erick now, could never look him in the eye, could never face his disappointment. Not after Bloodmark. I hadn't killed him to save myself, or Erick, or anyone else. I'd killed him because I'd wanted to. Because he'd deserved it, whether the Mistress knew that or not.

Erick would never understand that. Not if he thought Mari was a mark. Not if he couldn't see that she wasn't, even after she'd killed Rec.

There was nothing left for me here. Nothing at all.

So I turned and left the Dredge, moved toward the only other place I knew.

To the bridge leading across the River.

To Amenkor.

The real Amenkor.

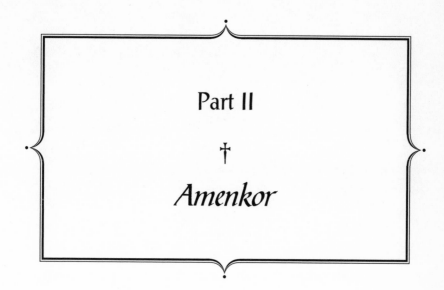

Part II

†

Amenkor

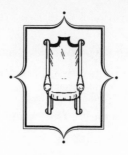

Chapter 7

A MENKOR.

The real Amenkor.

I stumbled to my knees in the half-light of dawn and vomited into the corner at the base of a stone-brick wall. My stomach cramped and I heaved again, muscles tightening in pain, but nothing came. There was nothing left in my stomach. Nothing but a horrible sickness.

When the spasms ended, I spat and crawled along the length of the alley to a barrel set near its end. I hunched back against the barrel, arms tight across my chest, as shudders ran through me. Reaction to the use of the river had never been this bad. But then, I'd never used it so heavily before, never kept myself submerged for so long. I'd never needed to use it so heavily.

I shuddered again, this time because of the image of Bloodmark choking on his own blood, and the sight of the Skewed Throne carved into the white-dusty man's chest.

I pulled myself hard against the barrel, eyes squeezed tight. I had no defense against the pain. The river, the run to Amenkor along the Dredge, the tension of waiting for the right moment to slip past the guards and cross the bridge and the real River, they'd all taken their toll. There was only weariness, an exhaustion that had settled into my muscles, into my bones. A weariness that dragged at me like a relentless tide.

I leaned my head against the stone-brick wall deep inside Amenkor and let the tide claim me.

†

A whip cracked, the snap startling me awake with a lurch.

"Hee-ah!" someone cried, and the clatter of hooves and wheels on cobbles receded.

I blinked into raw sunlight, eyes blurred, then shifted.

A boy stood before me.

I froze, muscles tensing.

The boy—no more than six years old, dressed in hand-stitched, fitted breeches, a vest, a white shirt; clothing far too fine for the slums or the Dredge—watched me with intent brown eyes. His hands were clutched behind his back, and he rocked back and forth, onto his heels and then his toes. A strange flattened hat covered shiny blond hair.

"Who are you?" he asked in a clear, precise voice. There was no malice, no fear in his round face. Nothing but curiosity.

I drew breath, my chest, my *lungs*, burning with the effort. But before I could answer—not even knowing what I would say—a woman stepped into view.

"Perci, what in the White Heavens are you— Oh!" The woman gasped, stepped back unconsciously, one hand reaching for Perci, the other reaching for the clasp on the dress near her throat. Her shocked face quickly hardened into something I knew, something I recognized:

Disdain tainted with fear. Mostly disdain.

My eyes narrowed, jaw clenching. My hand slid to the dagger tucked at my side. She wore a blue-dyed dress, fitted at the waist, with sleeves reaching to her wrists. Sandals with many straps covered washed feet. Simple clothes, not as fancy as Perci's. But there were no stains, no ragged edges, no wear marks. The clothes looked fresh, like puddles of water immediately after a storm, before scum slicked the surface.

My gaze returned to her eyes.

Some of the disdain slipped away, the fear edging forward.

"Come, Perci." The hand on Perci's shoulder tightened and she began to draw him toward the mouth of the alley, toward the bright sunlight.

Perci resisted, his face squeezing into a frown of defiance, but when the woman's hand tightened further, he let himself be dragged away. I slid into a crouch behind the barrel as they moved, relaxing only when they'd vanished into the flow of people at the edge of the alley.

The people.

My hand tightened on the dagger and I drew farther back behind the barrel. A fresh wave of nausea swept through me, more fear and dread than sickness from the use of the river.

On the street, men and women moved among carts pulled by horses. Most carried satchels and small bundles tied with twine. A few carried baskets, bread sticking out of raised lids. All wore unstained clothing in strange, bright colors—blues, dark reds, a width of bright yellow. The men wore breeches, boots, white shirts, vests, wide belts with pouches openly displayed. The women wore dresses with long sleeves and sandals, long hair tied back with thin leather straps, some with hats or folded scarves over their hair. They moved without rushing, with heads high, eyes forward. Tall.

They moved without fear.

A pair of black horses clattered into view, tied to . . . a cart. Except it wasn't a cart. It was a little enclosed room, a small door in its side. Through the window cut into the door, I could see a man with a thin, angular face.

When he turned toward me, I ducked behind the barrel.

The sight of the horse-drawn room, of the clothes, of the *colors*, felt like a kick to the gut. What had I done? This was not the Dredge. This was Amenkor. The real Amenkor. I didn't belong here, didn't know the streets, the alleys, or narrows. I didn't know the people, their patterns and reactions. They didn't dress the same, didn't even seem to move the same, the ebb and flow of the street subtly different, more sedate, less frantic.

A strong urge to retreat seized me, clamped onto my throat and held on tight. Run, flee, cower in the nether regions of the Dredge.

But as soon as the urge took hold, it was crushed by despair.

I couldn't go back to the slums. Not now. Not ever. Erick would be looking for me. The first place he'd look would be my niche.

Where he'd find Bloodmark. Erick would know that I'd killed him.

Guilt stabbed hard into my stomach. And shame as I imagined Erick kneeling over Bloodmark's body, checking out the wound, scanning the body for marks. But he wouldn't need confirmation of who had driven the dagger into Bloodmark's neck. He'd know as soon as he saw the body.

No, I couldn't go back to the slums. I'd killed so many for Erick, for the Mistress, but Bloodmark had been different. I'd killed him for myself. For the white-dusty man and his wife.

But mostly for myself.

I drew in two long, deep breaths to steady myself, felt the shame fade, replaced with regret. Not regret that I'd killed Bloodmark, but that somehow in the process I'd lost Erick as well.

I suddenly thought of that last vision of Erick at Cobbler's Fountain, of seeing him for the first time beneath the river, his essence a strange mixture of gray and red. No one had ever appeared both colors before. Those that were harmless or presented no immediate danger were always gray; those that weren't were red.

So what did the mixture mean? Could Erick somehow be both? Harmless and dangerous at the same time?

Or was it not that simple?

I thought about Erick outside the iron gate, stalking Jobriah, the first mark I'd led him to. He'd been dangerous that day, enough that I'd shied away from him. I'd seen that same black look in his eyes many times since then. And every time I'd shuddered, pulled back and away.

But I could still feel his arms around me as he held me and I told him about the ex-guardsman trying to rape me, of how I'd stolen the dagger and killed the bastard as the White Fire swept through the city. I'd settled closer to Erick then, had been comforted by him.

Was it possible for someone to be both?

I shook myself, thrust the unanswered questions away. Harmless or dangerous, red or gray, it didn't matter anymore. Erick was gone, lost, stolen from me. Just like the Dredge.

I shifted forward, stared down the length of the alley to the bustle of the street, to the ebb and flow of strangers in fine clothing and clean skin.

Who are you? Perci had asked.

I glanced down at my hands. Bloodmark's blood had dried into the creases of the palm, had caked between my fingers. I closed my hands into fists and felt flakes fall away, felt the dried blood like grit between my skin.

"I'm gutterscum," I murmured to myself.

The sensation of having been kicked hard remained, deep inside, the ache like a stone in my gut. I drew in a deep breath through my nose, snorted back snot and phlegm and swallowed it, coughing slightly.

I couldn't return to the slums, but I couldn't remain here either. I was too different. I'd be noticed the instant I entered the street. I needed to get cleaned up, wash the slums from my face, from my clothes.

I stood, slowly, with effort, feeling aches throughout my body, but mostly in my chest and stomach from where Bloodmark had kicked me. Back pressed against the stone-brick wall for support, I lifted my dirt-, blood-, and vomit-smeared shirt. A livid bruise in the shape of a foot lay in the center of my chest, black and purplish-blue, edged in a horrid yellow. Another bruise rose along my side.

I saw Bloodmark's foot stomping down out of the night, winced as I dropped the shirt back into place. I glanced down the alley again in both directions, frowned.

Something else was different here. Something I'd noticed the night I'd followed Erick to the bridge. Something that reinforced the fact that I was no longer on the Dredge with more power than the people on the street, or their clothes, or the strange room on wheels.

The alley had *edges,* seemed somehow more defined, more *there.* There were sharp corners at its mouth, clear recesses for windows, for doors, and none of the windows were boarded up. The cobbles that covered the ground were mostly intact; the path for the runnel of water down its center mostly straight.

Beyond the Dredge, the alleys and narrows were worn, rounded, *used.* The shit and piss and lichen that stained the stone and mud-brick was permanent. The slush of rotten garbage that slicked the niches, collected in the crevices and corners, only shifted. It was never removed.

And on the Dredge, there were no barrels. None completely intact anyway.

I turned to the barrel, leaned down over its opening. It was just over half full of rainwater. I stared down at the ripples on the water, at the face reflected there.

The hair was flat, slicked with mud, matted with splatters of blood. It hung in thin tendrils, like rat tails, shorn short and uneven, nothing reaching farther than the chin. It framed a thin face, mouth pressed tight into a thin line, most of the skin smudged with more dirt, more blood, all dried and flaked like the blood on my hands. What skin wasn't covered with grit—with the Dredge—was sallow, almost gray. And the eyes . . .

I flinched.

The eyes were hollow, wasted, crusted with dried tears. And in the muddy depths—

I stood a long moment, looked deep into the water, into those eyes.

Then I plunged my hands down into the water and scrubbed the blood away, scrubbed until my skin felt raw, until my ragged fingernails left marks. Then, before the water could settle and the reflection could return, I dipped my head into the barrel.

Water closed over my face and I shut my eyes, remembering Cobbler's Fountain, feeling again the terror of that six-year-old girl as she tripped, as the water enveloped her, closed up and over her head. . . .

I jerked out of the rain barrel, water streaming from my hair, down my face. I gasped, sputtered, but scrubbed at my skin and pulled at my hair before dipping back down into the barrel again to wash away the grime, resurfacing with another choked gasp.

"Where did you see this woman?"

The voice filtered out of the general noise of the street. I turned, hair still dripping water. I scanned the alley and realized one more thing that made the real Amenkor different from the Dredge.

The alleys had fewer darknesses, fewer hiding places. Windows and doors actually existed, were not simply empty openings leading to deeper darknesses. I had few places to escape to here.

"Down that alley," a woman said. I glanced back to the street and saw her—the woman who'd dragged Perci away. She stood with Perci, nodding toward the alley. A guardsman, dressed like Erick, but with finer clothing, more armor, and a sword instead of a dagger, followed the direction of her nod.

"And you say she had blood on her hands?" the guard asked. His voice sounded dubious.

"Yes. And on her face and clothes. And I think she had a knife."

The guard grunted and began moving toward the alley.

I turned and moved into its depths, moved without conscious thought. I didn't know where I was going, but I knew I couldn't stay here any longer. I'd have to finish cleaning up somewhere else.

†

The first time I tried to use the river after killing Bloodmark, a spike of pain slashed into my head behind my eyes and my stomach clenched so hard I collapsed to the ground at the mouth of the alley where I stood. I lay curled where I'd fallen, drawing in breaths in huge gasps. Panic smothered me as the pain escalated, the spike driving deeper, harder, turning white-hot.

I'd never had pain like this. Not *days* after my last use of the river. Especially not after the nausea and weakness had receded.

And then a horrifying thought surfaced, stilled my gasping breath with a twinge of pain in my lungs.

What if I couldn't use the river anymore at all? What if somehow in my push to find Bloodmark I'd overextended myself, burned myself out?

The thought shoved everything away, crushed everything but the spike of pain behind my eyes and a hollow sound in my ears. It left me stunned.

I couldn't survive without the river.

Someone touched me, a gentle hand on my shoulder.

I jerked back with a gasp, struck the wall of the alley.

"Are you all right?"

I could barely see the woman who knelt beside me, her hands lying cupped on her knees. A strange field of yellow, like a film of scum over water, covered my vision, pulsing with the pulse of the spike. Jagged little streaks, like flares of lightning, ran through the field of yellow.

"I'm . . . fine," I gasped, too frightened of what was happening in my head to really respond, to think.

The woman sat back slightly, her dress rustling, the sound unnaturally loud. "You don't look fine." Her voice seemed dull, faded, and seemed to come from much farther away.

I tried to focus through the field of yellow, pushed myself up onto my hands. The pulsing lightning began to recede. "I'm fine," I said with more force.

The woman frowned doubtfully and glanced back toward the street. Her dress was a plain brown, but still clean. Her long, light-brown hair was tied back with a simple green ribbon, pulled away from her round face. And she wore an earring in one ear—gold with a bluish-green iridescent bead.

It reminded me strangely of water.

Across the street, a man and two older boys were unloading sacks of potatoes from a wagon, tossing a heavy bag over each shoulder before toting them through a wide door into the building beyond. One sack had split while being hefted, spilling a few potatoes to the ground. The sack itself had been set to one side at the back of the wagon.

When she turned back, the woman with the iridescent earring scrutinized me through narrowed eyes. Her frown had deepened. Her gaze flicked to my clothes, to my hair.

Neither was splattered with blood now. After eluding the guardsman in the backstreets, I'd gone down to Amenkor's River, washed everything as clean as I could make it. On the Dredge, the clothes Erick had given me had seemed clean, almost too nice to be worn. But at the edge of the River, at the bottom of the stone steps that led down to its walled-in banks, I'd seen the stains, the tattered edges, the small tears.

I felt those tears, those stains, now, under the scrutiny of the woman. Tight anger burned in my chest and I pushed myself back onto my heels.

"I said I'm fine," I repeated, harshly.

Her brow creased. Then she stood and said, "Very well."

I flinched at the slight coldness in her voice, the remoteness.

She moved away, stepped back into the street, but paused when she saw the wagon again, the potatoes. The last of the sacks had been toted into the building and the older of the two boys was holding the split sack while the younger collected the dropped potatoes from the street. They cinched the sack closed as best they could and hauled it inside the building as well.

The woman turned back. "Perhaps . . ." She hesitated, seemed to reconsider, then added in a rush, "Perhaps you should try the marketplace. Or the wharf. You might have better luck there, on the docks."

Then she cut across the street, pausing only long enough to let a man on a horse pass.

I watched where she had vanished for a long moment, feeling a dull ache in my chest, for a brief moment smelling yeast, feeling a brush of oven heat against my face.

But I pushed the ache down, smothered the scents. The spiking pain had dropped down to a throbbing stab and my vision had begun to clear. I still felt weak, but even that was fading.

I stood carefully, then scanned the street.

People moved from shop to shop, building to building. They paused to talk, to laugh. Bells jangled as someone entered a narrow door in the building beside me. The smell of tallow drifted out. But not the harsh, oily tallow of the Dredge. This tallow was mixed with strange scents, wild foreign scents that prickled the inside of my nose. Across the street, another door opened and a roar of laughter escaped into the street, the man who had left waving to the others inside.

I'd have no luck hunting here. The closest I'd come in the last two days had been the split sack of potatoes, and even that would have been risky. That's why I'd tried to use the river. But this wasn't the Dredge. The people might not be wary, but they had nothing to fear. There were too few of them, nothing like the crowds on the Dredge. There were no places for me to blend into, no niches to hide in.

And then there were the guards.

I stepped deeper into the alley as two appeared on horseback. Like the guard the other day, these two were dressed like Erick, but cleaner. Edged, like the alleys. They held themselves stiff and straight, and their eyes . . .

As they passed, the closest guard's gaze fell on me. His eyes were like Erick's as well, but the danger, the darkness that I'd seen hidden in Erick's gaze was blunt and blatant. And arrogant.

The guard's eyes narrowed, as if it had finally registered that he'd seen something out of place, something wrong.

The two passed beyond the entrance to the alley.

I didn't wait for them to return. I moved back into the depths and began to work my way toward Amenkor's River. I'd stayed near the water the last few nights. Because the riverbank wasn't as active as the inner streets, it provided a few more places to hide. And because I could see the slums on the far side, the familiar sight was comforting. But the woman was right. I couldn't continue hunting in this area, especially if I couldn't use the river.

I halted, bit my lower lip, then tentatively tried to push myself beneath the surface. For a moment, the world grayed, noises receded to wind. But the sense was distorted, watery and indistinct.

And then the spike of pain returned, slicing down through my temple. Weakness shot through my legs.

I shoved the river away before the pain increased, sighed in relief as the searing spike began to recede.

When my legs felt stable again, I continued. I didn't know where the marketplace was, but the wharf. . . .

I'd seen it from the rooftops, seen it the night the ex-guardsman had caught me and dragged me there to rape me. I remembered the White Fire as it sped through the harbor, so cold and silent, remembered how it had engulfed the ships, the docks, before surging up onto the land. All I had to do was follow the River down to the sea.

I shivered, felt the Fire stir inside me.

I tensed, half expected the spiked headache to return and the nausea, but the cold flame of the Fire drifted away. Apparently, it wasn't affected by the use of the river.

My stomach growled.

I picked up my pace. I'd have better luck at the docks.

†

I knelt between two crates behind a pile of tangled netting on the wharf and watched a ship with three masts bump hard into the long wooden dock. A man shouted, voice hard and vicious against the slap of the waves, and men scurried as ties were thrown over the edge of the boat. The dock groaned as the ship drifted away, and then a plank slapped down and more men began unloading cargo, crate after crate hauled down to the dock. Some of the men unloading crates had dark skin—darker than could be attributed to exposure to the sun—their faces flatter and wider, bodies shorter, more compact. All of the darker-skinned men had straight black hair, cut to the nape of the neck. Most had tattoos on their faces and down their necks.

Zorelli. Men from the far south.

I eased forward, hoping for a better look.

It was chaos, men on the ship, men on the dock, the man barking orders left and right, motioning with an arm toward the wharf, toward the ship, arguing with another man who came down the plank as if he owned it. The man coming down the plank glared at the one shouting orders, then gave a curt command. The other man turned back to the boat, bellowing more fiercely than before, cursing, pissed off, taking it out on the crew.

The captain stepped off the plank, dipped his head toward another man waiting on the pier. Both wore fine breeches, heavy boots, shirts with unnecessary ruffles near the throat, and long jackets that came down to their knees. The man on the dock had a dark-red jacket, like blood, with gold threading in strange patterns down the arms and near the cuffs. He was mostly bald, a fringe of dark hair with shots of gray surrounding his head like brown stone around a fountain. He wore rounded wire on his face, with hooks that went around his ears. Every now and then, when he turned, sunlight would glint off his eyes, as if it were reflecting off water, only this reflection appeared flat and rounded.

The captain of the ship wore dark green, with less gold threading, but with more hair and no wires on his face.

As I watched, the captain and the man in the red jacket began arguing. When the argument ended, the captain of the ship stormed back up the plank, the man with the wires on his face watching him go.

Then the man with the wires on his face began moving down the dock toward me, his eyes narrowed in anger. Another man— younger, paler—fell in beside him, dressed similarly but without the horrible jacket.

"What's the matter, Master Borund? What did the captain say?"

The bald man growled. "He said he didn't have the entire shipment. Said the cloth from Verano is missing and the Marland spice couldn't be found. Someone in the city bought it all up before he could get any." He cursed, then drew in a deep breath to steady himself as the two passed by the crates. I'd sprawled back, head down as if asleep, but I needn't have bothered. They were too intent on their conversation to notice me. "This city is going to pieces, William. And neither Avrell nor the Mistress is doing anything about it. . . ."

Their voices receded.

I lifted my head to see if they were far enough away, then shifted forward and watched them merge with the crowd on the wharf, vanishing among the hawkers and dockworkers, the stench of seawater and fish. Then I turned back to the ship.

There was nothing on the ship for me, nothing I could steal. I'd already determined that. But I didn't leave. The ships in the harbor intrigued me. I watched the men unload the crates, watched the ropes and pulleys on the masts sag and dip in the wind. Waves slapped against the ship's sides, and now and then it bumped up against the dock where it was secured. Men shouted and cursed and spat and laughed. White-gray birds shrieked, dove for the water, for the men, before settling on the dock supports and flapping their wings. Someone dropped a crate and with a wrench and crack of wood it split, sending some type of brown, hairy, rounded fruit rolling along the dock.

I leaned forward, possibilities leaping upward in my chest, but forced myself to settle back.

I couldn't risk it. Not without the river. I'd learned that the first few days on the wharf. I could still feel the hawker's hand latching onto my wrist and jerking me around the first time I'd tried.

Where do you think you're going with that? he'd spat, his voice somehow greasy.

I leaned back against the crates, brought up a hand to wipe at where I could still feel the spit on my face. I'd said nothing, too shocked that I'd been caught to speak.

I'd never been caught on the Dredge. Not since I'd figured out how to combine the river with what Dove and his street gang had taught me. And especially not after the Fire.

But here I had to be more careful, had to take fewer risks. All because every time I tried to use the river that spike of pain returned. I couldn't tell if it was lessening as the days passed; it was still too sharp. So sharp that I hadn't tried to use the river at all in the last two days.

I pushed the nagging worry back, continued to watch the last of the crates being unloaded. The strange hairy fruit was being repacked.

I sighed and turned back to the wharf. I couldn't risk taking anything directly from the docks, where escape routes were restricted, but the wharf. . . .

I slid from my place among the crates and netting and merged with the crowd.

I spent the rest of the day on the wharf, shifting from place to place, watching the hawkers, watching the dockworkers, eyes sharp for the misplaced fishhead, the unwatched crust of bread. The crowds were slightly different here than on the Dredge. The majority of the people were the same—pale skin, darker hair in shades of brown and black, darker eyes as well—but there were more strangers on the wharf. Men with beads braided in their beards; women with feathers in their hair. Others wore cloth draped over them, secured with intricate folds and tucks, rather than being tailored. I saw a few with the blue paint smudge of the Tear of Taniece near the corner of their eye.

The streets and alleys just beyond the wharf were almost like the Dredge as well. The alleys were lined with bundles of netting and meshed crab traps with dried seaweed stuck to them, rather than heaps of broken stone and crumbling mud-brick. The stench: salt and dead fish, rather than shit and stagnant water. I'd even managed to find a new niche—the end of an alley, where crab traps had been piled high, covered over with a stretch of tanned hide against the rain. I'd forced a hole in the center, pulled traps out from inside, until I could squeeze into the narrow opening and move around beneath the tanned hide. It was much closer to the Dredge than the upper city, where I'd been before, where I'd woken to find Perci staring down at me.

I glanced away from the wharf, up past the buildings immediately next to the water to the slope of the hill behind. The roofs thinned as my gaze swept higher, the buildings larger, more ornate and isolated. At the top of the hill I could see three circular walls, the white stone of the palace gleaming in the sun in their center.

In the upper city, there were almost no foreigners, and almost no smells at all. At least nothing that stung the nose or made my eyes water.

My gaze dropped back to the wharf and I breathed in the stench of fish again.

A man cursed and the thud of a dropped bundle hitting the wood of the wharf drew me out of my daze. Night was beginning to settle, and clouds had begun to drift in from the sea.

It would rain tonight.

The man squatted down, began gathering up what had spilled from his bundle, the flow of the crowd parting around him. A few items had rolled. A flat package tied with twine slid against a dock support jutting up from the planking and the undulating water below.

For a moment, I tensed, ready to slip beneath the river, but stopped myself with a shudder, remembering the spiked headache.

I settled back against the alley wall and watched as the man grunted, reaching for a cylindrical package that had rolled farther away than the rest. Only the flat item that had slid to the support remained.

But the man stood abruptly, tossed the cylindrical package into the bundle, then swung it up over his shoulder and joined the crowd.

I stared in shock at the rectangular package he'd left behind.

Then, with a swift glance left and right, I shoved through the people to the dock support and snatched the package up.

Without opening it, I headed back to my niche, pushing through the crowd. Once in the back alleys, I slowed, relaxed, my arms tingling.

All I wanted was my niche.

I slipped down an empty street, toward an alley. Night had fallen completely now, and the first drizzle of rain began to fall. I'd almost reached the end of the alley, my hands still clutching the package, when someone stepped into my path.

I froze, water beginning to drip from the hair hanging before my face. Through the tangles, I could see the man's grin, could see he wore finer clothes than the dockworkers, than the hawkers. Breeches without stains, a leather belt with a dagger tucked into it, a dark shirt, a cloak against the rain.

"What have we here?" he murmured, and like the hawker that had grabbed my arm days before, his voice sounded greasy.

I took a step back, one hand dropping from the package to the dagger hidden beneath my shirt.

The man's grin widened, and even before I saw his eyes focus on something behind me, I heard a sound.

A footfall.

I spun, dagger half drawn—

And a fist crashed down against my face, striking hard along my jaw, so hard I stumbled backward, fell into a clutter of netting resting against a crate. My free hand groped at empty air, my head resting against the crate, a sudden dull roar filling my ears. I'd lost the package, but not my dagger. It was caught in my shirt, still hidden.

My hand found the edge of the crate and the disorientation vanished. Blinking against the rain, against the darkness, I shifted forward, dragged myself into a crouch.

Through the roar in my ears, I heard someone laugh, the sound dull and empty.

Anger flared, frigid and tinged with Fire.

I lowered my head, spat blood onto the rain-slicked cobbles of the alley—

And felt myself slip into the river. Smoothly, cleanly. Like a knife into flesh.

And without any pain. No spiked headache. No nausea.

I almost cried out in joy, hope and relief surging upward into my throat, but I choked it down.

"Come on, Cristoph," someone said. The second man. The one who'd struck me. "Take whatever she's got. It's not safe here."

"Shut up. It's perfectly safe here. No one will see a thing. Besides, this won't take long."

I lifted my head. The alley was no longer dark. I could see the wash of red that was Cristoph, another wash of red that was the second man. The rest of the alley was gray, but with a push I slid deeper, the gray taking on edges, and deeper still, until I could see the crates, the cobbles, the slashes of rain as it fell. The blurs of red deepened as well, until I could see the cloaks, the belts, the knives that had been drawn. I could see their rain-drenched hair, their faces.

Cristoph was moving forward, knife held ready.

The second man's face pinched into a frown. "What are you doing? Just take whatever she dropped!"

"I want more than just the packages this time."

The second man grabbed Cristoph's shoulder, brought him to a halt. "What do you mean?"

Cristoph jerked out of the second man's grip. "Don't touch me."

I slid my dagger out from under my shirt.

Cristoph turned back toward me and I could see what he intended, with a sickened heart could see how it would end.

Amenkor—the real Amenkor—was just like the Dredge. The streets might be cleaner, but the people were the same.

"Don't," I said, and I could hear beneath the warning in my voice an edge of pleading. "Don't," I said again, shaking my head. Softer this time, but more steeled.

Cristoph grinned and I shifted my weight.

He came at me in a rush, his knife forward but not ready to strike. He wanted me docile, immobile, not dead. At least not at first.

I stepped to the side, just out of his path, and brought my dagger around in a hard, vicious slash, all of the training Erick had given me in the depths of the Dredge sliding smoothly into place.

My dagger cut across his arm, high, near the shoulder. I heard him gasp, saw him stumble into the crate.

"Shit!" the second man cried out, then stepped to Cristoph's side, pulling him up roughly. "Stop this!"

"No!" Cristoph hissed as he lurched out of the second man's grasp, glanced at his torn shirt, at the stain of blood there.

Then his gaze leveled on me. "So the bitch knows some knife-play." With a wince of pain, he reached up and tore off the clasp of his cloak, freeing both arms.

"Oh, gods, Cristoph," the second man muttered, still leaning against the crate behind him.

Cristoph ignored him. He edged toward me, eyes intent, breath coming in short little gasps through his nose.

He lunged.

I stepped aside again, slashed, connected with his upper back, slicing along the shoulder muscles, but not deep. Cristoph grunted, spun, slashed low, across my stomach, but I'd already stepped back, out of reach. He changed tactics, tried to slash upward. I leaned back, felt his blade slick past my neck, nick a tangle of my hair, but my own blade had already risen, had slashed across his face, along one cheek. But without pause, without even a gasp, Cristoph pressed forward, forced me to step back, to one side, pushing me—

And suddenly I felt the second man's presence at my back, felt it like an undertow, felt his knife, *tasted* his knife—

I turned, ducking beneath one of Cristoph's slashes, and drove my dagger up into the second man's gut, up under the ribs, in and out with a single hard thrust, and then I stepped back, still half crouched.

The second man tried to gasp, choked instead. The arm that had been raised to slit my throat from behind dropped to his side. He stared down at the gush of blood that had begun to seep into his shirt, that had already spread down to his breeches.

He glanced back up and in a soft, confused, wet voice, said, "Cristoph?"

Then he dropped to his knees, hard, and fell back, knife hitting the cobbles with a thin clatter, body with a solid thump.

I turned to Cristoph. He'd stepped back, almost to the alley wall, and now stared down at the second man's body in cold shock. His knife arm hung at his side, and blood seeped from the slash across his face.

I straightened, and his gaze shifted to me, his eyes sharp and wide. He blew air out through his mouth, rainwater spluttering outward.

"Gods," he whispered.

And then he ran, heading toward the alley's entrance, leaving his cloak and the second man behind.

I watched him go, watched the empty entrance to the alley for a long moment, then realized that someone was watching me.

I turned.

At the far end of the alley, at the other entrance, two figures stood, one slightly behind the other. The second man held a lantern, the light almost white in the gray.

I let the river slip away.

The man at the end of the alley was dressed in a blood-red jacket with gold threading. When he turned, lantern light reflected off the wire he wore on his face.

I tensed, but the two men walked away, leaving me alone.

I stared down at the body.

I felt nothing inside except a cold, flat hollowness.

I thought of the boy, of Perci.

Looking down at the body, rain pattering against the fine clothing, a darker stain beginning to seep out from underneath along the cobbles, I said in a dull voice, "This is who I am."

I turned, picked up the package I'd taken. I ripped away the paper, felt the twine cut into my fingers. But I didn't care.

It was a book.

I flipped through the pages, stared blankly at the black markings.

I couldn't read.

I turned back to the dead body. "You died for a fucking book," I said.

I dropped the book onto his chest.

Then I walked away.

·⟨ *The Palace* ⟩·

"TOO late, too late, too late," I mumbled under my breath as I rounded a corner at almost a dead run. The linen closet should be inside the room just ahead. But I could feel the night sky pressing down on me even inside the palace, could feel time slipping away. I should never have been held up by Avrell and Nathem, shouldn't have paused in the concourse, staring at the immense hall, at the guards. I was going to miss the changing of the guard.

"Stupid, stupid."

I rounded the corner and almost slammed into the back of another servant.

Pulling up short, I slid back around the corner and pressed flat against the wall, listening. My breath came in barely controlled gasps. I'd sprinted from the waiting room where I'd overheard Avrell and Nathem talking.

In the adjacent hall, I heard the servant's footsteps pause and I held my breath. After an agonizing moment, the footsteps resumed, receding down the hallway.

I let out a long breath, stole a quick glance around the corner to make certain the corridor was empty, then ducked to the only doorway off of the hall.

It was open.

I slid through it, then closed it behind me and locked it. I scanned the darkened room after my eyes had adjusted. Some kind of library, shelves of books lining three walls. A large table surrounded by chairs filled the center of the room, books stacked haphazardly on the table among numerous candlesticks and half-burned, unlit candles. Parchment and quills and ink were placed before some of the chairs.

Against the back wall, inconspicuous among a few scattered plants and more comfortable reading chairs, sat a door with wooden slats and inset panels. The linen closet.

I bolted across the room. The door was locked.

Reaching into the inner pocket, I drew out the key Avrell had provided, thinking once again it was odd to lock a linen closet, then inserted the key and turned. The catch sprang and the door snicked open.

I stepped inside, closed the door behind me and took a moment to peer through the wooden slats into the library.

No one had followed.

Then I turned and my heart froze.

The closet was full of . . . of linens. Stacked floor to ceiling. No wall was bare. There was no entrance to the inner sanctum.

Horror set in—that I'd made a mistake, that someone had betrayed me. Taking a quick step forward, I grabbed a stack of linen and yanked. The stack gave way, collapsing with a low, rustling *whmmp* into the small space behind the door, revealing a rough stone wall. In the center of the wall, but low to the floor, a narrow aperture glowed with torchlight coming from the opposite side.

I drew in a steadying breath of relief, then crouched down next to the opening.

It was three hands high, almost two hands wide, and had originally been a slot for archers on the outer wall of the castle, a window so that they could fire down onto an invading force. For some unknown reason, during the construction of the newest parts of the palace, the archer's niche had not been filled in and sealed up. I knelt and placed a hand against the outside of the opening, felt the grit of the granite that had made up that original wall. Not the smooth white stone of the more recent palace. This stone was rough, flecked with impurities, colored a blackened and sooty gray by exposure to the elements, even though now it never saw daylight.

Through the archer's window I could see the small niche where the archer would have sat, ready to defend the wall, and beyond that a hallway. Shifting slightly, so that the torchlight from the hallway lit my face in a long thin bar, I could see a doorway guarded by two guardsmen. They wore the edged clothing of the guards of the real Amenkor, carried themselves with the same blatant sense of danger and arrogance, but they wore more armor. The Skewed Throne symbol stitched to their clothing was gold. Firelight from the palace's wide bowls of burning oil glinted off the metal of wrist guards, the pommels of sheathed swords, and shoulder guards.

Perhaps I hadn't been slowed down as much as I thought.

I'd just turned to settle in and wait when one of the guardsmen looked toward the other and sighed. "We've only just started and already I'm tired. It's going to be a long watch."

I fell back against the granite wall and said, "Shit," even as the other guard grunted in agreement.

I'd missed the changing of the guard after all.

Drawing in a deep breath, fingering the handle of my dagger, I grunted and bit my lower lip.

Shit, shit, shit. Now what?

Chapter 8

I WAS working the wharf, had been working the wharf for the past week, ever since killing the man in the alley. I was leaning on a support, the sounds of the docks a muted rush of wind in the background. Beneath me, I could feel the support quiver as waves slapped up against it below. The world was a wash of blurred gray, except for a narrow window of focus, where sunlight glared on a mostly-white cloth spread out over the back end of a cart. Stacked on the cloth were piles of vegetables and fruit.

In the sunlight, the colors of the fruit stood out vibrant and harsh. Everything looked perfect, the flesh smooth, unblemished. There were no scabs, no bruises, no softened spots of decay.

Since coming to the wharf, I hadn't seen anyone selling fruit. I'd seen nothing but fish—fish heads, fish bones, fish guts—and crabs, which smelled like fish but tasted sweet.

I glanced up from the apples, from *the* apple that had rolled slightly to one side, near the edge of the cart, and watched the man who knelt in the back of the cart behind his wares. He was arguing with a woman over the price of some carrots, but his eyes flicked toward everyone that came within two paces of his cart.

I frowned . . . and my stomach growled. I looked at the apple again, thought for a moment I could actually *taste* it.

The sunlight brightened, the narrow field of focus widening. More people slid out of the gray, and everything took on a sharper edge.

I pushed deeper, until the world in focus had sharpened so far it felt brittle.

Then I relaxed . . . and waited.

The crowds of dockworkers and fishermen, of fishwives and seamen, ebbed and flowed around the cart. The fruit seller eventually threw up his heavyset arms in disgust with the woman, tossing the carrots back onto the cart. The woman spat on the wharf, flung a rude gesture at him with one hand, and huffed off.

More customers came, and still the fruit seller eyed everyone who approached.

And then a woman towing three young children bled out of the gray.

I straightened, and with single-minded intent *pushed* at the river, forced it forward . . . and saw what would happen, saw how I could get the apple . . . how I could get more than just the apple.

I licked my lips as my eyes darted to the fruit seller, to the sour-faced man he was currently haggling with, to the woman who had just seen the cart, to the three children. The oldest boy reached out for no apparent reason and shoved the middle girl to the ground. Without turning, the mother cuffed him on the back of the head and said, "Leave your sister alone." Her voice sounded tired and bitter. The youngest boy hung back, out of the reach of both mother and older brother.

The mother swerved toward the cart and the three followed.

I pushed away from the support and began moving forward.

The fruit seller glanced from the man to the mother, then down toward the three trailing children, and frowned.

"How much for the turnips?" the mother asked. The daughter squeezed in front of her, her chin coming up to the lip of the cart. She reached for a turnip, but couldn't quite make it.

The fruit seller opened his mouth to answer. At the same time, the older boy reached around his mother and hit his sister. Her arm, straining for the turnips, jerked and sent the entire pile tumbling.

I heard the fruit seller shout, heard the mother spit out a curse, heard the daughter scream and begin to wail. The fruit seller lurched to save the turnips, the daughter spun, eyes flaring with anger. Everyone was turning toward the boy, toward the rolling turnips, toward the noise.

I was two steps away from the apple—from an armful of apples—with no one watching, when a hand closed about my upper arm.

I jerked and spun, dagger out before I thought. I would have killed him, thinking *This is who I am,* but just before the dagger drove forward, toward the midsection just beneath the armpit, I smelled oranges. Not from the fruit seller's cart. He had no oranges. I smelled oranges in the gray world of the river.

I pulled my thrust. The dagger sliced through the man's shirt, beneath his arm and across his chest.

The man gasped and lurched back, releasing my arm. He stared at me in shock, the hand he had used to grip me held out to stop me from a second attack. The other hand clutched his chest over the rent in his shirt.

I glared at him, saw that he was gray, harmless, and turned to leave.

"Don't!" he choked, stepping forward. "Just wait!"

I hesitated. Because even after I'd almost killed him, he'd stepped forward to halt me, not away. And because of the smell of oranges.

Behind me, I heard the mother bark at her oldest son, heard them drawing away. My chance for an apple was gone.

"What do you want?" I asked, shifting my focus completely toward the man. I suddenly realized I recognized him, recognized the finely-made breeches, the white shirt with ruffles at the throat.

It was the man who had accompanied the red-coated merchant I'd seen on the dock.

"I—or rather, someone else—wishes to speak to you." He straightened, his outstretched hand dropping, then winced. When he drew his other hand away from his chest, I could see a few rounded stains of blood against the white of his shirt.

I crushed a pang of guilt. "What for?"

The man hesitated, then said stiffly, "I don't know. You'd have to ask him yourself."

I frowned.

He had black hair, shorn short, wild and untamed, but not dirty or matted. His face was rounded, the skin a little pale. His eyes were green, shadowed with fear, still a little too wide from shock. They kept darting toward the dagger. But there was nothing else beneath the fear: no hatred, no contempt, no danger. And no pity.

I slid the dagger back beneath my shirt. "Where?"

He heaved a sigh of relief, tension draining from his shoulders. "Not far. My name is William." He held out a hand, as if expecting something, like a beggar on the Dredge.

I stared at it in confusion and said, "Varis."

After a moment, he withdrew the hand, coughed slightly into it. "Ah, yes. Varis. If you'd follow me?"

He began to move away, off the docks, along the wharf toward the real Amenkor.

I waited a moment, thinking I should slip away.

But in the end I followed him. Because of the smell of oranges.

†

We moved through the back streets of the wharf, William ten paces ahead of me. I followed warily, my eyes darting toward every blur of red. I felt unsettled, and moved slowly. William turned back once, his eyes catching mine, and he smiled encouragingly. The scent of oranges drifted over the sharper smells of sea and salt, like a breath of wind.

I halted uncertainly, struggling with a new sensation, something deep in my gut that trembled.

William's smile faded and he moved back toward me. "It's not much farther," he said.

He reached out as if to take my arm again, but I drew back, my eyes hardening.

"Go on," I said, and nodded down the street.

He continued, but not before giving me a confused frown.

He halted a few streets farther on at a door beneath a sign with a ship carved into the wood, its sails torn and ragged, the central mast broken. When he opened the door and gestured me inside, laughter and the sounds of a dozen voices rolled out into the street.

I stepped back, glanced toward William. I knew it was a tavern, had heard the raucous noises through opened doors before, knew the smells. But always from the street, from the Dredge. I'd never actually been inside one.

William's brow furrowed as he waited. He didn't understand my hesitation.

Before he could say anything, before the frown began to touch his eyes with real concern, I straightened and stepped past him into the inner room.

The sudden influx of sensation was overwhelming, the sound and motion and scents too intense. A dozen conversations, twenty voices or more, rushed out of the background noise, roaring forward like a gale, somehow trapped inside the little room, confined. A thousand scents struck like a blow—fire, ale, sweat, tallow, rot, cooked meat, bread, heat—all mixed and compacted, enough to gag. And through the sound, through the smells, in the dulled transition from sunlight to candlelight, people were moving: clapping each other on the back, stumbling up from tables, wandering toward the fire, reaching for food, coughing, carrying mugs of ale, drinking, eating, choking.

It was too much. The river began to close in, the water closing up and over my head, smothering me. My breath caught in my chest with a sharp pain and held there. My shoulders tensed. My hand closed in a death grip on my dagger. The room rushed in to crush me.

Then, with effort, I forced the darkening gray of the world to focus. I felt the river push back, resist, struggle—

Then the noise bled into the background. The scents slid away. And the giddy rush of motion pulled back, stabilized.

I gasped as the river gave way and began to balance, coughed as if water were caught in my throat, in my lungs—like when I'd surfaced from the water of Cobbler's Fountain at age six.

William stepped up behind me and I felt the light fade as the door closed. His hand moved as if to touch me, his eyes concerned, but he stopped himself at something he saw in my face.

"Over here," he said, and led me through the mass of people toward a table in the corner, where the man in the red coat sat. I felt confined by the low roof, the people, but when I saw the red-coated man, all of that sensation fled.

The scent of oranges grew so strong it dampened out everything in the room, so sharp my eyes began to water.

I slid from the river, and the noise of the tavern rushed back, the scents. But in the real world they were not as overwhelming. In the real world, they were no worse than the crowds on the Dredge.

William moved behind the table, to where the red-coated man sat. He leaned down to murmur something in the red-coated man's ear, but the red-coated man's eyes never left mine. He watched me intently from behind the wires on his face. When William finished, he only nodded, and William stepped back to stand behind his shoulder, arms behind his back.

The red-coated man motioned to the only other chair at the table. "Would you like to sit?" he asked. His voice was soft and hard at the same time, careful and wary.

I glanced toward the chair, felt the motion of the room at my back, the steady stream of people, and shook my head.

He nodded, as if he'd expected that response. Then, in a deeper voice, one much more dangerous than before, he asked, "And do you know who I am?"

I shook my head again.

He watched me for the space of two breaths . . . and then his gaze shifted out into the crowd behind me. "Moll, could you bring a plate of the pork and some ale. And bread with butter, of course. Enough for three."

I turned and watched a woman nod in our direction and hustle off toward a door.

When I turned back, the red-coated man was watching me again, this time with a frown.

"We saw you kill that boy the other night."

It was a statement, and when he reached beneath the table I tensed, a cold sensation rushing up from my stomach. But not the warning Fire. This was simple panic. My hand went for my dagger—

But then the red-coated man drew forth a section of black

cloth, finely-made—too fine for what I'd seen on the common people of the wharf. It was stained with mud, with blood.

It was the cloak Cristoph had dropped, the one he'd left behind.

The red-coated man pushed the cloak back down beneath the table.

"I sent William back for the body. He tossed it into the harbor, but he brought the cloak and the book to me. If the body is found, the boy's family will think he was roughing it in the wharf region for fun, that he got involved in something he shouldn't have—dice, too much drink, the wrong crowd—and that he was killed for his money."

"What about the other one, the one who ran away?" I asked.

Borund grimaced. "I don't think he'll cause a problem. He'd have to admit he was on the wharf in the first place, attempting . . . whatever he was attempting. I find that unlikely."

I shifted uneasily. "Who were they?"

"Does it matter?" When I didn't answer, he shook his head. "Merchants' sons. They shouldn't have been messing around on the wharf. They certainly shouldn't have been down here preying on the likes of you. Don't you agree?"

William snorted. The red-coated man frowned but didn't turn around.

"In any case," the red-coated man continued, "William has convinced me that you could be . . . useful."

I glanced toward William, but his face was blank, his eyes focused inward.

"How?"

The red-coated man drew breath, but suddenly Moll appeared with a tray heavy with shredded pork smothered in some kind of sauce. The meat steamed, the scent of heat and smoke and juice powerful, drawing a rumble from my stomach. She set the tray down with a grunt as a second, younger woman arrived with a huge pitcher of ale and three wooden cups—except they were larger than any cups I'd ever seen; deeper and with large handles. Yet another woman arrived with a flat board with bread already sliced and a bowl with butter in it. A small knife, as long as my finger and strangely flattened, was half-buried in the butter.

My stomach clenched.

"Will that be all, Merchant Borund?"

"For now, yes, Moll."

The three women nodded and wove back into the crowd behind me, but not before considering me with curious frowns. Moll nodded to me as she passed, with a tentative smile.

After they left, Borund sighed and relaxed back into his chair. Motioning toward the food, he said, "Please, have something to eat. You as well, William."

I hesitated, too shocked to move. There was more meat on the tray than I'd eat in a week, and the bread. . . .

William shifted forward, used the small knife to spread the butter over a slice of bread, then used something else with three small prongs to stab a chunk of the meat. He placed the meat on the bread and then stepped back to eat.

I watched a moment, still stunned, then stepped forward. I resisted the urge to grab the entire loaf of bread and run. Instead, I picked up a single slice and when no one reacted, stepped back. I half expected Borund or William to shout, or reach out and grab my arm as the hawker had done when he'd caught me trying to steal from his stall.

Instead, Borund leaned forward and said, "Here. Try some butter on that."

I held out the slice of bread I'd taken. Borund took it and slathered it liberally, then handed it back.

The bread was warm, and the butter had already begun to soak into the slice. It smelled sweet, tasted sweeter, soft and warm and smooth against my tongue. The flavor flooded my mouth, and a trail of it trickled down my chin like drool.

It was the best thing I'd ever tasted, sent tremors through my arms.

I stuffed the rest of the bread in my mouth, wiped the trail of butter away with the back of my hand while still chewing the last of it.

Borund leaned forward with a smile. "Now have some with the meat."

He waited until I'd gotten another slice, with plenty of butter, more than Borund had used, and some meat, then sat back while William poured three cups of ale.

"Amenkor is dangerous, Varis," he began, then hesitated. "May I call you Varis?"

I nodded around my third helping of butter, bread, and meat.

"Not just here on the wharf. It's dangerous in the upper city as well. Perhaps more so. Especially since the White Fire." He paused, grimaced to himself, then focused again on me. "I did not think it was that serious—not as serious as William claimed—until . . . until we saw you being attacked in that alley by those boys. I was willing to dismiss how bad things had become in Amenkor until then. But now. . . ." He shook his head, shifted uncomfortably in his seat, his gaze moving toward the crowd behind me.

I stopped for a moment, suddenly uneasy. Inside, I felt a tendril of the Fire flicker upward, there and then gone. But the motions of the room behind me began to filter into my awareness, no longer part of the background.

Borund's gaze moved from person to person.

"Now," he said, "I no longer feel safe. Even here, where I've come since my father first brought me to the wharf." He smiled, the gesture bittersweet and brief, and returned his attention to me.

"And that's where you come in, Varis. I need someone to guard over me, protect me."

I stopped chewing. Through a mouthful of bread and gravy, I sputtered, "What?"

Borund leaned forward. "I want you to accompany me to the wharf, to the city or palace, wherever I go, and make certain no one harms me. I know you can handle a weapon. I've seen it. I know you can defend yourself. That boy you killed . . . he was *trained*, Varis. He knew how to use a knife. And yet you bested him without any effort at all."

I swallowed painfully, the lump of bread too large and tasteless. "He was stupid."

"Perhaps. But in the end you walked away, not him. I'm willing to bet you can best almost anyone. Especially anyone that may be hired to kill me."

"Who would want you dead?"

William snorted again and took a long pull on his ale. William had drunk plenty of ale. I hadn't touched mine. Neither had Borund.

"Other merchants. Perhaps others from the upper city with power. People here on the wharf who have become . . . desperate." Now Borund reached for his ale. "There are plenty who might try." He drank, watching me carefully over the top of the cup, then set the cup aside. "See this jacket? The red signifies my merchant house, the color chosen typically as an indicator of the product I traded in when my house was first certified as a member of the guild. Mine is red because at the time I dealt mainly in imported wines.

"But my house has grown since then," he said. "I deal in many commodities now—spices, grain, cloth. The gold embroidery on the sleeves of the jacket and around the neck indicate all of the wares that my house has dealt in before." He pointed to his cuff.

"These three lines cinched tight in the middle mean that I've traded in flax, that perhaps I have a source if someone is interested. This elongated circle indicates I've dealt in silks from the eastern city of Korvallo, across the mountains. The more embroidery, the more powerful the house. The jacket and the embroidery are a necessary part of the work of the guild, are in fact essential if my house is to remain influential in the guild and in the palace. But it has a drawback. It announces to the world exactly how powerful I am. And it attracts . . . undue attention."

"It makes you a target," I said.

Borund did not respond, turned his attention toward the ring of spilled ale the cup had left on the table instead, began spreading the ale around with one finger in small circular motions.

"You would no longer live on the wharf, of course, in your little pile of traps. If you came to work for me."

My eyes narrowed, a pulse of anger uncoiling deep within.

He glanced up briefly, then continued playing with the ring of ale. "Yes. I had you watched. I had to make certain you were trustworthy. That you weren't sent by one of the other merchants, as a spy perhaps." He sighed. "If you are interested, you would have to live in my house in the inner city. Sleep there, eat there. My schedule is not fixed, so I'd need you close, in case I had to leave quickly. I would provide everything you needed, within reason." The small circular motions stopped and he lifted his finger from the ale, lifted his eyes to me. "It would be a much better life than stealing what you can from the wharf."

I hesitated. The anger that he had followed me, had watched me—that he had done so without me noticing—felt raw and hot inside me. I should have seen them, should have noticed whoever had been sent to stalk me.

And that's exactly how I felt. As if I'd been stalked.

Suddenly, the bread and meat and butter felt heavy and sour in my stomach. I felt sick, the air inside the tavern too close, stifling. The noise and motion of the people began to push forward again, overpowering, like when I'd first stepped into the room.

Feeling feverish, I stepped away from the table. "I don't know." I took another step, the urge to run creeping up slowly from inside, tingling through my arms, even though there was no warning from the Fire inside me, no hint of danger.

Borund stood as well, sharply, frowning, one hand slightly out-stretched as if to catch me before I fled. He seemed about to protest, but then he stopped, let his hand fall back to the table.

"Perhaps this was a mistake," he said.

And then the pressure of the room became too great, the noise and scents too harsh.

I turned, hesitated. . . . But in the end I slid through the crowd to the door and out into the new-fallen night.

✝

Once outside the stifling tavern in the night air, I moved swiftly toward my niche, past people I barely saw before swerving around them. My mind was blank, empty. There was nothing to feel except the heavy weight of food in my stomach, nothing to taste but a strange fear tinged with a sickening excitement, all flavored like butter, smooth and slick inside my mouth. . . .

I stumbled over a trailing length of rope attached to a crab trap, caught myself against a wall. My heart thundered in my chest, so hard it hurt just beneath my breastbone. I coughed roughly, then straightened.

Drawing in another deep breath, I leaned my head back against the stone of the wall behind me.

I could still smell oranges.

I drew in a few more deep breaths, coughed halfheartedly, and sank down into a crouch, weight on my heels. On the street before me, a few people moved. Some slowed, watched me warily. No one came close.

I closed my eyes. Against the darkness, I thought about William grabbing my arm, felt the instant surge of fear, of desperation, of dread that this was another rapist like the first man I'd killed . . . or another Bloodmark.

But William wasn't one of those men. I could see it in his eyes, in his confused expression, in his mussed, clean hair. I could see it in the way he'd held out his hand to stop me from attacking a second time. And it was in his smile.

I shifted uneasily, feeling again that trembling sensation deep inside, somehow warm and tense at the same time, and strangely guilty.

I turned away from the sensation, thought about Borund instead, about how he'd offered the food, about his eyes. He'd been wary, reluctant at first, the wrinkles near his eyes tight. But then he'd relaxed, smiled, put the butter on that first slice of bread. Not the slow smile of Garrell Cart before he'd taken the girl on the Dredge, before he'd killed her. No. Borund's smile had been amused as he watched me take that first uncertain bite, as he watched me slather the butter onto the second slice myself.

But he'd also had me followed, watched, stalked. Like I imagined that ex-guardsman I'd killed had stalked me, or like Garrell Cart had watched the girl with the green cloth. Predatory.

Wariness twisted my stomach, made worse by William's confused eyes, by Borund's smile.

And by the oranges.

Erick had given me oranges. I'd trusted him. I trusted him still, even though I felt that I'd betrayed him in some way by killing Bloodmark. Even though that last image of him, at the edge of Cobbler's Fountain, before we'd found Mari, had been gray mixed with red. I didn't know what the red mixed with gray meant exactly, but I still trusted him.

I squeezed my eyes tighter, felt tears near the edges, felt them burn.

I suddenly wanted Erick back, wanted him there, at the edge of Cobbler's Fountain, waiting. I wanted to see his hard expression, his dark eyes, his scars. Even if it meant that the moment he saw me, the moment he laid eyes on me, he denounced me. Even if all he did was cast me out.

But I couldn't get Erick back. Not now. I'd made my choice.

I opened my eyes, wiped at them forcefully, then glared at a man who'd paused on the far side of the street.

He turned quickly and moved on.

I glanced around, dipped beneath the river briefly but saw no red, then stood and began moving toward my niche.

†

Sunlight glared off the rolling waves of the harbor in flashes, forcing me to squint and raise a hand to shade my eyes. At the end of the dock, a ship with three masts creaked against its lines as workers—Zorelli and Amenkor natives alike—hauled boxes and barrels down the ramp to the dock itself. It was the usual chaos that normally kept me enthralled with a strange tingling excitement deep down inside my stomach, but today I wasn't interested. Today, only William and Borund held my attention.

Both stood at the end of the plank that led to the deck of the ship, Borund dressed again in the red coat. William stood back and to one side, in a white shirt with ruffles down the front and brown breeches tucked into boots. Both were frowning in thought as the captain of the ship talked. I could only catch a few phrases of the conversation at this distance, and none of those phrases made sense. But I couldn't get any closer without revealing myself. I wasn't well hidden as it was.

Borund's frown turned grim and he shifted so that he was looking out toward the sea, toward where the two promontories of land to the west of the city jutted out and curved toward each other, forming a narrow inlet into the bay.

The captain of the ship finished his report and even through the chaos of the unloading around them, I could sense the silence between the three men growing. The shipmaster's fingers nervously kneaded the edge of the hat tucked under one arm as he watched Borund's face.

Finally Borund sighed and turned away from the sea. Forcing a smile, he gripped the shipmaster's arm at the elbow, squeezed once as he said a few words, and then the two nodded to each other, the captain donning his hat as Borund and William turned away.

I pulled back behind the stack of crates and waited, breathing in the salt air and looking up at the blue of the sky, the bustle of the wharf a few paces away.

When William and Borund passed by, I waited until they'd moved twenty paces farther on, then slipped into the flow of the wharf traffic behind them, close enough to hear what they said, but far enough back they wouldn't notice me. I'd been following them for the last week, whenever I managed to catch them on the wharf.

". . . getting worse," Borund was saying. The grim expression I'd seen on the docks had returned. "Mathew says that all the ports are as bad off as we are. He's barely finding enough to trade and still keep his ship. If it doesn't pick up soon, he'll have to ground her or sell her."

"Perhaps you could buy it from him," William said. "Keep him on as captain."

Borund grunted. "Not if we can't get more trade going through the city. We've had to start cutting into the reserves as it is. There's just nothing out there. Too dry to the north, too wet to the south. And I don't know what the hell happened to the spice and silk routes through Kandish. The entire nation seems to have vanished.

Avrell announced to the guild that nothing's come through the mountains in the last three months—no emissaries from Kandish, no caravans. He hasn't even heard from his own diplomats, and you know how widespread his network is."

He glanced toward William. "Something is happening, here along the Frigean coast and on the other side of the mountains. We have to find another source for our staples. Mathew says that he grabbed the last of the wheat in Merrell, and nearly all of the barley—as much as he could load into the ship without foundering. He paid a hefty price, but I think it was a wise choice."

"Should I send it on to Richar in Kent? Raise the asking price to compensate?"

Borund hesitated, then halted, his gaze once again turning toward the harbor. The flow of people on the wharf parted around him, like water around a dock support.

Twenty paces back, I slid into place beside a cart loaded with dead fish, their mouths open, eyes filmed with white. The hawker glared at me a moment, then turned back to the passersby, shouting with a startlingly loud voice, "Fresh fish! Just from the ocean! Fresh fish!"

At the center of the flow of people, Borund turned from the sea, his gaze traveling over the city of Amenkor itself, taking in the far side of the bay, where the buildings at the edge of the bluff rose to the mismatched angles of the roofs behind. It created a strange pattern above the slate of the water, and as I followed his gaze I suddenly realized with a sickening twist in my gut that there, among those roofs, across the bay on the other side of the River, lay the Dredge. And that on one of those roofs, almost six years ago, I'd watched the Fire emerge from the west and cut across the harbor, consuming everything.

And then I'd killed a man.

"No," Borund said, and I tore my gaze away from the buildings and from memory to see that Borund was now staring at the people moving about him, watching them as they haggled and cursed and rushed along the wharf. His voice had sharpened somehow, and his gaze flickered from face to face. But he didn't turn toward me. "No. Don't send the grain on. Tell Richar we have none to spare. And tell Mathew to purchase whatever he can find, no matter the cost."

Borund caught William's eyes and something passed between them, William's back straightening.

"Very well," he said.

Borund sighed and glanced up at the sun, the skin around his eyes wrinkling as he squinted. "I feel the need to check the warehouses suddenly. Take inventory. See exactly what and how much we have in stock, ready for use."

William stepped forward and they began walking away. I stayed behind. I'd followed them to the warehouses once before. There were no people around, no places to hide. And both William and Borund had disappeared into a single building for four hours while I waited in the rain.

I glanced down as they vanished into the crowd and caught sight of a small fish at the edge of the cart, its one eye slightly sunken into its head. Its scales had dried in the sun.

I cast a quick look toward the hawker.

Five minutes later, I was deep in the back streets, headed toward my niche, the dry fish held loosely in one hand.

✝

Two days later, I settled into the edge of an alley across the street from the inn where William had first taken me to see Borund. It was early yet, the sky still blue, with thin bands of clouds, but within the hour it would be dark. I stared at the door to the inn, listened to the noise from inside spill out when someone entered, and tasted butter. Tasted it so badly I had to swallow.

I couldn't see far inside the inn, but Borund and William never showed up this early when they came. After a moment, I sat back on my haunches, leaned against the alley wall, and waited, closing my eyes.

William instantly rose to mind. His black hair, tugged by the wind coming in off the sea. His green eyes.

The liquid guilty sensation returned in the pit of my stomach, but this time I didn't force it away. It was strangely exciting. Different.

I found myself smiling for no reason.

And then the scent of oranges intruded.

I opened my eyes and sat forward. Twilight had settled onto the street, the sky gray now, the clouds tinged with the last of the sunset. Even as I inched forward, catching sight of Borund and William moving toward the door to the inn, the deep sunlight faded and died.

Borund halted at the door to the inn to talk to someone—another merchant by the man's dark green jacket, the amount of gold embroidery on his sleeves roughly equivalent to Borund's. But this merchant was accompanied by two other men. The merchants clasped arms, hands gripping forearms, and nodded to each other. William kept back a pace as they talked, but his attention was on the conversation. I watched him as he scanned the street around them, keeping a careful eye on the two men with the other merchant.

Perhaps I'd refused Borund's offer too quickly, I suddenly thought. I'd followed them for days, watched carefully to see if I was being followed still, tracked. But there'd been nothing. Neither Borund nor William had done anything aside from checking the docks, checking their warehouses, meeting with other merchants and with shipmasters on the pier.

I almost stood and moved across the street, moved to catch William's attention, but Borund ended the conversation with the merchant. He turned and motioned William inside, rough laughter breaking out from inside the inn as William opened the door. Borund nodded once toward the merchant with the green coat, who smiled and nodded back, and then the door closed and the laughter cut off.

I was just about to settle in and wait for Borund and William to leave, when the green-coated merchant turned.

The smile had vanished. In the last of the fading light, I saw the merchant's eyes narrow, his face harden with hatred.

A shudder slid through me and without thought I dipped beneath the river. In the rushing noise of the street, the merchant was mostly gray, but with faint traces of red at the edges.

Like Erick had been the last time I'd seen him.

I pulled back sharply, stared wide-eyed at the merchant across the street. For the first time since I'd killed Bloodmark and fled to the docks, I wondered what it meant. There'd been no need to wonder; I never expected to see Erick again, and I'd met no one else with the strange mix of red and gray.

But now . . .

I shifted forward, watched the merchant intently. He had a thin face, but soft somehow, not gaunt. His eyes were dark, but in the light I couldn't tell what color they were. His hair was dark as well.

For a moment, he searched the street, his eyes halting as he caught sight of a thin man leaning against a wall close to where I crouched. He pressed his lips together as if considering, then nodded once toward the thin man before turning away.

With a sharp gesture, the green-coated merchant called the other two men to his side. They left, moving swiftly.

I turned my attention toward the thin man leaning against the wall.

For a long moment, he did nothing but stare down at the cobbles of the street. Then he smiled and pushed himself away from the wall, moving sedately toward the inn. As he moved, he pulled a slim knife from his belt and tucked it up one sleeve of his shirt.

A shiver sliced through my gut, but before I could react, the man had opened the door to the inn, some type of music now mingling with the sound of voices spilling out. Then the door shut and the man was inside.

With Borund. And William.

I hesitated at the door to the inn, barely conscious of the fact that I'd crossed the street at a dead run, or that I'd slid beneath the river, deep. I shuddered at the memory of the last time I'd entered the inn, of how the people and voices and scents had overwhelmed me. But the memory lasted barely a breath before I pulled open the door.

It was as bad as the last time. Music, laughter, voices, belches, clattering pottery, creaking benches, all of it crashed into me, surged forward like a rolling wave on the bay, slapping into one of the dock's supports. And with it came the instant disorientation of the crowd, movement without purpose, without order, and the strong blanketing stench of sweat and smoke and ale.

But this time I forced everything into the background with a mental shove and focused, sifting through the noise and chaos.

The entire room . . . solidified. The blur of motion became bodies, servers weaving through the patrons with trays aloft, patrons clapping each other on the back or tossing back drinks. A man with garish clothing belted out a song while playing a strange instrument, and two women dressed like prostitutes but who weren't wove through the edges of the crowd, trailing filmy cloth, dancing. All noise bled into the background wind, making the foreground eerily silent. And the stench was damped, as if it had been shoved close to the floor—still there, lingering, but not strong.

A man staggered toward me and I stepped out of the way a second before he would have jostled into me. A look of annoyance crossed his face for a brief second, but he bumped into the next man through the door and stole that man's purse before leaving. My movement placed me in the midst of the crowd.

I spat a curse. I could no longer see, the people too close, blocking my view.

But I caught the scent of oranges.

Focusing on that, I sifted through the crowd, barely touching anyone. But the deeper I moved into the room, the greater the cold sense of urgency in my gut grew. I remembered the man's knife as he slipped through the door of the inn, could see his slow smile as he pushed away from the wall.

I gave up trying to go unnoticed and began shoving my way forward. The cold sensation flickered, then curled into a wisp of the Fire.

I staggered out of the press of bodies into an open area of tables. Gasping, I grabbed the back of a chair and scanned desperately for the thin man, for Borund and William.

I found Borund almost instantly, sitting at a back table. Moll, the woman who had served him before, was just setting down a platter of roasted meat and vegetables. I couldn't see William. Or the thin man.

I dove deeper into the river, going as deeply as possible, thinking of Garrell and the girl with the green ribbon. I hadn't been able to help the girl. I'd been too late. But I could help Borund.

I searched the crowd for splashes of red, realizing suddenly that I hadn't used the river outside when I'd seen the thin man. I'd been too shocked. Now I had no marker, no scent for him.

I latched onto a blur of red, almost lurched forward, hand already on my dagger, but realized it wasn't the thin man. Someone else, someone watching me closely, but too far away to worry about now. Another blur of red, and another, neither the thin man.

The Fire curled higher, grew, began to move up into my chest, toward my throat. The taste of oranges flooded my mouth.

There were no other splashes of red in the inn. The thin man wasn't here.

Unless . . .

I paused, realized that all of the men who appeared red were watching me, were focused on me.

The thin man wasn't interested in me. He was interested in Borund.

I hesitated a moment, then closed my eyes and drew in a deep breath, frowning as I concentrated. I could feel the Fire growing in my chest, tingling in my shoulders, but I ignored it, focused on the separate sensation of the river instead, on its flow as it pushed around me. I reached out and touched it, pushed it, tried to alter its focus, turning it away from me . . . and toward Borund.

When I opened my eyes again, the texture of the room had changed. Everything was still gray tinged with other colors, but now there were more of them. The three men who had appeared red before were still red, but now they were somehow removed and unclear, faded. Now, there was a new set of red, a darker red than the others.

The men dangerous to Borund.

I unconsciously stepped forward, scanning the new faces.

The Fire began moving along my arms.

At the table, Borund took a swig from his ale, his meat already half eaten. He reached for a chunk of bread.

And then I saw the thin man.

He stood just behind Borund, within five paces. As I watched, the Fire sliding down to tingle in my fingers, the thin man's knife dropped from its hiding place in his sleeve into the palm of his hand and he began to move forward.

At the same time, someone halted just beside me and in a startled voice asked, "Varis?"

I turned, saw William's surprised eyes, his brow wrinkled in confusion—

And then he saw the dagger in my hand. I didn't remember drawing it.

His eyes went wide, and one hand rose as if to grab me . . . or maybe to ward me away as he'd done on the wharf when he first grabbed my arm and I attacked him. But before I could find out what he intended, I bolted toward Borund.

I think William shouted in alarm, but it was too hard to tell, his voice drowning in the background wind. The thin man now stood a pace behind Borund, had brought his thin dagger up toward Borund's back where he sat. I could see what he intended: a quick thrust up between Borund's ribs, like the thrust I'd used to kill Tomas, the man who'd attacked Bloodmark. If done right, Borund would barely feel it, might think it was someone bumping into him from behind, but it would kill him nonetheless.

Borund saw me at the last moment, a forkful of shredded meat raised half to his mouth. He jerked back, shock and fear registering in the breath before I crashed into him, his chair, and the thin man.

All I could think of as the three of us tilted, Borund grunting at the impact, was the dead girl's body—the girl with the green cloth.

Then we hit the floor. The edge of Borund's chair ground into my hip and with the sudden sharp pain I lost the river. Sounds crashed down—the splinter of wood, gasps, a scream, clattering pottery, and close, the rustling of clothes and bodies. My face was crushed into the thin man's shirt, into his chest, and the stench of salt and dead fish blotted out even the scent of oranges. I gagged on the cloth—

Then felt the shivering touch of metal as a knife sliced into my side, not deep, but enough to draw blood.

I hissed and jerked back, one hand finding purchase on the floor, catching the thin man's face as he struggled to pull away from me, from Borund. His arm was trapped beneath Borund's chair, held in place by Borund's weight, but his knife arm was still free.

Without thought, barely on my knees and with only my own dagger hand free, I sank my dagger into the thin man's stomach and pulled up, cutting hard and deep. Blood instantly stained his shirt and he gasped, eyes flying wide open. He flailed for a moment, and then all of the strength left his arms and shoulders and his free arm sank to the floor.

"What the bloody hell!" Borund shouted, still tangled up in the remains of his chair.

I pushed back and sat up on my knees over the thin man's body. He was still alive, gasping harshly, head and eyes moving back and forth as if he were searching for something. His hand spasmed and he dropped his dagger.

His eyes caught mine, held there for two short gasps, and then he died.

Inside, the Fire pulled back from my arms, from my chest, and settled quietly in my stomach.

Then someone grabbed me from behind, jerked me to my feet. Others grabbed my arms. I let them, only struggling when someone attempted to take my dagger. They backed off under my glare without touching the blade.

William emerged from the crowd into the space around Borund's table and instantly dropped to Borund's side, helping him untangle himself from his coat and the chair. Meat sauce stained the front of his coat, blood stained the back.

As he helped Borund up, William's gaze fell on the bloodied

body of the thin man and he jerked back in distaste, cast a startled glance toward me.

The look in his eyes—fear, loathing, disgust—sent ice through my gut, as if someone had dashed frigid water up against my spine.

"What in hell is going on here?" Borund snapped the moment he was standing. He glared at me, until William leaned in close and whispered something in his ear.

Then his gaze fell on the body as well and the glare died in his eyes. He became suddenly very calm, no emotion showing at all, his back stiffening.

A man shoved through the crowd, his eyes angry. "What's the meaning of this?" he asked, but then he saw the body, saw me and the dagger. "Call the Guard."

"They're already here," someone said roughly, and two guardsmen pushed into the open. "What happened?"

"She killed him," someone said, and only then did I realize that the inn was silent. No music, no laughter, no voices. Only the rustle of bodies and a few taut whispers.

"Is this true?" one of the guardsmen asked Borund.

I watched Borund. I hadn't taken my eyes off him since William had helped him up. He stared at me intently, his face unreadable.

"Yes," he said. But before anyone could move, he added, "But she's my personal bodyguard, and this man was trying to kill me."

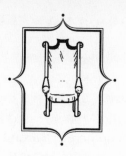

Chapter 9

"HE tried to kill me!" Borund spat. I stepped back from the violence in his voice, almost slid into the darkness of the alley at the side of the tavern and vanished, an instinctive response from the Dredge. But Borund's violence was without a mark, and tinged with shock. "He tried to kill me, openly, in the middle of a tavern!"

We'd moved out of the tavern, stood now outside the door. Borund had removed his blood- and sauce-encrusted jacket, had folded it and handed it to William. William kept back a few paces from Borund, his face white and shaken, eyes wide. Like when I'd spun on the wharf and almost sliced open his chest. The horror of what I'd done, that I'd seen in his eyes earlier inside the tavern, had died. This was delayed reaction.

He glanced toward me. I held his gaze, didn't waver, even though I felt sick to my stomach.

"You're hurt," he said, but his voice was distant.

I looked down, grimaced at my sliced shirt, at the cut that had already stopped bleeding. "I'm fine. It's nothing. Barely a scratch."

Borund didn't notice.

On the street, a group of raucous men passed, pausing at the door, and Borund moved farther down the street, watching the group warily. Some of the shock was beginning to fade, replaced by a heated calm. I could see it in his eyes, even in the darkness.

He remained silent until the roar and music of the tavern was cut off behind the group of men. "He wasn't acting on his own. I've never seen the man before. He must have been hired."

"I wonder who sent him," William muttered.

Borund turned toward William. "That is the question, isn't it?"

"It was the green-coated merchant," I said.

Borund turned toward me. "Charls?" he asked incredulously.

"The one you spoke to before entering the tavern." I could see him clearly, the thin face, dark eyes filled with hatred. Gray mixed with red.

Borund stood still, as if unable to move, his mouth slightly parted.

Then the tavern door banged open and the guardsmen stalked out. I pulled back unconsciously, but Borund straightened as they turned and nodded.

They glanced once toward me, eyes suspicious, mouths tight. A new fear clawed through me. I wondered if Erick had told them about me, had told them to watch for me, that I'd murdered someone and then fled.

But there was no recognition in these guardsmen's eyes, only a generalized distrust, as if they still didn't believe Borund's story, knew that something about it was wrong. But they couldn't figure out what. Not with William supporting the statement. No one else in the tavern had seen anything, or was willing to come forward.

The guardsmen nodded again and stalked off, heading toward the palace, its walls on the hill overlooking the city lit with oil light. I felt tensed muscles relax, in my shoulders, in my gut.

When the guards faded into the darkened streets, Borund turned toward William. "You tried to warn me before. Did you know it was Charls?"

William shook his head. "No. I only knew that it no longer felt safe to move around in Amenkor, especially at night. I didn't realize there was such a . . . personal threat."

Borund grunted. "Then it was good you brought up your concerns when you did, otherwise I'd be dead."

He turned toward me, his eyes intent, as hard and unreadable as stone. "And you," he said softly. "It was a gift of the Mistress that you were here. A very fortuitous gift."

I straightened under his stare and said, "I've been watching you, following you." The words were harsh, defensive, defiant.

"I see. Is that how you know it was Charls?"

"After he spoke with you, he motioned to the man who tried to kill you. Then left."

"And you followed that man into the tavern? To stop him from killing me?"

I drew breath to answer, then glanced toward William. He still seemed shocked, his hair appearing even wilder. But he was more focused now, paying closer attention.

Instead of answering out loud, I simply nodded.

Borund considered this, his gaze so intense I was forced to look away.

Finally, he murmured, "Fortuitous gift indeed." As if he'd reached a decision, he stirred, glanced once toward William and back. "Have you reconsidered my offer? I'm forced to agree with William now. A bodyguard is necessary."

I stood straight, hesitated only a moment, and said, "What do you want me to do?"

†

They led me through the streets of the wharf, beyond the warehouses, and up into the streets below the palace, into the upper city. Borund offered to return to my niche, to gather up whatever I wanted, but I had my dagger, my clothes. There was nothing in the space I'd formed out of crab traps and tarps. Nothing worth returning for.

We moved swiftly through the streets, William ahead while I trailed behind, both of the men tense, wary.

At one point, we passed the end of the bridge where I'd crossed the River from the Dredge into Amenkor. I paused, stared out over the expanse, over the river water, and thought of Erick, of the white-dusty man, of Cobbler's Fountain.

Then I turned away. Both Borund and William had stopped farther on up the road, were looking back at me, but neither said anything when I moved to follow them.

Carriages appeared, and men on horseback, and once two guardsmen. Each time Borund slowed until the men and horses had passed. The buildings—crowded and close at first, with narrow alleys—changed. Courtyards appeared, not ruined and decayed like on the Dredge, but with closed iron gates and trees. Alleys widened. Surrounding walls appeared, the buildings set back from the streets, enclosed and protected. And the stench of fish and salt and sea faded.

Then William paused on a corner, scanned in all directions, and moved purposefully across the street to a small gate set back inside an alcove in a wall. A moment later, Borund and I joined him.

As William unlocked the wrought-iron gate, Borund turned and muttered, "This is your new home, Varis."

We stepped inside a garden, pathways curling away in all directions, clear in the darkness because they were made of white stone and glowed in the moonlight. Trees, branches hanging down limply, sighed in a sudden breeze from the harbor, smelling of the ocean. Everything was shadowed, details hard to make out in the darkness.

Borund strode quickly into the garden, toward a building I could barely see, leaving William and me behind.

"What's wrong?" William asked.

I looked up into William's eyes, saw the stars behind him, and said, "There should be buildings here. It shouldn't be so . . . empty. It's unnatural."

William smiled. "It's a garden. It's supposed to be empty, without buildings." He shook his head, then moved out into the garden.

A twinge of guilt slid through me, as if I'd done something wrong. I watched him a moment before following.

We passed into the shadow of the building, to another door. Borund was waiting for us inside, at the beginning of a long hallway, along with an elderly man and a woman who carried a lantern. More light could be seen farther down the hall.

"Lizbeth," Borund said, and the woman dipped her head anxiously. "This is Varis. She's going to be staying here for the immediate future. Have a room made up, with whatever she requires."

Lizbeth turned her gaze on me, frowning. Her eyes were sharp, like Bloodmark's, catching every detail, noting every mark, every tear, every smudge and bruise. "Will she be needing new clothes?"

Borund turned to look at me, then smiled tightly. "Yes. New clothes. But nothing too removed from what she's wearing right now. No dresses. Nothing . . . ruffled or anything. Bring her a variety and let her choose."

Lizbeth nodded. "And water for a bath, I expect. Soap, too. Lots of soap."

"Whatever Varis wants, nothing more." There was a hint of warning in Borund's voice, and Lizbeth shot him a questioning look. "Varis is part of the household now."

"As what? We can't afford any more help."

A wave of annoyance passed over Borund's face and he frowned heavily. "Varis is my new bodyguard. She'll be with us whenever we leave the manse."

Lizbeth backed away slightly, her sharp gaze returning to me with renewed interest. "I see. I'll go get the water started in the bathing room. Is the east room acceptable?"

Borund glanced toward me. "No. The east room is too big. Give her Joclyn's old room for now."

"Joclyn's room? But that's just a serv—" Lizbeth cut off abruptly, going still as Borund placed a hand on her arm.

"Joclyn's room, Lizbeth. I know what I'm doing." There seemed to be something else in Borund's voice—caution or warning.

Lizbeth nodded, although her brow remained creased with a frown. Borund let his hand drop, and Lizbeth handed the lantern over to the other man, took Borund's stained jacket from William, then hefted up the edges of her skirts with her free hand and dashed down the hall, vanishing through a side door.

The rest of the group turned to follow. I trailed behind.

"Gerrold."

"Yes, sir," the older man answered.

"Have some food brought to Varis' room. Whatever you have to spare in the kitchen at this late hour. Bread, wine . . . no, make that water, and . . . and butter." Borund grinned and glanced back briefly. "Lots of butter. Once that's done, meet William and me in the office." And here, Borund's voice grew dark. "We have much to discuss."

"Yes, sir."

†

I was awake when someone knocked on the door of the room Lizbeth had led me to the night before. The room was too large, containing a bed, a desk, a chair, a lantern, and a tall piece of furniture with many drawers against one wall. A large bowl rested on top of this last piece of furniture, with a pitcher full of water.

"Varis?" Lizbeth called, her voice muffled by the door. "Varis, are you awake? Borund would like to talk to you and he asked me to get you ready."

There came another light tapping at the door, and then Lizbeth opened it, tentatively, and peeked in. When she saw the bed hadn't been slept in, she opened the door wide in alarm, then caught sight of me.

The panic on her face vanished and she raised the hand not holding a stack of clothes to her breast and sighed heavily. "Thank the Mistress! Is everything all right? Where in heavens did you sleep?"

My gaze flicked unconsciously toward the darkness beneath the bed, then back toward her as the muscles in my shoulders stiffened defiantly.

Lizbeth frowned in incomprehension, head turning, and then nodded. "Ah." Her expression softened. "Not used to beds? Nor baths either, I expect." Her eyes narrowed as she took in my hair, my face. She'd left me standing over a large tub of water the night before. I'd stared at the water a long time, thinking of the barrel of rainwater I'd used after fleeing the Dredge, wondering why this tub was so large. I'd dipped my arms into the water, shocked at how cold it was. After scrubbing at my arms, I'd discovered the steps on one side and realized I was supposed to climb into the water, like when I was six at Cobbler's Fountain.

"Looks like we'll be needing another bath," Lizbeth said at the door, more to herself than to me. "Apparently, all that murky water I drained away last night was only the surface dirt. At least today we've had time to haul in and heat the water." She came farther into the room and set the clothes down on the bed, moving carefully. "William explained the situation last night, after I left you at the bath. He said I was to help you . . . adjust."

She turned toward me, the harshness I'd seen in her eyes the night before gone. Then she stepped forward, stopping a few paces away with an uncertain smile. "He said to be careful with you. That you might not understand how things are done around the manse, and that anything you wanted was to be provided. Is there anything you'd like this morning?"

I didn't answer. She held my gaze a moment, but then her eyes drifted to my clothes.

"Nothing this morning? Well then, I brought you some new clothes, something better than those rags." Her eyes returned to mine, narrowed shrewdly. "And I expect you'd like something to eat? Eggs perhaps? Maybe some bacon?"

I shifted forward and my stomach growled, loudly enough for Lizbeth to hear. I frowned in annoyance, and Lizbeth smiled tightly, trying to control a grin.

"I thought so. Let's get you into a bath first, then try out these new clothes, and after *that* we'll see what they have in the kitchen. How does that sound?"

†

Lizbeth led me to a hallway outside a large wooden door three hours later, my skin feeling raw from the bath Lizbeth had presided over, my new clothes scratchy, loose, and smelling of soap. I wore a brown shirt, brown breeches with a thin leather belt, and sandals. My hair hung damply around my face in tendrils, my head aching from how often my hair had been pulled by Lizbeth. She'd finally given up trying to untangle it and had cut most of the length away with a pair of scissors. It now hung down to my chin, rather than past my shoulders.

I'd glared at her the entire time, but she'd ignored me. She'd ignored my grunting protests when she'd tried to dip my head underwater as well, simply placing her hand on the top of my head and pushing me under with surprising strength. She'd soaped up my hair before I'd stopped spluttering, talking the entire time about the manse and how it was run.

Now, she rapped on the large wooden door and cast one last

critical glance over me as I stuffed the last of the buttered bread into my mouth.

"You'll do," she mumbled, then caught my gaze and added sternly, "for now. I'll show you around the manse once Borund is done with you." She eyed me carefully for a long moment, and then her eyes softened and she relaxed. Like the white-dusty man had relaxed when he'd seen me take the rolls.

Something tightened at the base of my throat, hard and hot, making it difficult to swallow the last of the bread. I choked a little, turned away to cough as my eyes blurred with tears.

When I turned back, she was already halfway down the hall.

Then the door opened and instinctively I reached for the dagger and backed against the wall.

I caught myself just as my hand touched steel, recognizing William.

"Borund's waiting," he said, ignoring my sudden movement.

I straightened and followed him as he turned away, moving into a huge room. I'd thought the bedroom had been large until Lizbeth had led me to the kitchen. But this room was twice the size of the kitchen. The walls were lined with shelf upon shelf of small statues, wooden boxes polished to a high sheen, cut stone, glass vases, candleholders, and plants. A large rug covered most of one wall, above a stone fireplace with no fire, but stained with soot. A large sword, three times the length of my dagger, rested in a sheath on a shelf above the fireplace. The wooden floor of the room was scattered with chairs and rugs and small tables. Most of the objects were obviously from Amenkor, but a few were too exotic, the patterns too strange. An intricately carved staff leaned against one corner, the dancing figures clearly Zorelli.

Borund sat behind a large desk in the center of the room, papers spread out before him in every direction. William took a seat to Borund's left behind the desk and pulled a set of neater pages toward himself. He dipped what looked like a stick into a small black bottle and scratched at the pages.

I halted at the door, wary of the size of the room, then forced myself to move toward the desk.

Borund sighed in disgust as I approached. "Put half in the warehouse and send the rest on. Send all of the spice to Marlett."

"They don't want the spice," William said as he made more scratches. "They want the wheat."

"Well they can't have it. Not at that price. And they won't be willing to accept the price I *would* take for it, so they'll have to choke on the spice."

"What if they won't take it?"

"Then it will have to rot in our warehouse in Marlett rather than here. We don't have enough room here."

"We don't have enough room in Marlett either. Not for spice."

"Then let it rot on the ship!"

William stared at Borund with a frown and said distinctly, "Very well."

Borund drew in a deep breath, face darkening, then blew out the air in a rush, raising a hand to his forehead. He massaged his temple, then removed the curved wire from his face. This close, in the light streaming in through the windows to one side, I could see glass inside the wires and suddenly realized why they had flashed in the sunlight on the docks. I hadn't seen the glass in the tavern, nor on the streets outside. It had always been too dark, or I'd been too far away.

"Apologies, William. I think the attack yesterday has affected me more than I want to admit."

"You've been working all morning. You should take a rest."

Borund grunted. "If only I could. But it's become so much harder. It's already midsummer. Winter is approaching fast and we haven't half of what we need in the warehouses." He shifted all the papers to one side in a disorderly stack and turned his attention to me.

His eyes widened in slight surprise. "I see that Lizbeth has been at work. You look . . . like an entirely different person." He paused and I shifted my stance, weight settling slightly forward, arms spread farther away from my body. My eyes narrowed, face hardened.

"Ah," he mumbled. "There's the Varis I know."

My shoulder muscles tensed. "You never told me what you wanted me to do."

He smiled, leaned back in his chair. William had set his papers aside and was now organizing Borund's stack.

"I want you to protect me. It's as simple as that. Just as you did last night at the tavern. I want you to accompany me whenever I leave the manse, follow me, like a shadow. Warn me of any dangers, protect me if you need to. But I expect you to warn me first. Is that acceptable?"

I thought suddenly of Mari, saw Bloodmark kneeling over her, his knife cutting down sharply and deeply, heard her screaming. I saw her trying to push herself upward after Erick had knocked Bloodmark aside, saw her watching me.

And then, abruptly, I saw the white-dusty man's face, saw the blood splattered on his forehead and cheeks from the Skewed Throne symbol that had been carved into his chest.

I hadn't been able to protect them. But I hadn't realized they needed protection, especially by someone like me. I'd always assumed they could protect themselves.

I stared into Borund's eyes—a dark brown, like mud—then drew myself upward and said, "I can protect you."

For a moment, I felt a faint curl of the Fire deep inside me rise up, sending a cold shiver through my gut. But then it died.

"Good," Borund said, then rose from his seat. William rose as well, putting the neat sheaf of papers to one side. Borund reached for a small pouch on the corner of the desk, lifted it, and held it out for me.

I frowned, hesitated, then took a step forward to take the pouch.

It held coins. More coins than I'd seen my entire time on the Dredge.

Gutterscum didn't deal in coins.

I turned a confused glance toward Borund, then William.

"Those are your wages," Borund said quietly, his voice gruff, but undercut with a note of pleasure. "It's what you'll earn every month you're in my service. I'll provide room and board as well of course." He smiled. "And as much butter as you want."

I held the pouch, not knowing what to do with it, until Borund cleared his throat.

"I'll have Lizbeth put that in your room for you," he said, leaning across the desk to take the pouch back. "For now, let's begin with a courteous visit to our dear friend Charls."

His voice was light and carefree, but tinged with darkness.

We stepped out into sunlight through a polished wooden door twice my width, banded with iron. Three wide, curved, tiered steps led down to a white-cobbled path wider than the Dredge. It led straight through the garden I'd seen in the darkness last night to an open front gate. Trees rustled in the sunlight. Gerrold waited at the bottom of the steps with three horses and a young boy I didn't know holding the three sets of reins. One of the horses stamped its foot and shook its head.

My eyes narrowed as Borund and William moved toward the horses. I stayed on the rounded top of the stairs, by the door. On the Dredge, horses were to be avoided, unless they could be ducked under for a quick but dangerous escape. Most were larger than me, and definitely heavier.

Borund was already seated before he realized I hadn't moved. "I assume you haven't ridden," he said dryly.

"No."

He frowned. "That will have to change. But not today. We'll move slow enough you can follow." He turned toward Gerrold. "Gerrold, you should have known she couldn't ride."

The man ducked his head briefly. "My apologies. I didn't think, sir."

Borund nudged the horse toward the gate.

William mounted with smooth skill, then motioned the boy and the remaining horse along another path toward the back of the manse. He turned toward me. "The horse won't bite," he said. "Come and touch him."

Ahead, Borund had paused, had turned back in his saddle to watch, annoyed.

I came down the steps reluctantly, halted just out of reach of the horse. He snorted, nosed forward as if trying to smell me, but William kept him in check with the reins and a soft clicking sound. The horse's ears swiveled back at the noise, then forward as he lowered his head.

I had to look up into his eyes, but I reached out tentatively with one hand, glancing toward William. William smiled and nodded his head, so I touched the horse on its neck.

The horse remained still, not moving, a shudder running down the muscles in his neck. The short brown hair felt smooth and warm in the sunlight, taut with energy, ready for motion. I stroked the horse's neck and the creature snorted again.

I smiled and laughed, the sound strange and startling in the late morning stillness.

When I looked up toward William, he was grinning, his face open, easy to read, his eyes bright. "I never would have thought to hear you laugh," he said, and then *he* laughed himself, as if the statement were somehow absurd.

He turned the horse, slowly, so the movement wouldn't startle me. Farther down the path, Borund turned back to the gate. His annoyance had vanished, replaced by amused tolerance. I fell into step a few paces away from William and his horse, far enough to run if necessary, but close enough I could still smell the horse's dark humid sweat.

"The horse's name is Fetlock," William said as we caught up to Borund and entered the street, "and Borund's mount is called Brindle, because Gart—the stableboy—thought the horse's color was shit-brindle brown when we bought him. The name stuck."

Borund snorted and mumbled, "Bloody stupid name," under his breath, shaking his head. But he was smiling. He reached forward and patted Brindle's neck roughly, the horse nodding his head as if in agreement.

The streets of Amenkor this close to the palace were practically empty and I gazed up at the sky as I had done on the Dredge, raising one hand to shade away the sun. There were no clouds today, the sky a pure blue. A steady breeze blew in from the harbor.

I let my gaze drop to the water of the harbor. Borund's manse was situated high enough up the slope that I could see down over the rooftops to the wharf, could see the masts of the ships tied at the docks. More ships sat in the harbor itself, appearing calm amid the slate gray of the waves.

I ignored the far side of the bay to my left, across the River, where the Dredge ran. Instead, I turned my gaze in the other direction, upward, toward the palace.

In the sunlight, the walls seemed smooth, colored like brown eggshell, with only a few windows at the lower levels. There were three layers of walls, the palace offset from the center inside the third wall, a few towers rising into the empty sky. Flags and banners flapped in the wind, too far away to be heard, their colors bright against the light brown of the palace and the sky.

"That's where we're headed," William said beside me, nodding toward the palace and the walls. "The old city. It's where we're most likely to find Charls this time of day."

I stared at what I could see of the palace between the buildings and above the walls a long moment, then turned my attention to the street. We were moving from the mostly empty streets where Borund's manse lay into more crowded areas, and almost without thought I slid beneath the river.

It was just like the Dredge. Or the wharf. A world of gray and red, a wash of sound in the background.

The tension in my shoulders and back shifted, from nervousness about the horses and William and Borund, to apprehension about protecting them from Charls. I could still feel the tavern, the desperation as I'd fought through the crowded tables, searching. I glanced up to William to see if he'd noticed, but he was watching the street intently, frowning, as focused as I was. He could still feel the tavern as well. I could see it in his eyes.

So I turned back to the street and with a subtle push on the river felt it shift, new people emerging to the fore, those that were possible threats to Borund. Those that were threats to me—the guardsmen, men with visible weapons—mostly slid into the background, a bleached red.

I settled in to watch.

We emerged onto a wide, crowded street and turned into the general flow heading up toward the palace. The noise increased, people shouting, hawkers bellowing, men cursing. The crush of horses and men—many more horses than I was used to—forced me to walk closer to William and Fetlock, almost touching the horse's side. Up ahead, I could see the first wall, an arched gateway standing open to the street. As we approached, the crush of bodies grew worse, as bad as the press of the tavern, tight and restrictive. The background noise beneath the river tripled and I felt my control beginning to slip, felt sweat break out on my back, in my armpits, felt my breathing increase.

Then we were through the gate, past the wall, and the crowd fell back, loosened.

I blew out a held breath, then steadied. Neither Borund nor William seemed to notice me or the crowds, continuing on up toward the second wall.

I tried to calm myself, my heart still shuddering in my chest.

"This is the outer circle," William suddenly said, motioning toward the surrounding buildings, "or rather, outer oval. This is where most of the merchants live, along with a few of the highest-ranking Guard and sea captains. Those with some influence. Essentially it's a residential area, close to the palace for when there's a need for the merchants to speak with Avrell, the First of the Mistress—or, more rarely, the Mistress herself—about trade negotiations and how they might affect the city or our relations to the surrounding cities of the coast. It's also close to the guild halls in the middle circle, and the wharf and the warehouse district below, on the harbor. Borund could live here if he wanted, but chose to live below, in the city. He always felt that living here would distance him from the everyday man. He was raised near the wharf, built his merchant house out of nothing but spit and hard work." William had straightened in his saddle, watched the passing buildings with a strange hope in his eyes. Almost under his breath, he added, "I want to live here someday, though."

I glanced around and frowned. This close to the main street, the buildings were tight together, almost as tight as the Dredge, and each doorway had a painted sign over it, all with designs that had no meaning to me. Two crossed swords on one, a three-masted ship on another. One seemed to be three squiggled lines, like waves.

Through the paned windows, I could see mostly empty rooms, the only furnishings desks and chairs and high countertops. Shelves lined the walls, packed with statues and plants like Borund's room. A few had large sacks and barrels instead. Most had sheaves of papers scattered over the desks and on the walls. And then I noticed that here and there, almost lost among the rest of the shops, were a few empty buildings, doors closed, windows boarded up. The empty buildings sent a cold shudder across my shoulders, as if someone had just breathed against the nape of my neck.

The empty buildings reminded me of the Dredge. This is what the Dredge must have once looked like—its buildings intact, its streets full of merchants and shoppers. But now this street was beginning to decay, beginning to fade. The empty stores were simply the first outward sign. My frown deepened.

"There's nothing for sale in those shops," I said.

I meant the empty buildings, but William didn't seem to notice them, didn't even seem to see them. He smiled without looking down at me. "Ah, but that's the thing. Amenkor is the crossroads of the Frigean coast, the gateway to the nations in the east, on the far side of the mountains. *Everything's* for sale in these shops. You just have to know the right person."

I didn't answer, uneasiness settling into my stomach.

Up ahead, we were approaching another gate and the second wall. William turned away from the shops toward the wall. "And this is the middle circle. All the guild halls are in here. We'll find Charls at the merchants' guild, no doubt." His voice darkened when he mentioned Charls. "That's where most of the actual business of trading and selling takes place."

We passed through the second gate into a large, open, square marketplace with huge stone buildings on all sides, broken up by various streets. The marketplace was crowded, but there were fewer hawkers than on the wharf. They stuck mainly near the center of the square, around the towering fountain. I paused to stare at the three stone horses that reared toward the sky, a spit of water pouring out of the top, three more spouts of water emerging from the horses' mouths. The water collected in a giant pool at the base.

Cobbler's Fountain seemed suddenly small and insignificant, almost childish.

William and Borund continued across the square, toward the largest of the stone buildings, its front riddled with carved statues of men and women, lying down on stone benches, standing and reaching for the sky, most wearing nothing at all. Some appeared to move until we got closer and I realized there were birds in the crevices of the carvings. There were birds everywhere, on the cobbled square itself, lining the stone steps leading up to the doorway that seemed small in comparison to the rest of the building. They fluttered out of the way of passersby, muttering soft, throaty coos of protest.

I followed Borund and William numbly, but we didn't approach the steps. Instead, we moved toward a side street, passing beneath an arch and along a narrow until it opened up into a courtyard where men practiced with swords and boys rushed, running errands. As soon as Borund and William appeared and dismounted, two boys stepped forward and led the horses away.

Borund motioned to William as we entered the merchants' guild through a side door and began climbing stairs. "He'll be in the Great Hall now," he said, glancing back quickly toward me. His mud-brown eyes were hooded and dangerous, but not like Erick's had been. Erick's eyes had been cold, purposeful, casual. Borund's were heated and intense, angry.

We passed through a low-arched doorway and into the Great Hall and I tensed, the hackles on the back of my neck rising. I resisted the urge to crouch, to draw my dagger and slip back through the doorway. I couldn't stop a harsh hiss of warning, like a pissed-off cat.

In the swirling gray world of the river, almost everyone in the room was red. A shroud fell over me, covered me like a blanket, pushed me down with its weight. All of the awe over the size of the room—over the fountain and the buildings and the walls outside as well—died, replaced by the instincts of the Dredge.

"What is it?" someone murmured, the voice muffled by the pressure I felt from the river. Then someone touched my arm.

William. I could *feel* him, smell him. Borund, as well. But I didn't turn to look at them. Instead, I kept my gaze focused on the room, on the people milling about, on the soft background noise of their conversations.

"What is it, Varis?" Borund asked, his voice a little more commanding than William's.

"Everyone here is dangerous," I said.

He grunted. "How can you tell?"

"I can see it," I answered without thought. "They're all red."

A long, heavy silence followed, but I was too distracted by the pressure to notice until Borund spoke again, his voice tight. "I'm only interested in one of them today, and I don't see him. Do you?"

I drew a deep breath and tried to concentrate more. As I submerged myself deeper, the reds shifted into various shades, some darker, like blood, others more vibrant.

I focused on those like blood, pushed the others into the background. There were fewer of them, and one of them was Charls.

He wasn't a mix of red and gray now, but a deep red. Even when I shifted the focus of the river back to myself briefly.

"There," I said, and pointed.

Borund laid a hand gently on mine and lowered it slowly. "Don't draw attention. Just nod in the right direction. We don't want anyone here to know the real reason we came."

I frowned, then realized it was like the Dredge, like standing at the edge of a narrow, looking for a mark.

Borund wanted us to be gray.

I nodded in the direction of Charls, and with a swift look at William, Borund began to move through the room. I kept my attention fixed on Charls and the few other washes of blood red. Borund paused occasionally to speak with other merchants, some dressed like Borund in long coats of differing colors with gold embroidery. Most had less gold than Borund, and after a quick scan of each, I dismissed them as harmless.

We edged closer to Charls, moving in a wide arc.

"Borund!"

I turned to see a dark, blue-coated merchant approaching, arms held wide. He had a plain face, a wide grin, hazel eyes, dimples. His hair hung down to his shoulders and had been tied back into a ponytail. He had no trace of red to him at all.

Borund smiled as they grasped arms at the elbows and clapped each other on the back. "Marcus, it's good to see you! How's Marlett?"

A bitter expression crossed Marcus' face and he scowled. "The city's hurting. Not enough wares to be found. And what we can find is becoming too expensive to buy."

"Not much better here in Amenkor, I'm afraid."

Marcus turned serious. "I heard about the tavern."

"Word travels fast."

"Good you had a bodyguard, eh?"

There was a hint of something more behind Marcus' voice and Borund fell silent. I gave Marcus a dark stare. Unconsciously, he shifted away.

"Yes. My bodyguard."

After a moment, Marcus cleared his throat. "I also hear you have some grain in storage?"

"You shouldn't always listen to rumor, Marcus. Now spice! I have plenty of spice!"

"I don't need spice," Marcus protested darkly, and the two began bargaining, just like any hawker and his victim on the Dredge or wharf. I let the conversation fall into the background and turned back to Charls.

He'd shifted, moved to the edge of the room, toward one of the walls covered in tapestries. Most of the room was empty of furniture, the polished stone floor bare, but near some of the walls sat a few chairs. Light streamed through tall, thin windows, slanting across the floor at an angle, but Charls stood in the most shadowed corner of the room now.

He spoke with someone I could barely see. Someone as blood red as himself. Another merchant.

I stepped back from Borund, Marcus, and William and focused.

He wore a dark yellow coat, like mustard, covered with gold thread. Ruffles filled the neck, puffed out of the sleeves. His face was narrow, but not thin, his nose long. He had a mustache, neatly trimmed. His brown hair was streaked heavily with gray and hung down his back in a ponytail longer than Marcus'.

He seemed somehow vaguely familiar.

I felt William step up beside me and realized that Borund had broken away from Marcus and moved on. I turned back to Charls, drew breath to ask William who Charls was speaking to, but the mustard-coated merchant had vanished.

Charls had moved back out into the light when Borund finally approached him. He smiled graciously.

"Master Borund," he said, his voice deep and somehow slick, like the dead fish on the wharf.

"Master Charls," Borund murmured. None of the danger I'd seen in his eyes touched him as he reached out and grasped Charls' arm at the elbow, as he'd done with Marcus, the contact brief.

Deep inside, I felt the Fire stir, a shiver running down the backs of my arms. I shifted slightly forward.

"Rough crowd down at the Broken Mast Tavern, so I hear," Charls said.

"Nothing I couldn't handle." Borund grinned. "That's why I like the docks. Always something . . . unexpected."

Charls' eyes flicked toward me, absorbed me with one quick, careful, considering glance, then stole away, back to Borund. "Yes. Something 'unexpected' always seems to intervene when you least expect it." There was a tinge of sourness to the words. But then Charls shifted. "But Amenkor has become desperate. Roughness is to be expected, just to survive. Wouldn't you agree, Master Borund?"

"No," Borund said shortly. And now he let the anger inside darken his eyes, blatant and targeted. "No. And it won't be tolerated either. The Mistress will see to that."

Charls seemed surprised, but then his smile widened.

The tendril of Fire inside surged higher and my hand stole toward my dagger. William sensed the movement and shifted farther away.

"Ah, Borund," Charls murmured, his voice soft. "I think you place too much faith in the Mistress. I don't think she rules the city anymore. Haven't you heard? The Mistress has gone insane."

Borund snorted. "And now you deal in rumor?" An edge entered Borund's voice. "Beware of what you play at, Charls. There is more at stake here than just business. You're dealing with the life of the city. The Mistress will hear about the attack last night."

Charls chuckled. "Yes, yes. Tell the Mistress, if you can reach her. She doesn't grant audience to anyone anymore. To even get into the palace you have to get through Captain Baill and his guards. And then your chances of seeing Avrell, let alone the Mistress, are slim. The Mistress has never been this hard to reach in the past. I wonder why? And as for the city . . ." Charls leaned forward, his eyes going dark and tight. The Fire inside flared and I stepped forward, stepped between the two, near Borund's shoulder, my hand on the dagger hidden at my side.

Charls didn't flinch, his eyes fixed firmly on Borund.

"You would be wise to leave the city alone, Master Borund. Powers are shifting, have been shifting since the Fire scoured its way across Amenkor. You slipped through the net once; I wouldn't wait around to see if it happens again."

Charls backed off, smiled thinly and reached to brush nonexistent lint off of Borund's shoulder. I halted him with a look and a slight shift in weight.

His smile faltered.

Then he moved away, engaged another merchant in conversation, his laugh echoing loudly over the conversations in the hall at something the merchant said. The merchant looked confused, but Charls put his hand on the merchant's back and guided him away, head bent close.

He glanced back once, smile tight and self-satisfied.

Then he was lost among the crowd.

At my back, Borund trembled with suppressed rage.

·⟨ *The Palace* ⟩·

MY heart had barely begun to calm, back still pressed against what had once been a granite wall outside the archer's niche, when there were sudden hurried footsteps from the corridor on the other side of the little window.

I slid down close to the opening and peered into the hallway just in time to see the two guardsmen I'd noted before jerk to rigid attention on either side of the doorway they guarded. They'd barely managed to compose themselves when another guard appeared, approaching fast, almost at a run.

I saw him just before he reached the two guards and shuddered, drawing back from the old window.

Captain Baill.

Beside the archer's window, I cursed, then slid back to watch, eyes narrowed in anger and suspicion. What was Baill doing here now? He should be safely occupied elsewhere. In the city, on the walls, at home in bed—anywhere but in the inner sanctum of the palace.

Unless someone had warned him, had alerted him to my presence. But who?

Captain Baill wore all the armor of his rank, was moving swiftly, his eyes darkened with intense irritation and something close to hatred. His bald head gleamed in the torchlight, his face covered in scars. Old scars. *Earned* scars. They surrounded dark eyes that shifted restlessly even as he walked—calculating eyes that saw everything, and *remembered*.

He moved toward the two guardsmen with purpose, barked, "Has anyone passed by here in the last hour?"

"No one, Captain."

"Fuck!"

The two guards glanced at each other, startled. Baill stared at the stone floor a moment, one hand rising to rub across his bald head.

Then he glanced up, scarred face hard.

"Come with me," he said.

One of the guards began to protest, motioning toward the door they guarded.

"It's a fucking audience chamber!" Baill roared. "There's nothing in there! We've got bigger problems."

And he began moving away, fast. Toward the main entrance to the inner sanctum, the doorway that had once been an outer gate.

The two guards hesitated a moment, then followed.

Then they were gone.

†

I dropped back from the archer's window, heart suddenly pounding. *Did* Baill know I was here? *Had* he been warned?

The fear twisted into anger, the taste of sickness on my tongue now bitter, like ash.

Had Avrell had a change of heart and warned them? Had *he* betrayed me?

It seemed unlikely. He was the one who'd hired me. He'd been the one arguing so fervently with Nathem to convince him that the Mistress' death was essential.

But who else could it have been? No one else knew I was here tonight except Avrell. He'd seen me in the meeting room, knew exactly where I was. . . .

A sudden flood of relief washed over me. It *had* been Avrell. But he hadn't warned Baill to betray me. He'd done it to help. Avrell knew the plan, knew I'd been in the meeting room, *knew that I was behind schedule.* He must have assumed I'd miss the changing of the guard.

So he'd provided the guardsmen with a distraction.

My hand tightened on my dagger in determination and I spun back to the archer's window, gauged the narrow opening. It didn't matter if Avrell had warned Baill to help me, or if someone else had warned Baill to stop me. Whatever the case, this might be my only chance to get past the outer perimeter of palace guardsmen. And I *had* to reach the Mistress tonight. There was no more time left, not if the city was to survive the winter.

Placing one hand at the top of the opening, reaching through with the other, I shoved my head and shoulders through. If I'd had anything in the way of breasts, I'd have been fucked. It was the only reason I'd been passable as a page boy, and one of the only reasons the plan to get me into the inner sanctum of the palace would work.

I exhaled sharply, pushing all the air out of my lungs in one hard gasp, and wedged my chest through next. Pausing to get a better grip on the granite, I drew in a gulp of air, the window crushing me. Too tight. I couldn't draw in a full breath. Pain shot up through my lungs. I gasped, began breathing in short huffs, exhaled all the air again and shoved, the window's edge scraping down to my hips.

For a heartrending moment, I thought the opening was too small, my frame too big. I panicked. Sweat broke out in the pits of my arms, slicked my palms. I shoved again, strained against the granite, felt it grinding into my pelvic bones—

And then, with a sharp, stinging pain, my hips scraped through and I collapsed into the archer's niche on the far side with a hiss, legs still dangling out the other side, into the linen closet. I pulled them through, lances of pain shooting up my sides, but I shoved that pain away and crouched in the niche.

In both directions, the corridor was empty. But I could hear voices now, shouts, heavy boots running in my direction.

I darted across the corridor to the door of the audience chamber. The unguarded door opened without a sound, but slowly, the solid wood heavy. I ducked inside, pulled it closed behind me and turned.

I was inside the palace's inner sanctum.

And all hell had apparently broken loose.

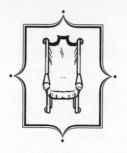

Chapter 10

WILLIAM thrust open the door to Borund's office with such force it cracked against the wall and almost rebounded back into his face. I'd moved halfway across the room without making a sound, dagger drawn, before I recognized him. Even after two months guarding Borund, I still hadn't relaxed when in his manse. Some habits from the Dredge were hard to break.

William stood in the doorway, mouth opening and closing, staring at Borund.

"What is it?" Borund said, rising from his seat behind his desk. His voice was steady, but since I'd been guarding him, I'd learned to read the undertones. They were touched with dread, as if he already knew the news, or already suspected.

William must have noticed as well, for he sagged slightly and drew in a breath. "Marcus is dead."

I frowned down at the floor, raced through all of the merchants I'd met. I'd accompanied Borund everywhere for the last two months—on excursions to the warehouses, to the docks to meet the ships, to the local taverns and the guild hall for meetings with merchants and captains and sources of information. I'd met dozens of merchants, some from the cities along the Frigean coast, others from more distant places, like Warawi, a city in the southern islands.

At first the outings had been tense, Borund expecting another attack. He'd gone to the palace to complain to Avrell but had been met by the palace guard instead. They'd sent for Baill, refused to send a message to Avrell or even the Second, Nathem, until we'd spoken to the captain.

I'd been on edge the entire time, eyes furtively scanning the guardsmen as they passed through the gates of the inner wall, expecting to see Erick, expecting one of the guards to gasp and point, then drag me away.

Instead, Baill had arrived, his bald head shiny in the sunlight, his eyes flat and impregnable. The moment I saw him, I knew we weren't going to see Avrell or Nathem. We weren't going to see anyone. Baill was a wall—dressed in armor, body solid, face scarred, but a wall nonetheless.

Borund sensed it as well. He straightened outside the gates, jaw tightening.

He told Baill of the attack at the tavern, told him of the attempt on his life, even implicated Charls.

"Can you prove it?" Baill had asked. His eyes were intent, attention completely on Borund and his story, noting everything—every frown, every glance, every nervous shift in position.

Borund motioned toward me. "Varis, my bodyguard, saw Charls outside the tavern, saw him give the order."

Baill turned his gaze on me and inside I felt myself cringe. Baill was the man Erick would report to. If Erick had told anyone about me, about how I'd killed Bloodmark, it would be his captain.

But there was no recognition in Baill's eyes. Nothing but the same harsh glare he'd given Borund. As if he were assessing me, deciding whether I was a threat or merely an inconvenience.

We were a distraction, one that he did not want to deal with right now. There was something else weighing on his mind.

"What exactly did you see?" he asked. His voice was low, rolled like thunder.

I told him—of the hatred in Charls's eyes, of the nod.

Baill grunted, turned back to Borund. "I can't arrest anyone based on a look and a nod."

Then he headed back inside the gates, the matter already dismissed from his mind. In that single unguarded moment, when he was turned away, I saw something in his eyes. Fear, concern, uncertainty. Nothing but a flicker, there and then gone.

Borund watched Baill's retreating back in shock.

Borund protested again, but there was no proof that the attack at the tavern had been anything but a simple theft gone bad, a consequence of the rich roughing it where they shouldn't be. And when no more attacks occurred against Borund, the matter was shrugged aside by the guard.

The Mistress wasn't informed. Any attempts to see her, or Avrell, or any of the rest of Avrell's staff concerning the attack, were blocked by Baill and the guardsmen. Access to the palace had been restricted. On the Mistress' orders.

Two weeks passed without anything suspicious occurring as Borund went about his business. No subtle threats except through words on the floor of the guild hall. No one following Borund or William on the streets between his manse, the wharf, and the warehouse district.

After a while, Borund began to relax, began to think that perhaps Baill was right, that perhaps having a bodyguard was unnecessary.

My stomach had tightened at the muttered thought, but he never approached me about leaving. He looked at me with a troubled glance, as if he didn't know what to do with me, as if he wanted to let me go but found that he couldn't.

Then the attacks had begun on other merchants. All of them had been described as accidents, or muggings. And all of them reeked of something else.

Borund stopped mumbling about letting me go.

He discussed the situation—Baill, the attacks, the threat—with William. We all knew who was behind it. But nothing could be proved.

Borund went back to the palace anyway, met with Baill again. But the answer was the same. There wasn't enough to convince Baill that these weren't simply random attacks. That had been four weeks ago, after the second death. Captain Baill had been so abrupt and condescending that Borund hadn't bothered when the third merchant died. The palace guard wasn't going to help.

Marcus. I suddenly remembered the dark, blue-coated man at the merchant's guild. The one with dimples. The one who didn't want spice. From Marlett.

The attacks were no longer restricted to the merchants of Amenkor. They'd expanded to include merchants from other cities along the coast.

I heard something fall heavily, like deadweight, and glanced up. Borund had collapsed back into his chair.

"Marcus?" He stared down at the papers before him blankly, then said again, "Marcus?"

William moved into the room, shut the door behind himself.

At the small noise, Borund looked up and he slapped his palm flat against his desk, sat up straight. "That's the fourth one since the attack in the tavern. And he wasn't even from Amenkor. This merchants' war has gone too far. It has to end."

"It's not going to stop," I said.

Both William and Borund looked toward me. I rarely spoke, kept myself in the background, uninvolved unless one of them addressed me with a specific question, especially when it dealt with Borund's business.

But this wasn't business. At least, not normal business.

Borund's eyes held mine, mouth pulled down into a frown. He didn't want to believe what I said, didn't want to think that Amenkor had degenerated that far.

"No," he said, turning away from my blunt stance. "No, it *must* stop. It's gone on long enough. I don't care how 'accidental' some of the previous deaths looked, they weren't accidents. And I don't care that we can't prove anything, that it's all hearsay and circumstance. Baill can just . . ." He paused, steadied himself with an effort, then asked in a harsh voice, "How did Marcus die?"

"Knife to the throat, on the docks. It happened a few days ago, or at least that's when he was last seen. They found him floating in the harbor this morning. It *looks* like another random mugging."

Borund snorted. "This was no mugging. We all know that. I'm beginning to think even Baill knows it, and he's simply choosing to do nothing about it, for whatever reason." The longer he sat behind his desk, the angrier he became. His fingers were tapping at the papers, his eyes flicking blindly from sheet to sheet.

Finally, he slapped his palm down on the desk again and stood. "No. It has to stop. Get Gerrold to ready the horses. We're going to the old city."

"The guild?" William asked, moving to the door.

"No. To the palace. I want to speak to the Mistress herself this time. Or at the very least Avrell. If I have to, I'll tell Baill it's guild related. He'll have to let me in then. It's my right as a member of the merchants' guild, damn it!"

William paused at the door, back rigid in shock, but nodded and left without a word.

†

"My apologies, Master Borund," Avrell, the First of the Mistress, said as he emerged from an open arch into the sitting room, "but the Mistress is not seeing anyone today."

Borund rose from his seat among the pillows, stiff with angry irritation. William rose as well. I was already standing, back to a wall so I could see the entire room. It was small, scattered with low seats, piles of cushions, and tables holding pitchers of water and plates of fruit. A few lattice-worked screens placed near the corners of the room sectioned off areas where people could meet more discreetly.

"I don't understand why it's taken so long for someone to see us," Borund said. "We've been waiting for an audience all afternoon!"

"I know. I was informed just now by the Second and came immediately." The First bowed his head and cast a measured glance toward me.

For a moment, he stiffened, his eyes widening slightly in surprise. Then he seemed to catch himself, his expression going blank, revealing nothing.

I frowned, felt a tingle of worry across my skin. I concentrated, pushed beneath the river.

The First swirled both gray and red. When I shifted the focus to Borund, the First was simply gray.

Avrell had raised his head and was now regarding Borund, but his attention seemed fixed on me, as if he were still watching, still . . . assessing.

I shifted uncomfortably. The First wore dark blue robes, an eight-pointed star symbol stitched on the chest in gold. His hands were clasped inside the wide sleeves, hidden. But he wasn't a threat to Borund, and wasn't an immediate or direct threat to me, if the red-gray coloration was any indication, so I forced myself to relax.

Instead, I took in his dark blue eyes, the lines of his face, his dark features, eyebrows and hair black. I listened to his voice, steady and soft, and watched his movements, every motion precise, considered. Occasionally, he would look in my direction. Nothing direct, but enough to make me stir. After a moment I realized why.

I never faded into the background for him as I did with almost everyone Borund dealt with. I never became gray.

Avrell was far too interested in me.

"I've tried to see you or the Mistress repeatedly over the last few months," Borund said, "and I've been turned aside by Captain Baill at every attempt. I'm beginning to think the rumors about the Mistress are true!"

Avrell froze, every muscle stilling with sudden interest. For the first time, his attention seemed to focus completely on Borund. "The Mistress is simply unavailable today," he said, voice hard as stone. "And, in general, I have been extremely busy. As you know, the coastal cities are in a stage of flux, everyone uncertain about the meaning of the passage of the White Fire six years ago. Now we've lost contact with Kandish and the other nations on the far side of the mountains, and winter is bearing down on us. . . . It is a difficult time. Surely, as a merchant of the guild, you see that?"

Borund sighed. "Of course. Business has been rough lately. That is precisely why I wanted to speak to you. Forgive my irritation, but Captain Baill. . . ." Borund clenched his jaw, shook his head slightly.

Avrell's stance relaxed, so subtly that Borund didn't seem to notice. The First seemed relieved.

In much too casual a tone, he asked, "Baill?"

"Yes, Captain Baill," Borund said shortly.

"He did not inform me that you had come to the palace to see me regarding guild matters before this."

Borund winced. "This does not pertain directly to the guild. I used the guild to gain access to the palace. To you."

Avrell did not react at first. "I see," he said finally. His brow creased in confusion. "So what did you need to see me or the Mistress about then, if not for guild matters?"

Borund hesitated, shot a quick glance toward William and me, then straightened. "I trust you will bring this to the Mistress' attention?"

"Of course."

Borund nodded in relief. "Another merchant has died. Master Marcus, a representative of Marlett."

I felt the air in the room grow tense.

" 'Another' merchant?"

Borund stared at Avrell in shock. "Yes. I would have thought you would have been informed."

"I *should* have been informed," the First said, his tone harsh. He stared for a moment at a blank wall, gaze abstracted and annoyed, as if he were looking at something deeper inside the palace. Unnoticed by Borund or William, he mouthed "Baill" as if it were a curse under his breath. Then his attention snapped back to Borund. "Captain Baill has not kept me informed of your . . . complaints," the First said. "Nor of the deaths of any merchants. When did this happen? How?"

Borund sighed, the sound short and sharp. "Marcus' body was found this morning in the harbor, a knife wound in the throat."

"And there are more deaths? How many have there been?"

"Four."

The First's eyes narrowed. "Four? Amenkor has become extremely dangerous for merchants lately."

Borund barked a short laugh that held no humor, then caught the intent look in the First's eyes and went still. They watched each other a long moment, something passing between them wordlessly. Borund's expression grew grim.

Eventually, the First stirred. "Thank you, Master Borund. I'll see what can be done. I'm sorry to say that I've been extremely distracted lately with other matters pertaining to the Throne and outside the guild. But perhaps I can pay you a visit sometime, so that we can discuss this problem," he cast a quick glance toward me, "and perhaps other issues, in more detail?"

Borund hesitated, then nodded. "Very well." He wasn't totally placated, that was clear in his voice, but he motioned William to his side. William nodded as well.

The First acknowledged them, then turned to leave, but not before glancing once more toward me.

I didn't move, kept my eyes hooded, unreadable, stance rigid.

A slight smile tugged at the corner of the First's mouth a moment before he passed through the arched opening into the next room. He seemed somehow satisfied, as if a nagging problem he'd been fretting over for days had just been solved.

†

"Do you think anything will change?" William asked Borund as we passed through the gates of the inner ward of the palace into the middle ward containing the guild halls. William and Borund were both mounted. I stood between the two horses and slightly forward, on foot.

"Perhaps," Borund answered distractedly. He'd been deep in thought since the meeting with the First. "There's more going on here than a shifting of power in the guild of merchants. Much more."

"But what?"

Borund shook his head. "I don't know. Something in the palace? Something to do with the Mistress? I don't know. If Avrell and Baill are involved, then it must have something to do with the throne." Borund's voice was lowered, as if speaking to himself.

I was more concerned about Avrell himself. He'd watched me too closely, had been far too interested in me for comfort.

They fell silent and I scanned ahead. We were on one of the narrow streets behind the guild halls, headed toward the large market square with the horse fountain. The last of the sunlight was fading from the sky, and the shadows were collecting beneath the buildings, dark and thick like on the Dredge.

The thought sent a shiver through me, and with a cold start I realized the Fire inside my gut had shuddered to life. Low, almost nonexistent, but there, trembling.

I straightened. But there were few people out this late, not in the middle ward of the old city. The old city was dead.

I shifted back, moved in closer to Borund, William, and the horses. None of them seemed to notice.

"What *can* they do to stop the killings?" William asked again a short while later.

Borund didn't reply. Not even with a grunt.

William sighed and gave up, staring forward into the darkened street.

The Fire was burning higher now, curling up into my chest. We passed a cross street and I tensed, glancing down the new street in both directions, but it was empty. Most of the windows in the surrounding buildings were dark as well, only a few glowing with internal candlelight. Torchlight flickered on the old city's surrounding walls, but it was distant, out of reach.

The cross street fell behind. I glanced back once, but saw nothing.

The cold Fire began to travel through my shoulders, prickled the base of my neck.

We passed into the shadows of the next building and I looked up, toward the thin band of the night sky, toward the stars. The stone of the buildings seemed suddenly too close, too confining, pressing down, cold and immobile.

And then I caught movement out of the corner of my eye.

My gaze snapped down to the street, to the sides of the buildings, and in the patterned gray I saw the darknesses: the arch on the left side that led to an inner courtyard, the niches on the right that led to small doors. The movement had come from one of the niches twelve paces ahead, but we'd already drawn abreast of the first niche, were pulling up alongside the arch to the courtyard.

The Fire inside suddenly flared, but it was too late.

I drew my dagger, yelled out, "Borund!" in warning, but the figures hidden in the niches and in the arch dove out of the darkness.

Borund's horse reared as he pulled on the reins, then it screamed, hooves kicking the air, and came down hard, caught one of the men with a crushing blow, trampling him underfoot. The sharp scent of blood flooded my senses, staggering in its intensity. I turned and surged forward, but Borund's horse foundered, fell to one side, knocked William's horse away. Startled, William lost his seat, slipped sideways in his saddle as it danced for footing, but the motion forced me back.

And then I felt the man behind me.

I stilled, plunged deeper, beneath the scent of blood, beneath the chaos of the men and the huff and stamp of the horses. Like that first fight on the wharf, with the merchant's sons, I sank deep enough I could taste the metal of the knives the men held, could feel their sweat, their desperation. Deep enough that I could sense their movements before they made them.

The man behind me swung, the blade silent as it slashed through air. With the cold grace and brutal quickness Erick had trained into me, I ducked to one side, beneath the man's too wide slash, and thrust backward, hard, felt my dagger slip in and out of flesh, scrape against bone, and then I shifted forward, before the man had even gasped. I felt his knees hit the cobbles at the same time as William's body struck the wall of the building to the right. For a moment, a horrible pain swept through my stomach as I thought he'd been crushed between the building and his horse, but Fetlock gained his balance at the last moment, William slipping gracelessly between the horse and the wall to the road, foot still caught in one stirrup.

One of the horses screamed again. The other snorted in terror.

My attention flicked to Borund. His horse had separated from William's. Borund and the horse stood in the center of the street, one of the attackers crumpled at the horse's dancing feet, three others closing in tight, hemming in the terrified horse. Of the three, two were too close, a danger to Borund. The third wouldn't get to Borund in time. I could finish him off later.

One of the attackers reached up to pull Borund from his mount, and I moved.

The first never saw me, never heard me. My blade slid across his throat even as he took a step toward Borund. The man gripping Borund saw the movement, released Borund and jerked back, his face startled, but he was too slow. I felt warm blood on my hand as my dagger darted upward and across into his exposed armpit, sinking deep. It slid out, slick and smooth and silent.

I turned toward the last man, on the other side of Borund and his horse, but he wasn't there, wasn't where I expected—

And then I *felt* William, felt the cold Fire surging along my arms, tingling in my fingers.

No.

I halted, searching, feeling too slow, the same terror I'd felt when racing across the Dredge toward the white-dusty man's house now mingling with the Fire.

William had regained his feet. His horse had moved a few paces farther down the street. William was still leaning over, gasping for breath, when the last man's knife sank into his side from behind.

I felt the pain, tasted it, like stinging, bitter sap. It seared through me, through the Fire, through the terror, slashed into my side like molten metal, and I gasped.

William arched back, the shock on his face clear, so close, almost tangible. Neck muscles pulled taut with pain, jaw clenched, he stared toward me, toward Borund, then sank to his knees, arms lax.

The man jerked the knife from his side, shoved him forward to the cobbles, then ran.

For a moment, the narrow street was silent, still, nothing but the nervous snort of the horses at the scent of blood. Then Borund shouted, "William!" and stumbled down from his mount. He tripped on the cobbles, but lurched to William's side.

Blood was already pooling on the street, dark and black and cold in the starlight.

The serpent of rage around my heart that I hadn't felt since the Dredge uncoiled and slid free. I tasted the blood—William's blood—tasted the scent of the man who had stabbed him.

The scent led into the night, down the street to another arch. I could almost touch it.

My nostrils flared. The same calm anger that had consumed me on the Dredge after finding the white-dusty man's body enveloped me. I could hunt this man down, could find him no matter where he hid. . . .

I'd made it to the arch, not even conscious of moving, when Borund snapped, "Varis!"

I glared back at him, saw him recoil at whatever he saw in my eyes, on my face. I didn't care. This was my hunt. This was what I was.

But then Borund gasped, "He's still alive! We need to get him out of here and I can't move him myself!"

The naked desperation in his voice, the pure pain and the force behind it, cut through the white-cold anger. My gaze flicked down to William's face, held in Borund's hands. Beneath the river, I could see William breathing, his breath like steam in the air.

"Please," Borund whispered.

With effort, I let the scent of the man slip away, shoved the anger aside, and ran to William's side.

"We have to stop the bleeding," Borund muttered, shrugging out of his jacket with the gold embroidery. The white ruffled undershirt beneath was already flecked black with William's blood. "Get his horse. I'll have to hold him in the saddle as best I can while you run ahead to the house and tell Gerrold and Lizbeth to find a healer and prepare a bed."

"I can get the guards," I said, rising, but Borund's hand clamped down hard on my wrist, halting me.

"Tell no one else!" he hissed, eyes black with anger. "Especially the guards. After what Avrell told us, and especially after dealing with Baill, I don't trust the guards. Only Gerrold, Lizbeth, and the healer."

I hesitated, ready to protest that there was still one man out there, that leaving him alone with William was dangerous, that the manse was too far away, but the desperation in his eyes halted me.

He'd never listen, and I already knew that the last man had fled.

We hefted William up into the saddle of his horse, Borund grunting with effort, Fetlock snorting and shying, eyes white at the smell of blood. I suddenly recalled carrying the dead girl back to her mother, remembered how weightless the girl had felt in my arms, as if she were nothing but an empty grain sack, loose and useless.

William didn't feel empty, nor weightless.

Hope surged through me, like warm water.

Then William was seated as best we could manage and Borund snapped, "Go! Tell Gerrold to fetch Isaiah. Quick!"

And I ran, faster than I'd ever fled on the Dredge.

†

I stood inside one of the empty bedrooms at Borund's manse, tight against one corner, and watched the healer lean over William's body. He moved frantically, sweat dripping from his face, even though he wiped at it continuously with a cloth. His eyes were wide but intent, trained on his swiftly moving hands as they ripped clothes, pressed clean rags against the flow of blood, held them until they were soaked through, then tossed them aside. He whispered as he worked, short, terse statements that sounded almost like prayer.

Already, the floor was covered with blood-soaked rags. A black-red fan of blood stained the sheets of the bed, dripped with slow, viscous droplets to the hardwood floor. I stood still in the corner and watched the blood gather at the edge of the bedsheet, form into a pregnant drop, then stretch.

"Blessed Mistress, help us! Why won't the bleeding stop?" Isaiah hissed to himself.

And suddenly it was too much.

I fled the room, startled Lizbeth in the hall outside as she rushed to the room with more linen. She called out, "Varis!" but I was already past.

I flung myself into my room, so small in comparison to the one that held William, but I wrapped the closeness about me as I crouched into the corner, pulled myself into a tight ball. Tears threatened, but I thrust them back, cloaked myself in the coiled anger that still simmered, hot and deep. As deep as the Fire.

In the harshness of the anger I saw the street again, saw the fight, saw the three men surrounding Borund's horse. I felt my dagger slit the first man's throat, shudder into the second man's armpit. And the third man. . . .

I heard someone open the door to my room, slowly, hesitantly, and I pulled deeper into myself, the skin around my eyes tightening. Footsteps crossed the room, light and careful, and then Lizbeth murmured, "Oh, Varis."

She hesitated a long moment, her uncertainty like a stench on the air, then touched my shoulder.

At Lizbeth's touch I gasped, choked on the taste of thick phlegm in my throat, and crushed my knees in close.

Lizbeth sat awkwardly on the floor in the corner, hesitated again, then pulled me close to her chest, brushed my hair with one hand.

"I thought the last man was going for Borund," I hitched between gasps, voice so thick the words were almost unintelligible. But I would not cry. "I thought. . . ."

"I know," Lizbeth said. "Hush now. I know." And she began rocking back and forth, holding me tight, like the woman on the Dredge had rocked as she held the dead girl with the green ribbon in her arms.

Slowly, reluctantly, I let the tension drain out of my body, curled tighter to Lizbeth's chest.

A long time later, when the anger had finally settled, when my chest ached and I felt empty and weak, Lizbeth still stroking my hair, I glared out at the floor of my room, unseeing, and said quietly to myself, "I thought he was going for Borund."

†

Borund sat at his desk in his office, the papers that littered his desktop forgotten. A large decanter of wine sat squarely on top of them, a glass to one side, mostly empty. Some wine had spilled, but Borund didn't seem to notice.

I stood against one wall, a few paces distant, where I always stood. The large room, with the chairs, the tables, the scattering of statues and vases and shaped stones, felt hollow and empty.

Borund reached for the glass without looking, tipped it back with a violent gesture, and swallowed the remaining wine, placing the glass back on the table gently. His eyes never left the blank spot on the wall in front of him.

I shifted uncomfortably.

"He began his apprenticeship with me when he was nine, you know," Borund said suddenly, his voice too loud in the silence.

I didn't respond, watching him warily. It had been two days since we'd brought William back to the manse and Borund hadn't left the grounds once. He'd barely left his office, Gerrold bringing him food and wine. Lots of wine. Borund had sent Gerrold and Gart back to the street where we'd been attacked with a cart to take care of the bodies, but when Gerrold and the stableboy returned, they'd reported they'd found only blood on the cobbles. No bodies. Someone had already carted them away. Charls wouldn't have wanted Borund's body to be found in the middle ward. Not when he needed everyone to believe that the deaths were accidents. He must have had a cart waiting, ready to transport the corpses.

He just didn't get the corpses he expected.

A few doors away, William slept fitfully and deeply. Isaiah had stopped the bleeding eventually, had cleansed and sewn shut the wound, but he'd said it was up to the Mistress whether William would live. The knife had gone deep, and William had lost more blood than he'd ever seen a man lose before and still live. There was nothing any of us could do now except wait.

Borund smiled. "I remember him standing at the edge of the desk, barely able to contain himself, his hands twitching as he clutched them behind his back. He'd glare at me when I ordered him to stand still. Oh, not openly. When he thought I wasn't look-

ing. And he hated keeping the records, writing down all those num-
bers in the logbooks, keeping track of the price of acquisition, the
price the goods were sold for, the amount of the sale and to whom."
Borund's smile widened. "But he got over that with time." His
voice was slightly slurred, the imperfections caused by the wine
barely noticeable.

He looked up at me. "You don't read or write, do you?" He
didn't wait for an answer, merely grunted, as if he were disgusted
with himself for not thinking about it in the first place. "We'll have
to fix that. But not today."

It's what he'd said about the horses. I hadn't ridden one yet.

His attention faded for a moment, then focused on the empty
glass. He shifted forward enough so that he could reach the decanter and poured himself another glass, taking a good swallow before dropping back into his chair with a heavy sigh.

"Nine," he muttered, and his eyes darkened. "The bastard."

I knew he wasn't talking about William anymore. Over the last
two days, he'd only talked of two things: memories of William. . . .

And Charls.

I shifted again, straightened slightly, suddenly attentive. The
last few days I'd moved around the manse in a state of shock much
like Borund's. This morning, something had changed. I'd had an
idea. But I didn't know if Borund would agree to it.

"The bloody bastard," Borund hissed. "Vincentt, Sedwick,
Terell, Marcus . . . all dead. Accidents, my ass." He took another
swallow. "Charls has to be stopped."

I shifted forward, hesitated barely a breath, then said coldly, "I
can do it."

He didn't seem to hear at first, his gaze fixed again on the blank
wall. Then he looked up, almost startled. But the expression faded
fast, smoothed out into cold consideration, the expression of a merchant, weighing options, gains, risks.

This didn't last long either. The cold consideration of the merchant slowly shifted into dark anger. An anger I recognized. It was the anger that had seized me on the Dredge, when I'd gone in search of Bloodmark that final time, the same anger I'd felt on the street in the middle circle, when Borund had called me back from the hunt for the man who'd stabbed William.

"You can kill him? Without being seen?" he asked.

"It will take a little time. I'll have to follow him, figure out his patterns. But I can do it."

Something between us shifted. For the last few months, he'd wavered between ordering me to do things, and asking me, one moment laughing and joking with me, the next wondering whether a bodyguard was necessary, worth the expense. It had been awkward and unsettling. He didn't know whether to treat me as family, like William, or as a servant.

But now, as he watched me, I saw his uncertainty over how to treat me, how to think of me, solidify.

He'd seen me kill before, had seen me stand over the bodies. And this was the image that settled into his eyes there, in his office, as he leaned slightly forward, one hand resting on the desk. He saw me as I was: a dagger, a weapon, a tool.

I'd never be family.

Some part of me twisted inside, tightened with regret. But it was small and was smothered by anger. At that moment, I wanted Charls dead as well.

"Then do it," Borund said, and there was no longer a slur in his voice.

I straightened, hand resting on my dagger.

I would have done it anyway, no matter what Borund said.

But it felt good to have his approval.

†

I followed Charls and his men for the next two weeks, noted the taverns he liked to visit, the streets he traveled to get to his warehouses and the wharf, his manse behind the first set of walls in the residential district. At first, I stayed back, over fifty paces, just close enough I could keep him in sight. It wasn't hard to track him; he always kept at least two men at his side, like that first night I'd seen him, outside Borund's tavern. Bodyguards, like me. Gutterscum. But after a while I realized his bodyguards weren't as wary as someone from the Dredge would be, and so I shifted closer. Not enough to catch their attention, but enough to note that I wouldn't be able to kill Charls on the street, or at the warehouses or wharf. Not without being seen.

That left only one option: his manse.

At the end of one of these excursions, coming up onto the gates of Borund's manse, I saw Avrell leaving through the side entrance to the gardens. He checked the night-darkened street, but didn't see me. Then he drew a hood up over his head and moved away, toward the old city, his pace quick.

I frowned, wondered what he had come to Borund to discuss. But I said nothing.

That was Borund's business. My business was Charls.

And I was ready.

†

I stood at the side of the bed and stared down at William, at his rounded face, his wild hair, his eyes closed in sleep. His breathing came in soft sighs, barely audible. Even in the moonlight that came in through the open window, I could see that the grayness of his skin had faded in the two weeks since the attack. He was still weak, could move about his room with the aid of the wall and the furniture, but it caused him extreme pain.

The anger inside me writhed as I remembered how his face had contorted the first time he collapsed. Sweat had drenched his skin just from sitting upright. His face had blanched. When he'd tried to shift his weight to his legs, his feet hanging over the side of the bed, they'd given out, folded like cloth.

He'd gasped as he was falling, but when he hit the floor, Borund not swift enough to catch him—

I flinched back, heard the scream again, heard the agony. And as I drew in a deep breath I smelled the stench of his pain—old sweat and rotten meat.

I shook myself. The anger held a moment more, then calmed. The remembered stench faded into the salt of the sea as a breeze pushed past the curtains at the window.

William.

His brow creased, face tightened. Sweat sheened his skin, and one arm twitched.

"No," he murmured. "No!"

I reached forward, almost touched his cheek, but halted at the last moment.

Something twisted in my stomach and I snatched my hand back.

I'd seen the way he looked at me at the tavern, after I'd killed that first man. Not fear. I'd seen fear plenty of times on the Dredge. No. William was more than afraid, he was terrified. Of me. Of what I could do, what I held inside. He was afraid of who I was.

I crouched down beside the bed, shifted closer so that I could see William's face better in the darkness. I could smell his sweat, his scent. On the sheets, in the air.

His face was still contorted, and this close I could hear him whimpering.

I'd come into his room every night since I'd offered to kill Charls, and every night William fell into nightmare. Borund didn't know, but Lizbeth did. I wasn't certain how, since I made certain no one was near before I came, but somehow she knew.

Leaning even closer, I said softly, "Tonight."

William shook his head, mumbled "No" again, but the tension around his eyes relaxed. His brow smoothed and his breath calmed.

I watched him a moment more, then looked up toward the window, out into the night.

Tonight.

†

Gerrold let me out of the side entrance, the one Borund and William had used to bring me to the manse. I stood in the shadow of its alcove and stared out at the side street. I wouldn't move until the patrol had passed by.

A few days after the attempt on Borund in the middle ward, palace guardsmen began to appear in the city. Patrols had wandered the city at random before; that had started even before I killed Bloodmark and fled along the Dredge. I remembered the woman who'd halted one that first day in the real Amenkor, remembered watching them move on the streets after that, some on horseback, others walking. But after the attack on Borund. . . .

Now the guardsmen were everywhere, their patrols passing through the streets of the upper city at regular intervals, a few patrols scouring the wharf and docks below. Neither Borund nor I knew who had ordered them, Avrell or Baill. Perhaps it had been the Mistress. The guardsmen did nothing except ride by, watching, their eyes hard and dangerous, cold, their horses' hooves clopping on the cobbles. No words were spoken, unless they were interrupting a fight. But they were *felt.*

Instead of making Amenkor feel safer, the streets now felt closed, somehow restrictive. As if the hand resting at the back of your neck, meant to be reassuring, had suddenly grown more viselike.

The first time Borund and I had seen them in the street, he'd watched them canter by with surprised approval. But when we'd passed the third patrol an hour later, he'd sent me a grim look, mouth pressed tight. "Heavy-handed," he'd muttered.

The rest of Amenkor agreed. I could see it in the people's eyes, in the way they kept their heads down, shoulders lowered. Hooded capes had become common almost overnight.

And it had made following Charls harder.

I pulled back deeper into the alcove as I heard clipped hooves on stone. A moment later, two guardsmen appeared on horseback, moving sedately down the street. One of the horses snuffled and nodded its head as it passed, scenting me, but the guards didn't pause.

As soon as they vanished around the corner of the main thoroughfare, I slid from the alcove and into the lesser shadows of the street. I knew where I was headed: the outer circle of the old city, where most of the merchants had their own estates, including Charls.

The streets of Amenkor were empty. Completely empty. It sent shivers down my back as I moved. On the Dredge and the wharf there were always movements, a sense of motion, even if the alley or street seemed clear. Things moved behind the walls, sometimes in the walls—dogs and rats and gutterscum.

Here, there was no life. Nothing but stone.

I moved swiftly, but slowed when I neared the gates to the outer circle.

They were open. Occasional patrols passed through them, the guards saluting each other or pausing to talk in low, mumbled voices to the two sentries posted there. The sentries stood to one side of the open arch, but they were relaxed, occasionally speaking to each other. Laughter broke out across the street as I settled into shadow twenty paces away from their position.

I glanced up to the night sky, toward the slice of the moon and the stars. There were no clouds tonight, nothing to obscure the light.

I suppressed a sigh and crouched low, grew still.

I submerged myself, deeper and deeper, until the balance felt right, until I could see into every shadow, see every guardsman's face as they passed by and the lines of exhaustion and boredom on the sentries' faces.

Then I focused, felt the currents alter around me, bend and twist, tighten, so I could see what *would* happen—

There.

I relaxed, shifted where I crouched, and waited. Guards moved, chuckled quietly, slapped their horses' necks, a steady flow. A few breaks occurred, where no one passed through the gate, but none long enough for me to move, and none where the two sentries were distracted.

A hundred measured breaths later, a pair of guardsmen disappeared down the street. As the last hoofbeat faded into silence, one of the sentries turned to the other, motioned out toward the city below, away from my position.

I moved.

As I slipped into the shadows of the outer ward, the gates behind me, I heard one of the sentries grunt and chuckle, slapping the other on his back. I paused a moment to make certain they hadn't seen me, then continued on.

The streets of the outer circle were subtly different. Closer, near the main thoroughfare leading up through the old city's walls, but then they widened out. As I moved, I found myself settling down into a familiar pattern, one I didn't recognize at first. But, pausing at a corner, I realized that the tension in my shoulders, in my legs as I balanced on the balls of my feet, came from the Dredge, from Erick.

I smiled slowly. I was hunting.

Sliding from darkness to darkness, I came up on Charls' manse,

stared up at the top of the wall above my head. Reaching for familiar handholds, I hefted myself up to the top. I watched the
building closely, my heart beating faster in my chest. As soon as I
slid down into the garden I'd be in unfamiliar territory. I'd only
come to the top of the wall in my previous excursions, watched the
house from a distance to get an idea of where Charls' rooms were,
to get a feel for the movements of his servants.

The manse should have been quiet, but candlelight glowed in a
few of the lower windows.

I hesitated, considered leaving.

I saw William's face, eyes closed in sleep, brows furrowed and
sweaty.

I dropped into the garden. The moment my feet hit the ground,
the Fire awoke, spreading cold across my chest. I ran across the garden to the house, toward a side door used by the servants to get to
the carriage house and stables. I sensed nothing, heard nothing.

The door opened easily.

Charls' manse was similar in layout to Borund's. I stood in a
servants' entranceway, a narrow door before me. Stairs to my left
ascended to the servants' rooms above. The kitchen stood on the
other side of the manse, with another set of servants' stairs there.
The door before me should open onto a long hallway running the
length of the house, intercepted only by the large open foyer with
the main stairs leading up to the second floor. Rooms opened up on
either side.

I stepped to the inner door, past the stairs, listened, then
stepped into the long inner hallway. Two doors down, candlelight
spilled out into the hall. I stilled, heart halting, but the hallway remained empty.

Silently, I edged up to the open doorway, heard voices as I
approached.

"Tarrence has seized all of the available resources in Marlett. It took him longer than expected though, even with Marcus gone. Some of what we expected to find in Marcus' warehouses had already been purchased by others."

"By whom?"

At the door, I settled down on my heels, one hand on the floor for support. I recognized the first voice as Charls, but didn't recognize the second. Sliding deeper beneath the river, I stole a glance into the room.

Four men, seated at a round table in a room like Borund's office, but more sparse.

"Regin, Yvan. And Borund." Contempt filled Charls' voice.

"Borund," the second man said flatly. He watched Charls carefully as he spoke. He had a long nose, mustache, gray-streaked hair pulled back in a ponytail, vaguely familiar.

I frowned, then remembered: the merchant with the mustard-colored coat from the guild hall. The one Charls had spoken to at the edge of the room, before Borund had approached him.

The other two merchants were familiar as well, people Borund spoke to in the hall on a regular basis. Both shared a glance and shifted in their seats, but said nothing.

I pulled back, contemplated moving back to the servants' entrance.

"Yes, Borund," Charls spat. "He's become increasingly annoying. If he'd only died that night in the tavern. Or at least during the ambush in the middle ward."

"But he didn't," the other merchant continued. "In fact, since that night, the other merchants have begun hiring their own bodyguards. And Borund has increased his purchases of essentials like grain and salt and fish, storing them in the warehouses here in Amenkor rather than shipping them out to the other cities. This is why he was to be eliminated in the first place."

"He's proving harder to get rid of than expected."

"Obviously."

I heard someone shift forward, his chair creaking.

In a much softer voice, the unknown merchant said, "In order for this to work, in order for us to gain and keep control of the city, our little group must be the only ones in the city with vital goods to sell. If we cannot get our hands on what Borund has stored away . . ."

He let the sentence trail off and I heard him shift again.

After a long silence, Charls said, "I'll take care of Borund . . . and his bodyguard."

A cold shiver of fear coursed through me, tinged with anger. Charls wasn't going to let it go.

Then, farther down the hallway, I heard footsteps.

I spun and headed back to the servants' entrance, closing the door softly behind me. But not before I saw a servant carrying a tray with a decanter of wine and four glasses into the room.

I paused in the small entryway, wondering if I should return to warn Borund that there were more merchants involved than just Charls. But I'd come for Charls, and now that I'd actually heard him threaten Borund, I found I couldn't leave.

Warning Borund of the others could wait.

I took the stairs two at a time, easing out into the hallway at the top. It was a servants' corridor, narrower than the one below, running the full length of the manse. The main hallway on the second floor paralleled this one, the two separated only by a wall. A single door on the left opened onto the main corridor at this end of the servants' hallway, other doors on the right leading to the servants' rooms.

Charls' bedroom was the closest on this side of the house, off the main corridor.

I pulled open the door into the main hallway and peered out.

Nothing. But the tendrils of Fire inside my gut increased slightly.

I slid out into the upper hall, stepped to Charls' bedroom door, and entered.

The room held a bed, a large chest at its foot, a desk, two chests of drawers, and a stone fireplace against the right wall. No candles were lit, but everything was clear. Papers and a small knife used to break wax seals sat out on the desk, everything organized and neat. Clothes were tossed onto the chest at the end of the bed. The curtains over the windows were drawn, letting in no moonlight.

There were no places to hide, no real darknesses except the room itself.

Frowning, I stepped to the side of the door and readied myself for the wait.

✝

I'd shifted into a casual crouch by the time Charls finally retired for the night, my legs beginning to cramp from standing. I didn't hear him approach. The door suddenly opened, swinging wide at my side, almost striking my knees.

I stood in one fluid motion, feeling the door before me, concealing me. On the other side, Charls sighed with exhaustion, stepped into his bedroom, and brushed the door closed behind him. No one else entered, and I heard no one else in the hall.

As the door swung away, revealing Charls, his back to me, I stepped forward, brought the dagger up, and sliced cleanly across his neck.

Charls hunched forward, a sickening gurgling sound filling the room as blood fountained, spraying his upraised hand, the edge of the bed, the clothes on the chest, the rug over the hardwood flooring. He staggered a step forward, stumbled to one knee, then twisted as he fell, a hand reaching toward the chest for support.

I stepped forward as he collapsed, his body turned toward me now, his eyes opened in shock, in terror, his face a cold white in the moonlight, the blood black in a sheet across his chest. I wanted him to see me, to recognize me. I wanted him to *know*.

And he did see. He jerked, shoulders pressing back, eyebrows rising.

Warmth spread through my chest, deep and satisfying.

I knelt a pace from him, a hard frown tightening my mouth, the corners of my eyes. "You should have left Borund alone," I said. But I wasn't thinking of Borund at all.

He sagged against the arm holding the chest, the other hand clutched against his throat. But the strength was leaving his body. He shuddered, lost his grip on the chest and fell to the rug. The blood began to pool, spreading.

The hand at his throat reached for me, trembling, grasping. His eyes caught mine, held me, pleading, and in their shimmering depths I saw—

I saw Charls. Not the businessman at the tavern, turning and nodding to the killer waiting for his instructions. Not the merchant on the guild hall floor, speaking quietly of threats and death. I saw none of these.

Instead, I saw Charls as he saw himself. A man who had clawed his way up into the highest ranks of the merchant guild. A man who had allied himself with someone too powerful for him to control and had found himself lost. A man who was even now trying to find some way to survive.

He'd let the face he presented to the world slip when he entered his own bedroom, had let it fall away when he knew he was a dead man but was unwilling to accept it.

I saw it all there, in his eyes. His dreams, his hopes, his desperation. He wanted to live, fought hard even as the strength drained from his arms and he sagged back against the chest. I saw the man beneath the merchant. The man I'd just killed.

The realization sent a shiver of shock through me, down to my core, and I jerked back. All of the satisfied warmth fled, gone in one gasp.

I stood abruptly, and Charls' outstretched hand dropped to the floor, all of the life, all of the straining tension leaving his body. I backed away from the corpse. Panic tingled through my arms, through my skin, prickled the hair on my arms, at the base of my neck.

When my back hit the wall, I gasped and grew still.

And then I ran, out into the hall, to the servants' passage, down the stairs, and out into the garden. I met no one, saw no one, not even as I dropped down from the wall surrounding Charls' manse. I fled through the streets of the outer ward, barely seeing where I ran, moving without thought, hearing nothing, smelling only the dark, viscous scent of blood. I saw only the bodies, all of the bodies, but mostly Charls, his eyes, the thick spatter of blood on his sheets, on his clothes, saw his mouth working to say something, to draw in breath when there was nothing left to do but choke.

I rounded a corner, entered the main thoroughfare near the gates, and slammed into a guardsman. The shock of the collision sent both of us sprawling, my body hitting the ground hard, head cracking into the stone cobbles of the street. My teeth rattled, bit the edge of my tongue, and I tasted blood, like bitter copper. Back against the ground, I swallowed the blood, heaved in deep ragged breaths and stared up at the moon and stars, stunned.

I heard the guardsman curse, heard shifting cloth as he climbed to his feet.

Then he leaned over me, blocked out the night sky, and I froze with a sharp, drawn breath.

He stared down at me in shock, one hand reaching tentatively for my face, reaching to brush away my hair. "Varis?"

Erick.

The panic returned, sharper than before, seizing my heart, my throat. I couldn't speak, and the breath I held escaped in a harsh rush that tore at my throat.

I had to get away. Guilt rose up, like acid, and I felt sick. I'd killed Bloodmark without Erick's permission, without the Mistress' blessing. Somehow, since meeting Borund, I'd managed to shove that fact deep down inside me, managed to forget it. I'd allowed myself to relax.

But now Erick had found me.

And I suddenly realized it was infinitely worse than just Bloodmark.

I'd just killed again. Not to save myself, not to save Borund. I'd killed Charls because I'd wanted to, because he'd hurt William.

I had to get away. The impulse was like a scream. I couldn't face Erick now, not with blood on my hands, on my shirt and dagger.

But I couldn't move. Erick held me with his eyes, softening from shock and irritation to something else . . . concern and wonder.

And then he touched my face, his fingers trailing down my forehead to my ear, and I broke, the tears coming harsh and hot and wet. My breath hitched in my chest.

"Varis," he said again, without question.

"I killed him," I sobbed, the words thick with phlegm, almost incoherent. "I killed him, I killed him, I killed him."

"Who?" He was cupping the back of my neck now, had lifted me to his shoulder, my eyes closed. I held him tight, feeling as if I were fourteen again.

"Bloodmark," I gasped into his shoulder. "Charls."

He grew still, but his hold didn't lessen.

On the street, someone gasped, and I drew back from Erick's

shoulder sharply, the tears choked back, abruptly realizing I no longer held my dagger. It had clattered to the street when we collided, lay just out of reach.

Vulnerability hit me, even as Erick rose.

Twenty paces away, a man stood at the edge of a cross street, wearing a cloak with the hood pulled back. I could see his face clearly in the moonlight, recognized the arrogant stance, the shocked look on his face.

The merchant's son, Cristoph. The man I'd fought in the alley on the wharf after first coming down to the docks.

I'd killed his friend.

And he'd heard me tell Erick I'd killed Bloodmark and Charls. I knew it as clearly as if I'd been beneath the river, had smelled it there. And there was something else, something that took me a moment to recognize.

Cristoph reminded me of the merchant with the mustard-colored coat, a younger version. That's why the merchant had seemed familiar at the guild hall talking to Charls, why he'd seemed familiar tonight.

Cristoph must be that merchant's son.

Erick took a single step forward and Cristoph turned and fled, his footsteps echoing off the outer walls before fading completely.

Panic seized me. I lurched toward my knife, grabbed the bloody blade in one hand and turned to face Erick in one smooth move. The urge to cry was gone now, the tears dried. Only a raw hollow near my heart remained, and I could feel myself pushing that away, discarding it, hardening myself against the pain. The emotion was useless.

I was no longer on the Dredge, no longer fourteen. I didn't need Erick.

We stared at each other a long moment, and then I said, "You can't protect me anymore."

And I ran.

I dodged into the street where Cristoph had vanished, eyes hard and intent, Erick shoved into the back of my mind. I'd deal with his reappearance later. For now, Cristoph was a threat. He'd seen me, had heard me say I'd killed Charls. I wasn't supposed to be associated with Charls' death at all.

I saw a flash of movement farther down the street as someone dodged into an alley, nothing more than a flicker of a cloak. I focused, drew the river up around me, but saw no one on the street. Nostrils flaring, I dashed down to the alley, ducked around the corner and searched the darkness.

Nothing.

I drew a deep breath, sorted through the scents on the river. But there was nothing I could attribute to Cristoph. I didn't remember him having a scent down on the wharf, when I'd killed his friend. But not everyone had scents.

Not willing to give up, I searched the alley, the recessed doorways, the alcoves. All of the doors were locked, and the alley ended at the edge of an empty street.

Shit!

The pressure of running into other guardsmen began to assert itself. And then there was Erick.

Would he send the guard to find me? Would he warn the sentries at the gate? He knew I'd killed someone. He'd seen the blood, heard me confess.

The guilt stabbed again into my gut, sliced through the last of my hesitation.

Cristoph had escaped. I'd have to deal with him later.

I headed back toward the gates, approaching warily.

The two sentries remained on duty. They didn't appear to be any more alert than when I'd passed through earlier that night.

I breathed a heavy sigh of relief, wondered why Erick had not warned them, but pushed the thought aside and concentrated on getting through the gates without being seen by the sentries.

I had to wait an hour, but eventually they were distracted long enough so I could sneak through. I headed into the outer city, back toward Borund's manse to report.

I did not see Erick or any other guardsmen along the way.

·⟨ *The Palace* ⟩·

I DIDN'T wait at the audience room's door. Instead, I moved immediately across the dark room, slipping between chairs and tables in the darkness, between vases of flowers, sculptures, and plants. On the far side of the room was another door, smaller, heading deeper into the inner sanctum, leading toward the throne room and the Mistress' chambers.

I padded toward the door, hesitated before opening it in order to listen. I couldn't use the river to see if anyone was on the far side since the door was blocking my view, but it was possible to pick up noises, scents. . . .

Nothing.

I was just about to open the door when something whispered at the edge of hearing. Stilling, I concentrated, let my breath out slowly and held it—

And heard a soft rustling, like dry leaves scraping across cobbles. I frowned, brow creasing. I'd heard this once before when inside the palace, during one of Avrell and Borund's meetings. But then it had only been a whisper, there and then gone. This was much louder.

Hesitating a moment, I focused.

The sound of leaves intensified, seemed to reach out toward me from a distance, and as it grew louder, the rustling sound began to resolve into voices . . . hundreds of voices all speaking at the same time, all clamoring for attention.

I jerked back from the door, but the voices vanished as soon as I quit concentrating, as soon as I let the river slip away. The room was silent. Dead.

Something clattered against the door on the other side of the room, where the guards had been posted. Without thought, heart thudding sharply in my chest, I pulled the door in front of me open and slid through, ignoring the strange voices for now. They would have to wait.

The door led to a narrow corridor, a hall for the servants that curved slightly away out of sight. I scanned in both directions. No one was in sight.

I bit my lower lip, took a moment to consult the mental map Avrell had given me. It wasn't as complete as the one for the outer portion of the palace, did not include all of the servants' passages.

I grunted in annoyance and turned right, slipping forward without a sound, one hand brushing along the rough granite wall to my left for reference. Ten steps farther on, my outstretched hand found the edge of a door.

I placed an ear to the wood, heard nothing on the far side.

I moved on.

Two doors later, the flickering light of a torch appeared at the end of the hall, around the edge of the curved corridor, followed by voices and the soft thud of a closing door.

I crouched down immediately, felt for the latch on the door at my back.

"What's going on?" someone demanded, his voice tired.

"Baill's got the entire guard out looking," someone else growled, "but he decided that wasn't enough so he called out all the servants as well." For a moment the torchlight flared, and in the brighter light I could see small bowls of oil lining the wall on either side.

They were lighting the sconces. The entire palace would be lit within the next fifteen minutes.

"And what in hell does he expect us to do!"

"Help him."

"And then what?"

I drew in a tight breath, then opened the door at my back and slid through it as the light of the torches and oil sconces grew, the voices getting closer. The door shut with a faint click, the wood muffling the conversation in the hall on the other side.

I waited until I heard their voices receding down the corridor, then turned to see where I was.

My stomach tightened.

"Shit," I muttered.

I'd backed myself into a storage closet with no other exit.

"Shit, shit, shit," I muttered under my breath, then turned back to the door. Pressing my ear to the wood, I listened intently for sounds in the corridor outside, but heard nothing. The men lighting the oil sconces in the hallway had passed by, but anyone could be out there now. The entire palace had been awakened.

I sighed heavily, cast an angry look at the door, then slid beneath the river.

The instant I submerged, I felt the strange whispering of leaves I'd heard in the outer room rushing forward. Only this time it was much louder, the hundreds of voices streaming out of the silence like a gale-force wind, reaching for me. I gasped, jerked back away from them, and at the same time shoved myself up and out of the river, hard, fast.

The real world returned with a lurch. I sat back on my heels, still gasping, felt sweat prickle my chest. Reaching forward, I hugged my knees to my chest until my heart stopped racing.

I had no idea what the leaf voices were, had no idea where they were coming from. But whatever they were, they wanted me. I'd felt them reaching for me, straining. And I'd felt the force behind them, a weight that could crush me.

I shuddered, pushed myself back up into a kneeling position before the door. I listened, using only my ears.

Nothing.

I nudged the river, as if I were at its edge and had dipped my toe into its waters.

Whisper of dead leaves, calling me.

I shivered, then leaned my forehead against the wood of the door. Until I knew what the leaf voices were, I didn't dare use the river.

Which made killing the Mistress that much harder.

I pulled myself upright, jaw clenched, then opened the door and stepped out into the hall.

No yell of alarm. No shrieks. The hall was empty.

But completely lit. The only places left to hide were the doorways.

I bit off another curse at Avrell, at Baill, at life in general, and continued down the hall at a brisk but quiet trot. No use skulking now.

I paused at the next door, heard muffled voices, and moved on quickly. The hall continued to curve, most of the doors on the left side. But, according to Avrell, they wouldn't lead me to the Mistress' chambers. Her rooms lay on the other side of the palace, to the right.

I came to another door on the right and paused again. Nothing. Opening it a crack, I peered into another antechamber like the first. Only someone had been here recently. All the candles were lit.

I closed the door quietly and proceeded down the hall.

Twenty steps farther on, I heard someone enter the hall behind me, heard the distinct sound of metal armor.

Guardsmen.

Without hesitation, I sprinted forward, eyes wide, heart pounding. The hall curved away, the right wall maddeningly empty, two doors, no three, passing on the left. The sounds of the guards grew louder, but I hadn't heard a shout. They were getting closer, though. I could hear their voices.

I'd almost decided to duck into one of the doors on the left, risk another closet, or something worse, when a door on the right appeared. The hall ended shortly after that, with one last door on the left. I darted toward the door on the right, grabbed its handle and eased it open smoothly. No time to listen for someone on the far side. The guards were too close.

I slid through, pulled the door closed behind me as quietly as possible, and then turned and halted, heart wrenching in my chest. I let out an involuntary gasp.

I'd entered a long, wide hall from a side entrance. To my right, four huge pillars stretched from the marbled floor to the ceiling. Another four pillars stood on the far side of the room. Shadows filled the recesses behind the pillars where I stood, and behind the pillars on the opposite side of the hall. Down the center, between the two rows of pillars, stretched a wide walkway, leading to two large wooden doors banded with metal.

Directly ahead, at the height of a dais, I could see the side of a throne lit by torchlight, the throne facing the walkway and the double doors.

The Skewed Throne.

My body shuddered and I blinked in the half-light, tried to focus on the throne, my eyes refusing to settle, the air distorted somehow. After a moment, I realized that the problem wasn't with my eyes at all, but with the throne itself.

It was a simple stone slab with no back and four supports, one on each corner. But even as my eyes held onto this image, it seemed to waver, twisting, one leg suddenly shorter but supporting a corner that appeared higher than all the others. The throne warped, turned in upon itself, the stone slab that formed the seat no longer flat, the edges that had appeared sharp and well defined before now smooth and rounded. Then it shifted again, now chipped and chiseled, rough-hewn.

The motion turned my stomach, sent a feverish heat tingling through my skin. I shuddered again and turned away from the throne, away from the dais and the three wide stone steps that led from the main walkway between the pillars up to the throne itself.

With a deep breath, I steadied myself.

And felt the throne at my back reach out toward me, felt it pushing against my shoulders, almost like a physical presence. The rustling of dead leaves returned, shivering through the air, growing even as the skin at the nape of my neck began to prickle. The voices emerged from the rustling sound, called to me, echoed in my ears.

I tensed in horror. The voices came from the throne. The throne knew me, had tried to call to me earlier, was calling to me now.

And I hadn't touched the river since the voices had rushed me in the closet.

I stepped back, tried to block the voices out—

Then I heard the clatter of the guards on the other side of the door, in the hallway behind me.

Not looking toward the throne, I darted to the right, down the long walkway, between the rows of pillars, across the half-dark room to the main entrance. I felt the throne behind me, a hot, scrabbling pressure against my back, felt it flowing from shape to shape, twisted and tormented, calling to me, the voices more urgent now, more desperate.

I gasped as I neared the doorway, passed through and out into the empty hallway beyond with a low, moaning cry. The gasp turned into a shudder of relief as I felt the ornate oaken door thud home behind me, cutting off the voices and the sensation of hands scrabbling across my back.

I leaned against the door a long moment, shudders running through my body. Sweat dripped down my face and I wiped it away with the back of my arm, heart thundering in my chest. I drew in deep, ragged breaths, steadied myself.

It took longer than I expected.

Then I straightened. I set the eerie sensation of the throne, of the haunting voices and their immense power, aside.

I'd reached the edge of the Mistress' private rooms. Time to shed the page boy disguise. It was almost finished.

My gaze hardened, face grim as I stepped down the unguarded hall to a new set of double doors, the *last* set of double doors, drawing my dagger as I went.

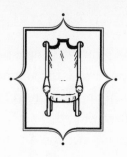

Chapter 11

"THE mustard-coated merchant's name is Alendor,"
Borund said, and sank back into the chair he'd had
moved into William's bedroom. "Cristoph is one of his
sons, the youngest. And if Alendor's involved. . . ."

He trailed off into silence. It was late morning, the day after I'd
killed Charls, and I'd just told him what I'd heard at Charls' manse,
and that Cristoph knew what I'd done. But I hadn't told them
everything. I'd only said Cristoph had seen me leaving Charls'
manse, blood on my clothes. I hadn't mentioned Erick at all.

On the bed, William struggled into a sitting position, using the
pillows and the headboard for support. He grimaced in pain as he
moved, a sheen of sweat breaking out on his forehead, but neither
Borund nor I moved to help him, careful of his pride.

When he'd made himself comfortable and caught his breath, he
asked, "So what does he intend to do? He's buying up all available
resources, gaining others from those who have it and aren't willing
to sell by intimidating them or killing them, but for what purpose?
A monopoly?"

"Yes." Borund nodded thoughtfully. "But a monopoly not just
on a single commodity. He wants to control everything. He's form-

ing a consortium, a small group of people that will control all of the trade in the city, perhaps in the surrounding cities as well if he already has Tarrence working for him in Marlett."

William snorted, then winced, one hand moving to his side. "That's not possible, not in Amenkor. And not anywhere else either."

Borund shifted forward again. "Isn't it? Look at what he's done so far. Besides Alendor, Charls, and the two other merchants Varis saw at Charls' manse, who else in the city has—or had—any stock of fish? Or wheat?"

William frowned in thought. "We do, in the warehouses on the docks. I think Darryn has some in storage as well. . . ." His voice trailed off, and then he looked toward Borund, eyes wide. "And that's it. Alendor controls almost all of the wheat and fish."

Borund nodded, his voice grim. "And what about other resources, such as fruits and vegetables? Or wine? What about cattle or pigs? There haven't been any drovers from the north since Regin purchased that herd in the spring. Since it's now almost winter, we can't expect to see any more herds like that for at least five months. Even non-food stocks, like cloth. We haven't had a shipment of wool or flax from Venitte in over four months, maybe even six."

"Six," William said distractedly. He'd sunk back into his pillows as Borund spoke. "And since it *is* almost winter, there won't be many ships in the coming months. We've only got a few weeks left of decent enough weather to risk sending out more ships, maybe a month at most. What resources we're going to have are already in the city."

They both fell silent.

In one corner of the room, I shifted my stance, uncomfortable. But not from the weighted silence. In my mind, I could see Charls reaching for me, his hand grasping at air. I could see his blood, black against his skin. Then there was Erick and—

"What about Cristoph?" I asked.

Borund frowned. "What do you mean?"

I straightened. "He knows that I killed Charls, knows that I killed his friend down at the wharf. He could go to the Guard."

Borund shook his head. "He won't. Alendor won't let him. It would attract too much attention to his house. Right now Alendor must be wondering whether you saw him at Charls' manse, whether we even know about the consortium. He'll want to stay out of sight until he knows for certain. Alendor will handle Cristoph for us."

I nodded, relaxed back against the wall.

That still didn't solve the problem of Erick. But he hadn't reported me to the guard after Bloodmark's death, hadn't warned the sentries at the gates last night. . . .

I sighed and closed my eyes, intent on pushing Charls' pleading gaze out of my head.

When I opened my eyes, I caught William watching me.

He flinched away, turning to look down at his feet.

My stomach clenched and I stared down at the floor, mouth pressed tight.

Into the awkward silence, a horn blew, long and hollow and forlorn.

Both Borund and William looked up toward the open window. It looked out onto the harbor.

With a frown, Borund rose and moved to pull back the curtains. I followed, stood at his side. The first horn was followed by others, the sounds filling the room in a strange cacophony of noise.

"What's happening?" William said. I could hear the impatience in his voice. He wasn't used to being restricted to a bed, unable to move about.

"Something in the harbor," Borund said.

"But what?"

"Wait," Borund said, his voice lowering, his forehead creasing in confusion.

On the slate-gray water of the harbor, ships flying the Mistress' colors of gold and white were preparing to make way on the docks. But these weren't the usual ships I'd seen off-loading crates and barrels. These were smaller, leaner, and somehow more dangerous, more purposeful, their sails crisp beneath the white-scudded sky.

And more maneuverable. As we watched, they pulled away from the docks and headed straight out toward where the spits of land on either side of the bay curved in toward each other, creating an opening to the ocean beyond. They passed a large merchant ship headed toward open water without pausing.

Gerrold appeared at the door to the room. "Something's going on in the harbor, Master Borund."

Borund grunted. "Yes, I see. Send Gart to see if he can find out what's happening. Quickly."

"Yes, sir."

Gerrold left, and Borund shifted forward, his stance going rigid, a dark frown touching his eyes, his mouth. "What . . . ?" he began, but didn't continue.

The Mistress' sleek ships began to slow, drawing up alongside the mouth of the bay. They began a slow pattern, weaving back and forth across the opening of the harbor. The merchant ship made slow progress forward, but when it got close to the line, one of the sleek ships broke from the formation and approached. The ships were too distant to see anything more than blurred movement on the decks. But there was movement, even as the merchant ship slowed to a halt, sails going slack.

Borund sucked in a breath, held it.

"What is it?" William barked.

Borund didn't respond, simply shook his head.

On the water, the sleek ship backed away and the merchant ship began to move again. But the sails didn't go back up in the same configuration.

The merchant ship began to turn, and Borund let his held breath out forcefully, as if someone had punched him in the gut.

Behind, I heard someone tearing up the stairs and down the hallway. The door burst open and Gart skidded to a halt just inside.

"The Mistress . . . has closed . . . the harbor," he gasped, eyes wide in shock, fear, and a child's uncontrolled excitement.

†

The gates to the palace were thronged by the time Borund and I made it up through the two outer wards. Most of the men yelling at the palace guardsmen lined up in front of the closed and barricaded doors were lesser merchants and representatives from the ships—both local and foreign—that were now locked inside the harbor, all with a sick desperation on their faces. Beneath the river, the mob was a nauseating churn of anger moving in strange, unpredictable eddies that tasted of salt and smelled of sweat. Tensions were so high I had edged in as close to Borund as I could get without touching him, leaving myself barely enough room to wield my dagger if necessary. He stayed back from the main crush of bodies, but even so I was jostled into his back once or twice.

Borund swore under his breath after scanning the mob, then thankfully turned and edged away from the gates. "We'll never get into the palace. Captain Baill must have shut the gates before he issued the orders to close the harbor, and this crowd isn't likely to disperse any time soon. Damn! I need to know what's going on!"

I continued to scan the crowd, shoulders tense, uncertain whether I should make any suggestions. That was William's job.

I caught Borund's eye, saw the stress around the edges of his face, the darkness from lack of sleep. The exhaustion was clear. I suddenly wondered how often he had gone in to watch William sleep late at night, as I had.

I drew breath to suggest we go to the guild hall, but someone stepped up to Borund's side, someone gray.

"Master Borund?"

The boy was short, dressed in ordinary clothes from the docks, with dirty hair and a round, grime-smudged face. His eyes were large and intent and flicked continuously over the crowd.

Borund frowned as he tried to place the boy. "Yes?"

"Avrell, the First of the Mistress, would like to see you," the boy said. "He said to give you this." He handed over a small chunk of stone, the outlines of an ancient snail embedded in one side, then darted back into the press of bodies near the gates.

Borund grunted. I recognized the piece of stone from Borund's office.

And I suddenly recalled seeing Avrell leaving through the side entrance to Borund's manse.

Borund motioned for me to follow.

The dock boy led us through the edge of the mob, at first heading toward the gates. But before the press became too close, the boy angled away and we passed into a side street of the middle ward running parallel to the wall enclosing the palace. Once we were free of the area in front of the gates, we moved swiftly, the boy motioning us forward while checking to see if we were followed.

I scanned behind as well but saw no one.

The boy ducked into a small building set back from the wall that was once a stable. The reek of manure still clung to the musty air inside, but there were no horses. Instead, the building was packed with marked crates, straw poking out through the cracks between the wood.

Borund gasped as the dock boy led us into a narrow space between the stacked crates. "Capthian red! Crates of it! I haven't been able to get this since last winter, not a single crate!"

The narrow path turned, branched once, then opened up into

a small niche that barely fit the three of us hunched over. The dock boy motioned us out of the way, then pulled at a chunk of the plank flooring. A section lifted away, cut with a ragged edge so that it couldn't be seen when set in place.

The boy motioned us down into the rounded opening below. I could see that it dropped down into a thin tunnel, even though there was no light.

Borund hesitated, glancing at me for confirmation.

"It's safe," I said. "It drops down to a tunnel. There's no one down there, and I can see a lantern ready to be lit."

Borund nodded and, with a bit of maneuvering, managed to lower himself down into the hole. The dock boy stared at me the entire time.

"How did you know there was a lantern?" he finally asked. "It's too dark to see it."

I didn't answer, simply dropped down smoothly after Borund once he moved out of the way. The dock boy followed, handing the lantern to Borund along with an ember box to light it. The ember inside was still glowing hotly.

The lantern flared just as the dock boy fit the cover to the tunnel back into place. Squeezing past both me and Borund, he took the lantern and said, "Follow me."

The tunnel grew narrower at first, until we had to proceed sideways, backs scraping the rough-chiseled wall, then branched to the left and right. We'd followed the left path for twenty paces before I realized the wall to the right was the same eggshell color as the wall of the palace, but darker, not as sun-bleached as the walls above. More tunnels branched off to the left, but we continued forward for another hundred paces before turning away from the palace wall. After two quick rights, we hit stairs leading sharply downward. The twists and turns, darkness and narrow niches, reminded me forcibly of the Dredge.

When we reached the bottom of the stairs, Borund turned back and murmured in a subdued voice, "We're passing under the palace walls."

After twenty paces, a new set of stairs led up to a door set in the ceiling. The dock boy set the lantern carefully on a shelf, then rapped lightly on the door.

It lifted open, light pouring down into the mostly darkened tunnel. Blinking away the sudden brightness, I saw a palace guardsman kneeling, holding the door, and standing above him was the First of the Mistress.

"Welcome to the palace," he said.

Then another guard leaned down into the tunnel with an outstretched hand to help pull us up.

†

"We haven't needed those passages in years," the First said, almost to himself.

We'd moved from the small room where we'd emerged, through a few short corridors lit with wide oil sconces, to a bare room containing wooden chairs and a table with wine and a platter of breads and cheeses. The room was dusty, the walls stained with old soot from torches.

I sat on my heels in one corner, quietly watching Borund and the First where they stood. The guards had been positioned outside, and the dock boy had split from the group on the way to the room. The only other person I'd seen was a woman robed in white who had brought the food and wine. One of the Mistress' servants. She'd smiled as she set the platter on the table, but the smile had faded when she turned back to Avrell and gave him a solemn nod before leaving.

Avrell's mouth had tightened . . . and then he'd pointedly ignored me.

"Why is the harbor closed?" Borund asked tersely. "Who ordered it?"

The First sighed and motioned to a chair. "The Mistress herself ordered it."

"What! But why?" Borund shook his head in confusion. "It doesn't make any sense."

"No, it doesn't," the First said flatly.

It took Borund a moment to catch all the implications the First had put into his voice, but when he did, he leaned back into his chair, the wood creaking in the heavy silence.

"So the rumors are true," he finally murmured. It wasn't a question.

The First nodded. "I wasn't certain, *can't* be certain, even now. The Mistress has been acting erratically since the Fire, but nothing alarming, nothing that couldn't be explained at the time as rational, if a little odd. But recently . . ." He sighed, his rigid stance sagging slightly. He moved to a chair. "Maintaining the Skewed Throne is not as simple as it would seem. The Mistress has always acted strangely in the past, given orders that made no sense at the time. But later you could always look back and see why the order was given. And none of the previous Mistresses . . . *changed* while seated on the throne. Not in any significant way.

"But since the Fire, this Mistress has. Her orders no longer make sense. There is no reason to close the harbor, and no real reason to saturate the city with the palace guard."

"So that wasn't you," Borund interjected. "Or Baill."

Avrell shook his head. "No, that came directly from the Mistress."

He paused, as if undecided whether he should say anything more. He watched Borund carefully, and Borund stirred in his seat under his gaze. Then he turned to me.

I held perfectly still, tried to remain expressionless.

Avrell considered me a moment more, then straightened and turned back to Borund, as if coming to a decision. "In the past few months, the Mistress' actions have shifted from simply eccentric to truly bizarre. She ascends to the tower and stares out at the sea at odd hours, even in the dead of night, in the rain, remaining there until one of the servants or the guards is forced to drag her back inside. She roams the halls of the palace, mumbling to herself, laughing, sometimes singing, sometimes growling, often in languages that no one understands. I've placed guards at the door to her chambers, to follow her, to make certain she does not harm herself, but somehow she manages to elude them. I ran across her in one of the gardens not two days ago, staring down at the roots of a tree when she was supposed to have been sleeping. She told me the sea was red with blood, the throne was cracked, and that the garden had once been a plaza. I took her back to her rooms, and the guards assured me they had not seen her leave. Nothing like that happened before the Fire passed through the city."

Borund had grown increasingly uncomfortable as the First spoke. "Why are you telling me this?"

The First kept quiet for a moment, then smiled grimly. "Because more is going on than it would seem. If it was the Mistress, and only the Mistress, I believe I could handle the situation myself. But no. There's too much going on in the city. You told me yourself about the attack in the Broken Mast, and the deaths of the merchants."

"Yes."

The First nodded. "I heard nothing of it until our meeting a few weeks ago, the night you were attacked in the middle ward and your assistant—William, I believe?—was wounded."

Silence, as both Borund and the First watched each other.

The First stirred. "There is a conspiracy among the merchants, an attempt to seize control of trade within the city at a time when trade, not only here in Amenkor but everywhere on the Frigean coast, is in peril. At first I thought it was something that should be left to the guild to be sorted out. Guild politics in play, if you will. But after speaking to you a few weeks ago at your manse . . ."

He let the thought fade, but Borund picked up the thread.

"You think that this conspiracy—I've been calling it a consortium—extends into the palace itself."

"Consortium," the First muttered, as if trying out the word for the first time. He smiled. "I like that. But, yes, I think this . . . consortium is much larger than a few merchants, and has connections in the palace. In particular, I think it includes the good captain of the palace guard, Baill." Avrell's voice twisted with distaste at the captain's name.

Borund's face darkened as well. Reaching for the glass of wine that had so far gone untouched, he drank, brow creased in thought. The First eased back in his seat and waited.

After a long moment, Borund glanced in my direction.

I dove deep beneath the river, shifting the currents toward Borund as I went, then turned toward the First.

In the swirling gray currents, the First appeared gray.

As I let the river go, I felt something tug at the currents, heard a vague noise, like the dry rasp of dead leaves blown across stone, like a voice . . . or many voices. But it faded.

I nodded to Borund, Avrell watching the exchange with interest. He said nothing, but his gaze was intent, much more focused than before.

I sat back and dipped beneath the river again, but the sound of dead leaves was gone. I shrugged it aside.

"Charls is dead," Borund began.

The First straightened slightly. "So I heard."

Borund grunted. "I thought he was the man behind the deaths of the other merchants, and in one respect I was right. He was the one organizing and ordering the deaths. He tried to kill me at the tavern on the wharf, but failed due to Varis' intervention. I suspected he was behind the deaths of the other merchants after that."

Borund paused, and the First glanced toward me. I didn't react.

"I see," he said. And he did see. I could hear it in his voice.

"Only after the fact did I learn that it wasn't really Charls giving the orders, that more merchants were involved."

"And do you know these merchants?"

"Yes. But the only one of consequence is Alendor. He controls almost half of the trade in Amenkor himself. If you factor in all of the other merchants I believe he has sway over . . ."

"He can control the entire city, especially if he feels he has power over the guard."

Borund nodded in agreement. "There are only three significant merchants left in the city *not* under his control: myself, Regin, and Yvan. I had thought that if the three of us allied ourselves together, we could send out what ships remained under our control still in the harbor before the weather changes. Perhaps we could find enough resources, buy enough staples, that the city could survive the winter months. William and I were just beginning to discuss this option when we heard the noise in the harbor."

The First grimaced. "By order of the Mistress, the harbor has been closed. Not even Baill expected this. He protested more than I did."

Borund leaned forward, placed his hands flat on the table. His face was drawn, his voice so intent it almost shook. "I've calculated what stores Regin, Yvan, and I already have here in the city."

"And?"

Borund shook his head. "The city will never survive the winter. There will be famine. At least half the city will starve, and that's assuming the winter is mild."

"And where there is famine, there will also be plague." The First frowned, looking down at the floor. "What of Alendor's stores? Would the city survive if we could seize control of what this consortium holds?"

"I cannot say. Based on what we know they hold, perhaps. But I don't have access to Alendor's books. Nor Charls'."

Avrell's frown deepened, his shoulders tensing as he thought. Anger and desperation flowed off him in waves, tightly controlled.

Borund stood. "We *have* to get our ships out of the harbor," he said, voice tight, "or the city will starve."

When Avrell glanced up, his eyes were dark. "I believe that Nathem, my Second, and I can deal with the Mistress. Somehow, we will get her to open up the harbor again. But even if we succeed with the Mistress, there is still the consortium. We need their stocks, and if Baill is in league with them, we cannot take them by force. We have to break the consortium itself. Now."

Borund nodded grimly. "In my opinion, the best way to do that is to eliminate Alendor."

The First's lips thinned.

And then they both turned toward me.

†

On the walk back to the manse, Borund muttered to himself continuously about what would need to be done once Alendor was dead, but I ignored him. I watched the street for threats, but did not see it. Not really.

I had agreed to kill Alendor. Another hunt, like Charls. Only this one would be worse. Because now I wouldn't see the man threatening Borund and William and the other merchants of the city. I wouldn't see the man attempting to gain control of all of the trade, the man willing to starve all of Amenkor to do it. No. I'd see the man underneath as well, the man that would plead for his life at the end if he had the chance.

We reached the manse, Gerrold opening the iron gate outside to let us in. Borund had ordered it kept locked since the first attack.

As we passed inside, something drifted through the river, a scent I felt I should recognize but couldn't, like lantern oil and straw.

I straightened, halted just inside the gate and stared out at the street, gaze flickering swiftly over the few people, scanning the few alcoves where someone could hide. But I saw no one, and the scent—so vague—was already fading.

"Varis?" Borund asked behind me. "Is something wrong?"

Frowning, I turned and said curtly, "No. Nothing's wrong."

He pulled back, hearing the lie in my voice. But he said nothing, confused, as I moved past him to the house, Gerrold shutting the gates behind us.

I went to my room, that had once been Joclyn's—a servant's—room, and stood inside the doorway. Nothing in the room had changed in the past few months except that now there were a few clothes folded in the chest of drawers. I moved to the chest and opened up one of the drawers, stared down at the pouches inside, pouches full of coins. Lizbeth placed them there on a regular basis, but I hadn't used any of them. Borund provided everything I needed: clothes, food. I'd never needed anything else.

Looking down at the pouches, I suddenly realized I didn't like Borund.

I closed the drawer, glanced once swiftly over the room, and then wandered out into the hall, turning toward William's room without thought.

William was sitting upright on the bed, sheets of paper scattered all around him. He smiled when I knocked and stepped inside the room.

"Varis," he said, his voice weary but light. Something had changed around his eyes though, something subtle. They were no longer wide and bright and open. Instead, they appeared pinched and dark.

It could have been simple exhaustion, but I didn't think so.

His smile faltered slightly, troubled, but remained. He motioned me inside. "Come in. I need a break."

I moved a few steps closer, but didn't approach the bed.

"Borund wants me to kill Alendor," I said.

His smile froze, then faded. His shoulders slumped and he turned to stare out the window. He'd had the bed moved since that morning, so that he could see the harbor and the Mistress' ships guarding the entrance to the bay.

"And what did you say?" he asked. His voice was flat, without inflection, without judgment.

I swallowed, standing rigid. "I'll need to know where I'll most likely find Alendor this evening. Borund said that you would know, that you know what inns and taverns most of the merchants frequent."

Silence. William didn't turn, but after a long moment nodded, as if to himself, as if he were finally accepting something that he had not wanted to believe. In a voice a little rougher and softer than the first, he said, "Alendor will be near the warehouses tonight. He usually checks on his own stocks, then finds his way to the Splintered Bow for dinner."

I nodded, then hesitated, waiting for more, but William stared stoically out at the harbor, what I could see of his face hard and harsh, closed off. All traces of the smile were gone.

I turned to leave, feeling a warm pain deep inside my stomach, as if I'd been stabbed and was bleeding on the inside. And the blood flow wouldn't stop.

I'd almost reached the door when William said, loudly, "Varis?"

I stood still, looking out into the corridor through the open door. I could tell by William's voice that he'd turned toward me, was staring at my back, but I didn't turn around. "What?" I was surprised at how thick my voice sounded.

"How . . . ?" he began, but he didn't continue, struggling.

I looked down at the floor and closed my eyes, then turned toward him purposefully. "When I was six, my mother was killed by two men when we were returning from a trip to Cobbler's Fountain. We lived on the outskirts of the slums, near the Dredge. Or at least I assume so, since that's where Cobbler's Fountain is. I don't remember much from before." I paused, seeing again in my head the two red men, heard myself say in a child's innocent voice, *Look, Mommy. Look at the red men.*

Then I focused on William's face again, on his steady, green eyes. "They killed her for what little she'd carried with her . . . some coin perhaps. They did nothing to me, left me with her body in an alley on a backstreet I didn't recognize. I didn't know what to do, didn't know where to go, where to run to, so I stayed there, next to my mother's body, until the guardsmen came.

"They didn't know what to do with me either. They were arguing about it, trying to decide, when a woman that my mother knew showed up and offered to take me in." I shuddered. "The guards handed me over without much hesitation—what else were they going to do with me?—and for a while I lived with this woman. She wasn't bad I guess, but she had five kids of her own already."

"But what about your father?"

I thought immediately of Erick, of the white-dusty man, but grimaced. "I don't remember my father. I don't remember much of anything from before Cobbler's Fountain and the night my mother was killed, mainly flashes of scenes, nothing significant. So I went with the woman."

I clenched my jaw at the memories—resentment and pain held tight but still leaking out into my voice. "After about a year—a year of defending myself from the other kids when she wasn't looking and fighting to get enough food to eat—I decided I'd be better off on my own. So I left. I ran away, moved deeper into the slums beyond the Dredge. I lived like an animal there, scrounging in garbage heaps, eating anything I could find, scraps you and Borund wouldn't even feed to a dog. I was dying and I didn't even know it. Then I ran into a street thug named Dove and his gang. They showed me that I could do much better if I was a little more daring. They taught me how to survive, how to steal, how to pick pockets, how to be quick and subtle, and how to distract. I was especially helpful to them for that. All I had to do was sit in the shadows of an alley and cry and someone would come in to investigate."

Some of the hardness had seeped out of William's eyes, but for some reason that didn't make me feel any better.

"So what happened?" he asked after a moment of silence.

I looked away from him. "Dove took one of the setups too far. One of the takes decided to run and it awoke something inside Dove that I didn't like. I told him I wouldn't help him hunt the woman down and so he abandoned me." I winced, feeling again Dove's fist as he struck me after I'd said no. "But it didn't matter by then. I was almost eleven and I'd learned everything I needed to know to survive in the slums."

The room fell completely silent. I could feel William's eyes on me, but did not look up. Strangely, the anger I'd felt had died, along with the tension in my shoulders, in my jaw. As if telling William had released me somehow.

"So why did you leave the slums? How did you end up on the wharf, where we found you?"

I did look up at this. I didn't want to tell him about Bloodmark, about Erick. So instead, I said, "Someone pushed me too far. And I finally realized that I didn't want to just 'survive' anymore. I wanted something else."

And now I found myself in the same situation, I thought wryly. I didn't want to go on killing. I wanted something else.

William said nothing, trying to understand, the intent clear on his face. "So you . . . grew up in the slums?"

I laughed, the sound without humor. "I *survived* the slums," I said with force. "Any way I could."

"But . . . how can you do it? How can you—"

"Because it's what I am. It's all that I know."

A pause, and I turned to go. Then, in a voice much less harsh, he said, "But you have a choice now."

I tried not to sigh. "No. I don't."

And I left.

†

I waited outside the Splintered Bow in a darkened side street, leaning against a wall. Outside the tavern, torches flared and spat in the breeze coming off of the water, and clouds roiled overhead, blocking out the stars and the moon. Winter clouds. The air tasted of rain, a cold rain, but it was still distant. Alendor had entered the tavern an hour before, with three others—another merchant, one I'd seen at Charls' manse, and two men I didn't know—and so I waited, trying not to think of William or Borund, Erick or the white-dusty man. I tried not to think of anything at all, submerging myself beneath the river, floating there.

On the side street, no one tried to approach me. A patrol of palace guards on horseback sauntered by, but they said nothing, only watched me with contempt before turning and vanishing up the main thoroughfare, heading toward the palace.

The tavern door banged open and I shifted away from the wall as Alendor moved out onto the street. He stood straight, a cloak draped over his merchant's coat. The other merchant followed a few steps behind him, like a mongrel. The remaining two men moved like guardsmen, casual and deadly, eyes always watching.

I frowned, suddenly glad there were clouds. I'd need the darkness. In the warehouse district, there were few places to hide. I'd discovered that when trying to follow Borund.

Alendor turned and said something to his bodyguards, then motioned back toward the warehouses near the docks. When they headed away from the tavern, I fell in behind them, far enough back that the guardsmen wouldn't see me.

At the same time, the Fire inside stirred. I'd been expecting it.

They moved slowly, warily, deeper into the warehouses, taking side streets, doubling back once. I pulled back even more, allowed them to get farther ahead. I knew the main thoroughfares here from accompanying Borund and William, but Alendor wasn't using the main streets. He used the narrows, the alleys between the large buildings.

As I followed, the Fire continued to grow, tingling down along my arms.

Ahead, Alendor and his group turned into another alley, this one half the width of the street we were already on. I waited to see if they would double back, one hand resting on the wooden wall of the warehouse to my left.

After twenty slow breaths, I sidled forward in a crouch, shifted around a rain barrel and glanced down into the alley.

Nothing but a stack of broken crates. They'd already moved out the far side. Or entered the building through a door I couldn't see.

I ran into the alley, already searching for Alendor's scent.

The Fire surged, burned down my arms to my fingers. I kept moving, thinking the sudden blaze was a reaction to Alendor's disappearance. I didn't realize it was something else until someone stepped out from behind the stack of crates into my path.

I slowed to a halt, the figure five paces away. I didn't recognize him, his face shadowed, dark with a trimmed beard and mustache, shaved head. A few scars marred his cheeks.

The Fire flared even higher as I plunged myself deeper, drawing my dagger, and I suddenly felt more men.

I spun, slipping into a crouch, as three more stepped out of the darkness into the end of the alley. Without turning, I felt more behind me, stepping up to join the man with the beard.

The Fire churned in my chest, and my stomach tightened, a different sour taste flooding my mouth: fear and despair, dark and wet and acidic.

It tasted of the Dredge.

My gaze flicked to the alley walls, looking for an alcove, a niche, a hole, a darkness. But this wasn't the Dredge. The buildings weren't crumbling to ruin, full of empty doorways and shattered walls.

The desperation clawed at my throat and I shifted my attention back to the three men before me, face hardening. My nostrils flared.

Then someone behind me laughed.

My head snapped back to the bearded man, to the two men who'd joined him. I thought it was the bearded man laughing, but it wasn't. Someone else stepped into the alley, wearing a cloak.

Cristoph.

I felt a sliver of surprise course through me. I'd expected it to be Alendor.

"It's not just me and a friend this time," Cristoph said. His voice shivered through me. I remembered it from the alley on the wharf so long ago, from that first kill in the real Amenkor.

The men began to shift forward, and Cristoph removed his cloak as he said, "Careful. She knows how to use that dagger."

I blew out a harsh breath through my nose and then dove deeper.

They came all at once, crowding into the narrow alley, laughing, bodies rushing. I felt them surge around me, felt their movements, tasted their blades, but there were too many of them. It became a mad rush and I spun, slicing out with short arcs, dagger gripped loosely because I had no real target, only a shifting, startling world of reds.

The dagger cut deep as hands grappled me and I cried out. The river was suddenly flooded with the stench of blood. And then even that was overwhelmed with sweat, with raw grunts and curses and shouts. I flailed, felt my dagger connect again, a shallow cut, heard someone bellow and felt emptiness as they pulled back, but then someone shifted and closed in and the river broke, became nothing but a wild current of sound and scent and rough skin.

The first punch caught me on the cheek and I gasped, growled low like an animal, and dug my dagger down and into someone's side. A scream and more copper-tasting blood, hot and fluid, and then a fist connected with my side, my shoulder, another to my back, low, and pain shot up through my spine. I cried out again, felt hands grappling with my arms, felt wetness against my side—someone else's blood—and then there was only weight, pressing me down, hard.

I hit the cobbles of the alley with a grunt, on my stomach, my face to one side, bodies crushing my legs, my chest, a hand splayed over my head. It gripped and lifted and thrust my face into stone, pain shooting down into my neck as my lip cracked and split, blood flooding down into my throat, coating my tongue. Someone laughed and then the weight shifted off my body.

I bucked, but there were too many on my legs, too many holding my arms, and then any thought of movement halted as a foot connected with my stomach from the side.

I gasped, sprayed blood and spit onto the cobbles from my lip, and couldn't catch my breath, my chest seizing. A sheet of white pain spiked into my skull, blinded me, and after a horrifying moment something in my lungs tore and I heaved in air.

A foot stomped down onto my back, flattened me to the cobbles, and I lost my breath again, coughed it out with a hacking wheeze.

A pause, but the hands on my arms tightened and the weight on my legs didn't move. I heard footsteps approach, realized I still held my dagger in one hand in a death grip.

Someone leaned down close, breath against my neck.

I strained, struggled to move, neck straining with effort. Someone chuckled and I spat out blood in frustration.

"This is for Bellin," Cristoph whispered into my ear. "And for Charls."

He shifted away, but not far.

A hand closed around my neck, tightened as I gasped and tried to pull away, then held me still.

Cold metal touched my throat.

In the chaotic roil of the river I tasted the blade, gasped in the sharp scent of lantern oil and straw: Cristoph's scent.

He hadn't had one before, but he did now.

I sobbed, the sound thick and distorted.

The blade began to press down, and then I scented something else.

Oranges.

"Let her go," someone said, voice calm and cold and dangerous, like the Dredge. And I felt a blade slip through the currents, swift and smooth, another dagger, distant—

And someone screamed, a gargled, bloody sound.

The knife at my throat jerked back suddenly, and Cristoph roared, "Kill him!"

And suddenly the weight holding me down released, pulled back sharply with the sounds of scuffling feet and grunts and the focused intensity shifted away from me, one step, two, down the alley.

I tried to roll onto one arm, felt pain sear through my chest from where the men had kicked me, and choked on my own blood. Pushing the pain away, I drew the river close, pulled it in tight, and concentrated on the struggle only three paces away.

Cristoph and his men had surrounded Erick. One man lay slumped to one side, his throat cut, but there were still six men left.

Too many for Erick to handle. Too many.

I rolled onto my side and gasped at the renewed pain but dragged myself up onto one arm, to one knee.

I still held my dagger.

I pulled myself into a crouch, turned toward the fight. The men were closing in.

And then Erick saw me. "Run!" he barked. His voice cracked with command, the voice he'd used to train me, to drill me, more a growl than a shout. His eyes flashed and he shouted again, "Run!"

One of the men turned—Cristoph—and I spun, stumbled, caught myself, and ran. I obeyed without thought. It had been drilled into me.

Behind, I heard a clatter of blades, heard Erick cry out in pain, heard someone roar in triumph.

And then I was in the street, fleeing down narrows and alleys I didn't recognize, running without a place to run to. Pain flared at every step, in my stomach, in my chest, across one shoulder. My face throbbed, and blood trailed down from my lip, down my neck.

I stumbled to a halt, gasping, in a narrow a hundred paces out when I realized no one was following me, leaned over near a wall, one arm out for support, and coughed. My eyes burned and my hair was tangled and matted. My lip throbbed with a pain unlike anything I'd ever felt before, and there was a thin sliver of cold pain up along my neck from Cristoph's blade, but the pain in my chest receded as my coughing fit ended, each breath no longer so piercing. I didn't think anything was broken inside, just bruised.

I drew myself upright, suddenly fourteen, back on the Dredge all over again.

And then I heard William's voice: *You have a choice now.*

My breath caught and I stared out into the black street. I choked, coughed hoarsely, and spat more blood, winced at the bruising in my chest, and thought about Erick, about Alendor, about Cristoph.

Suddenly, the pain in my chest didn't seem so harsh. Because I wasn't fourteen anymore, waiting for the next kick, the next shouted "whore!" Because I didn't have to listen to Borund . . . or Erick.

I shoved myself away from the wall, staggered back toward the alley. By the time I'd reached its entrance, I'd let the writhing snake of anger inside me uncoil and drawn the river and the Fire up around me like a cloak. It subdued the pain, pushed it into the background. But it was going to cost me. I could feel the nausea rising even now, a nausea I hadn't felt in over a year, since Bloodmark. But I'd never pushed myself this deep for this long into the river's depths since then.

And it didn't matter. All that mattered was Erick.

I rounded the corner, moving with the quick, quiet stealth I'd learned from the Dredge, as fluid as a cat. At the far end of the alley, I could see the men that surrounded Erick's body where it lay, laughing as they kicked him, muttering to each other, goading each other on. Cristoph stood back from the group. Only four men left, besides Cristoph. Two other bodies lay scattered through the alley.

Erick had little time. He'd be dead in the next twenty breaths if I didn't act. Cristoph would kill him. Even as I watched, Cristoph smiled. The same slow, cruel smile I'd seen on Garrell Cart as he gazed down at the little girl with the green ribbon.

I pushed away from the wall, the last vestiges of the pain smothered. Everything became focused, became clear.

Twenty breaths.

The first man died two breaths later, my dagger slipping up and in and out. He jerked forward, arched back, began to fall, but I was already moving. I felt Cristoph see me, heard his drawn breath like a gasp in my ear. But he was the farthest away, and not close enough to harm Erick.

The others first.

The second man heard the first one's startled gasp, but he wasn't fast enough. My dagger punched into his neck even as the muscles there contracted and his head began to turn. He staggered back, hands shooting to the spray of blood, struck the wall to the left of Erick's crumpled body, slid down its side. His pulse thrummed through my head, a dark ripple, and I tasted the heat in the air, the sweat.

Eight breaths.

" 'Ware!" Cristoph shouted, sharp and brittle with tension, anger, and terror.

I spun, caught his eyes.

He saw something there, deep inside me. The harshness tinged with annoyance in his gaze vanished like a burst bubble, replaced solely with fear.

He stepped back.

At the same moment, the third man snarled and lunged for me. Almost without thought my blade sliced up and into his side. I caught his weight as he fell into me, felt his last gasp of breath against my shoulder and neck. It smelled of garlic and potatoes.

He was heavier than I'd thought and I staggered, sliding to one side, out from underneath him as he fell. His blood coated my hand, slick and coppery.

Twelve breaths.

And then the river echoed with running feet. Slipping my blade free of the man's side, I rolled his body away from me, turned to see Cristoph and the last man dodging around the corner of the alley.

My nostrils flared and I drew in the deep scent of lantern oil and straw.

I smiled and turned away from the fleeing men, kneeling down at Erick's side.

His face was a bloody mess, cuts and gashes and dirt and pebbles mired across the scars he already had. The whites of his eyes were startling, his breath coming in short gasps. Blood dripped from his nose to the cobblestones, and his arms were hunched protectively about his body. Every breath he drew sent a shudder through his chest, his legs twitching.

"I told you to run," he wheezed.

I leaned in close and smiled. "And I told you you couldn't protect me anymore."

He stilled for a moment, regarding me, and then he chuckled, the sound wet and thick. The chuckle edged into a moan and he rolled onto his back, straightening slightly. "The Mistress' tits, it hurts," he gasped, then winced as he moved his arm.

I dove deeper, focused as I laid a hand on his chest to keep him from moving. Nausea bubbled up, but I thrust it aside. I still had work to do tonight. The scent of oil and straw pulled me.

I could see that Erick wasn't as hurt as he looked, beaten but not broken. Cristoph had been the real threat. Erick would survive if he'd stay in the alley and wait for me. No one would disturb him here.

I relaxed and leaned in toward him. "Don't move. Stay here and wait for me. I'll be back to get you."

He looked at me a long moment, surprised, but then nodded. "I'll stay," he muttered.

I pushed away, but he halted me before I'd moved two steps with a barked, "Varis!"

I turned back, face creased with annoyance. The scent of oil and straw was strong, almost overwhelming.

"He's a mark now," Erick gasped, so intent on what he said that he'd risen slightly, his upper torso wavering a few inches off the ground.

I smiled and nodded. "I know."

He collapsed back to the cobbles with a groan.

I'd reached the end of the alley and turned before I realized that I'd spoken to him with the same harsh crack of command he'd used to train me.

†

Lantern oil and straw.

I drew in a deep breath, glanced upward toward the roiling clouds. The pressure of rain weighed down on me, heavy and cold. I was barely keeping the nausea at bay now, drawing more and more on the protective Fire to keep it back.

I had to find Cristoph. I wouldn't be able to hold on much longer.

I dodged across a main thoroughfare, ducked through an alley and sped down the street on the far side. Cristoph was moving deeper into the warehouse district, traveling fast. The other man was still with him, his scent warm, like stagnant water, and not as strong. But Cristoph's scent intensified as I ran, seemed to be gathering like a pool of water not far away.

Another street, down the edge of a long warehouse, through another alley—

A warning pulse in the Fire and I slowed, felt a shudder as the scent of stagnant water suddenly sharpened. I tasted metal.

The man that had fled with Cristoph was quick. His blade flashed out from behind a stack of empty crates and caught me in the arm before I could jerk back. I felt the tug as it sliced through my shirt, through skin, tasted my own blood, but the silvery jolt of pain was smothered almost instantly by the Fire.

I stepped back from the crates as the man moved out of hiding. He growled, a low, dark sound, and his eyes flared with hate. But I could smell his fear in his sweat, thick and putrid. It was the bearded man, the one who had first stepped from hiding in the alley where I'd been caught.

He circled me and I turned slowly, followed him. In the darkness, he could barely see me, was listening more than he was seeing. I could see it in the turn of his head. His breathing was harsh, drowning out most sound.

"Where are you, little bitch?" he hissed, almost too low to hear.

I grinned.

He lunged forward, knife striking. I parried, ducked to one side, sliced up and out toward his chest, but he was already moving, grunting with the effort, pulling back.

My blade caught his shirt but nothing else and then we were circling again. My grin was gone. He was breathing harder, but there was a change in his stance. He wasn't trying to see me anymore. He'd given up, was relying on his other senses.

His nostrils flared and I suddenly wondered what I smelled like, but then he dove, moving in tight and close.

My blade grated across his and I felt his breath on my face, the stench of stagnant water overpowering. His free arm snaked around my back, jerked me in tight, our blade arms caught between us. Just as I began to twist out of the hold, his foot caught the back of mine. He turned, spun me in the direction I'd been about to twist, and I tripped over his foot.

I landed hard on my shoulder, gasped as numbness sank into my flesh, my arm going dead for a moment, then tingling along its entire length. I felt my dagger slipping from my numbed fingers, heard it clatter to the cobbles of the street, but I didn't hesitate. I rolled onto my back, reached up with my other arm and caught his wrist as he struck downward, dug my fingers into tendon and muscle. He hissed and dropped down onto my chest, knees to either side, but he didn't lose the knife. My grip was too tenuous, my fingers in the wrong place.

He leaned forward, arm trembling, and forced his knife closer. His other hand clamped onto my arm, tried to wrench it free, but I held tight. He snarled in frustration, his knees tightening about my sides. Sensation began returning to my useless arm, a horrible burning fire, but I fought it back and began scrabbling for my lost dagger. Giving up on wresting my hand free, he pulled back and punched me.

The sheeting white pain from my already split lip almost wrenched me from the river. The Fire wavered and I spasmed, bile rising to the back of my throat. I choked it down, seized the river again, the protective Fire returning just in time for me to halt his knife a few inches from my chest.

He shifted, laid his hand on my chest, and put his entire weight behind his knife.

It was too much. I couldn't hold it. My arm was trembling already, weakening. I could see the strength flowing out of it in tendrils. I could smell my own sweat, tainted with terror.

The knife lowered, touched my shirt, pricked my skin. Blood began to stain the cloth, and the man smiled, a wicked, vicious smile. I strained harder, the muscles in my arm burning, but the knife sank lower, digging in. The tip of the knife scraped bone.

The scent of blood intensified. White-hot pain began to flare through my chest, so hot the Fire couldn't hold it back. I gasped, my eyes going wide—

And I pulled the river close, formed it into a hard, solid ball between me and the grinning face of the bearded man, and punched it forward.

The man jerked back with a gasp, the knife tip sliding free of my chest as his arm went weak and I thrust him away. My other hand found my dagger and with a heave I pulled myself up off the ground and into a crouch, weight in my heels.

The bearded man never had time to recover. He was still gasping, arms cradling his chest where I'd punched him with the river, when I slit his throat.

I stepped back, staggered under a sudden weight of weariness, but forced that back as well as I caught myself against a wall. The scent of stagnant water was fading, the lantern oil and straw now so strong it overwhelmed everything else, even blood. Using the wall for support, I stumbled down the street, turned, and saw the door.

I halted. The warehouse took up the entire block and had two floors. Lantern light glowed through the few windows surrounding the doorway. The entire building reeked of oil and straw.

I pushed away from the wall and moved across the street. I was no longer moving fluidly. My arm still tingled with the last traces of numbness and my chest throbbed with a dull, hideous pain that the Fire could not suppress. My face had begun to throb as well. But the writhing coil of anger urged me forward.

I didn't hesitate at the door. Instead, I kicked it open.

At the far side of the little room beyond, Cristoph jerked around. He held a lantern and was just about to step through a second, open doorway into the warehouse itself. The room we were in held two desks and numerous ledgers on shelves.

When he saw me, Cristoph bolted through the door, taking the lantern with him.

I staggered past the desks to the door, stared out into the warehouse beyond. Crates filled the immense room, stacked high, so that the warehouse was nothing but a warren of narrow walkways and niches. But Cristoph's scent was strong, and I could see the flicker of lantern light clearly.

I slid forward.

Cristoph turned and twisted through the passages, ducked and doubled back. But he couldn't hide. Not with his scent so strong. As I got closer, I could hear his breathing. It was panicked, punctuated with gasps and moans.

I moved faster, my nostrils flaring. I was close. I could almost taste him.

Then the sounds of panic quieted. I paused, edged around a corner.

He stood in the short passage on the far side, and the moment he saw me he heaved the lantern at me.

I ducked under it, sped forward, heard it shatter as it struck the crates behind me. The scent of lantern oil was suddenly stronger, as intense as the blood earlier—

And then there was a faint whoosh of sound. A wave of heat washed forward and I paused.

Ahead of me, a look of horror passed over Cristoph's face as the sheen of light intensified. He held still in the flicker of flames, then dropped his gaze to me and fled to the left, down another passage.

I turned back, smoke suddenly choking me. The entire passage behind me was consumed in flame. And it was spreading. Fast.

The entire warehouse would burn. And it wouldn't end there.

I spun and rushed after Cristoph. He was too close to let go now. And he knew the quickest way out.

I caught up to him twenty steps farther on. He was trapped at a dead end, backed up against a wall of crates.

"Please," he gasped.

The wall of heat from the fire pulsed behind us and now the river was saturated with the sounds of wood crackling, splintering.

Cristoph glanced toward the fire, then seemed to sag, the panic pulling back. "We're trapped. The only way out was back through the fire."

I frowned, then stepped forward. He only had time to tense, to draw in a sharp breath, before I struck.

I made it as painless and quick as possible. He was a mark, nothing more.

When his body slumped to the floor, I stood over it a moment. But I felt nothing. No satisfaction. No anger. No remorse.

Then I turned to look at the fire. I could see its light at the end of the passage, could see the light flickering on the wood of the ceiling high above. I could feel it pushing toward where I stood, a ripple of heat and smoke and light.

I glanced up to the top of the crates. They were stacked high, but not all the way to the ceiling.

I was small, thin. I could fit through narrow spaces.

I stepped over Cristoph's body and began pulling myself up.

†

I stumbled out of the warehouse through a back entrance, where goods were loaded and unloaded. The smoke on the air was heavy and thick, cloying beneath the river, but I didn't dare let it go. I still had to reach Erick, and the fire inside was raging, had already spread to the warehouse on one side.

The entire warehouse district might go up in flames.

I shoved the thought from my mind, gathered the Fire and the river about me as tightly as I could, and set out at a half run toward

Erick. Halfway there, shouts began to rise in warning. Someone ran past with a bucket and I snorted, feeling a shiver of guilt. But there was nothing I could do. And the bucket wouldn't help.

I stumbled into the alley where I'd left Erick, half expecting him to be gone, but he wasn't. He was sitting up instead, back against the alley wall. I knelt beside him and he chuckled when he saw me.

"You look like hell," he said, and I grinned. But it was weak. I was barely holding on, the nausea and pain steadily overtaking the Fire.

"Come on," I said, pulling him upright. He groaned, rolled to his knees, and then with help managed to climb to his feet.

"What in the Mistress' name did you do?" he wheezed as we staggered out onto the street. He was supporting me more than I was supporting him. The fire could be seen clearly beneath the lowering clouds.

"Cristoph started a small fire."

He laughed, winced, then shook his head.

We made it to the edge of the warehouse district before I lost the river completely. It slid away without a sound, even as I reached for it, and the sudden pain and nausea was instantaneous. I vomited in a corner, Erick leaning over me, while people on the street panicked. The fire lit up the clouds behind us, thick smoke roiling skyward, reflecting the flames.

"What did you do?" Erick said again in awe as he watched.

From where I knelt, hunched over my own puke, I glanced up at him. I wasn't going to hold out much longer. "Get me to Merchant Borund's manse," I croaked.

He nodded.

I felt the first fat drops of rain strike my face and then I let the nausea and pain overtake me.

I never felt myself hit the ground.

✝

I woke when the first tremors hit.

Erick was carrying me. He clutched me tight at the beginning, but then the spasms became too violent, my arms twitching, my back arching, and he was forced to set me on the ground.

"Gods," he muttered. His voice was muted, as if coming from a distance. In the background, I could dimly hear screams, running feet, the roaring crackle of fire. Rain poured down, sluicing my face, dripped from Erick's hair as he knelt over me, his hands pressing me down, trying to hold me still. Fear was stamped across his face, stark and surreal.

Eventually, the tremors passed. The last thing I saw before weariness claimed me again was Erick, staring down into my half-lidded eyes, his face grim.

The second time, the tremors were worse. I never opened my eyes, *couldn't* open my eyes. My body was so taut I could feel the cords of muscle in my neck. My teeth were clenched so tight my jaw ached and tears squeezed from between my eyelids. Erick didn't set me down this time, and there was shouting.

"Open the damn gate!" Erick bellowed, but again everything was distant, removed.

A clatter of metal, a screech as I was jostled in Erick's grip, his balance shifting. He must have kicked the gate the moment it was unlocked. And the next instant he was running.

"What is this?" someone demanded, a voice I recognized, but it took a moment. Gerrold.

"Varis," Erick barked. "Are you Borund?"

"No."

"Get me Borund!" The training voice.

"What's this?" Lizbeth now, her voice harsh but shrill.

I felt the tension in my neck relaxing. The sensation of rain had stopped. We were inside.

Someone else approached. "What is the meaning of this?" Borund demanded.

"Varis is hurt."

"What?" Borund's voice moved closer. I felt a hand press against my face. "By the Mistress . . . Gerrold, go fetch Isaiah."

"But the fire—"

"Now!" I couldn't be certain, but I thought I heard true agony in his voice.

Perhaps I was something more to him than a tool, a weapon.

Receding footsteps. My neck muscles had almost completely relaxed.

"Lizbeth—" Worry now.

"Towels, hot water, I know." Not as shrill as before. Determined and grim. Even with my eyes closed I could see her hitching up skirts, darting off toward the kitchen.

"Right. Now. You, Guardsman—"

"Erick."

"Whatever. Follow me. We'll take her up to her room."

More jostling. We'd almost reached my room when I began to thrash.

"Gods!" Borund gasped.

Erick shoved someone out of the way and tossed me onto the bed. "Hold her, damn it! She'll hurt herself!"

Hands clamped down onto my shoulders, a body pressed down over my chest. More hands gripped my legs.

"Gods, she's strong," Borund muttered. One leg tore free. My knee connected with something soft and fleshy and I heard Borund bark, "Shit!" before he recaptured the leg.

I heard Lizbeth gasp as she returned, and then there was a flutter of quick movements and a moment later, still thrashing madly, someone pressed a hot cloth against my forehead, water drenching down into my hair.

"She's sweating up a storm," Lizbeth said.

Erick only grunted.

I felt the tremors easing again, felt the strength draining away, leaving me empty.

"I think it's stopping for now," Erick muttered, and he drew his body weight off me, carefully.

I began to sob, the tears hot and salty, my chest hitching painfully. I tried to speak, but the strength was draining away too fast.

"Shh," Lizbeth murmured, her voice close, her breath tickling my ear. "Hush, you're safe now."

Exhaustion dragged her away. Just before it claimed me again, I heard Erick say faintly, "That's not the end of it."

And it wasn't. I rode the waves of tremors and exhaustion as I'd done before on the Dredge, waking enough that I could hear things faintly. But the pain was too intense. I never opened my eyes, only listened.

". . . in bloody hells happened!" Borund, voice vehement.

"It was an ambush," Erick spat back. "They were waiting for her!"

"Who?"

"She called the one Cristoph."

"Cristoph? But she was supposed to be following Alendor!"

Erick grunted. "He knew. He must have led her to the alley where Cristoph was waiting."

Silence. Then Borund said, "Cristoph *is* Alendor's youngest son. Perhaps Alendor is more daring than I thought. Or more desperate."

Another silence. "She'd be dead if I hadn't intervened."

Someone else entered the room. "Master Borund. The fire has spread through the warehouse district and entered the wharf. All ships have taken to the harbor, but, of course, with the blockade none can leave."

Borund swore. "Damn Avrell! Why can't he get the harbor opened? All our ships are safe?"

"Yes."

Borund sighed, began pacing. "What about the rain? Is it helping? Are we safe here?"

"The wind is blowing the fire toward the wharf. There's a chance it will jump the river to the other side of the harbor, but the rain seems to be keeping the fire damped. It's hard to tell. . . ."

I felt Borund approach, stand over me. But I could feel myself fading. "We'll stay here as long as possible. I don't want to move her."

A breath against my face as someone leaned close. Then I heard Borund whisper, "You damn well better come back, Varis. I can't lose you. Not after almost losing William."

His voice was choked.

Darkness. Soft darkness, like cloth.

Then a patch of light.

"How long will she be like this?" Borund asked.

Someone's hand pulled away from my chest. The trembling fit had abated and I could already feel the exhaustion pulling me down, the cloth moving back over my head.

"Hard to say." Isaiah, the healer. "But the seizures aren't as strong now as before. She's recovering. . . ."

More darkness. I pulled its cloth close, smothered myself in it. But another patch of light intervened.

"And what about Alendor?" A new voice, smooth and careful. I struggled with the cloth of darkness, pushed it back. It was Avrell, the First of the Mistress.

"No one's seen him since the fire," Borund answered.

Avrell sighed. "Parts of the warehouse district are still smoldering."

"Thank the Mistress for the rain. All of Amenkor might have burned." Borund had moved closer. "But it doesn't matter," he added. "With the warehouse district gone, we've lost most of our food stocks. The consortium is dead whether Alendor survived the fire or not. There's nothing left in Amenkor for the consortium to control."

"He's still a danger."

"I won't kill him," I tried to say, but the darkness was returning. I couldn't tell whether anyone had heard me, whether I'd even spoken out loud.

Borund leaned in closer. "Not anymore."

I fought the darkness, screamed at its resilience. "I won't kill him!"

Avrell moved closer as well. "In any case, we still have the problem of the Mistress. Nathem and I have tried to replace her, to seat someone else on the throne, but it isn't working. And the current Mistress still refuses to release the blockade."

Silence. "And what do you expect me to do about it?" Borund sounded tired and distracted.

I felt Avrell leaning over me, felt his presence like a weight. "Remember our discussion when I came to your manse a few weeks back? You told me that Varis once said she sees people as 'red,' and that is how she knows who to protect you from."

Borund grunted.

"I questioned that Seeker who brought her to you. He told me a similar story, that Varis claimed one of the Mistress' marks that she helped him to hunt down was 'gray,' that Varis told him that meant the mark was innocent. I'd heard of this before, so when you and Varis came to the palace, I had one of the Servants check to confirm my suspicions."

I stilled, felt the darkness drawing in close and tight and struggled against it. But I was still too weak.

Avrell leaned back, his clothes rustling. "I know what needs to be done now."

Before Borund could respond, or Avrell could continue, the darkness claimed me. One last time.

†

When I woke again, it was from true sleep. No feeling of cloth darkness shoved aside for a brief moment. No patch of light. No uncontrollable trembling. Instead, there was weariness, sunk so deep into my bones I could barely move. But I opened my eyes.

Sunlight. It flooded the room . . . my room.

I blinked up at the ceiling, let the throbbing of my face, my chest, my entire body flood through me. The pain in my chest was edged and concentrated. The pain in the vicinity of my lip was dull and spread out. The rest of my body was simply bruised, muscles and flesh worn and tired and completely drained of strength.

I lay a long moment and simply breathed. The air was tainted with smoke.

"Welcome back."

I turned my head, ignored the warning pangs from my neck.

William sat in a chair on the opposite side of the room, watching me. He smiled, and I felt something inside the empty hollowness of my gut warm. "Aren't we the pair," he added, then laughed.

I smiled, or tried to. There was more wrong with my face than the split lip. I remembered the bearded man punching me and lifted one arm tentatively to my cheek. It felt swollen and hot to the touch.

I let my hand drop back, more for lack of strength than anything else.

"How long?" I asked.

William leaned forward. "Five days. The first two days we were afraid we'd have to move you because of the fire, but the rain halted that, or at least held it at bay. By then we realized that the seizures weren't as bad each time and were spaced farther apart. We figured it was only a matter of time." He hesitated, then asked, "What happened to you?"

I turned away, stared up at the ceiling again. A surge of fear rippled through me, but not as strong as I expected. I'd never told anyone about the river, about what I saw. Not directly.

But Avrell knew now, and I assumed Borund. I found it strange that they had not told William.

"I don't see things the same way you do," I said. I paused, but the ripple of fear was smothered by the warmth. "When I want to, I can make everything a blur, as if I'm staring through water. Only the things of importance are clear. But it isn't easy. Sometimes, when I push things too hard, or when I do something unexpected, something I didn't realize I could do before, I get sick."

I waited, not certain what to expect.

After a long moment of silence, I turned back to see William still sitting forward watching me. He smiled again, then stood.

Moving carefully, one hand holding his side, he came up to the edge of the bed.

"I'd better go tell Borund you're awake. He and Avrell want to talk to you."

My stomach clenched and I thought, *I won't kill him*, but then William reached forward and gently brushed my hair away from my face, distracting me. A light touch that sent shivers down my neck and shoulders and into my back.

I held myself perfectly still and watched as he left the room.

✝

I stood at a window in the palace and stared down at the city and harbor below. It had taken three days to recover enough so that I could get out of bed, and another two days before I felt well enough to come to the palace with Borund in order to see Avrell.

Borund had tried to push me. But I didn't listen to Borund anymore. I made my own decisions.

On the harbor below, patrols still blockaded the inlet, the sleek ships flying the Mistress' colors weaving back and forth beneath the sun. On land, a large chunk of the city close to the water was blackened, a few charred walls and half buildings still standing. Some warehouses had survived, and most of the docks, but close to a quarter of the city had burned.

I thought of Cristoph heaving the lantern at me and frowned.

I thought of Erick and bit my lip. I hadn't seen him since that night, had only heard him in the days that followed. And he hadn't been there at the end, when the tremors weren't as bad. I'd only heard Borund and Avrell.

Behind me, Borund suddenly blurted, "Where in bloody hell is he?" and stopped his pacing.

As if he'd heard, the door to the little room opened and Avrell stepped in. He was followed by Erick.

I shifted away from the window unconsciously, but halted. Erick's face was set, grim and determined and dangerous. The same face he wore on the Dredge, when he was about to kill a mark. As if he were about to do something he regretted, but that he felt was necessary.

His eyes caught mine but revealed nothing. He didn't even nod in acknowledgment.

I settled back as Avrell moved forward, suddenly uneasy.

Avrell approached Borund first, caught his gaze, and said simply, "It didn't work. We'll have to do what we discussed earlier."

Borund tensed. "Are you certain? There's no other option?" He did not look toward me as he spoke.

"I see no other way," Avrell said.

Borund sighed, shoulders sagging, and nodded. Then they both turned toward me.

I straightened at the looks on their faces, felt my bruised shoulders tense, felt my face set into a guarded expression. I watched Avrell, but it was Borund who moved forward.

"Varis, we need your help."

My stomach tightened and I drew in a deep breath, anger flaring, but before I could say anything, Borund continued.

"The fire that was started in the warehouse district . . . it burned up a significant portion of our reserves. The food we'd put aside, the food that had become scarce even before the fire, all of that . . . is gone. If we gather together everything that's left, from all the merchants in the city, and if we buy up and ship as much as we can from the nearest cities, we might be able to survive until the spring harvest. But in order to do that the ships *have* to leave within the next five days. They have to leave *now* or they won't make it back before winter makes the seas too rough. Do you understand?"

I shook my head, the tightness in my stomach beginning to sour. Because a part of me *did* see, already knew what was coming. "No, I don't understand."

He sighed heavily. "We can't buy up and ship what we need when the harbor is blockaded."

I glanced toward Avrell. "Then unblock the harbor. Let the ships out."

Avrell didn't move. "We can't. The Mistress ordered the harbor closed. The Mistress has to order the harbor opened again. Baill won't listen to anyone else, including me. He doesn't *have* to listen to anyone else, not when given a direct order from the Mistress."

My gaze darted back to Borund. "Then get her to change her mind."

"She won't," Borund said. "We've tried."

The room fell silent. I knew what they wanted, but I wanted to hear them say it.

"What do you want me to do?"

And now no one wanted to speak. Borund drew back, breath held. Avrell stilled. Erick stood by the closed door and watched me, his expression still hard, closed.

"She's insane, Varis," Borund finally managed. I was surprised. I'd expected Avrell to speak first. "We want you to kill her."

"No." I said it almost before he finished, and he stepped back at the vehemence in my voice. "No, I don't want to kill for you any-more. Find some other way."

"There is no other way!" Borund said. His voice became hard, commanding, desperate. "We've tried reasoning with her, we've tried countermanding her orders. We've even tried replacing her—"

"Enough."

Avrell's voice cut Borund short and he turned, angry and bel-ligerent, but Avrell ignored him. Instead, he watched me.

"You heard us discussing this before. The Mistress is insane. Something in the White Fire six years ago drove her insane. She or-dered the palace guard into the city, infiltrating the streets when there was no serious threat. She ordered the blockade of the harbor, for no reason whatsoever. But that isn't the worst." He stood, mov-ing forward, taking the place of Borund, who fell back.

Behind them both, Erick perked up, suddenly attentive.

Avrell stopped in front of me, held my gaze. "When the fire started in the city below, the Guard instantly responded. We moved to form brigades to the harbor, lines of men to pass buckets of water to help put it out, or at least try to contain it. But the Mistress ordered the guardsmen not to help. And so they didn't. I stood on the tower beside the Mistress, stood there in the rain, and watched the city burn, *let it burn*. Because that's what the Mistress had ordered. And do you know what she did as it spread toward the docks? She smiled." He paused, and I saw rage in his eyes. "She let the city burn, Varis. If I had any doubts about her sanity before, they're gone now."

"Then replace her," I said.

He shook his head. "I tried. Everyone I seat upon the throne dies. Horribly. The throne twists them somehow, tortures them without leaving a mark upon their bodies. Looking at the histories, no one has ever tried to replace a current living Mistress. The Mistress has always been dead before a new Mistress was named. No." He shook his head again. "No. The current Mistress has to die before I can replace her.

"I'm sworn to protect the throne, not the Mistress."

I looked into his eyes and saw how much it had torn him inside to admit it. A deep tear, as deep as anything I'd learned on the Dredge . . . or in Amenkor. Because in the end both the Dredge and Amenkor were the same. The *people* were the same.

My gaze shifted toward Erick, took in his rigid stance. "Find someone else to kill her. Like Erick. Make her one of the guardsmen's marks."

Avrell shook his head. "No. It has to be you, Varis." He shot a quick glance toward Borund, who shifted uncomfortably. "Borund told me that you see the world differently, that you say those that are dangerous to you and to him are 'red'. Erick says you told him something similar when you hunted for him on the Dredge."

I felt a hot shudder of betrayal snap through me, shot a glare at Borund, then Erick, but Avrell had already continued.

"The Mistress knows when someone is approaching, so someone like Erick won't be able to get close enough to kill her. No. The only one who might have a chance is someone like you, someone who uses senses other than the normal senses." Avrell had shifted close to me, stood directly in front of me so that I was forced to focus on him, not Erick or Borund. "I don't know how this . . . talent of yours works, but it's our only chance to kill her. You are the only one capable of getting close enough to try. It has to be you, Varis."

He felt me hesitate, and so added, "You wouldn't be killing her for us, Varis. You'd be killing her for Amenkor." Then he backed away.

I sagged slightly, turned toward Erick, appealing to him for help, for support.

His expression was set, hard and unforgiving. "I've seen her, Varis. She truly is insane. But you already know that. You saw it first, there on the Dredge. Remember Mari?" He drew in a breath, let it out slowly. "You told me she wasn't a mark. I didn't believe you then, but I do now. The Mistress was wrong. Mari shouldn't have died. Someone who can't see the difference shouldn't be sitting on the throne."

I frowned at Erick, feeling cheated somehow, the sense of betrayal deepening, and turned back to Avrell.

Something else flickered behind his eyes, something deeper, as if he hadn't told me everything, as if he were still holding something back, some hidden purpose.

"Find someone else like me," I said, but my voice was defeated. I'd already decided.

"No." He shook his head, a smile touching his lips, and I saw again that flicker in his eyes, as if he were leaving something out, as if he'd lied in some way. But he'd heard the defeat in my voice as well. "There is no one else. It has to be you."

I stared at them all, one by one—Borund, Avrell, and Erick. Something wasn't right, something that I couldn't see.

This is what I am, a small part of me murmured.

But this time it was my decision, my choice.

I sighed, the sound heavy, and asked, "How do you intend to get me into the palace?"

·⟨ *The Palace* ⟩·

TWO days later, I found myself tucked into a niche in the palace, squeezed into shadow, knees to my chest, looking down on a corridor lit by oil sconces. I'd come in through the passage beneath the wall. Avrell had given me a rough sketch of the palace, page boy clothing, and the key to a linen closet. I wasn't to be seen. No one was to know I was there, especially not Baill. And I had to kill the Mistress tonight. The ships had to be released in the next three days. There was no time left.

Almost the moment I started the hunt, a passing Servant saw me, asked for my help. But the marks were my choice now, and so after helping her with the baskets I let her go. I waited until she was gone, then headed for the linen closet.

I passed through rooms, gardens, halls. I slid into a familiar waiting room, ducked into shadow, listened to Avrell tell Nathem he had ordered the Mistress' death. After they'd passed, I slid from room to room with less stealth and more speed, until I'd found the linen closet Avrell had told me about, the one with the arrow slot I could squeeze through to enter the inner sanctum, the true palace.

I'd entered the throne room, seen the Skewed Throne itself, listened to it.

And now I stood before the Mistress' own chambers, dressed in a page boy's shirt and breeches. The hallway blazed with light, every sconce flaring high, flames flapping and hissing. The entire palace was lit, every hall, every corridor, every room. I could feel the energy in the building, people searching, scouring the halls, the audience chambers, the storage areas. I could feel them, guards and servants, everyone Baill could call to hand, even though I held the river at bay, the voices of the throne there too strong, too demanding for me to trust myself beneath its surface. I hadn't used the river since entering the palace.

No one stood guard over the Mistress' chambers.

I didn't hesitate, even when a shiver of doubt coursed through me. Someone should be here, watching. Avrell had said he'd placed guards here, to watch over her. But it didn't matter. Part of me already knew what I would find.

I plunged into the rooms, into the antechamber with trailing curtains, soft scattered pillows, tables of fruit and drink and platters of cheese. Empty. I slid without sound to the bedchamber, drew close to the veiled bed itself, drew back the curtains.

Empty.

And then I knew.

Baill wasn't hunting me, he was hunting the Mistress. She'd slipped past the guards at the door again, just as before, had hidden herself somewhere in the palace.

And I knew where she would be.

She'd been calling me all night. I'd just refused to listen.

·❮ The Throne Room ❯·

THE corridor to the throne room was still empty and I stepped up to the wide double doors without skulking, standing straight, back rigid, blade drawn but held loose at my side. I stood in front of the wooden doors banded with delicate ironwork for a long moment, staring at the subtle curves of the iron, the gleam of the rounded metal studs that held it in place, the polish of the wood beneath. Old wood, the age obvious. But the grain still glowed with an inner warmth.

The Mistress waited for me inside, with the throne. I hadn't seen her before, but I knew she was there. She'd been calling me with the voices—that dry rustling of leaves—since I'd entered the inner sanctum of the palace. Avrell had said she knew when someone was approaching, and she knew about me, knew I was here. The river hadn't masked me from her at all. Nor the Fire.

Fear crawled across my shoulders, making the muscles tense and twitch. My hand clenched the handle of my dagger, then released.

But then why were there no guards to protect her? Why hadn't Baill and a retinue of twenty guardsmen been waiting for me outside of the Mistress' chambers if she knew I was coming?

I glanced down the empty hall, suddenly wary. Someone should have been here. Unless . . .

I turned back to the iron-banded door with a frown.

Unless the Mistress *wanted* me to come.

I suddenly thought about the ease with which I'd moved through the palace, the lack of guards, the way Baill had drawn them away from the entrance to the audience chamber. At the time I had thought the lack of guards was fortuitous, or something arranged by Avrell himself, but now. . . .

What if the Mistress had arranged it all, instead of Avrell? What if she'd somehow led Baill astray?

I shivered, steeled myself, shoulders tightening. It didn't matter. I had agreed to kill her, to save Amenkor. If I could get close to her, I still might have a chance, whether she knew I was coming or not.

I reached for the ornate wrought-iron handle of one of the doors and pulled it toward me. The wood groaned, the sound loud in the empty corridor, but I didn't cringe, didn't duck into the nearest shadow. I stepped into the throne room instead, pulling the Fire that still curled deep inside me around myself in a protective wall.

The force that was the throne, that writhed and warped within the throne room and pricked the back of my neck, came suddenly, but I was expecting it this time. With a horrifying weight, it pushed me down, tried to force me beneath the river. For a moment, it almost succeeded, the Fire I'd raised to shield myself flickering as if doused with water. I grunted under the onslaught, brought my hands up to ward the intense pressure away, even though there was nothing physical for me to fight against, but the Fire held, drawing strength as the pressure relented, backing off.

But it didn't leave. I could feel it, filling the room, saturating it. I tasted it with every breath, felt it prickling against my skin, alive and predatory. It sent sparks of static through my skin, like lightning. I shivered at the sensation, tried to brush it aside.

I suddenly remembered that I'd felt the presence once before, weeks ago, when I'd come with Borund through the passage beneath the palace wall to meet with Avrell that first time. It had tasted me then, when I'd used the river to make certain Avrell was sincere. I remembered hearing the brush of dead leaves on stone.

It hadn't been certain then, had withdrawn, but it wanted me now.

The thought raised the hackles on the back of my neck, set every instinct for danger I'd learned on the Dredge on edge.

I could feel it pacing the room, felt its presence like the growl of a feral dog, but I forced myself to breathe, to scan the room.

Eight thick granite pillars rose to the vaulted ceiling, four on each side, resting at the top of three tiered granite steps, surrounding the wide flagstone walkway from the doors to the throne, just as before. But now every sconce along the hall had been lit, the throne surrounded by bright candelabra; only a few of the candles had been lit when I passed through the room before. The white-and-gold emblem of the Skewed Throne hung above the throne, the folds of the banner sharply defined in the light—a banner I had not seen before, in the darkness. I refused to look at the throne itself, at its shifting shape. I could already feel the feverish heat against my skin, the same heat I'd felt when I'd entered the room before.

The hall was empty, the two doors on the other side of the room— one of which I'd used to enter the throne room earlier—both closed.

A wave of uncertainty passed through me. I suddenly felt as if I were being hunted, as if someone were watching me from the shadows.

I hated being stalked.

I took one step forward, searching the darknesses behind the pillars to either side. The weight in the air surged forward like a tide, restless, the growl vibrating in my skin, but abated when I winced but did not waver.

My grip shifted on my dagger, slick with sweat.

I moved forward, not pausing now, searching the shadows behind the pillars, searching the niches. But the room was truly empty.

I halted in the center of the throne room, confused. I knew the Mistress was here, could feel her eyes on me. I could feel the throne as well, somehow heavy and solid, even though I could see it shift at the corner of my eye, could feel it gnawing at my stomach. It felt more real than the room itself.

I swallowed, turned away from the throne, back toward the door I'd entered through—

And a laugh echoed through the room, soft and cold. The laugh of a child. Behind me, the door groaned and pulled itself shut with a hollow thud.

My mouth went dry, my tongue parched. My breath quickened and something hard and hot lodged itself at the base of my throat.

The laugh came again, closer, and I spun, settling into a light crouch instinctively. I reached for the river, out of habit, out of necessity, and the pressure stalking on the air surged forward again greedily, rising high, the world shifting into gray and a roar of wind before I jerked myself back with a shudder. Pulling the Fire closer, I shot a glare of anger out into the room, drew myself up straight, and searched the room again.

The laughter had come from inside the room. Someone *was* here.

I stilled when a new voice filled the room, singing quietly to itself.

". . . o-ver the water, o-ver the sea,
Comes a Fire to burn thee.
White as whitecaps, harsh as the scree,
Here it comes to judge thee."

The woman's voice finished with a chuckle. The sound filled the room, throaty and deep. Totally unlike the child's laughter a moment before.

"It came for me, Varis," the throaty voice said. My flesh prickled, my hackles standing on end at the sound of my name. I tasted my fear, like old musty cloth. "Oh, yes, it came. And it destroyed me." Another laugh, this one bitter and choked, dying off harshly into nothing.

Calming myself, I grew still and listened instead. For a breath. For a rustle of clothing. For the tread of a foot. But there was nothing, the voice echoing strangely, seeming to come from everywhere and nowhere at the same time.

I turned. Someone watched me, was judging me, and I struggled not to slip beneath the river as I would have done on the Dredge, because I could feel the throne watching as well, circling patiently.

"What's the matter, Varis?" the woman's voice said smoothly, mockingly. "Can't you see me? Can't you find me?"

I clenched my jaw in anger, tightened my grip on my dagger.

Another chuckle, again soft and throaty, cut off sharply as the woman barked, "Perhaps you aren't using the right Sight!"

I halted my slow, careful spin and the voice laughed again, this time the sound draining down into choked sobs.

Enough, I thought.

Standing straight, I chose a random spot between two pillars on one side of the room and stared at it resolutely, my breath tight and angry.

The sobbing ended and the air in the room shifted from confrontational to curious. I felt the shift like a wind across my back and shivered.

"Not going to play, are we?" A different voice, aged but still strong. The voice harrumphed, like an old woman. "We'll see about that!"

I jumped, startled, my hand raising the dagger defensively. The last statement had come sharp and close, as if the old woman were standing right beside me. But before I could even catch my breath I saw movement at the base of one of the pillars, heard the rustle of cloth.

A woman uncurled from a hunched-over posture, the folds of her dress falling to her sides. She was clothed in white, with long hair as black as pitch, the simple dress stitched with smooth, curved lines of gold at the throat and at the hem, the lines curling upward like fire, as if she were surrounded in the vague outlines of flames. Her skin was smooth, not aged with wrinkles as the voice suggested, and her cheekbones were high.

But it was her eyes that held me. A depthless brown. The darkest features of her narrow face somehow, even against the ebon hair. They captured me, didn't allow me to look away. They commanded me, ordered me to obey even before she spoke.

"You've come to kill me," she said, her voice neither the child's voice, nor the singer's, nor the old woman's, but a strange mixture of all three, resonating with even more voices underneath. "So do it."

The muscles on my shoulders crawled, an unsettled feeling trailing down my back. I'd walked right past her when I'd searched the room, close enough she could have reached out and touched me . . . killed me. I hadn't seen her, hadn't even felt her. My back stiffened and I suddenly felt vulnerable, exposed.

And angry. She was toying with me, batting me about like a cat with a rat.

"Why couldn't I see you?" I asked, voice harsh. But inside I was reeling, trying to figure out what she wanted, what she needed. Was she insane? Or was she simply having a little fun?

Her brow creased a moment, but then she smiled. "Because you chose not to see me. You've come to kill me, but you don't want to. So much easier not to kill when you can't find the mark, isn't it, Varis?" Her head lowered, her eyes narrowed. "But you see me now. And you haven't got much time, Varis. I can occupy the guards only so long. They can't be held at bay forever. Even Baill."

As if she'd called them into existence, guards pounded on one of the side entrances to the throne room, voices muffled by the door. The door began to rattle as they tried to force it. The sounds echoed loudly in the room.

The Mistress didn't move. "Kill me now, Varis. They'll find their way in eventually."

But I didn't move. I didn't trust her. The image of the cat and the rat was too vivid in my mind.

The rattle at the side door stopped. Shouts rang out. Someone called for Baill, someone else for Avrell.

"You have to kill me," the Mistress said, her tone soft and reasonable. "You have to kill me or the city will crumble. It's already started. You've seen it. On the Dredge, on the wharf, even here at the palace." She raised her head, held herself imperious and still. "And I want to die, Varis," her voice still calm. "I *want* you to kill me."

Cold shock ran through me, from my neck down to my toes. The dagger felt suddenly heavy in my hand, weighted, my body somehow light.

"Why?" I asked, my voice sounding distant, removed.

She smiled, and at the edges of her eyes I saw the insanity I'd heard in the laughing child's voice, in the song, in the old woman's voice. I'd seen it enough on the Dredge, recognized it as easily as I recognized the feel and weight of my dagger, cold and deadly and familiar. I recognized it now, staring up into her face, and realized that she held the insanity at bay. Somehow the real Mistress had found herself amid the madness, and she was clinging to herself with a cold, granite desperation that was steadily slipping away from her. If I didn't act soon, she would lose control completely.

"I'm destroying Amenkor, Varis," she said, her voice strong but wavering. "The Fire did something to me and I can no longer control the throne. It's begun to take over, to consume me. You need to kill me before it takes over completely."

I hesitated, still uncertain, and her face suddenly hardened into a frown.

"Do it," she barked, her voice filling the room, the command clear in her voice, in her stance. "Please."

It was the tremble in the last word that convinced me, the way her lips pursed at the end, her muscles rigid with effort. I still didn't trust her, the cat and the rat image still too real, but I had to try. It was an opportunity.

I gripped my dagger firmly, stepped forward, up the tiered stairs, watched her warily as I moved to her side. She drew in a deep breath and as I shifted in behind her, I realized sweat lined her forehead, stained her dress with fear and the effort to control herself. She lifted her head, exposed her pale neck, her stance taut, breath coming in gasps through her nose, and closed her eyes.

I drew up close behind her, but halted.

She was too tall, at least a foot taller than me. I couldn't reach her neck.

I shifted my stance, changed tactics, adjusted so I could slide the dagger into her back, low and quick, but she must have realized my problem. She sighed and grabbed her dress in two fists, kneeling in front of me. Tossing her head back to clear her hair, back straight, she exposed her neck again.

"Do it now," she said, and the strain in her voice was clear, made worse when the main entrance doors began to thud.

The guards were at two of the entrances now, were trying to break through with what sounded like a battering ram.

"Quickly!" the Mistress spat.

I reached forward, around her head, one hand on her shoulder to steady her, the edge of the dagger against her throat. I felt her heat through the cloth of the dress, felt the embroidery. Her pulse shivered up the blade of the dagger into my hand.

I drew a short breath, tensed the muscles in my arm, but hesitated.

It felt wrong. Too deliberate. Too manipulated.

It felt like the eyes of a cat, watching coldly, body perfectly still, as the rat began to twitch, to gather its muscles for a darting escape.

It felt like entering the alley while following Alendor. An ambush.

Fear suddenly spiked through me and I tensed, muscles contracting, ready to slip the dagger across her throat in one smooth motion—

But I was too late, too slow. The cat pounced.

A hand clamped down hard on my wrist, locked so strongly I felt my forearm go numb. At the same moment, the Mistress shuddered beneath my other hand, her muscles pulling taut.

I had a fleeting moment to think, *Trap!*, a fleeting moment to feel terror cascading down through my muscles like ice—

And then the Mistress wrenched the arm holding the dagger out and away, snapped it around with enough force to pull me off-balance. I lurched forward into her back with a gasp, lost my hold on my dagger. It clattered to the floor, down the three tiers of steps to the walkway.

Terror slid into panic. I froze.

The Mistress reached around her own shoulder with her free hand and grabbed my shoulder. The shuddering thud of the battering ram echoed through the room. Wood splintered, groaned. Metal shrieked. The Mistress jerked me around in front of her, my arm twisting. She shifted her grip on my wrist, pulled it up sharply behind my back, and drew me in close, our foreheads touching. Her sweat dripped onto my cheek, her wavy black hair tickling my neck. She smelled of wine and cheese.

"Not quite yet, little hunter," she gasped in the throaty voice. "Not unless we have to. There's another way now that we've gotten rid of your dagger."

And I looked into her eyes, body still in shock, muscles still frozen in panic.

She hadn't lost control. The real Mistress still held the insanity at bay.

A sharp grinding pop filled the hall and the Mistress pulled back as something heavy and metallic hit the floor. The noise from outside in the corridor grew suddenly louder: shouts of triumph, a bark of command.

I recognized the voice. It was Baill's.

"Not much time at all," the Mistress murmured to herself, then turned back to me. With a thin smile she flung me down the tiered steps to the walkway, in the direction of the throne, away from my dagger.

I landed hard, unable to control the fall. But as I hit the flagstone, the panic that had seized my muscles released, replaced with anger.

She'd tricked me. And now I had no weapon.

I snarled, twisted out of the sprawl into a crouch, and caught the Mistress descending the tiered steps slowly, almost languidly. Behind her, my dagger lay on the floor, and farther down the hall a glittering hinge from the large doors. The base of one of the doors was skewed into the hall, wood splintered.

The door shuddered again, bucking inward. The men outside bellowed.

I focused on the Mistress. Her face had turned solemn, grim. "It's time, Varis."

My gaze flicked to my dagger, so far out of reach, then back to her face. Desperation clawed at my arms, at my chest. My breath came ragged and torn through my nose, my jaw clenched, anger a hot lump in my throat.

The Mistress halted between me and the door. The Skewed Throne stood behind me.

"It's time," she said again, with a hint of sorrow, and then she raised her hand.

I reacted without thought, not certain what she intended, what she could do, only knowing that without the dagger I had only one defense: the river.

I dove beneath its surface, pulled the Fire around me as closely as possible as I felt the currents envelop me, smother me, the world graying, drowning. I dove deeper, and deeper still, using the force of my anger, my fear, noting the details in the stone, in the door, in the floor, in the light, as they shifted and clarified. The sounds of the battering ram, of the men in the hall outside the two doors, of the guttering flames in the sconces and on the candelabra, collapsed into the vibrant background wind I'd known since I'd almost drowned in Cobbler's Fountain.

For a moment, the river held me as it had always held me, warm and comforting, like my mother's embrace.

But then the other pressure—the throne—pounced down upon me, a surging, growling ocean of sound and sensation. I screamed, the sound reverberating around the room, and drew the White Fire up as a shield against the onslaught. But the pressure, so vast, so dark, so like the ocean, smothered me, crushed me flat against the flagstone of the hall. Granite cut into my back, each minute crack in the timeworn flagstone like a chasm, each grain of dirt and grit like a boulder. I screamed again as the pressure built, but the scream faltered as the breath was pressed from my chest.

And then I realized that the Fire still held, that it formed a thin shield between me and the howling pressure of this other presence on the river. Trying to draw breath, strange spots already forming on my vision, I pushed the shield of Fire upward with all my strength, pushed it away a hair's breadth, another, then an inch. I gasped through clenched teeth, desperately sucked in air, and pushed harder, straining at the forces, at the eddies and currents that wove around me in a mad frenzy. I shoved the Fire upward until I could finally draw myself up and settle back onto my heels.

Breathing hard, I glanced up at the Mistress, my anger unleashed, coiling and spitting inside me. I intended to kill her now, no hesitations, no doubts.

She'd halted a few steps in front of me. Behind her, the door shuddered again, but the noise was relegated to the background, so muffled by the raging voices I held outside the Fire it almost couldn't be heard.

The Mistress frowned, her hands at her sides.

I didn't give her a chance to think, to respond. As I'd done with the bearded man on the street, I pulled as much of the river as I could as tightly to my chest as possible, compacted it down, and punched it toward the Mistress' chest, my eyes dark with intent.

She raised one hand casually, palm flat, facing toward me.

The hard ball I'd thrown at her hit an unseen wall a foot from her hand and stopped. A backlash of force surged toward me, hit me hard in the chest. I gasped, in surprise and in pain, landed hard on my ass, coming up sharp against the first step in the dais to the throne.

A cold wave of real fear coursed through me, cutting through the anger like a scythe.

The Mistress knew of the river, could use it as I could.

I licked at something warm at the edge of my mouth, tasted blood. Ignoring it, I narrowed my gaze, concentrated through the pain in my chest and the taste of blood, and focused on the area in front of the Mistress' hand.

Faintly, I could see lines of force, almost nonexistent, woven so elegantly and so tightly they seemed to merge with the raw energies of the river around her. The energies formed a solid wall.

The gathered ball of energy I'd flung at her seemed suddenly childish and frayed.

"What is that?" the Mistress asked quietly, advancing forward. Her tone was hard, demanding. "What is that around you? It tastes familiar. . . ."

I scuttled up the steps of the tier, to the base of the last step, but the Mistress continued her advance, the subtle wall protecting her moving with her. I could feel the Skewed Throne at my back. It was a vortex of energies, white and blazing, the focus of the prowling pressure that had tried to overwhelm me and still beat at the shield of White Fire that protected me.

The Mistress halted, the wall of force she held before her inches in front of me. I couldn't back up any more. The throne blocked my way.

The Mistress' frown grew deeper and then she locked eyes with me. "What is it?" she demanded again, voice as hard as stone.

I didn't answer. My eyes were hooded, the anger back. My gaze flicked toward my dagger, so clear beneath the river, too distant to retrieve, then returned to hers.

Neither one of us moved for a long moment, our breath the only real sound. Somewhere in the background, another grinding pop reverberated through the room, followed by a much heavier clatter. Ripples of force shuddered through the flagstone up the hall to the dais and the throne as one of the main doors pulled free of its last hinge and struck the floor. Men shouted, surged into the room. I could taste the steel of their blades, the tincture of their armor. I breathed in their sweat and fear and confusion as they halted, taking in the Mistress and me on the dais. I felt the air shift as they moved aside, letting Baill and Avrell move to the front of the room. But it was all muted, flattened somehow.

The only thing that mattered was the Mistress. Her eyes, her will, her intent.

She watched me silently.

Then her mouth tightened. "Never mind. It doesn't matter."

And she reached forward, her flat palm changing into a clawed grip. The wall she'd used to protect herself released and she grasped the front of my shirt, lifted me up, and thrust me back onto the throne.

For a moment, the room held, the Mistress taking one step back. No one else moved. The throne beneath me twisted and shifted, the sensation sending a feverish heat through my skin, making it crawl and shudder, prickle with sweat. The river held unchanged as well, the energies roiling.

Then the river exploded.

The Fire flared, rising to consume everything in sight as the swirl of gray energy that had once been the river blackened, charred, became a frenzy of pure motion that refused to resolve into images, into sight. The throne room fell away, and the voices that had plagued me since I'd entered the palace surged forward. As I cowered behind the Fire, I realized that was exactly what they were: voices. A thousand voices, more, all screaming to be heard, all hammering at the shield of Fire, demanding my attention, howling for it. It created a maelstrom of vicious wind, a hurricane force that threatened to overwhelm the Fire, to overwhelm me. And I knew with sudden certainty that it would have crushed me if not for the Fire.

I strained against its force, held the Fire rigid and impenetrable, and after a while realized the Fire would hold.

I relaxed, eased back within the confines of the shield. It still took effort, but not as much as I'd thought. I couldn't hold it forever, but for now. . . .

I drew a deep breath, let it out in a slow sigh.

Varis.

In the white of the shield, the voice was barely a whisper, a rasp of dead leaves blown against cobbles.

Varis.

I shifted toward the voice. The throne raged around me, the voices angry. Some spat curses, others howled, others whined. A group joined forces and surged against the Fire and I was forced to fight them back, tasting sweat against my lips, tasting blood. They retreated.

Varis.

I found the voice. A woman's voice, deep and throaty. A voice I recognized. It was the woman who had sung earlier. Not the child, nor the old woman. And not an amalgamation of many voices. A distinct voice, soft and calm, but tinged with fear.

Varis, there isn't much time.

I'm here, I thought, pausing at the edge of the Fire. The woman's voice came from the far side, among the whorl of the other voices.

A sigh, a hint of wine and cheese, of desperation. *You have to take control. I can't hold it any longer.*

I shuddered. *Control of what?*

The Skewed Throne.

I don't understand. The Fire wavered. I flung it back up, tasted more sweat at the effort, salty and sick.

The throne. That's what this is, Varis. All of these voices, all of these people. They are the men and women who created the throne, the women who have sat upon it since that creation. All of them—all of their thoughts, their hopes, their dreams. They are the throne. But they need someone to control them, someone to order them, keep them in check.

You control them.

A snort, a sigh. That scent of wine and cheese again. *I did control them. But not anymore. Something happened. Something happened to the throne when the Fire passed through it. But it was too subtle a change. I didn't notice it, not until later, when it was much too late. By then, there was nothing I could do. And the other voices—oh, gods. . . .*

Dread bled through the Fire, pooling like oil, thick and viscous. I heard sobbing.

You have to take control, Varis. I can't hold them together any longer. There are too many. Far, far too many! I barely managed to keep control in the throne room tonight.

I was already shaking my head. *No.*

You have to. And now the voice was harsh again, cold. The voice of a woman used to being obeyed. *You have to take my place, become the Mistress, or Amenkor will fall. I'll destroy it, without knowing what it is I'm doing. I'll destroy it, Varis, without meaning to. It's already started. You have to stop it.*

No.

Silence. *Then you'll have to kill me.*

I winced, felt sweat prick the corners of my eyes. I blinked back tears. *And if I kill you, what happens to the city?*

A pause. Something beyond the Fire shifted, a shuddering, gathering of forces that was vaguely familiar, something I'd done on the river many times, only this was much more powerful.

The Mistress pushed herself forward, to see what would happen. For a moment, the voices surging all around the Fire quieted, expectant.

The city will survive, the Mistress said with a heavy sigh, the energies shifting back. *But barely, and not as it is now, not as Amenkor. It will be changed, completely. And many will die.*

The voices hesitated, as if stunned, but then roared back to life.

Why?

Because the city needs a ruler. I've done so much damage—

No, I broke in. *Why me?*

Silence. *Because you have the Sight, what you call the river. Because you know how to survive.* The woman paused. *And because the Fire changed you as well. I felt it before I pushed you onto the throne, but I didn't recognize it. The Fire is protecting you. I can sense it clearly now. It has to be you, Varis. I don't think anyone else can handle the throne anymore. It's too powerful. It will kill anyone else. It has killed everyone else. Avrell tried with others that had the Sight, many times, but the throne overwhelmed them all. It crushed them. Killed them. But you have the Fire to protect you. They didn't.*

Her voice, so soft and clear at the beginning, had become strained.

I'm not going to be able to hold them off much longer, Varis. I felt a surge on the other side of the Fire, like a punch. The voice gasped. *Oh, gods! I can't—*

Then the voice was lost, torn away violently. I reached out, tried to hold on to her, my breath caught up short.

At the same time, a shudder ran through the Fire again and I was forced to hold the Fire steady instead. I stood behind it, frozen, feeling suddenly empty, drained, and lost. Abandoned.

Despair washed over me. I was trapped in my own little niche.

And then I thought about the Mistress.

She'd given me a choice.

I listened through the Fire to the voices. Thousands of them, howling and jabbering. Their noise increased, roaring even higher as they assailed the Fire. I felt it beginning to give. They wanted me, needed me. I could feel them pulling, trying to draw me in and consume me.

I shuddered.

Kill the Mistress, or take the throne.

There was no choice. Not in the end. Not if I could save the voice, the woman whose throat had already felt the touch of my dagger. Not if I could save Amenkor at the same time.

I rested my head forward, sighed heavily, then looked out into the black maelstrom that was the Skewed Throne, the thousands of voices that had sat upon it, that had become it. The thousands of voices that could consume me utterly, as they'd consumed the women Avrell and Nathem had tried to place on the throne before me.

For a moment, I heard those women screaming, so hard their own voices tore their throats. I felt them convulsing, muscles spasming, twisting them, contorting them. I tasted their blood as they bit out their own tongues, gouged out their own eyes, clawed their own faces.

Then I drew in a deep breath, steadied myself, and dropped the shield of Fire, exposed myself completely to the river, to the throne.

I didn't even have time to gasp. The throne pounced and sucked me in.

It was like the time I entered the tavern behind William. The sensations—the sounds and sights and smells—overwhelming. I thought I would be crushed, but it was infinitely worse. Instead, I was picked up by the maelstrom of voices, tossed about on the wind of their noise, turned and twisted until I was completely disoriented. My breath came in short little gasps and I felt my chest constrict, my throat tighten.

And then the images began. Only they were more than images. They were parts of the voices, parts of their lives.

And I didn't simply witness them, I was forced to *live* them.

✝

A scream and I stared across a wide round room made of black stone toward Silicia a moment before she collapsed to the floor, a trickle of blood snaking from her mouth where she lay. But there was no time for concern. The power in the room was too great, shuddering beneath our control. I winced as it stabbed a dagger of raw hate down my left side, the pain visceral, enough to make me stagger, but I held firm. My gaze flicked around the room, toward the five others that still stood with me, encircling the two thrones that stood in the center of the room.

The power grew, surged higher, oppressive and dark, and as one, those of us that remained focused the power on the thrones, concentrated it, wielding it like a sword or hammer.

Sweat broke out on my brow, and another sheeting dagger of pain coursed down my side. I gasped, felt my hands clench into fists, felt my back arch as every muscle in my body pulled taut. But still I forced the power down, compacted it, squeezed it into the granite of the two thrones.

Thunder rolled through the room, vibrated in the obsidian floor. Someone else cried out, the shout cut short. *Garus,* I thought, *my love.* A different pain shot through my heart, but I couldn't turn to see him. Not now. The power was too intense, the construction of the two thrones almost complete. A moment more, just a moment, and we would be finished. . . .

Something slipped, a barrier dropping away as the power culminated, crested, and suddenly it began to funnel into the thrones, fast, faster than we had calculated. Those remaining in the group gasped as one, and through the sudden funneling roar of energy I felt one of the others—Atreus?—struggling, trying to pull herself out of the construct. But it was too late, far, far too late.

The funneling of power increased, surging forward, sweeping down and down until it split into two distinct vortices, one for each throne, the power seeping into the simple stone of the two thrones, saturating them, and still the thrones wanted more.

I began to feel it pulling at me, felt myself caught at its very lip. With a gut-wrenching churn of despair, I knew none of us would escape. The thrones needed too much. But I began to struggle anyway, like Atreus, tried to draw myself up over the edge of the funnel, the whirlpool of energy. New pain shot into my side, paralyzed my left arm with a burning tingle. I collapsed to the floor, juddered there, seizures racking my body. My head pounded into the black stone. I felt blood seep, felt my hair grow matted, felt warm coppery wetness slip down my back.

Then the funnel took me.

I screamed, my roar echoing in the cavernous room, and for an instant I saw my lifeless body crumbled to the stone, saw my empty eyes, saw my face stained with blood, my silk shirt soaked, the fine yellow stained a deep red.

I had a moment to think, *We are the last. What have we done?*

†

And then I gasped, the vision tattering away as I wrenched myself from the maelstrom.

I had time for a single desperate breath, a single desperate thought—*Two thrones?*—and then

†

Someone wrapped their thick-fingered hands around my throat from behind and squeezed.

I gagged, hands flying up to scrabble at the heavily-muscled forearms, managed to suck in a strangled, weak sliver of air—

And then the muscles in the arms bunched and the man flung me into the wall to the right. I struck the rough eggshell-colored stone hard, my head cracking against an edge, and then I was falling, slumping downward, my vision spinning.

It's dark, I thought, staring up into the night sky. Through blurred vision, disoriented, I noticed stars, saw the edge of the palace. I recognized the architecture: one of the balustrades before the palace, on the promenade. Flames from the oil sconce flapped raggedly in the wind, like a banner.

Then someone kicked me, the pain sharp, drawing me up out of the daze, and I screamed, the terror I'd felt an hour before as the strange White Fire swept over the city returning. I could feel the city surging in my blood, could feel its terror, and I screamed again as the foot dug deep into my side, rolling me over onto my stomach.

The blood-pulse of the city thrummed in my ears, and beneath that the thousand voices of the throne, all screaming, all horrified. But I still held them under control, still contained them.

Then the hands returned to my throat, crushed it closed. I gagged again, felt the hands shift until only one held me by the neck, fingers large enough to squeeze out all but the barest of breaths. The other hand began tearing at my robes, ripped them back from my shoulders, the man behind me, pressing his weight down hard into my back, grunting with the effort.

The hand at my throat lifted me roughly, my back arching. The other hand reached around and cupped my exposed breast, then squeezed it with bruising force.

"This," a ragged voice hissed in my ear, spittle flecking my cheek, "is for refusing me."

My eyes widened in shock as I recognized the voice.

Neville.

Neville twisted my captured breast viciously, then thrust me hard to the stone of the portico above the promenade, hand still tight across my throat.

A fumbling of clothes, a shifting, and I felt night air against my exposed legs. Blind spots began to appear in my vision and I sucked in a hard breath under the grip of Neville's hand.

And then he thrust, penetrated with a guttural, visceral grunt of pure pleasure, and I screamed, screamed so hard my throat tore, his hand jerking my head so far back I could no longer breathe.

The scream cut short. The blind spots wavered and grew as he thrust again, crying out. Something tore, deep inside, and I felt blood, but the blind spots were widening, reaching out to engulf me. Another thrust, another tearing, and the voices of the throne inside me screamed.

†

I spun away, caught and pulled and throttled by the maelstrom.

Panic began to set in. I felt myself fraying, felt everything I knew—the Dredge, the wharf, Amenkor—losing cohesion, tattering and ripping under the force of the voices.

I was losing myself to the throne. I couldn't control it.

It was going to win.

✝

I stood on a tower overlooking the night harbor. Light reflected on the water from lanterns on ships. Lights glowed in the windows of the houses below the palace.

A breeze touched my face and I lifted my head to meet it, closed my eyes.

In the darkness of my mind I could hear the throne, could feel the entire city resting below me. It throbbed and flowed, beat with its own pulse. A living thing that I could feel in my blood. Amenkor.

I smiled, drew in a deep satisfied breath of clear, salty sea air.

And then, far out over the sea, there was a pulse of power.

I opened my eyes, the smile fading away. I watched the horizon.

An invisible wave, like a ripple on a pool of water, rushed out from the ocean, brushed past me with a gust that pushed me back a step. I blinked at it, frowned at its taste.

Something powerful, something immense. Something greater than the throne itself. Older. Ancient.

I waited. Dread stirred in my stomach, thickened in my throat.

In the back of my mind, the voices of the throne paused.

Some of them recognized the taste of the power, but not what it was for. One of them knew it personally, had seen it before.

It had spelled her doom.

I leaned forward, hands resting on the top of the tower. I waited.

There.

The western horizon was tinged with white, as if the sun were beginning to rise.

But the sun rose in the east.

My hands tightened against the grit of the stone wall.

The white light grew, spread across the sky, a wall of pure white Fire. It swept in from the sea, swift, stretching from the ocean to the clouds, immense and horrifying.

The voice in my head that had seen it once before cowered before it in gibbering fear.

The Fire struck the bay, surged through the harbor, seared its way forward, utterly silent. It swallowed up the ships, swallowed the docks, scorched onto land, up toward the palace, sweeping forward with swift, cold intent.

I gasped the moment before it consumed me, stepped back—

And then it filled me, burned down to my core, wrenched me open and exposed me, exposed all of the voices of the throne. For a moment, everything was silent, the voices stilled for the first time since they'd tossed me on the throne to see if I'd survive. I tasted the Fire, felt it burn deep, deeper, felt it judge me.

I felt its purpose. Nothing to do with Amenkor, nothing to do with me. It was residual energy, the remains of an event so powerful it had stretched across the ocean, burned across the sea from a distant land. The consequence of a magic that no one in the throne knew the intent of, that was totally unfamiliar. It was nothing to us.

I felt it beginning to fade, felt the voices of the throne returning to normal.

Then something inside the throne twisted and tore.

Pain lanced up from my stomach into my throat and head and the Fire left me, passed on, sweeping across the city behind and onward, toward the mountains. I staggered into the stone wall, felt its rough surface bite into my arms, and almost vomited over the side. Breathing shallowly, I pulled myself upright.

The pain receded, drew away almost as swiftly as it had come.

I frowned, tested the throne, tested the voices. They were quieter than usual, but that wasn't unexpected. The one that had recognized the Fire was utterly silent.

When I freed her, I found her lying on the steps of the promenade leading up to the palace, her robe torn and ragged about her waist. There were bruises on her neck, on her breasts. And there was blood.

I pushed her back, shuddered at her pain.

The Fire had destroyed her. The guard Neville had raped and killed her over a thousand years before.

I turned and stared in the direction of the mountains. The Fire was a white light beyond their rim, fading even as I watched.

I reached for the city, felt its pulse. I could hear screams already, could see lights appearing in all quarters. The people were panicked, some driven mad. I could feel the disturbance, the throb of the city swift and erratic. It would take time to settle.

But at least the Fire, wherever it came from, whatever it had done, had done no harm here.

†

I cried out, wrenched myself away from the maelstrom and the memory of the Mistress. My breath came in ragged gasps. More memories surged forward. I saw a thousand deaths, saw the city burn, the palace gates collapse, walls crumble, the palace rebuilt, the palace expanded, another tier of walls go up, all in a blinding flash. Sunsets roared across my vision, starscapes, gardens, streams, grottoes, storms, lightning flaring sharp and smelling of seared air. I was slapped, choked, knifed, spat upon. I was kissed, hefted up into an embrace, dropped down to a bed, to a rug, thrust to a stone wall, onto the seat of a rattling carriage, onto cool grass. I was held to a wall and lashed, held to the ground and raped as I screamed, moaned and bucked, gibbering in fear. I was tortured, hot iron pressed into flesh, charred and blinded, my toenails ripped out, wood shoved under my fingernails. I was kicked, feet driving into my stomach. I was drowned, water closing up over my head, cold and terrifying and inviting. I heard my mother's laugh.

I latched onto the memory, onto Cobbler's Fountain. I latched onto the sensation of water, filling my nose, my ears, muting out the sound of the world, everything collapsing down into a blur of wind, a wash of gray filled with ripples from the surface of the water above. I saw shadowy shapes there, saw sunlight reflected, refracted, dazzling and bright. But that was above the water, removed.

Beneath the water, it was just me. Not the man being sucked into the two thrones at their creation. Not the woman being raped above the steps of the promenade. Not the woman who'd witnessed the Fire from the tower of the palace.

Just Varis.

I felt something else struggling deep inside me, pushing forward. Someone young, no more than six. Someone who had died that day at the fountain, when she had witnessed her mother's death in the alley at the hands of the red men.

Ash.

The name was no more than a whisper, spoken with my mother's voice. The name I had been given, that I could not reveal to Erick when he asked. But the little six-year-old girl who had tripped and fallen in Cobbler's Fountain eleven years before stood beside me now. I could feel her.

We were both drowning. Varis and Ash. We were dying inside the throne, together, as one.

I could let the throne consume me. There would be no more deaths then, no more marks. There would be nothing.

But then the Mistress would not be released.

No, not the Mistress. Her name was Eryn. Eryn would not be released.

And then what of Amenkor? The Mistress had said it would survive, but barely. It would survive but would not be the same.

I stared up at the shapes moving above the water, blurred beyond recognition. The shapes of the people inside the throne, those that had created it, those that had sat upon it or touched it since its creation.

If I stayed, I needed to find a way to control them, and I suddenly realized I knew how. It was just like the crowd at the tavern. It was a choice. I could be Ash, sit back and watch, hover around the dead body of Amenkor and do nothing, let the throne overwhelm me, let the guards send me where they willed.

Or I could be Varis. Ruthless. Hard. Forceful. I could seize control. *This is who I am.*

I drew a deep breath and pulled everything that I thought of as myself, all of my memories of the Dredge, all of my emotions, everything that was *me* together, wove it tight.

And then I pushed myself up through the water. I left my mother behind. Left the six-year-old girl named Ash behind. That wasn't me anymore. I'd changed.

At the last moment, just before I breached the surface of the water, I felt the Mistress' hands—Eryn's hands—reach down to grab me beneath my arms and help pull me up into the sunlight.

Welcome to the throne, Varis.

And it *was* just like the tavern.

✝

I opened my eyes to the throne room in Amenkor. Baill and Avrell stood a few steps down from the dais, watching me carefully. Baill's sword was drawn, but he was a step behind Avrell, the First of the Mistress holding him back with one hand. The rest of the guards were farther back, clustered around the broken throne room door and the pillars to the right and left.

I glanced down. The Mistress had collapsed to the floor, her figure crumpled. Her face was worn, sheened with sweat and tears.

Beneath me, the throne no longer twisted and turned, warping itself into different shapes. It had solidified into a stone curve with armrests and no back, the edges of the armrests curled under. My arms rested lightly on its edges, hands gripping the ends. My back was rigid.

I felt a heavy throb beating all around me, recognized it from Eryn's memory of the tower.

It was the city. Amenkor. From the Dredge to the palace. A steady pulse of teeming life. I could reach out and touch each one of those lives if I wanted, could watch them live, could help them. Those in the slums, rooting through garbage. Those on the wharfs and in the ships blockaded inside the harbor. Even those sorting through the burned-out rubble of the warehouse district.

I drew in a deep breath, felt the city warm and vibrant inside of me.

I let the breath out with a sigh. The city could wait.

I turned toward the Mistress, who began to stir. On the river, lines of energy entrapped her, bound her to the throne. I began to pull the threads apart, carefully. The voices fought me, but I knew myself and ignored them, thrust them into the background as I'd done my entire life with all the noises of the Dredge that were unimportant. Just like the tavern.

By the time the Mistress roused completely, sitting upright with a groan, she was no longer the Mistress. She was Eryn again, wholly her own.

She raised a trembling hand to her head and gasped, shooting a glance toward me. Avrell stepped toward her, one hand outstretched.

"Mistress?"

She turned toward him, then shook her head. "No," she said, then sobbed, hiding her hands in her face.

Avrell's hand dropped and he stood up straight, turning toward me. His face became a solemn mask and he folded his hands formally before him. He bowed his head slightly.

"Mistress."

I turned to Baill, eyes hard and intent.

He glanced toward Avrell with a frown, then lowered his sword and sheathed it. He bowed down, the motion quick and barely deferential. "Mistress."

Behind him, the guards that had gathered, mixed with a few white-robed servants, bowed down as well, a clatter of sound and shuffling cloth.

I wondered briefly how many of those servants were true Servants, young girls and women who had a touch of the power like me, who had been brought here to be trained with the hopes that one day they could control the throne.

I wondered how many of those Servants had died on the throne when Avrell and Nathem had tried to replace Eryn.

Avrell stepped forward to catch my attention.

"What of the city?"

I felt the city rushing inside me, hurt but vital, beaten but not destroyed.

I smiled and thought of the Dredge, of the wharf, of the palace itself. I felt the scar of the fire in the warehouse district, felt the ships gliding on the waters of the bay, felt the River surging through the center of the city. I heard the steady pulse of its blood in my ears, full of heat and strength.

"It will survive," I said, and behind my voice I heard other voices, all of the women who had sat on the throne after its forging, all of their strengths, all of their memories.

It would not be easy.

But it would survive.